The Waxen Image

*To Herb —
my tennis
partner —*

THE WAXEN IMAGE

a novel by

Rudy S. Apodaca

Titan Publishing Co., Inc./Mesilla, N.M.

To my beloved Nancy

PROLOGUE

West Africa, September, 1926

THE outline of the figure approaching Andrew Borlin grew obscured against the dense foliage and trees spread throughout the slope of the darkened hillside he had just crossed.

Babatundé Ejugu?

Andrew Borlin considered calling out. They should move quickly, he thought, for there was little time to do what had to be done. The figure was still some fifty yards away. Borlin decided against shouting, for he could be mistaken—it might not be his servant, Babatundé Ejugu, who was advancing toward him. But who else might it be, then? Had something gone wrong? No, Borlin thought, it had to be the native who was coming in his direction. Only moments before, Borlin had heard the crackling sound of rifle shots coming from an area below the steep mountainside; he guessed the servant would be appearing any moment now. The night was dark, although there was the dim light coming from the thin crescent of the moon a few degrees above the western horizon.

The figure grew larger, and Andrew Borlin could not now

mistake the singular manner in which his faithful servant scrambled through the jungle.

"Babatundé, hurry!" He spoke softly. The figure was now only a few steps away. "What in heaven's name kept you so long?" Borlin grew impatient for the native didn't answer. "Speak up, man! What were those shots all about?"

"I almost caught, *Tuba*," the native replied. In West African, the word *Tuba* referred to boss or employer. Babatundé breathed heavily. "I escape just in time. Image not there, *Tuba*. Must be in Bangurah's hut. We must go there."

Andrew Borlin cursed under his breath. "Shit," he said out loud. "Are you sure, Babatundé? We must get our hands on it." He sounded desperate.

"I sure, *Tuba*. I look place all over. I know where it must be, if it there. Babatundé know place inside out, but not find it. There only one other place; image must be where Bangurah sleep." He spoke slowly, pronouncing every word distinctly. The native invariably spoke somewhat methodically, his speech seemingly unaffected by emotion.

"Come then, lead the way. We don't have much time. Your having been found in the village will mean they'll soon be sending out a search party. They might even report it to Bangurah tonight, rather than wait till morning. So we must get there first."

The native had already begun moving down the slope and Andrew Borlin followed.

Andrew Borlin was thirty five years old. He was big-boned but slim and wasn't a large man. His long, black hair was extremely thick at the back and covered his neck, overlapping his shirt collar. His bushy eyebrows almost touched just above the nose. He was ordinarily light skinned but the hot sun of the African jungles during the last twenty months had darkened him considerably.

He followed closely behind Babatundé, although with some difficulty. The native hardly made a sound as he moved down the slope. He appeared to be gliding two or three inches above the ground, Borlin thought. Babatundé knew his way around the dense jungles of West Africa better than any other native Borlin had ever come across during the almost two years he had spent on that continent. Indeed, Borlin was glad he had the native with him tonight. "Good old faithful Babatundé," he said to himself. "You're a life saver." He realized he meant that literally, although he hadn't intended it that way.

In a few minutes, the two men had reached the eastern edge of the slope and then they began climbing the crest of a small hill. They stopped midway up the hill. Babatundé went down on his knees and turned to Borlin.

"Here we are, *Tuba*," the servant whispered, in that same slow, deliberate speech of his which he used only when he spoke English. In his native tongue, he spoke much faster. He was full negroid, but for some reason Borlin couldn't explain, the only negroid features he possessed were his stiff, short hair and his dark skin. His lips and nostrils, for instance, were smaller than Borlin's, and even his dark skin was lighter than the skin of some Caucasians.

"Bangurah live only a few yards away there behind the thick brush, below the top of that hill," the native continued. He gestured with his hand. "You wait here, *Tuba*. I be back soon." He turned and started up the hill again.

"Babatundé!" Borlin cried out. The native stopped and turned around. "Be quick about it, Babatundé. And remember, you must kill him. Be certain of that." He paused, as if to emphasize his words. "And be careful."

"I will *Tuba*. Babatundé will not fail you." He disappeared up the small hill.

Borlin crawled along the edge of the hill toward the stump of a large tree and leaned against it to rest. He felt tired and for the first time since he and Babatundé had left his quarters, he realized he was perspiring heavily. He took out his handkerchief and ran it over his forehead, collecting the tiny droplets of sweat that had accumulated there.

He closed his eyes for a moment and remained sitting there quietly for several minutes. Suddenly he cursed the circumstances which had brought him here to the crest of this hill and which, in a few minutes, would make him a cold-blooded killer. "Blasted country," he said to himself. "I've made a fucking mess of twenty months of experiments in this place." And it was all the result of one, rotten, bloody brawl in a drunkard's hangout. His thoughts wandered off to that one night a few days ago which had been the beginning of this incredible nightmare. His thoughts stopped the sounds of the night in the jungle. Off in the distance, he heard the horrible laughing-like noise of a hyena. It was one of the few sounds of the jungle he had grown to despise. He heard some sound coming from his left. He looked into the darkness, trying to detect the faintest movement, but he could see nothing. Then his thoughts wandered off to that night.

It had begun as a perfectly normal evening and after dinner, he had promised Babatundé they would visit their usual hangout, outside the small village of Melfi, along the West African coast. "The place where they sell fire water," Babatundé would say. Borlin and his servant had frequented there before and had spent good times there together. There was little else to do in that particular part of the country with one's spare time, and Andrew Borlin had grown accustomed to going there, if only to have one or two drinks and maybe chat with some of the other Americans living in the area. But he had grown lonely and there were times he would drink heavily to fill the vacuum caused by his wife's absence. She had come to Africa with him originally, but after the first few months, it became evident things weren't working out. She had grown to loath the place and then, to compound the problem, she had taken ill and finally, the doctor advised him his wife should take the next vessel sailing for the States. Borlin had reluctantly agreed for he knew he would miss her terribly.

And he had been right. He had slept with other women since his wife's departure, if only to satisfy his sexual, animal desires. But time and time again, he had ached to be close to his wife—to feel her soft, tender skin next to his. He required the physical closeness of a woman and any woman would do to satisfy his physical hunger. But there was an emotional emptiness when that woman was not his wife, for he loved her deeply. He was not a religious man, but he had even made some futile attempts at prayer to quell the loneliness; he had been unsuccessful. In a few short weeks, he would be with her again and he grew impatient.

Thoughts of his wife were with him that fateful night,

when he and Babatundé arrived at the tavern. That was one of those nights he wanted to get pathetically drunk, and so he drank the cheap vodka served there, to rid himself of the miserable feeling of loneliness. Babatundé was drinking little and Borlin unsuccessfully attempted to get him to drink more. The native simply covered his glass with his hand when Borlin tried pouring more vodka into it.

"Oh, Babatundé, what a sight for sore eyes, you are," Borlin remarked merrily. Borlin was on his sixth drink of straight vodka. "My faithful Babatundé. You abstain from too much of this fire water just enough to make sure you're in perfect shape to take care of one who's overindulging in it. You take care of me tonight, you hear!" He placed his hand on the native's head and tried unsuccessfully to muss what little hair was there. The native always displayed a long, bright smile across his face when Borlin would say that, his narrow lips becoming still narrower.

It was as they were about to leave the tavern that the fight started outside. The noise attracted the tavern patrons, including Borlin and Babatundé. The fight seemed harmless enough and Borlin always enjoyed a good fistfight that didn't involve him, especially when he was helplessly intoxicated.

But this particular fight, he soon discovered, wasn't the kind he enjoyed, for a small, frail boy of some fifteen or sixteen years of age was being brutally beaten by two older, much larger men. Borlin recognized one of the men. He was the son of Bangurah Krubally, one of the natives. Bangurah, much to Borlin's dismay, had grown to dislike the American since shortly after his arrival in the Melfi province. Borlin was dismayed because he had hoped for complete cooperation from the local tribes in conducting his experiments, and Bangurah was looked upon by his fellow men as a leader, so it had seemed at the onset important to strike a good relationship with him. He didn't learn immediately the reason why Bangurah disliked him. But two or three months after his arrival, when he had gained the confidence of Babatundé, he finally learned from his servant that Bangurah was an extremely jealous man and his jealousy was directed at Borlin simply because he felt Borlin had alienated the natives of Bangurah's tribe against him. Borlin had, from the beginning, treated the natives with kindness and for this, he earned their respect. It was the kind of treatment they rarely saw coming from an American. Before Borlin's arrival in the province, Bangurah was respected and a popular figure with the tribes in the area. He was the kind of individual who welcomed and cherished this feeling of importance. Soon after Borlin's arrival, the local natives grew to trust him. Yet, Bangurah's position remained unaffected and his popularity with his fellow natives continued. But he wasn't ready to share this respect and popularity with anyone else, least of all a foreigner, and finally Bangurah's blind jealousy proved too much for him to control and so he turned his unending hatred toward Borlin. The feeling, of course, wasn't mutual and Borlin had made several overtures in an attempt to end the native's hatred toward him, but the native had been unresponsive to his efforts.

The young boy in the fight was a helpless victim. Borlin couldn't bear it any longer, for the liquor he had consumed appeared to intensify the anger he felt toward the two assailants. He shoved his way past several onlookers and lunged at the two men. The boy sobbed in vain.

Borlin flung himself at one man, turned him around and struck him across the face. The man sailed through the air, landing at the feet of several spectators. The man didn't move nor did he attempt rising. When Borlin swung around to face Bangurah's son, he found the native with a smirk on his dark, sweating face. In his hand he held a long knife which he moved back and forth, threatening, the blade glistening in the light coming from the bare bulb above the tavern entrance.

"Don't be a fool, put that knife down, son!" Borlin ordered. "Before someone really gets hurt." He could see clearly into the eyes of his young aggressor. He had, many times before, seen the same wild, frenzied look that he now saw in these eyes—they were the eyes of one who had taken morphine or heroin. He guessed that this had some connection with the seemingly unjustifiable attack on the young boy. Borlin quickly realized his opponent would not listen to reason.

"Babatundé!" Borlin yelled at the servant, whom he saw behind Bangurah's son. "God fetch the constable, quickly!

Hurry, Babatundé! Through the corner of one eye, he saw the native run up the path leading to the village.

To Borlin, it seemed hours passed and Babatundé hadn't returned. The young man remained standing there, as if ready at any moment to lunge forward with the weapon. Several times, Borlin asked him to put the knife away, but Bangurah's son had ignored him, forming that same smirkish look with his mouth. Finally, the inevitable happened—the man came at Borlin, the long knife held in front of him. Quickly, Borlin stepped aside as the assailant attacked, but the knife caught his shirt and as Borlin barely spun away, the knife ripped through the cloth, nicking the skin under the arm. No sooner had he stepped aside when he saw his assailant coming at him again. This time, Borlin knew he must hold his ground. His legs spread apart, he squatted to help maintain his balance. He had studied judo and other forms of self-defense, and he shouted some unrecognizable sound as he stretched his arms forward, grabbing his attacker around the wrist of the hand holding the deadly weapon.

Instantaneously, he turned his body sharply, twisted his assailant's arm, and pulled with all his strength. Immediately, the native became airborne, going over Borlin's head, and in a jack-knife position, fell hard on the ground. Borlin slowly walked up to where the man lay on the ground and turned him around. He noticed immediately Bangurah's son hadn't released the knife. There was a heavy mumbling of voices as the crowd's eyes came down upon the knife still clutched in the man's hand. It had entered the body, near the heart. The man's eyes remained open—the terrified look of a man who had realized for one split second before death that he was about to die. Borlin looked down at the knife plunged into the heart, then again at the wide-opened eyes. He let the body fall and turned away from the nauseating sight, his body shivering with guilt.

He heard yet another mumbling of voices coming from behind and he turned around. He immediately recognized one of the voices—it belonged to Bangurah Krubally. Borlin surmised someone had summoned him. When Bangurah reached the scene, his eyes came to rest upon the inert body of his dead son. Although the body was slightly twisted downward, the knife was clearly visible even in the dim light. And so was the blood that was now flowing freely out of the wound, soaking the dead man's shirt, and dripping onto the ground.

Bangurah rushed to his son. He knelt next to the body, disbelief in his eyes. Slowly, he pulled his son's body toward him. It was then he saw the wide-opened eyes; he let out a shriek of terror and began moaning and wailing uncontrollably as he pressed his son's body to his. He began saying something in his native tongue which Borlin couldn't understand.

Within seconds, Bangurah let go of the body, stood up abruptly and turned. He stared angrily at Borlin. Borlin would never forget the look in the eyes of this man who had lost his only son.

Suddenly, the man began hurtling angry words at the man he blamed for his son's death. Borlin comprehended only some of the words, but the rest were undistinguishable to him.

The people in the crowd began whispering among themselves as they dispersed. For an instant, Borlin turned to see what the commotion was all about and he spotted the constable approaching. Babatundé Ejugu, a somber expression on his face, followed quickly behind.

By this time, Borlin had become shaken, unable to put events together in proper perspective. He appeared terribly confused and recalled only vaguely hearing the constable speak to Bangurah in an attempt to control him.

Babatundé disappeared and returned shortly with a tall glass of water for Borlin. It was then that Borlin noticed the servant was shaking. He was afraid. Borlin knew it wasn't for himself he felt fear, but for his master. And he sensed this fear was connected to something Bangurah had said to him.

The following afternoon, the constable paid Borlin a visit to notify him the magistrate had ruled the death justifiable homicide—Borlin had acted in self-defense. The news did little to relieve him of the uneasiness and anxiety he felt, for earlier that morning, after he and Babatundé had testified at the hearing held in the magistrate's office, Borlin learned from his servant why he had displayed such fear the prior night.

"Bangurah vowed vengeance to the gods above for his son's

death," Babatundé explained when the two of them arrived at Borlin's office.

"Well, I figured that much myself," Borlin said, "after listening to all that filth he kept shouting at me. I'd never seen such anger in my life."

"He no mean ordinary vengeance. He mean witch doctor vengeance. Bangurah is *duma*—witch. He vow to the gods he cast an evil spell against you. A curse by use of image. Image of Andrew Borlin."

"You don't mean something like voodoo—a voodoo doll?"

"Yes, *Tuba*. A doll made of wax. Bangurah swear to kill you by destroying image of you. By destroying image, he destroy you. He practice witchcraft. He plan to do away with you, *Tuba*."

Borlin stood there horrified. If Babatundé had been telling him this when he first arrived on the African continent, he would have simply dismissed it as a completely harmless, native superstition. But he had been in Africa for a considerable length of time now and during that period, he had visited dozens of villages where witchcraft was indeed practiced, and moreover, he had seen the terrifying results of African black magic. With his own eyes, he had seen what could be done by mortal men who called upon evil spirits and demons to give them the power to bring harm or death or sickness to an enemy. He had seen the effects of black magic when it was used to cast a spell on someone against whom vengeance was sought, and it had quickly made a believer out of him. He realized immediately what had to be done before the servant spoke again.

"We mustn't allow to happen," Babatundé pleaded, his voice shaking. Borlin knew what the servant's next words would be, for they had already entered his own mind; he too knew there was only one solution. "We must get rid of Bangurah, *Tuba*. There no other way, but to kill him before he kill you."

Nevertheless, Borlin searched his mind for a way to avoid what seemed the inevitable. "But I'll be leaving in a few weeks," he said nervously, attempting to put the matter aside casually. "If he does nothing before I leave, I'll be safe once

I'm gone."

"No matter where you are, black magic so strong it reach around world. Distance across deep oceans not stop magic of Bangurah. His magic very powerful. This is why we must waste no time. Bangurah make doll quickly. Babatundé has seen black magic with waxen image work before—many times. It causes horrible death."

Two facts became clear to Borlin after his talk with Babatundé. If Bangurah did in fact make such an image, and the curse placed upon it, then the image must be stolen to insure that it wouldn't be harmed or damaged. For it was through damage of the doll that eventual death struck the person it represented. But that was not enough, for most important of all, Borlin hesitatingly acknowledged, Bangurah would have to be killed to prevent him from carrying out the curse against him by simply creating another wax doll.

Borlin shuddered a few days later when he learned from his servant what they had been waiting to hear—Bangurah had completed the image—Borlin's image. There was now no alternative left to them; they knew then what they must do.

Andrew Borlin's thoughts returned him to the present. He waited, seated against the tree stump.

His thoughts were suddenly interrupted by the sound of two shots coming from the direction the native had taken only minutes earlier. Soon he heard the heavy rustling up ahead, caused by the scraping of a man's body against the thick reeds and brush on the hill. The noise grew louder, and then, Borlin made out clearly the silhouette of Babatundé.

"Did you find it?" Borlin cried out. He no longer whispered. The tone of his voice revealed his nervous anticipation.

"Yes, *Tuba*," Babatundé answered tiredly. "But there trouble before I able to kill Bangurah with knife. He wake up before I get chance and we struggle. Had to use pistol, *Tuba*. Good idea I take it along." He paused for a moment to catch his breath, then continued. "Found image, *Tuba*! It hidden in back room."

"Was it damaged in the fight?"

"No. It in good shape. Here it is, see for yourself." He slowly brought his hand forward and extended it toward

Borlin. He cupped his hand and in it was the image.

"Here, let me see it, Babatundé."

The native carefully handed him the object. Borlin took it and held it delicately with both hands.

He began inspecting it. He could barely see it by the dim moonlight. It certainly looked innocent enough, he thought. He began feeling it carefully. It was delicate and soft, and was made of beeswax. It had been dressed in miniature cloths made of khaki material, the same material found in Borlin's clothes.

"Bangurah bother you no more, *Tuba*," Babatundé said softly. Borlin detected a certain jubilance in his voice. "You need not worry about his black magic now. I take care of that for you, *Tuba*."

"Yes, you're so right, Babatundé," Borlin agreed. He took his eyes away from the image and glanced up at the servant. "My faithful friend. Thank you, Babatundé. I'm so grateful to you—I owe you my life." The native smiled and nodded approvingly, satisfied he had pleased his master.

Borlin returned his eyes to the wax object again and he began examining it once more. He still held it in both hands, cradling it like one would a small child. Yes, he thought, Babatundé was right—Bangurah no longer posed a danger. He was harmless—gone—dead. But in his hands, Borlin held the evil which Bangurah had created and that posed a danger still —a danger he realized he'd have to contend with—for how long, he wasn't certain. Now that Bangurah was dead and Borlin had gained possession—now that he held the image in his hands, a dreadful, terrifying awareness took hold of him— an awareness which forced him to realize he was now confronted by a similar, if not greater, danger. The doll was made in his own image and he would have to take painstaking care that it was never damaged, even slightly, for should anything ever happen to the image, Bangurah's spell would surely and inevitably cause the death of Andrew Borlin.

Was there a way the spell could be overcome or broken? Did someone—somewhere—know how to reverse the curse? He wondered. He would have to find a way.

But before that time would come—he would have to protect the image with extreme caution. In the days or months or even years ahead of him, lay the important task of preventing harm to come to the image he now held in his hands.

CHAPTER 1

July, 1976

ROSS Blair felt an aching tiredness sweep through him as he readied himself for bed. Once in bed, he found he couldn't sleep. He tried clearing his mind of the happenings of the long day. But the thought of three individuals remained with him —Carol Lockwood and his daughter Carrie and surprisingly, Andrew Borlin. He tried concentrating on the sleep his body longed for, but sleep wouldn't come. Instead, from some deep recess of his mind, he would see a shape take form; it was that of Carol. He was somewhere within that twilight area between the world of sleep and wakefulness.

He pictured Carol vividly, sitting on the lounging chair in the hotel patio downstairs; she was speaking to him. She was telling him of Carrie and about her father, Andrew Borlin. A weird fellow, Ross thought. Then his thoughts passed on to Carrie and he saw the vague image take shape—a young girl possessing beautiful long hair. But he couldn't make out the face—it was vague, yet he knew it was Carrie whose image he saw as he lay there, sleep evading him.

She too was talking to him; telling him she loved him and

that she had missed him terribly all those years. What her mother had done was unforgivable, she was saying. She should never have kept them apart as she had for so many, many years. And now, for having done all of that to them, she wanted to punish her mother. Her mother had not allowed her to know him. But now that he was here and would find her, everything would be fine and she would change her ways because of him —to show her love for him.

The image of Carrie was erased from his mind. He suddenly became aware of his surroundings; he knew he was in a hotel room in a small town in New Mexico and then he remembered that Carol Lockwood was asleep downstairs. He thought of Carol again. He recalled their conversation of the past evening and he began wondering what the following day had in store for them. What, if anything, would they accomplish? Was Carrie actually somewhere around this little town? Or somewhere else? He thought of the professor — Arthur Conrad, whom Carol had accused of influencing Carrie astray into a world of drugs. Did he know where Carrie might be?

Such thoughts persisted as he lay there awake for what seemed hours.

Finally, he began falling into a light sleep. But then, he thought he heard voices coming from somewhere downstairs; he wasn't certain from where they originated. He listened carefully for the voices again but there was only silence. He decided he had been imagining them. Minutes later, as he felt his body slowly relaxing itself into sleep, he thought he heard voices again, louder this time, but he was now too sleepy to arouse himself, so he allowed his body to relax even more as he continued falling deeper to sleep.

When he next awakened, he had lost track of time, for he didn't know whether he had been asleep for only minutes or for hours. He opened his eyes and it was then he became aware of what had awakened him; it had been a loud noise. It had sounded as if it had come from somewhere in the building. It was a sharp, crackling sound. Yes, he was sure of it now. A shot—he had heard the blasting noise of a gun or rifle going off. Quickly, he jumped out of bed and reached for his trousers. He left his pajama shirt on and hurriedly slipped into his slippers. He rushed to the door and opened it.

A few dim lights had been left on in the lobby. Looking over the railing below, he caught a glimpse of the head of the old man as he disappeared below the second floor corridor. The hotel operator was walking hurriedly toward the passageway leading into the patio. Shoving from his mind the dreaded thought that the shot was in someway connected with Carol, Ross ran awkwardly through the second-floor corridor, went down the stairs, and turned sharply at the foot of the steps, heading toward Carol's room.

Immediately upon entering the narrow corridor, he noticed the door to her room open. He knew then his fears were realized. When he reached the open door, he stopped; he saw the old man kneeling near the foot of the bed. He was speaking in a whisper and Ross couldn't make out what he was saying. Lying on the floor near the bed was Carol's lifeless body. Ross rushed to her. He noticed immediately a slight motion of her body and that her eyes were slightly opened; they looked up at him as he stood over her.

The old man took his eyes off Carol momentarily and looked up at Ross, despair in his eyes. "My God, she's been shot!" he said slowly. His voice trembled. Awkwardly, as if to prove his statement, he pointed at a spot on the bathrobe which Carol wore; it was stained with blood. He stood up. "I'll go fetch a doctor right away. She's hurt bad." He walked hurriedly past Ross and disappeared down the corridor.

Ross knelt beside Carol and quickly took her hand. He felt miserable, watching the pathetic, helpless look on her face as she looked into his eyes. Desperation came over him as he thought of what he might do to help her, but he was too shaken to think of anything. He saw her lips move slowly. She was trying to tell him something but only a weak sound came from her.

"What are you trying to tell me, Carol?" Ross asked frantically. "I can't make out what you're trying to say." He leaned forward and brought his head closer to her face. "Please try speaking a little louder if you can."

Again, her lips opened, trying vainly to form some word; trying desperately to gather sufficient strength to utter some recognizable sound. Ross turned his head and placed his ear only inches away from her lips. Finally, he recognized the words she was barely uttering. *Picture. Wallet.*

He raised his head and looked down at her again. "Picture in your wallet, is that what you're saying?" he asked. He quickly realized what she was referring to. "Yes, I understand." Earlier, when he had said goodnight to her, she had offered to show him Carrie's photograph so he would know her. He was about to stand up to search for the wallet, but before he did so, his eyes came across it; Carol was clutching it in her hand. She held the wallet loosely in her left hand.

Gently, he raised her hand. The wallet was held open with her finger; he took it from her and opened it to where she had half-opened it. His eyes came across a photograph of a young, teenage girl. It wasn't a snapshot but a studio portrait, and it showed the attractive face of a young girl with long, dark brown hair, wearing a dark knit sweater, a custom pearl necklace around the neck.

Quickly, Ross turned the picture so that Carol could see it. "Is this the picture you wanted me to look at? Is this what you meant?"

She appeared weaker now, for she didn't even bother moving her lips, but only nodded her head. Immediately, Ross noticed she was trying vainly to tell him something else; the expression on her face showed pain, but it also told Ross that whatever she was trying to convey to him was important to her. He could see that in her eyes. He wanted to cry out to her; to help her along with whatever it was she wanted to say to him. But there was nothing he could do—he knew that. She lay there helplessly.

Her tired eyes looked up at him despairingly as if trying to communicate with them, but to no avail. Finally, in one last effort, her lips parted, and her eyes opened wide, as if reacting to the agonizing pain she felt inside, but then her eyes slowly closed and her head turned suddenly and went limp. The hand Ross held became heavy. He realized she was dead and he immediately released her hand.

He stood up, unsure of himself. He noticed movement at the doorway and he turned around. Several tenants, awakened by the noise and commotion, had gathered at the door. One of them was the tourist gentleman Ross had seen earlier sitting in the lobby with his wife. The man asked if there was anything he could do to help, but Ross shook his head. He asked them to please return to their rooms and then he closed the door. He returned to where Carol's body lay. A feeling of despair and confusion came over him.

The question which kept pounding in his head was *why*— what possible motive? What reason could there be for this seemingly senseless death? Was it something Carol knew? Was her death in someway connected with Carrie or Carrie's group? *God, don't let that be.*

As these unanswerable questions poured through his mind, he recalled the voices he thought he had heard earlier while attempting to fall asleep. Yes, yes! He had heard them—voices. One had been Carol's. He was certain of that now. Had the other belonged to the person who had murdered her? Had Carol known her assailant? He concentrated on the voices to see if he could recall anything that had been said. But he had been half-asleep. He couldn't even begin to guess if the other voice had been that of a man or a woman.

He stared down at Carol's lifeless face and remembered that many years ago, her face had looked sullen but starkly beautiful when she slept, and a slight shudder crept through his body as he thought that her face looked the same way now. A bitter taste came to his lips.

He was still standing over Carol's body when the old man returned.

"I've called a doctor," the old man said. His voice wavered. "He's on his way. Should be here in a few minutes."

"It won't do any good, I'm afraid," Ross said softly. "She's dead." Saying the words only forced him to glance down once more at Carol's body to reconfirm the cold, hard fact that he spoke the truth. How cruel life can be sometimes, he thought. How utterly cruel.

"I'll go back and call the sheriff," the old man said, his voice still quivering. "I forgot to do that a moment ago. I imagine he'll want to know about this now." His last words tapered off as he left the room and started down the corridor.

Ross took the photograph from Carol's wallet and placed it inside his pants pocket. He waited for the old man to return. Ross asked him to stay in the room and not let anyone in until the sheriff arrived. Then he walked slowly back to his room to get fully dressed.

The doctor had arrived when Ross returned downstairs. A few minutes later, the Sheriff of Sandoval County, Bartolo Dominguez, arrived. He was a tall man; tall and muscular with extremely broad shoulders. He was neatly dressed, his clothes appearing newly dry-cleaned and pressed.

The Sheriff appeared alert as if he had just begun a new work day. Before he closed the door behind him, he asked another group of onlookers which had gathered in the hallway to return to their rooms. Dominguez then went immediately to where the doctor was crouched over Carol.

The old man was there too, standing next to Ross. Ross assumed the old man had told the sheriff about him, but now wasn't sure, as the sheriff hadn't appeared to notice him. Ross was about to introduce himself when Sheriff Dominguez turned to face him. He addressed Ross by his last name and introduced himself. Immediately, he began interrogating Ross. What exactly was his relationship with Carol Lockwood? Did he have any idea who might have committed the act? Had Carol located her missing daughter? Could she be mixed up in all of this? Ross answered each question as briefly as he could and explained Carol's plea for help. After asking several other questions, the sheriff told Ross he'd like to have a written statement from him, but that it could wait until morning. Ross said he could make arrangements to be in the sheriff's office any time.

"Yes, yes," Sheriff Dominguez said, "that'll be fine, Señor Blair. Could you please be at my office at, let us say, ten o'clock?"

"Yes, I'll be there."

"But I do have a few more questions I'd like to ask you tonight, if you don't mind. Questions which I feel are necessary at this time."

"Surely, I understand."

"Where were you when Mrs. Lock—when the shot was fired? You did hear the shot, didn't you?"

"I was in my room—asleep. Yes, I heard the shot. I didn't know what it was at first, but it awakened me."

"Is your room upstairs or downstairs?"

"Upstairs."

"One of my deputies should be here soon. When he arrives, would you mind accompanying me to your room so that I may take a look around?"

"No, I don't mind, but—"

"Pardon me. In all fairness, I must tell you that you don't have to grant me permission to do that, should you not—"

"Of course, Sheriff Dominguez, I realize that, but I don't mind if you look around. It's fine with me."

"My apologies, Señor Blair, if it should seem to you I'm being overly suspicious of you. Believe me, I have not the slightest reason to doubt for one moment that you are telling me the truth when you say you were in bed at the time this unfortunate incident happened, but it is not necessarily to convince myself that I am asking this of you, but only to convince the public that has seen fit to elect me to this office—to convince it that I am doing the job I am being paid to do. Sometimes it means offending people who don't appreciate being suspected of anything. Please understand, Señor Blair, I am asking only that you allow me to do what is my duty— nothing more, nothing less. You understand, of course?"

"Yes, I understand completely," Ross answered. "Please feel free to look around. I'll stay down here until your deputy arrives, then we can go up together. Or you may go up now alone, if you wish."

"No, that won't be necessary, I can assure you. I'd rather you accompany me. So we'll just—Ah, it won't be necessary for us to wait, Señor Blair. Here is my deputy now." He looked toward the doorway, through which a medium-sized man had appeared, dressed in the same khaki western shirt and trousers worn by the sheriff. He too wore a tan western hat. "Rodriguez, you stay here with the doctor in case he needs anything. Make sure nothing is touched and no one else enters the room. An ambulance will be arriving shortly. I'll be upstairs with Mr. Blair should I be needed." He walked over to the doctor and said something to him Ross couldn't hear. Then he turned again to Ross. "Let's go, Mr. Blair. It'll only take a moment of your time and then I'll be out of your way. Until later this morning at my office, that is."

"Yes, certainly," Ross said. They began walking down the hallway.

Upstairs in Ross' room, Sheriff Dominguez continued his apologetic manner in explaining the need to search the room.

"It's wiser to be sure about such things from the onset, Mr. Blair," he was saying as he rummaged through a suitcase which Ross had brought out of the closet. "You know, later one might began to think of what one would have found, and the thought is always up there in some corner of the mind creating worries because he failed to do something he later regrets not having done." As he spoke, he was careful to put back everything in the suitcase neatly in place. When he had finished, he closed the suitcase. "Besides, the innocent man, I have always contended, has nothing to hide and therefore, it behooves him to cooperate with the authorities, lest they suspect he has something to hide. Yet, it does not make my job any easier, doing all this. Snooping, some might call it."

"I understand perfectly, Sheriff Dominguez," Ross answered, in a tone of voice intended to convince the sheriff he didn't mind the search at all. "I'm sorry if I've given you the impression that I think you're intruding. I agree with you it's wise for you to do this. After all, if it helps clearing me from suspicion, it's fine with me."

"I appreciate your cooperation, Señor Blair. I'm glad you look at it in that way. If you only knew how little of that kind of cooperation my office receives around here, then you'd surely know how much I'm very appreciative when I meet someone like you."

"Thank you."

Sheriff Dominguez walked to the closet with the suitcase and placed it down on the floor. He remained in there for a moment, searching the top shelf. "You know, Mr. Blair," he said as he closed the closet door and walked up to Ross. "I've known you for only a few short moments and already I feel much at ease talking with you. I'm beginning to like you. It takes a rare man to make me react like that." He pulled a package of Viceroy cigarettes from his shirt pocket.

"Thanks for the compliment. You don't know how glad I am you feel that way, my being in a strange town and after what's happened to Carol."

"Well, I meant what I said." He held the package of cigarettes up to Ross. "Cigarette?"

"No, thanks, Sheriff Dominguez, I've got some of my own." He stepped over to the night stand and picked up a cigarette. When he turned around, Dominguez had his cigarette lighter lit and stretched toward Ross.

"Please don't think I'm just prying unnecessarily into your personal life, Mr. Blair," the sheriff continued, "but had you and Mrs. Lockwood been divorced long?"

Ross fixed his eyes on him. Sheriff Dominguez, he thought, had to be one of the most apologetic persons he had ever met. He too was beginning to like this man standing before him and whom he had met unexpectedly.

"Yes, we had, a long time," Ross finally answered. "Almost twenty years ago. In fact, yesterday, when she placed a call to me in San Francisco, was the first time I'd heard from her since our divorce." He noticed an expression of surprise on the sheriff's face.

"Yes, I would have to agree that *is* a long time. And did you also say you hadn't heard from her at all during all of that time? Not once?"

"That's right. Not until yesterday."

"Didn't you know her whereabouts?"

"No." Ross noticed the puzzled look in the sheriff's eyes. "Oh, she had her reasons for not revealing to me where she and my daughter were living; she explained that tonight. She herself admitted to me that the reasons she thought she had weren't good ones, but they had seemed to be at the time. She evidently thought I'd interfere in the raising of our daughter Carrie."

"Ah, Señor Blair," Dominguez said, "I'm afraid I'm more bewildered now than before about this situation." He raised his hand and scratched his head, shaking his head slightly. "Look, I'm through here for tonight. Suppose I leave you alone and let you rest. You must be very tired, I'm sure. Then, later this morning, you can come to my office and over a cup of coffee, you can explain all of this to me. Both of us will have rested by then. Is that all right with you, amigo?"

"That'll be fine, Sheriff Dominguez. I'll be there at ten."

"By the way, did your ex-wife have any other relatives in Albuquerque aside from your daughter? Or anywhere else? They should be notified."

"I don't know, to be honest about it. I was planning on checking that out tomorrow. Her husband, or maybe her ex-husband, might be in Albuquerque. She never told me whether or not she was divorced."

"Yes, of course, I suppose it will have to wait until then. There's little we could do at this time of night, anyhow."

"I'm sure you're right."

"Well, Señor Blair," Dominguez said as he walked toward the door, his back toward Ross, "if you should oversleep in the morning and be running late, it won't matter if you get there later than ten. I've plans to be in my office all morning, anyway. Much paper work to do, I'm afraid. And then with this unfortunate tragedy happening, this weekend will prove a long and busy one for me." He opened the door and turned to Ross. "Also, Señor Blair, if you'd like, I'll put one of my men on special assignment to see if he can help you locate your daughter. I'm not sure we can be of much help, but we are always at your service and willing to try. I want you to know that." A somber expression came to his face.

"Thank you, Sheriff, you're very kind."

"Tell me, Mr. Blair, this business about your missing daughter. Do you suspect that what happened tonight might be connected with this group she has been hanging around with?"

"I wish I knew, Sheriff. There doesn't appear to be anything that ties Carol's death to it. Of course, it's possible, but it's difficult for me to comprehend why it happened."

"Well, we'll continue our discussions later. My apologies again, Señor Blair, for having kept you, and most of all, I want you to know how sorry I am for what has happened to Mrs. Lockwood. We'll do everything we can. I've already placed a request for an examination by the county coroner. He should be here by mid-morning. Most likely he'll want an autopsy performed. It's usually done in cases such as this. And who knows, that might give us some clue in finding the person who did this. Rest assured, we'll certainly do everything we possibly can."

"I'm sure you will, Sheriff. Thanks again. Goodnight."

"Goodbye." His face displayed a deep gracious smile as he closed the door between them.

Ross momentarily kept his eyes fixed at the closed door. His mind was on Sheriff Dominguez. He felt a sudden sense of satisfaction in having made friends with the sheriff, and he could also see plainly why it was Carol had liked the man.

He turned away from the door and walked to the bed, where he sat down. He drew one last puff from his cigarette before stubbing it out in an ashtray. He was uncertain whether he should try going back to sleep. He was extremely tired but he wasn't sleepy and he knew he would have difficulty falling asleep. But he needed the rest and even though he might not be able to fall asleep, lying down would provide some rest.

Carol's sudden death was still very much in his mind. The confusion of the night was beginning to give him a headache; countless, repetitive questions still kept pouring into his mind. Who killed her? And why? Why? Each question kept creating and exposing other questions equally as puzzling. It was exasperating not having any of the answers—not even parts of answers. He was convinced he had been correct about the voices he had heard; one had been Carol's—the other, her killer's voice. It had to be someone she knew personally. The question he dreaded the most was whether the killing was connected with Carrie or her group, directly or indirectly.

What about Arthur Conrad, the professor Carol had told him about? Did he really have some magnetic stronghold over his student followers, including Carrie; something approaching that of Charles Manson's hold over his "family" in the Tate-La Bianca mass murders. Carol might have been wrong about the professor's role; or maybe, without consciously knowing it, and suspecting the worst, she had exaggerated the relationship between Carrie and Conrad and his influence over her and the group.

Finally, he undressed and got back into bed. He closed his eyes, the unanswered, piercing questions still racing through his mind, faster and faster now.

There was probably much about Carol's life that he knew absolutely nothing about; and now, would never learn. She had revealed part of it to him the day before, but probably she had only scratched the surface; there were matters she herself would never have revealed to him under any circumstances. Much could happen to a person in a period of twenty years, and he could only surmise that much had happened to Carol during that time. There had been persons in her life he would never meet. He thought again of Carol's second husband. Was he still alive? And if so, where was he living? In Albuquerque? He would have to find out soon, hopefully tomorrow. The murderer had been someone she knew—it had to be. He thought once more of the voices he had heard while in the twilight of sleep. Over and over again, the same questions returned, taunting him.

Sleep wouldn't come as he twisted and turned in bed. Below, in the lobby, he could hear the mumbling sound of someone talking, of people moving about. But the noise didn't bother him. Tomorrow would be a tiring and long day, he thought, and he had to get some rest. Sleep would have to come eventually; he would force it to come.

He thought of the events of the past few days, when this nightmare had begun. But for that phone call from Carol, he'd be back in San Francisco. That damn phone call, he moaned. His thoughts carried him back to the past Tuesday, the day he had met Monica Ashley for lunch at the Hotel Oxford.

CHAPTER 2

IT had been an unbearably hot summer; finally the first rains came during the first week of July. The moisture of that week was welcomed by Bay Area dwellers as they were relieved by the return of cooler weather. Their relief was shortlived, for the heat returned once the sky had cleared, and the combination of the rain and heat resulted in an unwelcomed, suffocating moisture which filled the air.

The clouds returned once again to hide the city from the hot, scorching sun, and so San Franciscans gained momentary relief from the humidity. It began raining again during the early part of the second week and some were talking of going to higher, cooler country for the weekend—Lake Tahoe to the west and Carmel and Monterey to the south.

The cab quickly slowed down as it moved toward the curb alongside the wide sidewalk on Market Street. It pulled up across the street from the Hotel Oxford, one of the tallest buildings in the city. It was past noon and the traffic in the streets was heavy but normal, as motorists went along oblivious to, and unhindered by, the slick streets. Downtown traffic in San Francisco always remained unchanged, regardless of the weather, and it wasn't any different this Tuesday.

Ross Blair opened the back door of the taxi and handed the cab driver a five dollar bill. He remained seated as he waited for his change, for it was raining steadily. He stuck his unopened umbrella out the door and tried vainly to open it; the latch was stuck halfway up. He looked at it annoyingly.

The cab driver turned around to give Ross his change. He held the change for Ross, who was still occupied with the stubborn umbrella.

"Things always seem to happen that way, buddy," the driver sighed impatiently.

Ross Blair looked up and gave the man a hurried glance. "What?" he asked. "I beg your pardon, I didn't hear you." He saw the driver holding his hand out. "Oh, sorry." He took the dollar bills and left the small change as a tip.

"Thanks," the cab driver said nonchalantly. "I said things happen that way," he repeated. "I meant you having trouble with that there umbrella, and the rain and them fellows back there waiting for me to move out of here so they can get in." He gestured to the rear, where other taxis had begun piling up.

"Yea," Ross said apologetically. Finally, the lock gave and he stepped out of the cab. He began walking to the corner of Mason and Market.

He smiled as he thought of the cab driver's impatience. He had always considered cab drivers, with few exceptions, notorious for being rude and discourteous. But they were merely something else to put up with if one chose to live in the big cities, along with air pollution, traffic congestion, and lack of wide-open spaces and fresh country air. But he wasn't about to let any of this, or the cloudy, rainy day, spoil his day, for he was in an extremely happy mood.

He was a man in his middle forties, but didn't appear his age, for he had retained a vigorous, youthful appearance. He had numerous skin wrinkles to the sides of his eyes caused by the squinting of his sensitive eyes at the sunlight through the years, but even that didn't detract from his young, healthy character. He stood slightly over six feet tall. Although he wasn't a muscular man, his body possessed a firm and strong complexion. He had gone through several years when he was approaching forty staying in good physical condition by jogging and by doing other forms of strenuous physical exercises, but now, he managed to keep his robust nature by playing tennis during the warm months and hand ball at a downtown health club during the colder weather.

He entered the hotel lobby, greeting Mr. Leonard, the elderly door man, as he walked toward the elevators. He met Monica Ashley at the restaurant located on the top floor of the hotel.

Monica waited for him at the far corner of the restaurant, at the table they used often when they ate here. She worked only a few blocks away on Montgomery Street and the restaurant was a convenient place to meet when they lunched together. She had walked from work in the rain.

Ross approached the table, leaned over, and planted a kiss on her cheek.

"Hi," she said and gave him a big smile.

"Hello, darling," Ross said, almost in a whisper. He struggled to get out of his raincoat. "It's this damn humidity that makes it stick to me." He took the raincoat and placed it over the back of an empty chair.

"You needn't remind me of the weather."

"My arms feel sticky under this suit." He pulled a chair back from the table and sat down.

"Don't expect me to feel sorry for you if it makes you feel uncomfortable," Monica said. "Really, Ross, I can't understand why you insist wearing long sleeve shirts during the summer when you'd be much more comfortable in short sleeves."

Ross grinned. He picked up the two menus which had been placed on the table and handed one to Monica. "Well, let's not go into that again. If I recall correctly, we've been through that little discussion several times before, haven't we?"

Monica opened the menu and began looking through it. "Yes," she replied. "And I'll probably keep bringing it up until I finally convince you you'd be more comfortable if you followed my suggestion."

"If you'd like a drink before lunch, I'll call the waiter—do you?" He was about to summon the waiter.

"No, thanks, Ross, not today. I've got loads of work to do this afternoon and I should keep a clear head."

"O.K.," he said as he shook his hand at the waiter, who had already noticed him. He glanced back down at his menu. "Yes, you're quite persistent all right," he said, continuing their discussion. "Tell me, do you get that from your mother or your father?"

Monica glanced up. She saw the teasing smile on his face. "And just what is that remark supposed to mean, Mr. Blair? Are you by chance criticizing my personality?"

He laughed. "Not really. I was merely posing the question as to which side of the family your strong persistence comes from. If you'd ask me, I'd say it was from your mother, from what little you've told me about your parents. Am I correct?"

"Probably. She *is* quite stubborn at that. It used to get me terribly nervous and uncomfortable when I was going to school and living at home. Anytime there was something she thought I should do in a particular way, she'd always keep at it trying to convince me she was right and I'd finally give in out of sheer exhaustion. Then after college, I became just as stubborn, in self-defense, I guess, and when she would start working on me, I finally learned to ignore her and proceed to do what I wanted. It used to get her awfully angry when I began doing that."

She looked up from the menu and noticed an inquiring look on Ross' face.

"Please don't misunderstand, Ross. I love my mother very much and I don't mean to sound critical of her. It's just that I didn't either like or appreciate that particular trait of hers. She had other faults, of course, like anyone else, but her stubbornness in particular used to infuriate me."

"I didn't misunderstand, darling. The thought occurred to me, though, that you've never told me much about your family. I mean—I know you have a father and mother and two sisters, but that's about all I know."

"Now that you mention it, I guess you're right. But then, you've never asked me."

"No, I haven't."

"From whom do you get yours?"

"From whom do I get what?"

"From which one of your parents did you inherit *your* stubborness? Now don't tell me you didn't know there was a streak of it in you."

"Well now, if you're going to put it that way, of course I know. But I usually try hiding it, haven't you noticed?" He laughed.

"Yes, I have. It doesn't matter anyway." She started laughing too.

"What are you laughing about?"

"You and me. We always seem to be a good pair for conversing in small talk when we can least afford to. I'm half-starved. Let's order!"

"Yes, let's do." He motioned to the waiter.

The waiter came and took their order.

"I'm sorry I was late getting here," Ross said. "I was afraid I'd have to call you to cancel our luncheon date. But I finally managed to break away."

"I'm glad you were able to make it."

"I gave you such short notice."

"It wouldn't have mattered if you had asked me two weeks ago to have lunch with you today, the way things have been at the office lately."

"Have things there been that bad?"

"Well, I wouldn't say bad. It's just that I've been so much on the go the past several weeks. And you know I don't mind staying busy. I've been extremely busy since Dick Blanchard gave me those two large accounts I told you about—remember them?"

"Yes, vaguely. Is there some problem?"

"No, no problem at all. But it's taken me some time to plan the layout. My clients are adamant they want all of the programmed TV commercials to tie in with each other's product during the next two television seasons—on both weeklies, no less. I'm afraid I'm running out of ideas."

"Have you much more to go with it?"

"I'd guess another month or so. I've been working at it constantly, and I think I'm about ready to slow down the pace a little. Dick's approved of most of the ideas I've submitted. I never thought I'd be able to get the wheels rolling on this one after I started out so sluggishly."

"Dick has a rather high regard for your business acumen,

you know. I can tell by the way he talks about your work. I'm proud of you, Monica. Most women your age get the hell out of the advertising business because they simply can't take the competition, the pressure, and the hard work that's required. But you—you've got what it takes, darling."

"You're so sweet, Ross. Thanks for the encouragement. But you deserve a lot of the credit for what I've been able to accomplish."

"In what way?" He offered her a cigarette which she declined. He took one himself and lit it.

"Simply because of that long, serious talk you and I had a few months ago, remember? It was that little pep talk you gave me."

"You mean the night after the party at Gary's. The night you were a little bit on the blue side because you felt you had been responsible for losing one of your firm's oldest clients?"

"A little bit—that's an understatement. As I remember, I felt so down in the dumps that night I even cried."

"Yes, I remember. I've fond memories of that night. You looked so lovely, even if you did feel down in the dumps, as you say. It also happened to be the first night I kissed you, remember?"

"Yes, I certainly do." She stretched her hand across the table and placed it on top of his. "But it was also the night you gave me the moral boost I needed to regain my self-confidence."

"I'm afraid you're giving me somewhat more credit than I may deserve. As I recall our conversation, any discussions we had on the advertising business most probably were intended to impress you with my—let me say—'boundless wisdom' in the field."

"Oh, Ross, I don't believe that. You're not the type who goes around trying to prove yourself to others in that way."

"No, not consciously, maybe. But subconciously, it's a different story. I couldn't help but try impressing you then." He gave her a serious, penetrating look. "Anyway, I'm glad you feel I helped you. You know I'd want to help anytime you felt you needed it." He took her hand and squeezed it affectionately. He smiled at her.

She returned his smile. "Thanks, you just don't know how much I appreciate knowing that. You're awfully good to me, darling." Then, changing the subject, she said, "I didn't know you studied psychology."

"What do you mean?"

"I was referring to your profound statement about you subconciously trying to impress others."

"Oh, that. Didn't I ever tell you that my minor in college was psychology?"

"Honestly, Ross?" He nodded. "I would never have guessed."

"I've always been interested in human behavior. Even as a small boy, I remember sitting for hours at a time in a small park near my parents' house, watching the people sitting on the park benches and strolling through the park. Mostly, I enjoyed listening to them in conversation and it was always amusing to me to watch their facial expressions or reactions to what others would say to them, especially the elderly. Ever since then, I've always believed that a person can learn a lot by simply watching people. Don't you agree?"

Monica grinned. It always amused her to listen to Ross tell her a tale of his childhood days. "Sounds to me as if you liked to snoop into other people's lives when you were a little boy." He laughed softly at her remark. "I'm afraid my knowledge of human psychology is skimpy," she continued, answering his question. "Besides, I've always had a difficult time trying to analyze myself, much less trying to analyze others."

Ross laughed again. "You're absolutely charming, Monica, the manner in which you say things sometimes."

"Honestly, Ross, I'm not the highly intelligent girl you sometimes think I am. I don't want to disappoint you." She spoke as if she were apologizing. "Don't let that Radcliffe degree fool you. I've seen some real dummies graduate from there. Besides, I got one of my worst college grades in psychology."

"You'll never disappoint me, darling. Just simply remain being the person you are and I couldn't ask for more. That's not asking too much, is it?" He stared deeply into her eyes.

She returned his serious look. "No, it's not," she replied and smiled.

Monica Ashley was 36 years of age. Her dark hair was combed in whirls neatly back and around it she wore a light, transparent yellow scarf. Although the skin on her face was quite white, it didn't have that unhealthy appearance which white skin often took in others. She had high cheek bones. Her facial skin was firm and hardly had any cosmetic make-up at all, except for mascara on her eyelashes and around her dark brown eyes, which emphasized the deep, penetrating beauty of the eyes. Her eyelashes had often been mistaken as being artificial, for they were extremely long. There was a certain quality of elegance and refinement in her face, but not excessively to the point of making her appear unfriendly or even snobbish.

The restaurant was extremely busy this Tuesday and it took unusually long before they were served. The waiter finally brought their dinner at a quarter of one.

"I'm absolutely famished," Monica said when the waiter had finished serving. She looked down at her plate. "So much so this doesn't look as if it's going to fill me."

They spoke very little as they ate, not rushing through their meal, and afterward, they took time to enjoy a cigarette. It was one thirty when they rode the elevator down to the ground floor.

The rain had lessened when they exited the hotel. Ross hailed a cab.

"Oh, I almost forgot," Monica said before Ross entered the cab. "What time will you be picking me up for the play tonight?"

"It starts at eight, doesn't it?"

"Yes."

"I'll pick you up somewhere between seven fifteen and seven thirty. That should give us plenty of time to get there, don't you think?"

"Yes, I'm sure it will. See you tonight, then. Bye, darling."

"Goodbye, Monica."

She waved goodbye, then turned and began the short walk to the office.

CHAPTER 3

MONICA Ashley was the second of three daughters of a Presbyterian minister and his religiously devout wife. She grew up in a Boston suburb. Following in her older sister's footsteps, she had attended Radcliffe, graduating with the class of '61. Shortly after graduation, she took a job as a copywriter for a Boston advertising firm and managed unhappily to stay on with that firm a little less than two years. Because of mounting dissatisfaction with her work and her having to put up with a continuing strained marital relationship between her parents, she finally quit her job and moved to California. The move had been the biggest decision in her life but she was determined to get as far away from her family as she could. At first, she had considered going abroad, but several job opportunities in Europe she thought she might be interested in fizzled out and she didn't have the courage to go there blindly, hoping to find a job that would suit her once she arrived.

A close friend she had known at Radcliffe had done just that and had come back several months later, the victim of disenchantment. Monica didn't want to make the same mistake. The excitement of living and traveling abroad was tempting to her and she had always wanted to visit Europe, but something in the back of her mind told her it wasn't the way to go about it. She felt secure staying within the boundaries of her own country, with people she knew and understood. Then, a few years later, she convinced herself, when she had managed to save a little money she could live on, she would make a few inquiries, and might make the trip across the ocean to whatever opportunities or disappointments might cross her path there.

Unexpectedly, shortly after she had been notified that the positions with the firms in Europe had been filled and she had already resigned herself to accept the somewhat inevitable fact that she would have to remain within close proximity of her family, she received an offer from Clayborn, Whitten, Smith & Associates, a New York based advertising firm with extensive subsidiary offices in San Francisco. The firm offered her a position in the San Francisco offices and she quickly accepted, although the starting salary wasn't as appealing as she would have liked. She wanted out from New England life, which is all she had ever known, and she wanted to move away from the family, particularly her mother, who apparently wanted to control and dominate Monica's life more so than ever before. She had grown to resent this part of her mother and it bothered her to feel this resentment.

She still remembered how difficult it had been to hide the relief and happiness she felt during those last few days in Boston when she prepared for the move to California and when she had said goodbye to her mother and father. Her mother had cried and stood shedding tears when Monica said goodbye at the airport. She had wanted to say goodbye to them at their home and take a cab to the airport, but her mother had insisted they drive her to the airport to see her off. When she had climbed the stairway leading to the airplane entrance, she had turned back to wave to them and she had seen clearly the pathetic look on her mother's tearful face as she returned her wave. It was then that for the first time in her life, Monica had felt sorry for her mother.

Her departure had affected her in a manner she couldn't understand completely. She guessed it might be because for the first time in her life, she felt she was finally cutting away at the remnants of emotional ties which still existed with her family. But whatever the reason, she also felt somewhat guilty on the flight to San Francisco. But all that was gone the moment she had stepped off the plane, and although she was a little homesick the first few weeks it took for her to get settled down in an apartment, her new job and in a different city, she quickly left her past where it belonged, in her memories, and began thinking of the future.

All that had happened slightly over twelve years ago. Since then, she hadn't completely abandoned her family, for she wrote to her parents often and telephoned them at Christmas and on other special occasions. She had also made it a practice to fly back to Boston and visit with them at least a week each year. She still loved her parents. It hadn't been the lack of love that had caused her to make the break from them. In fact, she was convinced now she had made the right decision and that the physical break had done much to insure that her love for her parents continued. She would have hated herself had she allowed that love to have vanished. She had also grown to appreciate them more now that they lived hundreds of miles away from her. During her thirteen year absence, her parents had been able to solve at least the major part of their marital problems which had in the past made life for them close to intolerable.

It had been a desire for a different life that had brought her to California—it was a life she could enjoy because it was based on independence and individualism, two basic traits she had always admired in others. And now she too had been able to gain her independence and emotional contentment. She had never known this feeling of independence through her high school and college years. Although she fully knew the meaning of it, somehow it always had managed to evade her during her earlier years, but now she had found it.

She had been extremely happy during the past thirteen years. She found her work both enjoyable and rewarding, and that was important to her. There had been several promotions along the way and one couldn't have expected life to look any brighter than it looked for her, she would say to herself, whenever she paused to contemplate how lucky she was to be so happy.

She thought of Ross as she turned onto Montgomery Street.

She glanced quickly at her watch—she was late for an appointment.

Ross Blair was one of the reasons why during the past several months she had experienced much happiness. There had been other men in her life before him; other romances—some brief—some for an extended period of time. But for whatever length of time they had lasted, none of them had survived the test. There had been offers of marriage from several young men with promising futures, but she had been unsure about the relationship and hadn't been entirely satisfied she was ready for marriage. There was always that lingering doubt that persisted. She had always believed that when the right man came along, there would be no doubt in her mind—none whatsoever.

Ross was an avid sailor and used to own a twenty-two foot sloop a few years back, but he had sold it because it had been both costly and time-consuming to maintain. Instead, he would now travel the short distance to one of two harbors he would frequent on weekends, and rent a small sailboat. He could spend an entire two-day weekend on a sailboat, he used to tell Monica, completely oblivious to anything else but the boat and the water. It was a sport he enjoyed immensely.

He had taken Monica sailing a few times on weekends and she immediately realized his strong love of the sea. He absorbed himself in the mechanics of the sport. There was little time for conversation; unless the sea calmed for a considerable length of time or they were on a straight tack heading back to the docking area. She found sailing hard work, at least during the times she had been out at sea with him, but there had been gusty winds and white caps, and that had made the boat difficult to handle. She had felt a slight fear. Ross had only laughed when she told him one time that there was so much to handling a boat that one had little time to enjoy the sport. But she had only said that in jest and she realized that whether or not he found it hard work, *he* enjoyed it, and she easily understood the feeling of contentment sailing provided for him. To him, he had told her, sailing was a total release from the everyday tensions of the grinding and competitive world of advertising. He would squeeze every drop of pleasure he could get from the moments of tranquility the open sea provided him.

He had been a member of the university sailing team at UCLA. Twice, he skippered his team's boat to victory at the annual Southern California sailing regattas. He confided to Monica once that during his senior year at the university, he became so discouraged with life and the conditions of the country, and more importantly, his uncertainty of what he wanted to make of his life, that he almost quit school, leaving the college degree and the competitive world to others. He had thought seriously of joining the crew of some large sailing vessel chartered to sail around the world. But the feeling had quickly passed and he had become more ambitious than ever.

He laughed on one occasion when Monica told him he would never have lasted wasting his life away on a ship. But he often wondered what would have become of him had he decided to become a professional sailor and live the life of a seaman. He wondered whether he would have been happy or whether he would have turned into one of those sailors he had seen often down at the wharf spending all his hard-earned money on booze upon returning to port.

Now that she had met Ross, Monica was certain he was the man she wanted to spend the rest of her life with—there were no doubts.

They had met at a dinner party given by a mutual business acquaintance, several months ago. Ross was an advertising executive with one of the largest advertising companies in the country. A strikingly handsome man, he had originally begun his career in advertising many years before in San Francisco and had spent a considerable number of years there but then had been transferred to New York City for several more years with the same company. Less than a year ago, he had been promoted to a new executive position in the firm's San Francisco offices. He was born and raised in San Francisco, and aside from his four years at UCLA and a two-year tour of duty with the Army in Korea, he had never been out of his home area.

When Monica was first introduced to him, she immediately became aware of a strong, submissive attraction toward him, an attraction she had never quite felt before with other men. This attraction had affected her strongly and she had caught herself staring at him during most of the evening. He hadn't seemed to have paid much attention to her except for displaying a friendly attitude when they were formally introduced. Consequently, she had been pleasantly surprised when he walked up to her later that night as the party was near its end and began a conversation with her. Then he had surprised her by asking if she would permit him to take her home. His query had taken her by complete surprise. That, plus the fact that she had been admiring his poise and good looks all evening, made her accept his offer before realizing she had. She felt slightly guilty and forward when she had wished he would suggest stopping somewhere to have coffee or a nightcap. But he hadn't suggested anything of the sort. When he had said goodnight to her at the door to her apartment, she didn't want the evening to end and she had been almost tempted to ask him in for coffee, but her strong upbringing took hold of her and she decided against it. All she could hope for was that he would be interested enough in her to call her some night.

Slightly more than a week had gone by since their first meeting, and Monica had almost given up hope they would ever see each other again or that he would ever call. Ross surprised her one day outside the building where she worked, as she was leaving work. He made no secret of the fact he had been waiting for her to come out of the building. He had only minutes before finished a conference with a client in the same building, he explained.

She thought he was teasing her. "Oh, come now," she had said to him, teasingly, "how did you know I'd come out through this particular exit at this very moment?"

"Because I've seen you leave the building before," he had answered. "You've always come out on this side—that is, you have when I've seen you. Now, as to the time element, I must admit I wasn't sure you hadn't left yet."

"I had no idea you even knew where I worked. How is it you've seen me here before?"

"Oh, I knew. I found out at the party we met. I'd seen you come out of this building on several occasions, even before we met at the party." He noticed the curious look on her face and gave out a slight laugh. "I don't want you to get the idea I've been spying on you. It's all been rather coincidental, really. I've been spending a lot of my time during the last month in this area. I've got a new client up on the tenth floor of this building —Camaron Products. You've probably heard of the company, even though it's fairly new—manufacturer of electronic equipment."

"Yes, I have. Be careful, Mr. Blair, you're treading on your competitor's territory." She gave him a teasing smile.

"If my client being in the same building Clayborn & Associates is in, then I guess you're right." He returned her smile. "But let's not let that come between us, shall we? I was waiting for you for a different reason and it has absolutely nothing to do with business. How about having dinner with me tonight?"

Once again, he had caught her by surprise and she had quickly accepted with a tone of voice that did little to hide her excitement. It embarrassed her, for he had noticed her elation.

That had been the beginning of their close relationship. And for Monica, their meeting had been the end of the seemingly unending search for emotional contentment in her romantic life.

Underneath the entrance canopy of the Hutton Building, she paused to close her umbrella.

She wore a bright yellow raincoat which fit perfectly over her shapely figure. She had an extremely small waist line and the raincoat had a wide belt which accentuated the smallness. The clinging, synthetic material of the raincoat made quite noticeable the deep curves of her bust and the firmness and roundness of her buttocks, but not in a crude manner.

She squirmed her way through the crowd in front of the entrance and then quickly walked through the rotating doors.

CHAPTER 4

THE opening act of the play began half an hour behind schedule. To add to the audience's discomfort, the theater was hot and stuffy as it awaited the play to began.

Monica noticed Ross' agitation increasing as they sat there, for apparently the delay affected him more than it did her.

Even during the intermission prior to the third and final act, he was unusually quiet as they both stood smoking in the crowded lobby. It was much cooler in the lobby than in the auditorium, but nevertheless, Monica sensed Ross had the urge to get away from the unwanted crowd, as far away as he could. But he said nothing, although he was well aware he wasn't being good company.

"Let's go have a drink at the Villa Roma on the wharf," he suggested as they left the theater. He tried hailing a taxi but it stopped for another couple. "Want to?"

"Not tonight, Ross," Monica answered. She gave him an apologetic stare. "You don't mind if we skip that tonight, do you? It's getting a little late and by the time we get there and back, it'll really be late. Besides, it'll probably be crowded there too."

"No, of course I don't mind, darling. I've made a terrible

companion tonight, I'm sorry."

"Please don't be. We all have our bad days. Tonight happens to be yours. You needn't apologize. Besides, I was about to offer a better suggestion."

"And what's that?" He waved at a cab. The cab driver quickly steered the car alongside and they entered the taxi.

"Let's go to my apartment and we can have a drink there." She moved over on the seat next to him and placed her head on his shoulder. "And I promise," she continued, "my air conditioner is working—not like the one back there. And more importantly, we'll be alone."

He placed his arm around her and rubbed her chin playfully. "That's a great idea." He gave Monica's address to the cab driver.

Monica Ashley lived in one of three high-rise apartment buildings, part of one apartment complex known as the Lincoln Park Apartments, located in the northwest section of San Francisco; various apartments had sprung up in the area during the past several years. The apartments were actually closer to Golden Gate Park, lying only a few blocks south, than to Lincoln Park located to the north. Monica's apartment wasn't spacious but she had selected it for its charm and mostly because of the big picture window in the living room facing northeast, from which one could view the San Francisco Bay area and the Golden Gate Bridge stretching majestically across it to the north to Sausalito. One caught more than a glimpse of the Pacific Ocean and at night, one could clearly see the lights of the huge tankers and ships moving out to sea or coming into the bay harbor.

In recent months, the one feature Monica had grown to dislike about the apartment was its location relative to Ross' apartment. Ross lived across town on the southside, in an apartment off Skyline Boulevard, just south of the city. It wasn't that she wanted him closer to her simply because of their relationship, but the distance between them had proven inconvenient, she had told Ross, especially to him, who had to travel clear across town everytime they made plans to go out somewhere. Even though Ross would often stay late at the apartment, not once had he complained about the long drive back to his apartment in the small hours of the morning.

"Ross, have you given thought to my suggestion that you try finding another apartment closer to mine," Monica said as they exited the elevator and walked down the long hallway to the apartment. "It'd be so much more convenient for you— you wouldn't have that drive clear across town."

He smiled. "You know," he began, "I was thinking about what you said the other night, wondering what it was that made it so difficult for me to decide whether I should move to this part of town or not. I think I have the answer."

"What is it?"

"Well, at first I thought it was just that I had grown too attached to my neighborhood. I think that's partially the reason but the major reason, I think, is that I'm afraid we'd begin taking each other for granted if I lived closer to you."

"You believe that?"

"I think we'd have a tendency to. Don't you?"

"No, I don't. And I think you're being silly in thinking that. Honestly, I don't know why you'd think—" She stopped abruptly and looked at him. She appeared upset. "Are you by chance implying that you're afraid we'd see too much of each other?"

He laughed. "Of course not, darling. I wasn't implying anything of the kind."

"Well, it seems to follow from what you said about taking each other for granted." She spoke sedately but she suddenly gave him a soft smile. "You think I'm kidding, don't you," she said as she placed the key into the door lock. She opened the door and they walked in. Monica turned to face him, not bothering to turn the light on.

He had stopped laughing now but his face still possessed a slight grin, the kind he always displayed when he was amused by something she had said.

"No, of course not," he finally answered. "I don't think you're kidding." He placed his arms around her and looked down at her. "But, I meant to imply nothing else," he continued. "The way I feel about you, darling, I don't think I could ever see too much of you and honestly, I can't see anyone ever taking a wonderful woman like you for granted." He paused in thought. "I guess what I really should have said is that there might be a tendency for us to take each other for granted, not that it necessarily would happen."

His smile had vanished and he now looked at her with serious eyes. Her eyes met his. They were standing there in partial darkness, the only light coming through the open doorway.

He bent down and pulled her toward him so that her face came close to his. Their lips touched, softly at first. Monica wrapped her arms around his broad shoulders. He pressed his lips harder to hers and she opened her mouth submissively.

He loosened his caress and withdrew his lips from hers. But before he let go of her completely, he gave her a soft kiss on the tip of her nose. It was something he would do often. He admired the shape of her nose. It was her beautifully shaped nose and her soft, white skin, he had said to her once, that made her look so pure and angelic. "Well, I'm not pure and angelic," she had replied and laughed when he had said that to her. "You've taken care of that, I'm afraid."

"Oh, Ross, my darling," she said softly to him as they stood in the semi-darkness. "I love you so much."

"I know, sweetheart," he replied. "And I love you. God only knows how much I love you." He kissed her again.

"We'd better change the subject for the moment," she said. She released him and walked to the lamp on the table near the sofa. She turned the lamp on. "You very conveniently interrupted our discussion."

"What discussion?"

"The discussion we began when I asked the question for the zillionth time about when you were going to look for another apartment. Really, Ross, I don't mean to sound possessive. It's simply that I'm beginning to feel I'm a terrible inconvenience to you when you have to travel all the way across town every time we go out somewhere. Don't you ever get tired of it?"

"No, darling what ever gave you that idea. You've never heard me complain, have you?" He walked up to her and placed his hands softly on her shoulders.

"No, I haven't, but that doesn't mean it doesn't enter your mind."

"Please don't worry about it, hon. I'd tell you if I minded.

Besides, have you ever stopped to think I wouldn't ask you out as often as I do if I really cared about the drive?" He searched her eyes.

"It's occurred to me." She thought for a moment. "You know, I must admit, we *have* been seeing quite a lot of each other lately. Maybe I *am* acting the possessive girlfriend in trying to get you to move out here, and I don't realize it."

"Oh, darling, but you're not—you're not being possessive. You're not the type."

"I'm not?"

"Oh, come now, shouldn't *I* be the judge of that."

"It occurred to me you might think I was trying to be possessive."

"Have I convinced you otherwise?"

She looked up at him, then placed her head on his chest and squeezed him tightly. "Yes, darling. I won't say anymore about it."

They parted and she took a few steps backward toward the bedroom. "Why don't you take your coat off and make us a drink while I go into the bedroom and freshen up a bit? O.K.?"

"What'll it be tonight—a martini?"

"Yes, please, darling. Make it extra dry. I could use it."

"Me too," he said and smiled.

She disappeared into the bedroom. Ross took his coat off, hung it in the guest closet, and walked up to the portable bar, where he poured gin into the glass pitcher.

A few minutes later, Monica entered the living room. Ross had already poured the two martinis and had set them on the coffee table in front of the sofa. He was seated on the sofa when she returned. She walked to the wall near the kitchen and turned on a light dimmer switch, turning on the indirect lighting on the opposite wall near the ceiling. She turned the switch so that the light was low, barely lighting the room at all.

"That's much better," Ross said.

The curtain over the large picture window was pulled open and they could now see the lights of the wharf on the extreme right and slightly to the left, the lights of the tiny cars crossing the Golden Gate and the many lights reflecting off the bay. The dark sky was slightly hazy and only a few dim stars were visible.

Monica returned to the couch and sat down beside Ross. She took off her shoes and raised her legs on top of the cushion, curling them under her. Ross handed her the drink on the table and took his.

"Cheers," he spoke softly.

"Cheers," she replied. They both took a sip. "Ummmmm, you make the best martinis, darling. Where did you ever learn to make such good ones?"

"I learned from an old friend of mine at the wharf. He works in one of the taverns down there."

"Fisherman's?"

"No, the small wharf up north a bit where I usually go sailing."

"Oh. You've never taken me there."

"No, I haven't. It's not exactly the kind of place a decent fellow would take his girl. I don't think you'd care to know it, darling. It's a sailor's hangout—nothing fancy. I used to stop in there sometimes after an afternoon of sailing, mostly to say hello to Joe. It's kind of an old dump, really. Mostly a place where winos hang out, and a few sailors and seamen who've just come in to port after being out at sea."

"Is Joe the friend you mentioned?"

"Yes. Joe Bertolina. Italian fellow. I've known him for a long time, ever since I used to hang around the wharfs and sailing vessels as a kid. He doesn't really need to work—he's on a sailor's pension—but he says he wants to keep himself occupied, so he works as a bartender. Anyway, it was from watching Joe that I learned how to make martinis. If you think the ones I make are good, you should try Joe's. Now there's a fellow who makes a mighty good drink—any drink."

He drank from his glass. "If you'd really insist, I'll take you there some day, so you can meet old Joe and try one of his martinis."

"All right by me, if you promise you'll protect me from the winos."

"I promise."

The drinks soon relaxed them. Ross made himself more comfortable by taking his tie and shoes off; he extended his legs, placing his feet on top of the coffee table. Monica leaned her head against his shoulder. They had done this often—sitting there, not saying much of anything—it wasn't an awkward nor embarrassing silence. Monica especially cherished this trait of theirs.

She soon felt the effects of her second martini. She didn't feel sleepy nor tired—only a happy, reposed state of mind. Ross' body felt comfortably warm and she pressed the side of her face to his chest. She wanted him tonight and she knew he wanted her. She realized she would soon be relenting to his desires and give her body to him.

He was already on his third drink. He drank it down and placed the empty glass on the table. Then he took Monica's drink from her hand and set it on the table.

"Come here," he whispered softly. "I'm terribly hungry for you."

She turned around so that the back of her head was now resting on his lap. She was looking up at him. "I know it," she said softly. "I want you to be."

He drew her up to him and they kissed.

She didn't mind his saying he was sexually hungry for her. It aroused her desire for him when she knew he wanted her. She wanted him to yearn for her and she didn't feel cheap because of it. When they made love, even the first time Monica succumbed to his advances, it was more than just physical desires they satisfied; there was always a mental, emotional contentment experienced along with their physical satisfaction. It made her happy to know he wanted her because of whom she was and that it wasn't only her body he wanted.

His demands excited her; a tingling sensation ran up her spine everytime she was aware of his animal desire for her. She wanted his demands. Her love for him was strong, and it was this love he demanded from her, as well as her body. And so she gave herself totally to him tonight.

She weakened, becoming more aroused as he pressed her soft body against his and ran his strong hands underneath her blouse. She became overwhelmed by the ecstasy of anticipation. He unclipped her bra and began fondling her breasts, which had grown with the excitement and the nipples were now hard. He caressed them gently so that it sent a wave of craving desire through her entire body. She grew slightly impatient and she suddenly wanted him in her. She reached down and began unbuckling his belt.

"Oh, Ross, my darling," she whispered into his ear as she kissed it. "Come inside me now. Now, my darling. I want you this instant."

"Yes, love."

And then in another moment their bodies became inseparable as they ascended higher and higher into an unreal ecstasy which no one could ever take away from them. Their bodies throbbed with intense pleasure each time he entered her. She wanted to cry out to him—to endear him with words of her love for him, as he penetrated seemingly deeper and deeper into her body, and then, their two bodies melted away as he poured of himself into her and their love for each other now permeated a fervor of exaltation she didn't want to ever end.

The bliss was soon over, though she had not wanted it to be. They rested, lying side by side, embraced, their warm bodies touching.

Monica closed her eyes and almost fell into a light sleep— she could have easily but she caught herself and opened her eyes. She saw Ross had his eyes closed and he was breathing hard on her breasts. She was suddenly aware of the stillness in the room. She felt both lazy and rested now and she slowly slipped her arm from under his. He appeared asleep for he didn't move nor make a sound as she stood up. She walked to the small table against the wall, where she picked up the pack of cigarettes, took one, and lit it. As she inhaled, the red glow of the cigarette threw enough light to allow her to glance briefly at the reflection of her nakedness in the wall mirror. She was proud of her body—proud that she could satisfy a man as she had moments ago satisfied Ross. And she was determined to keep her body sexually attractive and vowed she would never let it degenerate into an unappealing, unattractive mold of flabby skin. She returned to the sofa and looked down at Ross. Even in the darkness, she noticed he now had his eyes open; she realized he had been watching her.

"I thought you were asleep," she said. She sat down beside him on the edge of the couch. He moved over slightly to give her more room.

"I was certainly getting there," he said. "I feel so relaxed but decided I better not go sleep lest I wouldn't want to get up when it's time to go. Then you'd get angry with me." He was lying on his side and he now turned on his back so that he was looking straight up at her.

"I wouldn't get angry." She inhaled her cigarette and blew the smoke away from him. "You've been watching me, I see."

"Uh huh. I've always enjoyed watching you walk around in the nude. You have a beautiful body."

"Thank you. I'm glad you think so. I'm quite attracted to yours too, I believe you've noticed."

"Naturally, just a little."

"A little, hell, you stinker!" She bent down and kissed him. She drew back and shook the ashes from her cigarette onto the ashtray on the coffee table. Then she took a puff. "Would you like a cigarette?"

"Yes, I think I will. Mine are right there on top of the table. I'll get them." He started to rise.

She held him down. "Don't bother. I'll get them." She stood up quickly, reached for the pack of Pall Malls and pulled the coffee table closer to the sofa. He took a cigarette from his pack and lit it with hers.

"Come lie down beside me again," Ross said, exhaling the smoke from the cigarette. He patted the cushion next to him.

She cuddled up to him. They lay there silently for a long while. Monica was staring up at the ceiling.

"Mind if I ask what you're so wrapped up in thought about?" he said and slightly nudged her with his elbow.

"Oh, nothing too important," she answered. "Just day-dreaming, I guess."

"What about—us?"

"Yes."

"Then it *must* be terribly important." He grinned. "Come, darling, out with it. We keep no secrets from each other, re-member?" He dragged at his cigarette, then put it out on the ashtray Monica was holding up to her bare stomach.

"I'm not keeping any secrets from you, darling. But there's some things that aren't easily explained and sometimes even better left unsaid, especially when one's motives can be misunderstood."

"I promise I won't misunderstand."

"Well, I was thinking how much I care for you and love you and that I want to love you always. And for some reason, I thought of our discussion this afternoon about the time you gave me that pep talk, as I called it. That kind of thing is proof that I've gotten to be extremely dependent on you, Ross."

"And what, may I ask, is wrong with that?"

"Nothing's wrong with it in and of itself, I guess. Most people need to depend on others, lean on someone's shoulder once in a while, if for no other reason than to remind themselves they're not self-contained. I think it's great having someone to depend on when the going gets rough."

"So what's wrong if you depend on me—or I on you for that matter? I want you to feel you can depend on me."

"I know that, Ross. It's wonderful to know you're there whenever I may need you. But then one gets to a certain point where too much dependence may hurt a relationship."

"And what point is that?"

"I'm referring to the point in time when a person is emotionally dependent on another all the time. I don't want to start leaning on your shoulder too much or for too long a time, because I'll never know if—" She stopped abruptly. "Oh, don't pay any attention to me. I doubt if I'm making any sense at all."

"But you are. I think I know exactly what you're getting at."

"What?"

"My guess is you were going to say you don't want to depend on me too much because you're afraid the day might come when I might call it quits between us before you realized what hit you." He paused, then added, "Am I right?"

"Well, sort of. Except I wasn't going to say it as bluntly as you've put it."

"Maybe not, but I guessed right, didn't I?"

"Yes."

"But you should remember, darling, it's a two-way street. Let's face it, hon, each of us can become the victim of the other unilaterally terminating our relationship. Haven't you stopped to think I too must face the possibility that *you* may someday lose interest in me?"

"Oh, darling, don't ever think that. There's no way that would ever happen."

"But, Monica, you realize it's a possibility. You and I can be certain only of how we feel about each other today. But that's now. At this moment, you find it difficult to see you could lose your interest in me someday. But people change—you and I included. That's why the question of marriage—" He stopped suddenly.

"Oh, Ross, there you go making assumptions—I said absolutely nothing about marriage. I knew you'd misunderstand my intentions. Now you're making me feel as if I were hinting of marriage when I meant nothing of the sort."

"Darling, I didn't mean that at all. I don't feel you're forcing me to propose marriage." He sighed deeply. "But you know something—my having brought up the question of marriage has revealed something to me about myself."

"What do you mean?"

"First, let me assure you that I love you deeply, darling. I love you more than I could ever dream of loving anyone.

"And I've thought often of asking you to marry me. You don't realize how close I've come to asking you, but I—"

"Please, Ross," Monica interrupted. "You don't owe me an explanation of—"

"Let me finish, Monica, I'd like to explain. I'm convinced now that what I had earlier only suspected is true. I realize now the reason why I haven't asked you to marry me—the truth is I'm actually afraid to—I'm afraid of marriage. Even as much as I happen to love you, I'm afraid because I don't want to ever lose you like—"

"Darling, please don't say that because it wouldn't happen."

"Maybe it wouldn't. But the possibility bothers me because of the failure of my first marriage to Carol. It's terribly immature, I know, and it's embarrassing to admit it, but I think it's the truth."

"But darling, that marriage was so long ago and you and Carol were young."

Ross' marriage during his twenties was something he and Monica had never discussed at length. Soon after they had known each other intimately, he had casually mentioned to Monica his marriage to his college sweetheart almost twenty years ago. Monica had never purposely inquired about the marriage. She had learned from him that a child had been born to Carol a few months before the divorce and that he hadn't seen the child nor Carol since the divorce.

Ross had spoken to her about the marriage almost without feeling; without emotion. It would have been difficult to have guessed then, when he had first told her about it, that although he had long ago accepted failure of the marriage and the divorce that followed, and it was now only a small part of his past, it would now come back to haunt him in a disguised form.

"I've never discussed at length my marriage to Carol, have I?"

"No. But I've never wanted you to feel you had to."

"I know. But I think I should tell you about it so you'll understand what I'm getting at."

"All right, darling, if you think it'll help."

"During the next half hour, she listened as he spoke of the marriage long ago.

"Anyway," Ross said when he had finished, "I used to ask myself why it was I hadn't asked you to marry me and the most obvious reason I could think of was that after so many years of being a bachelor, it's difficult to think of myself as a husband with different responsibilities than I've been accustomed to during the last twenty years. And yet, I'd think that with time, I'd be able to adjust to the change. But deep down inside, I now honestly think there's that other reason I mentioned—my fear of marriage—that's a reason that's not so obvious, but now I'm sure it's there."

"Oh, Ross, but that marriage took place ages ago, even though the divorce may have hit you hard at the time. And it's water under the bridge. Besides, you don't hear me complaining about your not having proposed to me, do you?" They both laughed.

"Let's not talk about it anymore," she continued. "I'm sorry I even brought it up."

He said nothing.

She placed her soft hand on his chin and turned him so that

he was facing her. Even in the darkness, Ross could see a bright, fresh smile on her face. It was that loving smile her face always possessed when she wanted him to know she was content and happy.

He returned her smile. "Well," he said softly, "at least I got it off my chest and I'm glad for that."

"So am I."

"You know, our talk about the fear that one's love may end for another brought to mind something I once read. Wasn't it Somerset Maugham who once wrote that the essential element of love is a belief in its own eternity?"

"I wouldn't know, darling."

He leaned forward and kissed her gently. "My precious Monica," he whispered, and then he took her in his arms and kissed her. As he held her, her naked body suddenly relaxed momentarily, and he felt her quiver with excitement as he pressed his lips hard to hers and ran his hands down her bare back.

Later, as he dressed, she went into the bedroom and returned wearing a light blue pajama nightgown. It was made of a transparent material and her skin beneath it looked both delicate and beautiful.

She made coffee and they sat and talked as they drank. It was two o'clock when they finally said good night to each other.

CHAPTER 5

MONICA'S work day began earlier than usual the following morning. She awakened at six, for she had to be in the office by seven. She had scheduled an appointment with a prospective client at nine o'clock. An executive meeting was scheduled for ten thirty and so she decided to start the day early to catch up on her work.

So it was going to start off as that kind of day, she said to herself irritatingly, as she stood in the corridor outside the company's offices, searching through her purse for the office keys, only to find she had left them at home. No one usually arrived at the offices until seven thirty at the earliest. It took her several minutes to search the building for one of the janitors, who had a set of master keys. She found him five floors below, mopping the hallway floors.

When she finally began working on the accounts material, she was surprised to find herself vigorously attacking her work, for she was not yet fully awake.

She stopped momentarily to warm up the day-old coffee she found in the small kitchen, poured it into a small server and took the server with her to her desk. She lost track of time as she tackled the accounts once again.

The phone startled her when it rang, for she had been completely absorbed with her work. She was surprised to find Mollie, the receptionist, at the other end, informing her that her nine o'clock appointment was waiting for her in the reception room. Monica quickly looked at her watch. It was three minutes of nine.

"Please ask Mr. Keever to have a seat," she said to Mollie, "and tell him I'll be right out. Thanks, Mollie."

She picked up her purse and slipped away from her office through a private exit into the ladies' room to freshen her makeup.

She had anticipated that her appointment with Mr. Keever would take what remained of the morning prior to the executive meeting, and consequently, she was surprised when by ten o'clock, Mr. Keever stood up to leave, apparently pleased with what Monica had presented. He bid farewell to Monica by tipping his hat as he lifted his small frame off the chair. He extended his hand to her. She smiled, shook his hand, and accompanied him into the reception room.

She returned to her office and looked at her watch. She had plenty of time to phone Ross and to put her notes together for her report. Although she would be seeing Ross that night at dinner with Gary and Brenda, she wanted to see him before then. She couldn't quite put her finger on the reason behind her strong urge to see him, but strongly suspected it had to do with their discussion of the night before. The discussion had left her somewhat uneasy but she didn't know why.

"Good morning, darling," she spoke softly into the telephone when Ross answered.

He seemed surprised to hear her voice. "Oh, good morning, Monica," he finally answered. "I didn't expect to pick up the telephone and find you on the line, dear."

"I didn't interrupt anything too important, did I, Ross?"

"No. Ed Parker and I were just sitting here discussing business. He says to say 'hi'."

"Tell him hello for me too."

"Just a minute, Monica; Ed is leaving." She heard Ross' muffled voice. "Monica says hello, too," she heard him say. "Well, I guess that wraps it up, Ed. Why don't you dictate a letter to Morton along the lines we've discussed and we'll wait to see how it goes from there."

Ed Parker was Ross' associate. They had also been the best of friends for a number of years, and once or twice, Ed had joined Ross and Monica for an evening dining together. A confirmed bachelor, or so he said, he was in years younger than Ross, but in appearance seemingly much his senior.

Ross was back shortly on the telephone. "Sorry, hon. You called just as Ed was leaving."

"Are you sure I didn't cut your discussion short?"

"Yes, we were finished, honestly." He paused for a long second. "And to what good fortune do I owe the pleasure of hearing your lovely voice so early this morning?"

"Early, you say! Listen, early riser, not in my book, it's not. I've been in my office since seven."

"You're kidding?"

"I most certainly am not."

"And to think I felt guilty last night for keeping you up so late."

"You needn't have felt that way. I think I was mostly to blame. As a matter of fact, I was about to apologize for that."

"Well, I guess our apologies cancel themselves out. Fair enough?"

"Fair enough."

"That's not really why you called, was it?"

She laughed. "No, it wasn't. I thought we might have lunch together today. I'd like to see you."

"Gee, Monica, I'd love to, but I just don't see how I'll be able to. I'm swamped with work here." He paused awkwardly. "Some unexpected matters have come up and I've got appointments clear through six, hon."

"That's too bad, darling. I'd really like to see you, if only for a short lunch."

"I'm afraid that won't be possible, darling. Honestly, you know I'd do it if I could. I'll probably have someone pick up a sandwich for me which I'll gulp down between appointments. I won't get a chance to go out of the office."

There was a sudden pause. Monica didn't speak for she sensed Ross was on the verge of saying something else; yet, he said nothing. She perceived also that although he spoke in a pleasant tone of voice, there was something peculiar about his voice. There was something strange about his reaction to her telephone call this morning which escaped her. She sensed that he had something in his mind that was bothering him. The awkwardness didn't pass unnoticed to Monica—she knew him too well. She realized for the moment it was best not to let him know she suspected anything.

"Well," she finally said, "I'm suddenly talking like a young school girl who hasn't seen her beau in months. After all, we'll be seeing each other tonight."

"We will?"

"Well, of course. Have you forgotten about our having dinner with Gary and Brenda tonight?"

"Oh, yes. Would you believe I had forgotten all about it?"

"You better make a note of it, dear," she said, trying to sound casual and to hide the slight annoyance she now felt for not knowing what was bothering him. There definitely was something which had suddenly come between them that made their conversation this morning sound almost artificial, as if each had suddenly run out of things to say to the other.

And yet, she may have picked a bad time to telephone him. In his own good-natured manner, possibly he was trying to remain pleasant with her while his mind struggled with some knotty problem. But even the thought that there was a satisfactory explanation for the sinking sensation she now felt at the pit of her stomach did nothing to satisfy her curiosity, so that she was compelled to ask the question that had been nagging at her mind.

"Darling, is there something the matter?" she said, unable to resist any longer.

"Why no, hon. There's nothing the matter—why?"

"I can't help but sense something's bothering you."

He forced a laugh. "Oh, well—that. It's the busy day I have in front of me, I guess. That's all, darling."

"I thought it might be something else." She paused. "Anyway," she went on, changing the subject, "it's not always that I get to cook a complete dinner for you. I'm making your favorite—meat loaf and that New England recipe cake you've always said you liked. That's one of the reasons we're having Gary and Brenda over to my place, remember. You insisted they try my cooking." She laughed awkwardly.

"Yes, darling, I remember I'm the one who invited them. I simply forgot it was tonight. You've never minded my showing you off a little. I want others to appreciate your good cooking too."

"If it makes you happy, I'm satisfied. I'm looking forward to seeing Gary and Brenda tonight, aren't you? It's been a long time since we were together with them."

There was a slight pause again.

"Yes—yes, I am. And I'm also looking forward to one of your delicious dinners."

"I'm sure you are, darling," she said. "I love cooking for you." Then, very abruptly, she said, "Ross, are you sure there's not something the matter that you'd like to tell me about?"

"Nothing to worry about, darling. Something's come up here which has created a slight problem—something a little out of the ordinary. But I can't tell you about it now—it'll have to wait, hon. I'll explain later tonight."

"All right; but it's nothing too serious, is it?"

"No, doll, it isn't. I'll tell you all about it tonight, all right?"

"O.K." She looked at her watch. There were only a few minutes left before the meeting was to begin. "Well, I better let you go. You've got work to do. And so have I, for that matter—have a meeting to attend in a few minutes. See you tonight, darling."

"I promise I'll be there on the dot." He paused. "Thanks for calling, Monica. And I'm sorry I can't make lunch today, hon—honest I am."

"I know you are. Bye."

"Goodbye, darling."

For a moment, she stood there in thought, holding the telephone receiver in her hand. Then she became aware of the sound of the dial tone in the quiet office and she replaced the receiver.

What problem had come up which had made Ross sound so strange? She had no basis for assuming the problem wasn't related to his work. Yet, she had called him many times before when he had been under pressure and he had never sounded as he had today. No, she thought, it was something more than that.

If the problem he had referred to wasn't connected with his work, the only possible explanation for his odd behavior was the discussion they had had the night before. Was something about the prior night bothering him now? Had he been honest with her about his feelings?

She was suddenly confused and uncertain whether or not she had used good judgment the night before—whether Ross had been wrong in his explanation of how he felt about marriage—more importantly, why he felt the way he said he did.

Much to her dismay, she realized she would have to put the matter in the back of her mind for the remainder of the day, for there was much work to be done.

She looked at her watch. She had only seconds to get her notes and account files in order for the meeting that was about to begin. She let out a deep sigh as she stood next to the large window of her office. She was staring down to the street below, watching the miniature cars and buses and tiny people that crawled about. They appeared to be barely moving from the top of the high building.

She moved slowly away from the window, picked up the file folders and notes from her desk and walked rapidly out of the office to the conference room. As if to gather strength and determination with which to tackle the day and work ahead, she thought of the times in the past she had undergone worse days at the office and had managed with apparent ease to get through them. She told herself today was no different.

CHAPTER 6

THE telephone rang as Monica prepared the dinner salad in the small kitchen of her apartment. It rang three times before she was able to leave the kitchen to pick up the telephone.

She picked it up carefully with her thumb and forefinger, her hands still gummy from the salad ingredients and the special dressing she had prepared.

"Hello," she spoke sharply into the telephone.

There was a pause at the other end. "Monica, is that you?" It was Ross.

"Ross, yes, of course it's me, silly. Who else did you expect?"

"No one else, but you didn't quite sound like yourself." He hesitated another moment.

"Is anything the matter, Ross?"

"No, nothing's the matter. Why?"

"Well, you calling, for one thing. It's already six-thirty. You're due here at seven. Gary and Brenda should be here soon. They're always so punctual. Besides, this is the second time today you've apparently failed recognizing my voice." She laughed jokingly and waited for Ross to say something, but there was another pause. "Well?" she finally said.

"Well what?"

"Will you be getting here at seven? Where are you, any-way?"

"Oh, I'll be there five or ten minutes late, Monica. I'm still at the apartment. That's really why I called, to let you know I'd be a little late."

"All right, Ross," she said, "but please try not to make it any later than that. We'll barely have enough time for a cock-tail before dinner."

"I promise I won't, darling."

She waited again for him to say something else and again, she felt as she had earlier that day—that there *was* something he had on his mind, and although it distressed her, she was more mystified than anything else. Oh, well, she thought, she would find out one way or another later that night what was troubling him. She wanted to say goodbye and hang up so she could finish up in the kitchen and so he could start on his way, but she didn't want to appear abrupt.

"Were you delayed at the office?" she finally said softly, finding little else to say to him.

"Yes, I'm afraid so. I've just showered and put on a new set of clothes and am about ready to leave. But I wanted to call you up before to let you know I'd be a few minutes late." He hesitated again. "I better hang up now so I can finish up and be on my way. Bye."

"All right. See you in about half an hour, darling. Bye."

She heard the sharp, loud click on the telephone line as Ross placed the receiver down.

She walked hurriedly into the kitchen. She began tossing the salad once more and added a few spices and the dressing. As she rushed through last minute details, she thought of the telephone call. The strangest part about the call was the fact that Ross had been late to engagements before, but never had he bothered to call her to say he'd be tardy. She had long ago recognized promptness wasn't one of his virtues. It had never irritated her and in fact, she had been amused at his total ina-bility of preventing time from passing him by.

Why now, then, for the first time, had he bothered to call simply to say he'd be five or ten minutes late. My darling, she thought, something was bothering him terribly. And again, she thought of their talk of the night before, which she now believed more so than she had that morning, had some connection with Ross' strange behavior.

Having finished in the kitchen, Monica went into the bedroom where she slipped into a floor-length hostess gown. Gary and Brenda arrived a few minutes early. Monica was still in the bedroom putting on the finishing touches to her makeup when the doorbell rang.

Ross arrived a few minutes later. Gary and Brenda welcomed him with open arms, as they hadn't seen him for several weeks. But the two guests noticed immediately that Ross wasn't his usual self tonight; he was extremely quiet after a bit of small talk. Brenda remarked about it to Monica as she helped her in the kitchen, before they sat down to eat.

"So you noticed it, too," Monica answered, saying nothing more, convinced now more than ever she hadn't been imagining things. She now had resolved herself to expect the very worst.

Gary Cohen was usually talkative, especially when he had had a few drinks and tonight was no exception—he monopolized the entire conversation during dinner. To Monica, this simple fact became agonizingly apparent as she saw Ross withdraw from the group, only nodding and smiling and on occasion, forcing a laugh in reaction to Gary's natural wit. But his mind was obviously elsewhere tonight and when he spoke, he did so almost too mechanically, as if it were something expected of him.

Monica could tell Gary and Brenda too felt extremely awkward, even though they were trying not showing it. The two of them, and especially Gary, kept the conversation going, but even then there were those perplexing, brief periods of silence. Monica found it difficult to become stimulated by the conversation, for Ross' moodiness had infected her.

Not surprisingly, when the guests had left earlier than usual, the apartment became extremely quiet. Aware that Ross was still standing next to the door, watching her, Monica avoided him, and walked away to the dinner table where she began picking up the remaining dishes.

She piled the dirty dishes to one side of the table and began picking up the place mats. Ross hadn't moved. Through the corner of her eye, she noticed he began walking toward her. She didn't bother turning around but continued with what she was doing. He placed his hands on her shoulders. He began speaking quietly.

"I'm terribly sorry for this evening," he said in a low tone of voice. "You must believe me. But I wouldn't blame you if you asked me to leave. I probably deserve that." He held her loosely and delicately, as if he expected her at any moment to push him away in anger.

But she didn't. She stood there, holding the place mats she had gathered off the table and staring onto the blank wall across the room.

"No," she said. "I feel you should stay awhile." Her eyes registered disappointment as she turned finally and looked up at him. "I think we better have a talk. We owe each other that much." She didn't wait for an answer but left him standing there and she walked into the kitchen with the dishes and mats in her hands. She returned within seconds and went directly to the couch in the living room where she sat down. Ross sat down at the other end of the couch. As he sat down, she turned toward him and gazed into his eyes. She broke the silence first.

"Ross," she began, "what exactly happened at the office today—I wish—"She suddenly was at a loss for words.

"Please, Monica," he broke in, "let me say something first. You don't have to ask any questions. I know exactly what's going through your mind. So please let me try to explain, O.K.?" He looked at her wearily.

"Of course," Monica said coldly.

"Well," he said gravely. He seemed to not know quite how to begin. "To begin with, I want to say that it would have been much better had I not come tonight. It turned out to be a bad mistake after all, my coming. I started to break our engagement tonight. That's why I called you earlier this evening. To—"

"Why didn't you, then? It certainly would have saved us the embarrassment with Gary and Brenda. They're certainly undeserving of behavior such as you displayed tonight. Whatever gripes you might have with me certainly shouldn't be directed at our friends, least of all Gary and Brenda. It was so cruel, Ross." She had begun speaking softly but as she spoke, her voice rose slightly and Ross could tell she was disturbed.

"Please, Monica," he spoke out exasperatingly, "hear me out first, won't you, before you condemn me for my behavior tonight." He looked sternly at her and she momentarily returned his stare with what he thought was a void expression on her face. She then avoided his glance.

"I'm listening. But I wasn't trying to sound disagreeable."

"The reason I called you was to call off our dinner engagement. Because of the way I felt, I didn't look forward to this evening at all and I suspected I might spoil the night if I came at all. But then I changed my mind about cancelling when you answered the telephone. I thought maybe I was wrong—that I would snap out of it once I got here and then, of course, I felt rather foolish calling you at the last minute. As it turned out, I was wrong in not coming out with it and so I managed to spoil the evening after all." He didn't take his eyes off her.

"And," he went on, moving closer to her, "I thought you might misunderstand the reason for my juvenile behavior tonight." He chose his words carefully. "You mentioned something a moment ago about it's all right directing my gripes at you but not at our friends. Darling, I've absolutely nothing to direct at you but my love and respect. You can blame me for spoiling the evening for you tonight—of that, I'm guilty. But you'd be wrong in thinking I spoiled it because of something having to do with you. The thought entered my mind earlier today that I hadn't succeeded in keeping anything from you this morning when you called me. This afternoon, I realized you might have thought the way I acted this morning had something to do with the discussion we had last night."

"As a matter of fact, I *did* think that," Monica said bluntly. "Now honestly, Ross, what else was I supposed to think? There was no other reasonable explanation I could think of."

She now saw in his face an expression she recognized—an expression that in the past had denoted both anxiety and exasperation directed at something unknown.

"Anyway," she went on when he said nothing, "I saw no other reason." She paused and looked at him inquiringly. "Is there?"

"Yes, Monica, there is, and I should probably have told you sooner, but this morning wasn't the right time. Nor was it something I could speak to you about over the phone. And I was too swamped with work this afternoon to make any time —so it had to wait until tonight."

He paused to clear his throat. "The way I acted this morning and this evening had absolutely nothing to do with our discussion last night nor with any problem connected with work. I guess you could say I was in a state of shock when you called this morning and I did a poor job of covering it up." He looked deeply into her eyes. "I heard from Carol this morning, Monica."

"Carol?"

"Carol—my ex-wife."

It took a few seconds for what he had said to register in her mind. "I can't believe it."

"You're not alone. Neither could I this morning when she called."

"But how did she know where you worked, after so many years?"

"I didn't think of asking her about that. Believe me, it was all quite a shock."

"It must have been. But it sounds so incredible. And to think we were talking about her only last night—what an extraordinary coincidence." She was anxious and curious to learn more about the telephone call. "Is she in San Francisco?"

"No. She called from some place in New Mexico. A little town somewhere north of Albuquerque. I don't remember the name—I made notes at the office."

"I can see how it must have surprised you when she called you just like that—after so many years of simply not hearing from her. What in the world did she want?"

" 'Surprise' actually doesn't describe the way I reacted to her call. I was utterly shocked by it. She seemed desperate. She called to ask me to go to New Mexico and meet her there."

"What in heavens for?"

"She didn't know who else to call, I imagine. Anyway, she wanted me to go down there to help her locate Carrie." He noticed the inquiring look on Monica's face. "Carrie's my daughter," he explained. "I'm sure I've mentioned her by name before."

"Oh, of course you have. Please go on." She was growing impatient.

"Carol's been looking for her. Evidently they had some disagreement and Carrie's left home. She also said Carrie's in some kind of trouble. She wasn't too explicit about it at all. Besides, we had a bad connection, which didn't help matters any, and I was on my way to a meeting. But I could definitely tell she was nervous and terribly concerned. I was so stunned by the telephone call that I simply couldn't think of many questions to ask her. Besides, she seemed so confused and it was difficult for me to get even some idea of what she was talking about. I don't mean to say she was hysterical or anything like that. But she made it clear that it was important to her that I go there as soon as I could—that it was a matter of life or death."

"Do you really think it's that serious?"

"Carol seemed to think so. She used those words exactly. It *must* be critical, at least in her eyes. And she was never one prone to exaggeration. At least, not when I knew her." He paused for a moment, as if reliving the telephone conversation. "And she also sounded very much afraid — fear was something I rarely saw her experience. She used to be almost excessively courageous and daring about things. She'd always shrug off any risk or danger to herself or to others. I remember it used to irritate me a little when she displayed this laxity—this indifference—about problems or danger. She's either changed a lot in the past twenty years *or*—she really meant it when she said it was important to her that I go there immediately."

"Twenty years is a long time. People can change drastically in that period of time." Monica paused and looked at Ross with bewildered eyes. "But, what I don't understand is, how does she expect you to help locate a daughter you haven't laid eyes on since she was only a few months old. Why, she's a grown woman now! And she wouldn't recognize you. What exactly does Carol expect you to be able to do?"

"Yes, you're right, I wouldn't recognize her or know her

at all—she'd be a complete stranger to me."

"Is Carrie in New Mexico?"

"Yes, I would think so. That's the reason Carol was in this small town she called from. She thought she might find her there. Apparently, someone told her Carrie might be staying there." He stopped. "Carol and Carrie have been living in Albuquerque all this time."

"You mean that's where Carol went to when she disappeared from here?"

"Yes, I was able to get that much out of the conversation. Evidently, they've been living there ever since."

"But why Albuquerque? Did she have relatives there?"

"Not that I ever knew about. I never did learn much about Carol's family, except that she was an only-child. She hardly ever spoke about her parents. Her mother died two or three years before Carol and I met. The only living relative I ever knew she had was her father, Andrew Borlin. A scientist in biochemistry or something of that nature. The guy was a weirdo. Actually, I only got to meet him a few times when he would come to California to visit with Carol. I used to get the impression he never cared much for me. He'd correspond with her once in a while and she with him and then suddenly his letters stopped coming and her letters to him came back unclaimed and Carol never heard from him again during the time we were married. But if I recall correctly, he was living out east somewhere when he last came to visit Carol. I don't have the faintest idea why she moved to New Mexico."

"But why did she leave without telling you where she was going? Didn't she explain that?"

"No, and to tell you the truth, I didn't think of asking. I don't have any of the answers, do I? That phone call has gotten me terribly on edge, and the whole thing's been bothering me all day. I really should have told you about this before now and we could have avoided this disastrous evening with Gary and Brenda. It left me with a bad taste in my mouth. I hope you understand now why I've acted the way I have."

"Oh, Ross, you poor darling. Of course I understand. But to think I believed it was because of what happened last night. I'm terribly sorry, darling. Suddenly, what happened tonight at dinner is unimportant. I'm so relieved it has nothing to do with last night." She paused momentarily, then gazed into his eyes. "It appears I'm the one that should apologize for jumping to all sorts of wrong conclusions."

"No, darling. It was perfectly natural for you to react the way you did." He shook his head and managed to smile, if only slightly. "Who would have guessed in a million years that after so many years of not hearing from someone I used to love—or at least, thought I did—and a daughter I haven't seen for twenty years, I would one day suddenly learn about them, much less under these mysterious circumstances." He was looking away from her, gazing down at the floor, as if he could see far beyond it.

Not finding what else to say, Monica asked, "You're not really seriously considering going there, are you Ross?"

"I don't honestly know," he answered softly and without conviction. "I must admit I've mixed emotions about the whole thing in general and about going there in particular. I've just got to find out more about it. I told Carol I'd call her back tomorrow morning and let her know whether I could get away or not, and give her some idea when I could leave."

She moved next to him, took his hands in hers, and held them on her lap.

"Even after all these years, I'm sure you must be terribly worried about Carrie, if it's as serious as Carol said it is. Didn't she give you even the slightest idea what she meant when she said it was a matter of life or death? Surely she would realize you'd be concerned about your own daughter, especially when she's kept her hidden from you all these years."

"Well, as I said a moment ago, there was considerable static on the line and we couldn't hear each other that well—and, too, I was rushed to get to that meeting. I finally asked her to give me her telephone number and I'd get in touch with her later on in the afternoon, but she said she was leaving for Albuquerque. There were a few things she needed to take care of there and she didn't know exactly when she'd be back to-night. So she asked me to call her tomorrow morning at the hotel."

"I hope you get the answers to some of these questions.

Don't you think Carol should explain to you what it is—"

"Yes, Monica," Ross broke in, somewhat impatiently, "that's what I hope to do tomorrow. I'm concerned about Carrie— deeply concerned, even though I haven't seen her in all these years. But I definitely want to learn more from Carol to see whether I'd be of any help should I decide going to New Mexico. There'd be little sense in my going there if I believed there was no way I could help, no matter how concerned I might be. But Carol herself must have strongly felt I could help in some way; otherwise she wouldn't have called."

"What about the police? Haven't they been able to find out anything?"

"That's one of the first things I asked Carol. She hasn't reported it to the police. She said she's afraid to."

"Afraid to!" Monica exclaimed. "But that's one of their duties—to locate missing per—"

"Evidently, this isn't simply a missing person case—there's more to it than that, I'm afraid. It has something to do with the trouble Carrie's in. Carol's afraid that if the police enter the case, they'll learn about Carrie's problem and matters might get worse instead of better."

"My heavens, Ross, what sort of trouble could it be?"

He shrugged. "I don't have the slightest idea."

"Oh, darling, I know it must be a terrible strain on you. But surely Carol will give you some idea what it's all about tomorrow when you call her back."

"I'm not so sure she'll explain everything that thoroughly over the telephone. I'm certain she'd have a lot more to tell me once I got down there."

"When do you think you'll definitely decide whether you're going or not?"

"I don't know. It's so confusing to me at the moment. I'll think about it some more tonight and tomorrow after I learn more from Carol. I'm sure I'll decide something by tomorrow night."

With that, they brought to a close their conversation about the mysterious phone call, and although it was difficult for her to do, Monica changed the topic of conversation. She was determined to try taking Ross' mind off the phone call, if only for a short while.

She remembered there was still some martini mix left in the pitcher which Ross had placed in the refrigerator. She went into the kitchen and was back shortly with two filled martini glasses. She handed one to Ross.

She would have wanted Ross to make love to her tonight but she sensed he wasn't in a romantic mood. Even though she now shared his anxiety, she wanted desperately to comfort him and she knew the best way to do that was to get him talking about something else. She partially succeeded doing that throughout the remainder of the night, but she was aware it would take much more than that to clear up his mind.

She had been wrong about his sexual inclinations, for, without encouragement from her, his desire for her grew and she gladly gave herself to him. For that one moment during which their bodies were fused together, the problems that had been suddenly thrust upon him that day became non-existent, cast aside by the fulfillment that filled his mind.

CHAPTER 7

ROSS Blair smiled at the young girl standing behind the counter. Her lips formed a bright smile.

"Thank you for flying TWA, Mr. Blair," she said. She turned and glanced up at the large clock on the wall. "Your plane will be departing in thirty minutes. You'll be boarding at Gate 26."

"Thanks," Ross answered.

"Have a pleasant flight, sir."

"I'm sure I will. Thanks again." He placed the ticket envelope in his inside coat pocket and walked toward the spacious air terminal lobby of the San Francisco International Airport. He was hungry and decided he had time to eat a sandwich at one of the terminal restaurants at the far corner of the lobby.

He walked swiftly through the maze of people in the lobby and entered the restaurant. The place was filled with people but he quickly spotted an empty counter stool at the far end. He sat down, hurriedly picked up a menu and placed his order.

He had barely finished half a cup of coffee when the waitress returned with the soup and sandwich he had ordered. He thanked her and then began eating hurriedly. He looked at his watch. He was rushing himself as usual. He had been to the

San Francisco airport many times in the past and it now registered in his mind that Gate 26 was located at the far end of
one of the longest wings of the air terminal.

As he thought of the long walk to the gate, a male voice
came crackling over the ceiling speakers. "May I have your
attention, please. Trans World Airlines announces the departure of Flight 760 non-stop, jet service to Albuquerque at 1:45.
Passengers may now board at Gate 26."

He would have to hurry. As he started on the sandwich, he
thought of the telephone call he had made to Carol that morning. He had finally reached her a few minutes before noon. He
had tried placing the call several times earlier in the day but
she wasn't in her hotel room. The desk clerk the operator had
spoken to was an elderly man. Ross had asked the operator to
have Carol paged and the old man had replied, "There ain't
no use paging her, Mister. This here's a small hotel and she'd
either be in her room or not here at all. Besides, I saw her leave
early this morning and I'd know if she'd returned. Been sitting
here at the front desk since early this morning."

"Did you hear what the desk clerk said, sir?" the operator
asked Ross.

"Yes, operator, I'll try again later, thank you."

"You're quite welcome, sir."

A few minutes of twelve noon, he tried again. The same
elderly gentleman put him through to Carol's room.

"Hello," Carol's voice came over the telephone. She appeared out of breath.

"Long distance calling for Mrs. Carol Lockwood," the operator said.

"This is she, operator," Carol answered, catching her breath.

"You may go ahead, now, sir," the operator said to Ross.
"Your party's on the line."

Ross didn't reply, but instead spoke to Carol.

"Carol, this is Ross," he said nervously.

"Yes, Ross, I thought it was you." She paused to catch her
breath again. "Have you been trying to reach me?"

"Yes. Twice before. I got a little concerned when I didn't
find you in."

"I'm sorry I wasn't here. I had just entered the lobby when

the desk clerk saw me and told me I had a long distance call. I ran up to the room and that's why I probably sound a little out of breath."

"Have you found out anything else about Carrie?" Ross said anticipatingly.

"No. I really didn't have much hope that I would. That's what I've been doing this morning. I spent almost the entire morning at the sheriff's office."

Ross was surprised. "I thought you didn't want the police in on this?" he asked. He noticed that his voice quivered a little, and wondered whether Carol noticed his nervousness.

"I still don't, really," Carol said almost in a whisper. "But after having spoken to you yesterday, I thought of how you might feel about my calling you after all these years and I prepared myself for the possibility that you'd decide not to come. To be quite honest, Ross, I wouldn't have blamed you if you hadn't called me back this morning. I finally came to the conclusion last night that my calling you yesterday had been a stupid mistake. I had no right doing that under the circumstances."

He wished she hadn't said that. He felt no ill-feelings toward Carol at all—he was sure of that, so that couldn't have been the reason why he suddenly felt an uncomfortable, odd sensation. What probably *did* give him that weird, seemingly unexplainable feeling was the fact that he was speaking with a person whom he had known intimately long ago. He was talking to the woman he once thought he loved deeply and one for whom he would have done anything in the world, but after the years had passed, that feeling had now vanished completely. There wasn't even the slightest hint within him that it had ever existed at all, and yet, the memory of it was still there. It was that memory of his past love for her, he was certain, and the lack of any feeling now as he spoke to her, which created the eeriness that appeared to be hanging over him now.

"Well, it doesn't make any difference," he finally answered after a long moment of silence, "whether you feel it was wrong to call me. The fact is that you did and we can't change that. Besides, I'm glad you did. I care about Carrie, of course, and if she's in trouble, I'd like to help." He paused. "That is, if I can," he added. "What happened at the sheriff's office—anything you feel you should tell me over the phone?"

"No, not really—hardly anything at all. The sheriff wasn't in when I got there and I waited nearly two hours by the time he arrived. He's an extremely nice person and I'm sure he's quite willing to help but I seriously doubt he'll be able to help much. Not with the limited information I was willing to give him, anyhow. It was a mistake going there."

"Why? Didn't you tell him everything about Carrie?"

"I told him I was trying to locate her and that I had heard she might be staying here in Esperanza, but I told him little else and actually, I didn't come right out and ask him to help me find her."

"Why not?"

"Because I wanted to hear from you first. I didn't know what would be the right thing to do. I'm terribly confused at this stage, I'm afraid, and I'm getting to the point where my mind's not functioning properly.

"I gave the sheriff Carrie's name and asked him if he could tell me if recently she or any of several others I mentioned to him had been picked up by one of his deputies or whether he was aware of a group of college students staying anywhere in the area. He personally didn't know but he checked his office's reports just in case and called the town police. He confirmed that no arrests had been made and that neither his office nor the town police had any report of the group being here.

"Anyway, the sheriff was extremely kind and courteous and very much the gentleman. Then he asked me rather routine questions like how long Carrie had been missing, her age, and things of that sort. I told him I didn't exactly consider Carrie a missing person but that I was concerned about her. He said unless I turned in a missing person report, there was little his office could do to help, since Carrie wasn't considered a juvenile under state law and therefore couldn't be charged with delinquency; unless she was breaking some law, there's no reason for his office stepping into the case. But he said if anything else came up concerning Carrie, not to hesitate getting in touch with him. I finally thanked him and left."

Ross realized that although they had been on the telephone

now for at least two or three minutes, he didn't know any more about the situation than yesterday. Carol's reference to the group of students increased his curiosity.

"Carol," he said somewhat impatiently, "that's one point I'd like for you to explain. What exactly is the trouble Carrie's in?"

"Well, I think I better give you some background, Ross," Carol began. "During this past school year, Carrie's changed an awful lot. Suddenly, she's made a complete 180 degree turn and she's taken a totally different outlook on life and—well, I know parents nowadays keep using this as an excuse for their children, and avoiding the real problem, but with Carrie, it seems appropriate to say it—she's been going around with the wrong kind of people—a bad group—people she's easily influenced by and it's not for the best. Carrie's always been easily influenced by others and it really hurts me to see her influenced by the wrong kind of person."

"What exactly do you mean by the wrong kind of people?" He stopped and waited for an answer but there was a long pause. "Do you mean hippies or hippie-types?" he finally asked.

"Yes," she said hurriedly. "But it's actually much worse than that." She stopped for a moment, then began speaking deliberately. "Ross," she said, as if building up the courage to say what she knew she had to say, "I didn't want to tell you all this until you arrived here, that is, if you decided to come, for fear you'd blame me or much worse, blame Carrie, and decide not to come at all." She paused again, then blurted out what she feared saying. "Ross, Carrie's using drugs—involved in drug abuse." She stopped abruptly, as if to allow Ross to digest what she had said.

Oh, God, Ross thought, is this really happening to me, after all these years. He viewed the drug scene as a thing of the past. "Are you sure?" he asked.

"Yes, Ross, I'm certain. That's the reason why I don't want the police involved. I'm afraid they'd find out about her using drugs and that she'd be arrested. There's no telling exactly what kind of people she's with and what the police might find in their possession if they should find her before I do. And the worst part of it is that I'm not so sure it would do any good if I were to find her first—I don't think she'd go back home with me—even if I got down on my knees and begged."

Her voice suddenly broke and for the first time in their conversations of yesterday and today, she lost completely whatever composure she had previously managed to retain. She began crying softly.

Ross didn't know what to say. "Carol," he finally managed to say, "please try to keep calm. You won't help matters by crying."

"Oh, Ross, if you only knew what I've been through these past few months, telling myself I must keep calm about this whole mess. And now that Carrie's gone and I can't find her, all of the confusion I've felt since I first found out about her using drugs has suddenly multiplied and it's just getting so unbearable." She was still crying quietly. She cleared her throat. "I can't seem to remain calm anymore. Oh, Ross, I didn't know who else to turn to except you. I know I don't deserve any help from you, after the way I disappeared from your life and took Carrie away years ago, but it's for Carrie's sake, not mine, that I've called you. I confess I've done wrong in keeping her from you all these years and much worse, in keeping your whereabouts from her secret. It sounds terrible to say all she knows about you is your name and what you looked like twenty years ago. She's got an old photograph of you—keeps it in her wallet.

"Carrie and I used to be happy together. I've brought her up the best way I knew how and we've always been able to understand each other in the past. But she's always resented the fact that I've kept from her information about you. It's because of the way she feels about you that I called you, Ross. Even though she's never really known you, I know she'll respect your views and understand your concern for her. I'm not just concerned with locating her. What's really got me worried is that once I find her, that won't be the end of it unless she changes her attitude and is made to realize she can't go on messing around with drugs and pot and doing the other things she's been doing. That's why I thought you might be able to help. I feel you'd be the one able to influence her—to make her understand that what she's doing is ruining her life." She had controlled her sobbing now and stopped crying.

Ross appeared stunned when she had finished. As if from out of nowhere, he had been suddenly confronted by what appeared at first glance, a problem belonging to someone else —to some other person.

"Is it *pot* she's using?" he asked. "From what I hear, every other kid is smoking it nowadays."

"No, Ross, it isn't just that. Carrie's into other drugs."

A depressing, lonely feeling crept over him. There was a long moment of silence. Finally, he broke the quietness.

"How long has this been going on?" he asked solemnly.

"I don't know exactly, Ross," Carol answered warily. "It was sometime after Christmas that it all started, I'm sure. I learned about it by accident one night when she came home much later than she was accustomed to. I had been reading and decided to wait up for her. She appeared surprised that I was still up. I noticed immediately that she wasn't herself. The first thought that came to me was that she had been drinking but I couldn't smell any liquor on her breath. She went straight to her room and it became quite apparent to me she was trying to avoid me. She became irritable when I walked into her room and began questioning her and then suddenly she became hysterical and finally broke down and wept. I was terrified and she too seemed afraid of something. Suddenly, her body began shaking uncontrollably, as if she were chilled, and it was then I suspected she had taken something other than liquor. I stayed up half the night with her and the next morning she broke down and told me she had been using drugs. I was terribly shocked and couldn't believe it at first. That day had to be one of the worst of my life. Even now, when I think back on that day, I relive it."

He and Carol spoke a few minutes more. She asked if he would help. Even when he had picked up the telephone to call Carol, he hadn't made up his mind then what he was going to do. But the telephone conversation had abruptly changed that. He had known then what he must do. He told Carol he would try catching the next plane to Albuquerque and hopefully meet her that same night at the hotel. He feared that if he rejected her appeal, it would haunt him the rest of his life.

CHAPTER 8

HE walked hurriedly down the corridor and finally reached Gate 26. He withdrew his ticket envelope from his coat pocket and handed it to the youthful-looking ticket clerk standing behind the counter at the entrance to the gate concourse. The clerk quickly tore out the ticket, stapled a boarding pass to the packet, and returned it to Ross.

A smiling stewardess met him at the front of the plane and led him to his seat in the first class section. He always traveled first class, for he disliked the feeling of being too crowded in an airplane.

The Boeing 727 began moving and taxied down one of the runways until finally, he was pushed against the back of the seat by the force of the plane as it gained momentum for take-off.

As the aircraft became airborne, the *No Smoking* light went off and Ross took a pack of Winstons from his shirt pocket and lit a cigarette. Earlier, the stewardess had asked him if he wished to order a mixed drink but he had thanked her and said no. He had been tempted to order a martini, for he felt tense and he knew the drink would relax him, but he didn't much care for the thought of having to depend on a crutch like liquor to ease a case of bad nerves. It was an easy trap to fall into and in his profession, he had seen many of his business associates and acquaintances get caught in it, more often than he would have cared to have seen.

As the plane rose higher and higher, he sat there reclining comfortably against the thickly cushioned seat, his arms resting on the arms of the chair. The dark blue, pin-striped suit he wore made him stand out against the dull, cream-colored upholstery of the seat. He wore a light blue shirt with french cuffs extending an inch beyond his coat sleeves, thus giving him a refined, well-dressed appearance.

He hadn't had time to change into a clean set of clothes before he left his apartment. He had rushed home from the office after talking with Carol, pulled out a couple of suitcases, and hurriedly packed a few of his suits and enough shirts and underwear to last him a few days. He actually had no idea how long he would be gone, but had left word with Ed Parker at work he would be back at the office Monday morning. The thought now crossed his mind, however, whether he was getting involved in something more than he had bargained for—something that would take him from his work for a much longer period of time. He now wondered whether he had acted too impulsively. He felt slightly guilty for questioning his decision to make the trip and finally convinced himself he was doing what any concerned parent would have done under these unusual circumstances.

He inhaled his cigarette, and turning to the small window, he let out the smoke in a narrow stream against the layers of thick glass. He stared out the window. The plane had risen above the clouds and was still climbing. Below, some two or three thousand feet, he saw the glistening white sea of thick, mushrooming clouds. They appeared as a continuous layer of pleasant, rolling hills, without a break. Far off in the distance, he could clearly see the edge of the white hills, and beyond, the light blue tinge of the open sky.

His thoughts were suddenly on Monica. He realized that upon learning of his departure, she would be angry at him, not simply because he had decided to make the trip, nor because Carol's phone call had resurrected, temporarily at least, a part of his past when he had loved someone else, but because he hadn't told her of his decision to make the trip before departing.

Actually, he had telephoned Monica's office several times that morning to let her know not only that he had decided to go but that he was taking the next flight out of San Francisco. She had been out of the office and no one there had known where she might be reached. He had left word for her to return his call, but she never did. But he had taken the time to write a quick letter to her explaining his sudden departure; he sealed it in an envelope and deposited it in the mail.

His thoughts returned to Carol Lockwood. She had remarried a long time ago, she had explained to him during yesterday's telephone conversation. She had apparently found it necessary to mention her second marriage to him when she had told him where she could be reached. She had given him the name under which she was registered at the hotel in Esperanza.

Upon reflecting on the prior day's conversation, Ross now wondered about Carol's remarriage. He recalled specifically that she had used the past tense—"I *was* married," she had said. Had her second husband died, or had the marriage ended in divorce? Or for that matter, had it been her only marriage since their divorce? He felt a little ashamed for suddenly becoming what he considered unreasonably curious about a matter which was none of his concern. He smiled to himself. After all, he could hardly say he was surprised to learn she had remarried, for she was only in her early twenties when they were divorced. Aside from that, she had been an attractive and appealing woman, mentally as well as physically, and so it seemed inevitable that she would remarry.

A brief thought crossed his mind whether she had changed much in appearance during the extended period of time they hadn't seen each other. He didn't think he had changed much physically in that span of time, aside from appearing a little older and heavier physically, maybe, but then, that was his own, subjective opinion—others might think differently. But there were some people whose physical appearance changed considerably in twenty years and he wondered if Carol was one of them. Until now, he had thought of her as she had looked twenty years ago. Her voice appeared much the same over the telephone. The thought of seeing Carol after so many years intrigued him. She meant absolutely nothing to him now, in a romantic, emotional sense, and yet, thinking of her stirred his curiosity and desire to learn about her life during the gap of twenty years.

His thoughts carried him back in time to when Carrie was born — it was August — August of 1956. He and Carol had married soon after he returned from serving with the U. S. Army in Korea. They had met while both were attending college and their relationship then had become intimate. But Ross, partly impelled by a strong sense of patriotism, and tired of his school studies, quit school and enlisted in the Army. The two of them had kept in touch by mail during the time Ross was stationed in Korea. In fact, it had been then that he proposed to her in one of his letters. When he was discharged and he returned to California, they were married within the week.

Both were extremely happy during the first months of the marriage. But of course, that was the expected beginning. They agreed not to have children during the first three or four years of their marriage. They discussed that aspect of their relationship thoroughly, and planned accordingly, but then, unexpectedly, Carol learned she was pregnant. Ross had mixed feelings about the pregnancy, but it was Carol that it hit the hardest— she didn't want to accept the fact that she was expecting a child. She grew terribly upset and there were periods of depression. The thought of it worked on her mind day after day and Ross tried hard to cheer her up, but with each day that passed, she appeared to fall deeper into a state of despondency.

He became angry at himself for letting this unwanted, unplanned pregnancy happen, when he saw how it was affecting Carol. Their relationship soon became strained. Ross hoped that once the baby was born, their relationship would improve; that Carol would change her attitude, but if anything, matters became worse after Carrie was born, until finally, one day when he returned home from work, he found Carol extremely quiet and moody—more so than usual. She hardly spoke at the dinner table. Later that night, she told him she wanted a divorce.

She had said it very simply and automatically, as if she were relating to him that they needed a new car or a new dinette set for the kitchen.

Even so, Ross hadn't really been surprised that she wanted a divorce but he reacted with dismay and shock at the casual manner of her remark. The statement opened up her mind and she was no longer silent; she talked for hours that night. They spoke openly to one another and Ross asked countless questions. Primarily, he wanted to satisfy Carol and himself that she had thought the matter out thoroughly and that she was certain she wanted the divorce. She was quite sure, she had answered candidly. She had spent long and lonely moments thinking about it and she had finally made up her mind. "I don't love you anymore, Ross," she had said softly. "I don't know what has happened to make me feel this way, but I just can't live with you anymore. I'm sorry, but that's the way I feel. It's all my fault, not yours. I don't blame any of this on you—you've been a wonderful husband." After she had said that, he questioned her no further.

But at the beginning, he wouldn't accept that she didn't care for him anymore. After they had separated, he would occasionally go visit her in the apartment she lived in with Carrie. He didn't know why he would go visit her except that he hoped to regain at least some of the rapture which had filled his heart when they had been very much in love, or had thought that they were. And many nights, laying awake in bed, he tormented his mind with the thought of how a person could change so abruptly as Carol had in her feelings toward him.

The divorce was mutually arranged without disagreement. Carrie was only three months old when the judge granted the divorce to Carol and approved the property settlement the two had agreed upon.

Carol, of course, was awarded custody of Carrie. Although it had been painful for Ross to part with his infant daughter, there was never any dispute over who was to get custody. Ross was allowed to visit with Carrie. The attorney had emphasized to both of them the importance of their cooperating with one another with respect to visitation rights and that he was certain the two of them could make suitable arrangements so that a problem didn't develop, as so often happened when the couple still held grudges long after the divorce. Ross too, felt confident that he and Carol could work out the matter between them and that she wouldn't deny him his right to see his daughter whenever he wanted to, so long as it didn't unreasonably interfere with any of Carol's plans. But what happened next proved him wrong.

A few days after Carol had called him the day of the divorce hearing, Ross made attempts to contact her, only to find she had disappeared. She hadn't bothered telling him she was leaving town. Something unexpected must have come up, he told himself, and there was no need to worry. But then a few days passed. Then a week—a month, and yet not a word from her. He became worried.

Carol had moved into a furnished apartment shortly after their separation. After the second week of her absence, Ross spoke to her landlord. He explained his concern for his ex-wife and his daughter and managed to talk him into opening the locked apartment. Upon examining the apartment, to their bewilderment, they found it empty. The closets and drawers were bare. Carol hadn't taken any two-week trip—she had gone permanently, without a trace.

Ross was close to panic in the confusion. Desperately, he began calling all of their past mutual friends to see if Carol might have left word with any of them or if she might have hinted to them where she was going. None had seen her for well over a month or knew anything of a planned trip. He even contacted some of Carol's old school friends—friends that, to his knowledge, she hadn't been in touch with since college. He felt ashamed contacting these old friends of Carol's but he called them nevertheless. There had to be some reasonable explanation for her sudden disappearance; someone had to know where she had gone.

Grasping desperately for anything that might lead him to Carol, he even filed a missing person report with the San Francisco police. But he could give the police few leads and he knew there was little they could do. If she had ulterior motives in keeping Carrie from him, she wouldn't have stayed in San Francisco, and probably, not even in the state. Of that, he was certain. But he had absolutely no idea where she might have gone.

His mind was in a state of turmoil when he thought of Carol's father—Andrew Borlin. He was the one person who might know where Carol was. But he realized that was a long shot. Carol hadn't heard from her father in quite some time. So he was right back where he started from—Andrew Borlin's whereabouts were equally unknown to him. Thinking of Carol's father, he remembered the letters he had written to Carol—she had kept them in a box full of old correspondence which they had kept strictly for sentimental reasons. They had even kept all of the letters they had written to one another when Ross was in Korea. He recalled that the box had been placed in an old storage chest Carol had bought in a second-hand store. She had stored many other personal items belonging to her. But were Borlin's letters still there? It was worth a try. The letters might produce an old return address, or even the postmark of a town or city which might lead him to Borlin's whereabouts.

Ross remembered that when he had helped Carol move into the apartment, there hadn't been room in the apartment for the large wooden chest. But there was a storage room in the basement provided for the building's tenants, and Ross remembered carrying it down there. Had Carol taken it with her?

Ross paid another visit to the landlord and told him about the wooden chest in the basement. Had Carol asked for the key to the storage room before her disappearance? No, the landlord said, she hadn't. Ross found the chest still in the same corner of the room where he had set it. He opened it and carefully, began going through each letter. There were seemingly hundreds of them. Not one could he find that had come from Andrew Borlin. He dropped the last letter into the chest and closed it, his hopes dimmed that he would ever hear from Carol again.

And now, cruising at 35,000 feet in the streamlined jetliner, Ross Blair was only hours away from meeting the woman who had vanished so mysteriously from his life so many years ago—someone he had never expected to see again the rest of his life. And maybe, if he wasn't too late, he would also get to know his daughter Carrie, whom he remembered only as a three month-old infant. She was now a grown woman. Time had erased the torment he had experienced at the beginning so long ago when he was forced to accept that he would never lay eyes on his daughter again. He had thought of her often, but only as one would a loved one who had died many years ago. Suddenly, this once-lost loved one, long buried from his life, had suddenly reappeared, and he now sensed a cold shiver of emotion throughout his entire body as he thought of meeting his daughter face to face.

CHAPTER 9

THE approach to the little town of Esperanza in Sandoval County was a narrow road. To get onto the road, one had to leave the interstate highway connecting Albuquerque and Santa Fe.

The approach—the surrounding countryside—vaguely reminded Ross of the terrain surrounding a small town in southwestern Colorado where he had attended a boys' camp as a youngster for several summers. He couldn't recall the name of the tiny Colorado town but the image of the camp's rolling hills was still vividly implanted in his mind, for he had grown attached to it as a young boy.

He was now approaching the outskirts of Esperanza. He had rented a car at the airport in Albuquerque and the young lady behind the car rental desk had provided him with a road map and directions. There had been a mixup with the baggage and he was delayed over an hour at the airport, before he was able to get on his way.

Ross glanced briefly at his watch. It was already six forty-five. The drive from the airport had taken him a little over an hour.

He slowed the car down as he passed the first building

marking the edge of the city. He noticed a small sign to the side of the road. In white letters on a green background, it read:

TOWN LIMITS
Esperanza
Elevation   5,167
Population   2,148

A hundred feet ahead, his eyes came upon a much larger sign—it was a billboard sign and it read in big, colorful letters: *WELCOME TO ESPERANZA, WHERE 2,000 PLUS, FRIENDLY PEOPLE BID YOU WELCOME—BIEN VENIDO, AMIGO.*

The narrow road widened into a four-lane street, with curbs and sidewalks to each side. There was little traffic. A traffic light up ahead turned red as Ross approached the intersection, and he brought the car to a stop. He lit a cigarette and glanced around. So here he was, he thought. Esperanza—somewhere in this little town was Carol. He felt a tingling sensation as he thought of her—of her presence here. The town looked small. It didn't seem like a town of some two thousand inhabitants. Ahead, he could see the edge of the downtown area where the buildings dwindled and the street narrowed, continuing on toward rolling hills ahead, where it disappeared in the distance.

On the corner, to his right, was a Shell gasoline station and right next to it, a small restaurant. There was still some daylight, but it had already begun to darken rapidly. A neon light above the entrance of the small cafe was lit: Larry's Cafe. Next to it was a bar—Larry's Bar & Lounge. The neon lights blinked off and on. Across the street were several stores—a five and ten and a J. C. Penney store alongside of it. These were followed by Turner's Dry Goods and Bumper's Watch Repair Service, and a little further ahead, standing by itself at an isolated intersection, El Chamizal Mexican Cafe. Only a few other structures lay beyond.

As he noticed the traffic light changing, Ross glanced down the narrow intersecting street and there, a block away, he spotted the large, vertical sign which read: SANDOVAL HOTEL. The two-story hotel was an old-looking edifice, appearing to have been recently white-washed or painted over. Yet, close to the edge of the roof, large chunks of stucco and plaster had fallen off, leaving visible the bare adobe brick beneath. The upper portion of the hotel was partially hidden behind two, tall cottonwood trees and through the limbs and leaves, Ross could make out the tiny rays of light coming from one of the windows of the hotel. Carol's room? Not likely, of course, but the picture of the lit hotel room reminded him again that Carol was somewhere in that hotel and that they would soon meet.

The light had turned green and someone honked behind him. He accelerated the car, allowed a motorist on his right to overtake him, and then proceeded to switch over to the outside lane to turn at the next corner.

He pulled over to the curb alongside the hotel and stepped out of the car. He walked down the narrow sidewalk toward the front.

He hesitated a moment at the entrance, then walked in. The entrance led directly into a small entryway. Two swinging wooden and glass doors leading into the hotel lobby were held open against the walls of the foyer. He stood in the entryway and studied the decorative hotel interior. Immediately, he felt as if he had stepped into a hotel in the late 1800's—as if taken back in time from the hustle and bustle of modern living in San Francisco into this sleepy town in the old West, of which this ancient hotel was a part.

The lobby was empty. He didn't move, apparently awed by what he saw. From an extremely high ceiling hung two rows of antique chandeliers—the kind that had been fashionable sometime in the late 1800's. Midway toward the ceiling, to each side of the lobby, stood decorative oak railings alongside narrow corridors running the depth of the lobby. The corridors provided access to the hotel rooms located to both sides on the second floor. Each doorway, stained a deep oak finish, stood out clearly against the background of the slightly yellowed walls.

Above each doorway, was a small wooden plaque with a name painted in gold script letters. Above the door nearest him, Ross could make out the writing—on each plaque was written the name of a woman, signifying the name of each room. To his right, above the first door, was *Carmelita;* the name above the next door was *Maria Elena,* and to his left was *Angélica.* The other rooms had similar names.

On the walls to each side of the lobby were dozens of framed photographs mounted on a white background. The pictures in them were small and Ross couldn't make out the subject matter of each, but he guessed they were pictures of old buildings and homes in Esperanza, depicting the town as it had looked some seventy years ago, and of the people that had formed a part of its past and history. Along the walls, there were what appeared to be old Indian relics and pottery inside glass showcases. There were numerous objects scattered throughout the lobby, giving the place an extremely cluttered appearance. In essence, the hotel was a small museum with numerous collections of objects representing the town's past. The effect of it was to give Ross an eerie feeling he had turned back the calendar and had stepped back in time.

The creaky hardwood floor of the lobby, which was stained and marred with use and age, extended back almost the depth of the building itself. Only the middle of the floor was covered with a large, wornout, tightly woven rug, made up of faded colors.

The place was empty and quiet, so quiet that Ross wondered if the place had been abandoned. The chandelier lights threw long, dark shadows along the wooden floor of the empty lobby.

Ross stepped forward out of the foyer.

Immediately to the right of the lobby entrance was an area which had been enclosed by an oak railing some three feet high. Inside, near the front railing, was an old, heavy wooden desk. A few feet behind this desk, against the far wall, was an old-fashioned, roll-top writing desk. Above the desk was shelving forming narrow pigeon or cubby holes, obviously for the room keys and mail of the hotel guests, for these too had the same feminine names found above the doorway to each room of the hotel. Most of the cubbyholes appeared unused. The hotel apparently had few guests.

A discolored lamp lit the front desk and to one corner was a disorganized pile of correspondence and envelopes, weighted down by a brass paperweight. There didn't appear to be a

modern-day object in the entire place. Even the typewriter setting on the desk was one of those heavy, obsolete black models
manufactured in the 1920's.

Near the front edge of the desk was an office bell. Ross
tapped the bell several times. In another moment, there was a
shuffling of feet. The sound of footsteps came from the direction of a doorway opening into the railed-off area. There
appeared an elderly, white-haired gentleman dressed in a
wrinkled white shirt and heavily worn-out pants. The trousers
were pleated and extremely baggy in contrast to the small
frame of the gentleman. He appeared to be in his early seven-
ties. The light reflected off what few white hairs could be seen
on top of his balding head. But to the sides and back of his
head, the man possessed a substantial quantity of hair—it was
snowy white, the man's dark complexion making it appear even
more so.

His shirt sleeves were haphazardly rolled up his arms to his
elbows, displaying small, veined arms and gnarled hands. His
feet dragging, he walked with slow, but steady steps toward
Ross, apparently in no hurry to get to the newly-arrived hotel
guest.

"Sorry to have kept you waiting," the old man spoke. He
looked up at Ross, his eyes squinting behind the rimless glasses
he wore. Above the glasses was a green visor—the kind that as
a small boy, Ross had seen train and postal clerks wearing at
the window of an ancient train depot or post office. "Was out
in back catching up on a few household chores." He studied
Ross. "Now—what can I do for you, sir?" He sat down behind
the desk.

"I'd like to register, please," Ross said. "Have you any
vacancies?"

"Sure do—lot's of them." The white-haired man looked up
at Ross again from where he sat. The visor he wore didn't
quite block off the light, for he wore it too high on his forehead, and he squinted from the glare of the ceiling lights. He
smiled slightly, but it was difficult to tell that he was because
of the many wrinkles surrounding his mouth. He glanced down
almost absentmindedly and picked up a small, white card from
the corner of the desk. He pushed it along the desk, picked up

a pen and handed it to Ross. "Just yourself, is it, sir, or do you have the Missus with you?"

"No, just myself," Ross said. He smiled at the man as he took the pen from him and began writing.

The old man leaned forward and watched Ross fill in the blank spaces. He held his head back sharply however, as he looked through the lower portion of his bi-focals. "I'd appreciate it if you'd *print,* if you don't mind. Makes it easier for me to read."

"I'll be glad to," Ross replied and grinned.

"Thanks," the old man whispered. "Yes, that's fine. When a person gets way up there in years, like yours truly here, eyes start playing tricks on him. And for darn sure, it don't stop there. Things get so that an oldster like me starts wishing he could turn the clock back and be young again—" He paused and looked Ross over from head to foot. "Wishful thinking it is on my part, but I surely wouldn't mind being as young as you again." He gave out a short laugh.

He took the registration card from Ross and examined it for a moment. "Ross Blair," he pronounced slowly. "Hmmmm, from San Francisco, I see."

"Yes."

"You're a pretty good ways from there."

"Yes, it's far."

"Didja just now get into town?"

"Just drove in."

"Well, we're mighty happy to see you picked the Sandoval Hotel to stay at. I trust you'll have a pleasant stay here." He squinted his eyes once more. "Is this a one-nighter or you planning on staying longer?"

"I don't know. I might be staying on for a while. Do you want me to pay in advance for the room? I'll be glad—"

"No, Mr. Blair, that won't be at all necessary. Suppose we wait until you get ready to check out. That'll be fine with me." His face displayed a broad smile which disclosed his extremely even and polished dentures.

"By the way," the old man continued, "you've got your choice, Mr. Blair—we've plenty of vacancies. Would you like a room on ground level or up on the second floor? Not much difference between them except for a few pieces of furniture here and there."

"Oh, I think a room on the second floor will do."

The man nodded, walked toward the back of the office and took a key from a cubbyhole. He returned and handed the key to Ross. "Here you are, young man."

"Thank you."

"Are you in Esperanza on business or pleasure?"

Ross hesitated. "Business."

"Course, it's none of my business, really. In fact, the Missus gets annoyed with me when she feels I get too inquisitive with guests. I tell her that isn't it at all—that is, my being nosey. I'm plain interested in people. Around here, we don't ever get many travelers coming through, being as we're off the interstate. We used to, long ago, when the old highway going up to Santa Fe passed right through town. Well, anyway, I always like to try making our guests feel at home."

"I understand. I appreciate good hospitality away from home." Ross paused as he slipped the key into his pocket. "I guess I should have checked with you before registering. I'm looking for someone who's expecting me. Do you have a lady registered by the name of Carol Lockwood?" He took out a cigarette and lit it. "*Mrs.* Lockwood," he repeated, unsure the old man had heard him.

The old man glanced up at him and behind the visor and large pair of eye glasses, managed to reveal a pair of twinkling, smiling eyes, and then he formed a broad smile but only for a flashing moment, for it vanished as quickly as it had appeared. Sorry, you mischievous little old man, Ross thought, it's not what you're thinking.

"Yes, we certainly do," the man finally answered. "Came into town a couple of days ago. From Albuquerque, she said she was. Are you from there?"

"No, I'm—"

"No, of course not, San Francisco. We were discussing that a moment ago, weren't we? How forgetful! I'm telling you." He shook his head as if displeased with himself.

Ross was amused by the old man's forgetfulness and his face broke into a slight smile. "Could you tell me if Mrs. Lockwood is in her room at the moment?"

"Oh, yes, you asked about Mrs. Lockwood, didn't you." He paused, lowered his head and brought his hand up to his chin. "Now, let's see—hummm. She comes in and out all times of the day, it's kinda hard to keep track of her." He paused momentarily in thought once again. "Yes—yes, that's right! She's not in at the moment, come to think of it." He nodded. "Yep, saw her go out not more than an hour ago and I'm sure she hasn't returned, 'cause I remember she left her room key here on my desk and she hasn't picked it back up yet. I put it up in her box there just half an hour ago." He stepped back to where he could see in the box. "Yep—still here where I put it."

"If she should happen to come in while I'm unpacking and cleaning up, would you let her know the room I'm staying in?"

The man nodded. "I certainly will. Be happy to, young man."

"What room is she staying in, by the way?"

"She's got a room all by itself out there in back on the ground floor. Said she wanted it that way. You go straight to the end of the lobby there by the corner in the back and there's a narrow passageway that leads you right straight to the room. It's the only one there, so you can't miss it. It's also the only passageway leading to the back—if you keep following it on down, it leads into a courtyard we have back there.

"Your room, I should have told you, is up there to the left. Just go up the stairway there at the rear and turn left and then left again. It's the third door coming back this way. I don't know if you've noticed or not but our rooms here don't have numbers—just names. I gave you *Verónica*—name's right there on the key I gave you in case you can't remember it."

"Yes, I've noticed."

"It gets kind of confusing for some people but we've had it that way for so long, kinda hard to change it now." The old man began walking in the direction of the doorway where he had earlier appeared, but he stopped and turned around. "If you should need me, just ring that bell there and I'll be out in a jiffy."

"Thanks," Ross said. He turned and walked out the front door and to his car to get his belongings.

Half an hour later, he was unpacked, had taken a quick cold shower, and was now getting into a clean set of clothes. The cold shower had relaxed him, at least momentarily, but he was now beginning to feel the tingling sensation of nervousness in his stomach caused by the anticipation of meeting Carol.

He was pleasantly surprised by the appearance of his room —*Verónica's* room. He grinned when he thought of the room in that way—a woman's room. It wasn't a large room, but the furniture had been arranged so as to make the most out of what little space there was. The room contained a double bed, for which he was glad. The bathroom was extremely small—large enough only for a crowded shower and sink but no bathtub. But in spite of its smallness, the room was refreshingly furnished, properly ventilated by central cooling, and more importantly, possessed an atmosphere of warmth and comfort which Ross appreciated away from home.

It startled him when he heard the knock on the door, and he stood there momentarily frozen. It must be Carol, he thought. He sensed the same eerie sensation which had overcome him when he had first heard Carol's voice on the phone only the day before; that same sinking sensation at the pit of his stomach.

He stared at the door as if expecting it to open suddenly any moment. The knocking came again, this time much louder.

Finally, he stepped quietly to the door. He swallowed hard and opened it.

They were face to face. The sensation he had felt only moments before remained with him, but had become more intense. He stared straight into the face of Carol Lockwood. At the moment his eyes met hers, he couldn't have looked away had he wanted to, for the two of them stood there magnetized, unable to look elsewhere.

It was strange to see her for the first time in twenty years. He was overcome by this strangeness—he knew her and yet he didn't—unexplainable feeling. Bewilderment. No recollection —no remembrance—however vivid, of those days so long ago —could have prepared him for what he now experienced. There, standing before him was Carol. His mind was suddenly filled with memories of the past. They engulfed him with nostalgia of something so far away and long ago.

She stood but a few feet away—the woman who had been a part of his past—there was that same nose, same eyes, mouth, attractiveness—everything in place, exactly as he had remembered her face. Remarkably, the years that had been added to her age had done little to change her facial features. Even her skin possessed that same exquisite softness and translucency he still remembered. She had aged, of course. What was there about her that seemed different, though? Was different. Her hair—only her blond hair was different. He now saw a woman with her hair cut short and slightly curled out at the ends. The Carol of long ago had long hair—silky and soft. It appeared coarser now, as if from being bleached again and again, and it had lost that smoothness he remembered.

He found himself slightly irritated by his sentimentality.

In another moment, inconspicuously, he glanced down briefly at her body. She was slightly broader and heavier than when he had last seen her, but not excessively so. Hiding behind the smile her lips formed, Ross could clearly see a gaze filled with desperation.

A few words. Someone would have to speak—to say a few words. In an attempt to undo the awkwardness which now had formed between them as they stood there simply staring at each other, Ross spoke.

"Hello, Carol," he said softly, then smiled. His voice trembled slightly and he cleared his throat, hoping she hadn't noticed. "Please come in. I was almost through getting cleaned up a bit after the trip." He opened the door wide for her.

"Hello, Ross," Carol said as she stepped inside. They didn't bother shaking hands. Her eyes had remained on his as they stood there, but she glanced away as she walked into the room. He offered her a chair and she sat down.

"How was your trip—did you have a pleasant flight?"

"Yes, I did, thank you."

Silence.

Again. "Did you have any trouble finding this place? The town, I mean."

"No, not at all." There was another pause. Finally, Ross

spoke again. "Pardon me for a minute, Carol," he said and he disappeared into the bathroom. He was in there for only a moment and then reappeared. He walked immediately to the dresser where he picked up his watch and ring and put them on. From the moment he had re-entered the room, he became aware that Carol had been watching him.

"You've hardly changed in all these years," Carol said. She considered him once again and smiled. "Except, of course, you are much more mature-looking. You're looking remarkably well, Ross. Age has done very little to you."

He looked down at her and smiled. "Nor *for* me. Thanks for the compliment, though. It's not often one gets a compliment like that from someone he knew from way back. I was about to say the same thing about you. You're looking fine yourself, Carol. Extremely well." He lied a little, for she appeared tired. "I guess we could say time has been good to both of us." He sat down at the foot of the bed, close to her. "I certainly wish it were under different circumstances that we were meeting for the first time in all these years."

"Yes," she agreed, "I'm sorry for that too." She looked somewhat haggard.

The preliminaries had been gotten rid of. Now, he was anxious to inquire about Carrie. "Which brings us, I guess," he said, almost methodically, "to the reason I'm here. Have you found out anymore about Carrie since we talked this morning?"

The question affected her profoundly, and a sudden change came over her. Her face quickly took on a tired, almost lonely, appearance, as if his question had plunged her back into a torrent sea of loneliness, and her eyes filled with tears. She shook her head and looked down at the floor.

"N—N-No," she managed to murmer. "Not a thing. Nothing." Immediately, she took out a Kleenex from her purse and began wiping away the tears, trying to compose herself. "I—I-I'm sorry for acting so emotional, Ross."

"It's quite all right, Carol. You needn't apologize."

"I find myself nearly at the end of the rope, I'm afraid. I'm trying to remain calm, honestly. If I ever want to find Carrie, I'll have to." She wiped away what tears remained and looked up at him. "I promise I'll try not to lose my composure again. I guess just seeing you again under these circumstances has caused these tears. I've been holding them back for too long. Oh, Ross, I'm so terribly happy you're here."

Again, she couldn't stop the tears from appearing. She cried softly—quietly.

As he sat there watching her cry, he became convinced his coming here hadn't been a mistake. He cringed at the thought that but for that one telephone call from her yesterday, he would have proceeded, in routine fashion, to live a life of normalcy in San Francisco, satisfied—content—happy, completely unaware that someone he had loved so deeply long ago was going through the living hell and torment he now saw Carol experiencing. She loved Carrie deeply—it wasn't difficult for him to see that.

He wanted to seek a way to comfort her but he didn't know what to say nor how to say it, nor did he even know where to begin. Finally, he reached toward her and held her gently by the arm.

"It's all right trying to keep calm in a situation such as this, Carol," he finally said, "but only if you can manage to do that. You shouldn't try stopping those tears from coming if you feel like crying. It might make you feel better, you know. It's no good keeping that tension locked up inside of you. Sooner or later it's got to find a release somehow, and if crying's its escape, don't hold it in. Let it out."

Somewhere in some dark secluded corner of his mind, what he now said to her triggered an awareness in him of a tiny flicker—a kindled memory—of having once told her long ago the same thing. In different words, perhaps, but words containing the same meaning. He now remembered that in the years they had known each other, he had never known her to have ever cried. Not a true, honest-to-goodness, healthy cry—not ever. Yes, she had somehow changed in all these years.

She now managed to smile at him slightly. She forced it, trying to show her appreciation for his thoughtfulness.

"Oh, Ross, you know me. I've never been one for too many tears. I don't honestly know why I'm doing it now all of a sudden."

"It's fine, don't worry about it." He felt a slight, moving pain in his stomach; he realized he was hungry and that Carol might be also. "Have you had anything to eat yet?"

"No, I haven't," she answered softly. "I'm not very hungry, though. Have you?"

"No." He stood up. "But you should get something to eat, anyway, whether you're hungry or not. What do you say I give you a minute to go to your room if you'd like to freshen up a bit and I'll be down shortly so we can go have a bite to eat. Do you know of a good place to eat that's close by?"

She stood up and began walking toward the door. Ross followed. "There's a small restaurant down the street a couple of blocks away. I've eaten there several times. The food's good."

"That must be the place I noticed when I first got into town. Does it have a lounge right next to it—Larry's Place— or something like that?"

"Yes, I think so."

"Good. Then we can have a drink before dinner. It'll relax you." He smiled at her and she managed to smile back. "Then I'd like for you to tell me everything there is to know about Carrie. There's much you couldn't even have begun telling me over the telephone."

Their eyes met.

"Yes," she agreed. "There certainly is."

He opened the door for her. I'll see you in, say—five minutes. Will that give you enough time?"

"Make it ten. I've a completely new face to put on after all these tears." She tried laughing but she only uttered a sound. It made Ross suddenly feel sorry for her.

"All right. Ten minutes, then."

"Bye, Ross."

"Bye, Carol. See you shortly."

He closed the door and heard the muffled sound of her high-heeled shoes as she walked down the corridor.

CHAPTER 10

THEY walked the short distance to the restaurant. The sun had set fully now, and the sky had turned a dark, but vivid blue, with a countless array of clear, bright starts interspersed throughout, the view unhindered by the slight glaze from the few lights of the little town.

It was a warm night, but Ross nevertheless felt comfortable as there was little humidity in the night air—a change from the hot, moist air he had left behind in San Francisco.

The restaurant and the lounge next door had a connecting entryway and liquor was served on the restaurant side. They ordered a cocktail before ordering from the dinner menu.

Carol was halfway through her bourbon and seven when Ross finished his. He ordered another drink for himself and one for her, although she said she didn't care for another one. "You don't have to drink it right away," he said to her. It'll relax you. You need that at a time like this. I can tell this thing's got you all tensed up."

She didn't answer him but forced a smile. They sat there quietly for a moment and after the waitress had served the second round of drinks, Ross broke the silence.

"Needless to say, Carol, I'm anxious for you to tell me

about Carrie's problem." He spoke firmly. "But first, rather than you starting with the immediate problem, I think it'd be better if you could answer a few questions, the answers to which aren't clear in my mind."

"Such as?" Carol asked softly.

"Well, for openers, where have you and Carrie been living?"

"In Albuquerque," Carol answered. "Ever since—" She paused, looked deeply into his eyes, then suddenly looked away. "Ever since I left San Francisco," she finished. "Or maybe I should say ever since I took Carrie from you. That's getting closer to the truth, isn't it?" She continued looking away, and absently, began stirring her drink with a plastic straw.

"Carol, let's not make things difficult for ourselves. That was ages ago. It's over and done with and I didn't come down here demanding an explanation from you for what may have happened in the past. Tell me about Carrie. Did this problem of hers start in Albuquerque?"

He offered her a cigarette and took one himself. Carol took a sip from her glass, then nodded. She dragged on her cigarette and let the smoke out quickly.

"Yes," she said, clearing her throat. "Carrie's 19 years of age now. Actually, she'll be twenty next month. She'll be starting her third year at the university in Albuquerque this coming fall." She paused. "What I mean is," she continued, "she was *planning* on attending."

"What university?"

"The University of New Mexico."

He nodded.

"Anyway, Carrie's been doing extremely well in school the past two years. I've always been proud of the way she's applied herself in her school work. Even in high school, when most girls her age were trying to get her to go some place with them —to some dance or school function, or just to go out for a Coke, she'd usually stay home studying for an exam or doing her homework. She always displayed an extraordinary amount of self-discipline.

"She didn't overdo it though. She always showed good judgment in deciding when she could or couldn't afford to have a good time with her friends." She tapped the ashes of her cigarette into the ashtray and then looked up at Ross. "Ross, I'm telling you all this because I want you to understand that basically, Carrie has—in the past anyway—been a good daughter. An excellent student. Oh, she's had her share of growing-up problems and we've had our differences, she and I—I'll get to that later—but nevertheless, I've had no complaints to speak of. I want you to know that."

"I understand, Carol." He paused, shook his head, then added, "It always happens that way, from what little I know of the problem."

"What do you mean?"

"Drug abuse. It seems one always hears that it's the good kids that get involved with drugs nowadays—whatever their background."

"Yes, that does seem to be the case, doesn't it." She stopped. He noticed a change come over her. Her voice sounded differently, as if she had lost the nervousness she had displayed earlier.

"I guess," she continued, "that I fit into the category of parents who react with disbelief and dismay when they're told their son or daughter is using drugs. I hadn't really stopped to think about it."

He nodded in agreement. "I'm sorry I interrupted. Please go on."

"Carrie's real problem began the start of the past fall semester, I think. Somehow, she met these new friends. I don't honestly know how it was she first got involved with this group, but I knew right away when I first met some of them, when she brought them to the house, that they appeared to be the wrong kind of—" She stopped abruptly. She was aware that Ross was carefully scrutinizing every word. "Oh, Ross, I don't want you to get the wrong impression. I don't mean to sound like a parent who's making excuses for her daughter. By blaming it on others. I'm not blaming anyone but Carrie—and part of the blame, I know I must cast on myself. Where exactly I've gone wrong, I haven't found out yet, but I hope to soon, and I pray to God it's not too late for that."

Ross said nothing. He wanted Carol to speak freely—openly, with as little interruption as possible.

"I can't comprehend it. Her attitude seemed to have changed so suddenly. It's almost as if it all happened overnight. Apparently, for some reason unknown to me, she's let go of her old friends—she grew apart from them, and has made new friends with this other bunch. It was almost as if she were suddenly rebelling against something, someone. Against me, maybe. I don't know what exactly—it's so difficult to understand, much less trying to explain it.

"I've already told you about the night I found out for the first time she was taking some kind of drug. That's when I became aware of the nightmare that had been there all the time. I never did ask her how long it had been going on. It seemed so unimportant at the time. What *was* important to me was the fact that she was involved with drugs. The thought terrified me.

"That night she confessed to me, she seemed sincere enough about it all. We had a real heart to heart talk and she admitted to me and more importantly, to herself, that she had done a stupid thing and that she didn't want to hurt me anymore than I had already been hurt. She was terribly ashamed about my finding out. She promised she'd straighten up. I thought then she was being honest with herself and with me but I found out soon enough—only a week or so later—that she apparently hadn't meant what she had said that night. Either that or she had gotten herself so involved with this group and with drugs that she couldn't break away from either of them.

"Anyway, from then on, our relationship dwindled down to practically nothing—no relationship at all. Slowly, as each day went by, I noticed a change come over her—a cooling of our relationship—and she became irritable with me on numerous occasions and she even appeared to go out of her way to act rude. It was as if she resented me for having found out what she had been doing. She began keeping irregular hours, and she ignored her school work. I sensed she was punishing me for something I had done wrong. And that's why I feel so guilty about this situation. Somehow, somewhere, something went wrong between us and I can't help feeling she blames me for it and now she's rebelling against me." She stubbed out her cigarette.

"Oh, Ross, that's what makes this all so painful—wanting to help her as much as I can, and yet, knowing she doesn't want my help. I'm terribly afraid she'll absolutely refuse any help whatsoever.

"And that brings me to the reason why I felt I had to call you. I didn't know how you'd react to my calling you after so many years. You may not believe this, Ross, but it took a tremendous amount of courage to telephone you. You'll never know how much. But I knew I had to; it was the only way. You see, I was afraid that even if I found Carrie, she would never listen to me. She'd fight me, I know she would. So believing this, I began thinking of someone who could help me. Someone close to her—someone she would listen to. And the only person I could think of was you—even after all these years.

"As I said on the telephone, she's always seemed to have strongly resented my keeping your name and whereabouts from her. In fact, I've even wondered if this may be what's behind her change in attitude. This may be her way of getting back at me. But honestly, Ross, my taking her away from you wasn't based on purely selfish reasons—not at first, anyway. At first—"

"Carol, please," Ross broke in, "you shouldn't feel as if you must apologize, or even explain your departure. Besides—"

"Oh, but I do—I absolutely must. *I* feel I owe it to you, *now* more so than ever."

He noticed in her eyes a twinge of remorse.

"You might even say," she went on, "that it's a guilt-burden that's been with me ever since, and I'd like to get rid of it once and for all. I don't want you to think I'm asking for some kind of forgiveness, so please don't misunderstand my intentions."

"I won't." He shrugged slightly. "Well, if you insist, I won't stop you. I want you to know though that as far as I'm concerned, you owe me no explanations."

"I appreciate that, Ross, I really do."

"But before you go into that, I'd like for you to finish telling me about Carrie. Let's get down to her disappearance and what you've done since you first started looking for her. Have you tried locating any of her friends? Any of the students she hangs around with, or at least, used to—anyone that might know or have some idea where she might be?"

"Yes. That's how I happen to be here in Esperanza. One of her school friends told me I might find her near here. There's a few places around this town, I've since found out, that have become popular with hippies and students from the university. I'm told the university students come up here mostly during weekends, but sometimes, they skip school and come here weeks at a time.

"I learned from a friend of Carrie's that Carrie had been here several times before. Other than what this friend of hers told me, I don't have anything else to go by. She said Carrie had mentioned to her that she might be coming up here to stay a few weeks before school started this coming semester. Of course, Carrie's plans were to come later on in the summer but when her friend found out Carrie wasn't at home with me, she thought Carrie might have changed her plans and come up here earlier.

"Actually, there *is* one other person I tried to get in touch with who—" She stopped suddenly. Ross immediately sensed that she was preparing herself for something she was about to reveal to him, but she didn't know quite how to begin. "I might as well tell you now," she went on, "and get it over with." Again she paused. "You see, I suspect Carrie's got some romantic attachment to this professor at the university. He's a much older man—I'd say in his late forties—early fifties."

"Do you mean it's mutual—it's not just some school-girl infatuation of hers?"

"I'm afraid it isn't just that. I wish that was all there was to it, but it's not, from what I've been able to learn about their relationship.

"She took a course under him last year. At first, I'm sure it *was* simply an infatuation. She couldn't stop talking about him. I've inquired among some of the students who were acquainted with Carrie and some of her old friends. They've all been candid with me for they were concerned and disturbed about her growing relationship with this professor. I think that might have been one of the reasons why she and her old school friends had a falling out. Frankly, they were all of the opinion that Carrie's involvement with this man was more than a school-girl crush." She stopped for a moment, then continued speaking softly. "There's one more thing about this professor that I must tell you, Ross. He has a reputation around the university campus of involvement with LSD and other hard drugs."

"And *pot,* I suppose," Ross commented, "if he's into the hard stuff."

"And, if that's the case," Carol continued, "I'm sure he's had a lot to do in influencing Carrie's involvement with drugs. I learned that this professor's a member of this group I told you Carrie's been hanging around with. In fact, he's the one who started coming up here near Esperanza and holding these pot parties and the like."

"That's disgusting. What's his name?"

"Dr. Conrad," Carol replied softly. "Arthur Bradley Conrad."

"But how in the world can a fellow like that continue teaching at a university? Don't the school authorities know about him?"

"I don't honestly know whether they do or not. You would think that if word about what he's doing has gotten to the students, one way or another, the administration would hear something too."

"But didn't you speak to any of the school officials about him? Let them know what you heard about him; or find out if they're doing anything about it—possibly they know nothing of the man's activities."

"No, I didn't. I was so involved in trying to locate Carrie that I didn't think about doing that. That didn't concern me—finding Carrie did."

"Naturally."

Carol picked up her glass and sipped slowly from it. She brought the glass down on the table and then looked up at Ross. He was watching her intently in the dim light. In the middle of the table was a glass centerpiece containing a lit candle. The glass was red and the flickering light of the candle through the glass made the table surroundings appear reddish. An eerie feeling came over Ross as he studied Carol's face. In the dim reddish light, her face displayed a certain youthful appearance and she looked almost as she had many years ago, even before they had married.

"What courses does this Dr. Conrad teach?" Ross asked. He casually picked up his glass and drank what remained of the scotch and water.

"Carrie was taking a philosophy course under him," Carol answered. "I don't know what else he might teach. Anyway, I called his office a couple of days ago before I came up here. But he wasn't in. I didn't know what I would have said to him had I found him. To tell you the truth, I felt somewhat relieved when his secretary told me he wasn't there."

"Do you seriously believe there's some romantic link between Carrie and him?"

"Well—yes. Carrie's old friends seem to think so. And the way Carrie used to talk about him last semester when she was taking that course under him, it was obvious she liked him quite a lot. As I said earlier, at first I *did* think it was just a school-girl infatuation, but—well, the way this group of friends Carrie's been hanging around with—well, they've just got loose morals and Carrie's bound to be influenced. I think you know what I mean."

Ross simply nodded.

Carol took another drink and swallowed hard.

"So it *does* look bad, doesn't it?" Ross said. He looked down at the candle centerpiece, the flame flickering through the red glass and casting shadows on the wall.

Carol nodded, realizing he hadn't expected an answer.

They sat there in silence.

"Well," Ross fiinally said, "let's stop talking about it for a while, anyway, and order something to eat. Shall we?"

"Yes, let's do."

Ross summoned the waitress when they had finished perusing the menu and he ordered for both of them. He was barely able to finish the steak he ordered. Carol had ordered a chef's salad. As he ate, he noticed her mostly just picking at the salad, not eating much of it. When they had finished their dinner, he persuaded her to join him in having an after-dinner drink. They both smoked cigarettes as they drank the liqueur. There was silence, almost as if they had terminated the conversation for the night, but Carol finally spoke. She took a drag of her cigarette and exhaled the smoke to one side.

"Ross," she said, "a few minutes back I told you I wanted to explain how Carrie and I ended up in New Mexico." Her voice now sounded more relaxed and Ross was sure her strained nerves were becoming slightly unraveled. Knowing that relaxed him even more.

"O.K.," he said. "You've been wanting to do that all evening." He smiled at her. "If you feel you must. I'm listening."

"Thanks. To begin with, you probably think my disappearance with Carrie was part of some scheme of mine tied in with the divorce and that I had planned it all along."

She had been looking down as she spoke, her eyes on the table. She lifted her gaze and looked into his eyes. "But it wasn't, Ross," she continued softly, almost inaudibly. "I know you probably don't remember my father too well, but if you should be able to remember even some part of him, it would be that he was somewhat of a loner—even mystifying at times. In fact, you may remember my complaining more than once that he even kept *me,* his own daughter, in the dark about where he was or what he was doing. He cherished seclusion and privacy, to say the least."

"Yes, I remember vividly that part of him. But if you'll recall, I only met him a few times and you actually never spoke much about him."

He returned her gaze. "What about your father?" he said curiously.

Carol inhaled her cigarette, letting the smoke out slowly.

"Well, he's the reason why Carrie and I ended up here." She noticed Ross' puzzled expression.

"My father," she explained, "telephoned me about two weeks before I went to court on the divorce. As a matter of fact, I was just thinking—it's coincidental but yet, ironic—he called me from this place—Esperanza. He used to live here."

"Really?"

"Or a few miles from here, rather." She put her cigarette down on the ashtray. "He didn't know anything about our separation or the upcoming divorce when he contacted me. His telephone call couldn't have been more ill-timed, for he wanted me to go to him immediately.

"He said it was extremely urgent that I come down here to see him. He seemed terribly disappointed when I explained to him why I couldn't leave San Francisco just then—I told him about the divorce proceeding that was two weeks away. Then he practically swore me to secrecy—about his telephone call, I mean. He got me to promise him I wouldn't tell anyone he had even called—not even you. Then he asked me to come down here as soon as I could after the divorce. It was all so mysterious and when I asked what it was all about, he said he couldn't tell me over the telephone; that it would have to wait until I got here. So he gave me instructions how to get here."

"You mean that's all he said—no explanation?"

"None whatsoever. But I kept prodding and he finally told me that it had to do with his health. But he wouldn't say anymore about it. Naturally, I was concerned when I learned he was in poor health. That definitely threw a different light on things and so I told him I would postpone the divorce hearing and go to him right away, but he insisted that I not do that—that I wait until after the divorce. Nevertheless, he was emphatic that I not delay coming here as soon as I could after the hearing.

"I want you to believe me that I would have told you then about Daddy's phone call, Ross, honestly I would, but I was afraid that if you learned I was going away with Carrie, even if only temporarily, you'd change your mind about the agreement we had made in the divorce action and that somehow that might delay everything. I honestly didn't know what to do. I'll have to admit that my not telling you was purely selfish on my part. I didn't want to delay the divorce at all. I thought it was best for the two of us to get it over with as soon as possible. And besides, I knew I'd probably be returning to California soon. It's true I didn't know exactly when I'd be returning, but believe me, Ross, at first, I never intended to keep Carrie away from you permanently."

What she had just said bothered Ross slightly and for the first time since he had heard from her, he resented her, and it surprised him that he experienced this resentment. It disturbed him and he tried not showing it.

"Why did your father go through all the secrecy?" he asked. He avoided her glance.

"I don't know," Carol replied softly. "I never was able to find out; it always remained a mystery. You see—when I arrived here, Daddy had passed away." Her voice shook a little.

"I'm terribly sorry," Ross said.

"Thank you. It really doesn't matter now."

Ross suddenly realized it was inappropriate paying his respects for a death that had happened almost twenty years before. But Carol's revelation of her father's death had aroused his curiosity.

"How did it happen—accident?"

She shook her head. "No, I was told he had a weak heart. He died of a heart attack. I found out he suffered the first one a week or so before he telephoned. He was in bed recovering from that one when a second attack came shortly before I arrived. 'Coronary thrombosis' the death certificate read." She picked up another cigarette from the pack on the table and Ross lit it for her. He didn't light one for himself.

"Was he buried here in Esperanza?"

"Yes. In a small cemetery just outside town. I've visited his grave a few times since his death. I haven't come up here as often as I should, really. A few years ago, I purchased a marker for it."

She thought for a moment. "It's strange, isn't it, how present problems can occupy a person's mind. I was thinking that I've been here several days and it hasn't even entered my mind to go visit Daddy's grave. My mind's been occupied with locating Carrie."

"That's understandable." He paused briefly, watching Carol's eyes in the dim light. "What had your father been doing here? Did you ever find out?"

"Not exactly. I did find out he had worked for a long time in Los Alamos — at the Los Alamos Scientific Laboratory. You've heard of the place, I'm sure."

"Yes. That's the place where they developed the atom bomb, wasn't it?"

"That's right. It's not far from here—up north about twenty

miles from Santa Fe. Anyway, Daddy's work there had something to do with radioactivity. But that was a couple of years
before his death. In going over some of his papers after he
died, I found the names of several of his associates at Los
Alamos. I corresponded with two of them, trying to find out
something about Daddy's last years. I even traveled up there
one time to visit one of his old associates. I learned from him
that Daddy had been conducting experiments with some kind
of newly discovered metal which had previously been believed
extinct. Plutonium Two—something or other, it was called.
Anyway, the discovery was an important one, this associate of
Daddy told me, because it had never before been found in its
natural state.

"He also told me Daddy had become interested in some
sidelight of some experiment he had been working on with
Plutonium—something having to do with the genetic structure
in human beings and the effect radioactivity had on chromosomes and genetic make-up. According to what this one scientist told me, Daddy supposedly discovered something else quite
by accident in working with this metal. He suddenly became
absorbed in it but it carried him away from what he was doing
for the laboratory. He became frustrated because he knew
he had his regular experiments to conduct and yet he was so
absorbed and interested in what he had discovered, but couldn't
find the time to work on it. Finally, he quit the lab and came
down here to Esperanza where he set up his own laboratory
and worked on this independent experiment of his. He kept his
discovery a secret even from the people he had been working
with at Los Alamos."

"But why come here, to this little town?"

"I don't know. He wanted seclusion, I guess."

"Your father certainly was a strange man, wasn't he?"

"I'm afraid so. When I first came here, I thought at first
that what he had wanted to tell me was in connection with
something he had discovered in his experiments. But then I
decided that wasn't the case at all. I believe he must have lost
interest in these experiments of his long before I arrived here."

"What made you think that?"

"For one thing, I visited the place where he had been

working, and it didn't impress me as a place a scientist would seriously consider using to work on important experiments. And then, of course, aside from learning from one of Daddy's associates what he was supposed to be doing down here, I found no notes or any other evidence that he was in fact conducting experiments. What I actually think was happening—" She stopped rather abruptly.

"You're probably going to think I'm crazy for saying this, but what I really think is that Daddy was involved in the practice of witchcraft."

"Witchcraft!" Ross exclaimed. "You've got to be joking. What in the world ever made you suspect something like that of your father?"

"Because of certain things which I'll get to later. First, let me tell you what happened when I first arrived here and learned of Daddy's death. Of course, his not wanting to reveal too much over the phone was in itself a mystery. You can well imagine, then, how I felt when I got here and learned Daddy had died.

"It was a shock and I felt completely lost. Being in a strange place, with strange people, coupled with his mysterious phone call—and—on top of that, never learning what he had wanted to see me about. I'm sure you'll agree, that was enough to get a person terribly upset, and needless to say, it made me a nervous wreck."

She paused to take one last puff of her cigarette and then she put it out.

Before she could continue with her story, the waitress approached the table and asked if they wanted to order another drink. Ross quickly asked Carol if she cared for one. She shook her head and thanked him.

Ross gave the young waitress a twenty-dollar bill and she disappeared through the doorway leading to the lounge. Carol excused herself and went into the ladies' room. When she returned, Ross stood up and left the waitress a tip.

"You look a little tired," Ross said to Carol. "Why don't we head back to the hotel and you can finish telling me about your father there. Besides, it's getting a little stuffy in here."

Carol nodded. "That's a good idea. I *am* tired, but I do

want to finish telling you. There's a small patio in back of the hotel near my room where they've got some lounging chairs. We could go there, if you'd like. Even though I'm tired, I couldn't go to sleep this early. I'm sure it's not too late. What time is it?"

"It's ten-thirty," Ross said, looking at his watch. The two of them walked out of the restaurant and into the refreshing night air.

CHAPTER 11

BACK at the hotel, they walked past a middle-aged couple seated in the lobby. Carol led Ross through a narrow corridor leading to the outside in back of the hotel. The old man who had greeted Ross earlier was nowhere in sight.

Carol pointed to a door as they passed through the crowded hallway. "That's my room."

Ross nodded.

The corridor led to a large patio at the rear of the hotel. It was full of shrubbery along the plastered, adobe walls surrounding the courtyard. Cypresses lined the high outside walls of the hotel. In the middle of the courtyard were two gigantic elm trees partially hiding the sky. The trees' leaves made a rustling sound as a breeze blew momentarily across the open patio. The only light came from two small light fixtures—one on the wall above the corridor exit from which they had entered the patio—the other attached to the top of a wrought-iron pole at the far end of the courtyard.

The patio possessed a pleasant, warm atmosphere and a fresh, sweet odor filled the night air. Ross could feel the strong effect of the liquor and for the first time during the last two days, he could definitely say he felt completely relaxed. It relieved him to know he could experience relaxation in the midst of the confusion of the past few days.

They sat down on two patio lounging chairs located near the center of the courtyard. Carol pulled out a cigarette and Ross lit it for her.

"I was out here last night," Carol said, drawing on her cigarette. "I enjoy the peace and quiet this place has to offer. It's nice out here, don't you think?"

"Yes," Ross replied. "It's pleasant."

"I love it here. The serenity's quite a contrast to that dark cloud of turmoil that my mind's been in the past few days. Keeps me from forgetting there's some people out there somewhere enjoying themselves—life—this very moment."

She sighed softly. "I suddenly feel guilty dragging you into this."

It irked him somewhat to hear her say that. She looked up at him from where she was lying on the reclining chair. She couldn't see his face too clearly but she nevertheless noticed he appeared upset. He was hunched slightly forward on the edge of the chair, his elbows leaning against his thighs. He was aware she was waiting for a response.

"You needn't feel that way, Carol." He emphasized his words. "I told you before I'm glad you called me. I'd like to help and that's why I'm here. After all, I too care about what happens to Carrie, you know."

"I'm sorry, Ross," Carol said apologetically. "I didn't mean to imply that you didn't care. Your presence here certainly speaks for itself. Even if we never were to find Carrie, or things turned out for the worst, I want you to know I'll always be appreciative for your having come. I don't think many others would have done that."

"Oh, I don't know about that. Anyway, I'm glad you did call me and I'm glad I came."

"I am too, Ross. You'll never know how much."

"Why don't you finish telling me about the time you learned your father had passed away?" Aside from wanting to satisfy his curiosity which Carol's story had created, he was attempting to set aside the topic with which they had begun the conversation.

"All right. I already told you how much the entire matter had upset me. Even though I had never considered Daddy and me close, still I found myself shaken by his death. I discovered a few days after the funeral that Daddy had had some business dealings in Albuquerque and had some funds deposited in a bank there. So I went there and learned that he had an attorney there also. So I looked him up.

"I found out Daddy had executed a will a few months before he died and had left everything to me. A substantial amount of the property he had owned was real estate located in Albuquerque. The lawyer told me he'd start probate proceedings immediately and that I'd have to remain in town at least for the time being. So he helped me find a temporary place to stay, and since I was Daddy's only beneficiary under the will, the attorney made arrangements for me to draw some of Daddy's money from the bank.

"When I found out it was going to take six to seven months to probate the estate, I had second thoughts about staying, but Daddy's attorney advised me the proceedings would go much smoother if I were physically present to handle the estate. I debated about staying, but finally decided to stay as long as necessary. Once I decided that I was going to stay, the next decision I had to make was whether I should call you and let you know what had happened. Several times, I almost picked up the phone to do just that. But the more I thought about calling you, the more terrified I became."

"Terrified? About what?"

"Oh, Ross, it must sound terribly childish and silly to you now, but at the time, it made sense. I convinced myself it was better if I didn't call you. My thinking that way had to do with the divorce not being final yet. You'll remember the attorney who represented me said that the divorce actually wouldn't be final until after a year had elapsed from the date the judge signed the decree—what was it called? An interloc—something or other."

"An interlocutory decree."

"Yes, that's it. Well, the attorney told me some things having to do with Carrie's custody. He said that as Carrie got a little older and circumstances changed, such as my leaving

Californa to live elsewhere, you could always petition the court to modify the decree with respect to your right to visit with Carrie. I kept thinking that if you found out I was here, you'd institute some kind of proceedings. In my mind, you suddenly became some kind of ugly monster—an enemy. It was all so cruel of me to think of you in that way. But at the time, it didn't seem that way at all. The way I felt must have had something to do with Daddy's death. You see, when he died, I suddenly treasured life very much; my own, of course, but more importantly, Carrie's. She was only a few months old then, a new life just beginning. I had grown very attached to her, especially after Daddy died, and I grew to love her a great deal. I just couldn't bear the thought of being without her even for a day. And I imagine that because of the distorted, confused perspective of mine, I was convinced you threatened all of that.

"When Daddy's estate finally was closed and I was free to leave, my fears about losing Carrie to you remained. In fact, they were stronger for I thought that my absence from California might work against me if you decided to petition the court to modify the visitation rights and to prevent me from leaving California again without first working out some kind of arrangement with you about Carrie. And by then, too, I had grown attached to Albuquerque; I had found a nice place to live. Not only that, but I had inherited Daddy's real estate holdings there and a few leases which were producing income. I felt it important to remain and look after my interests rather than leave it in the hands of someone else. It was all terribly selfish of me, Ross, and I know that only too well now. Actually, I knew it then too, but somehow it didn't matter then. I even rationalized my actions time and time again, by telling myself that Carrie was only a baby and that you wouldn't miss her as much as I would, but all of that was so wrong of me. I wouldn't ever ask you to forgive me. I wouldn't deserve it."

"Carol, that was all a long time ago—it's water under the bridge now—and I see no reason to discuss it. I wish you'd stop bringing up the past." He stared at her intently. He was slightly disgusted with her now for having returned to the subject of her disappearance from his life.

"Why don't you finish telling me about your father's

death?" he continued. "Is there anymore to tell?"

"Yes. I'm not so sure you'll think there was something mysterious about what I'm about to tell you but I certainly did when I first arrived here. And I still do, although it really doesn't matter anymore. Nevertheless, I felt a strange sensation those four or five days I spent in Esperanza before I finally left for Albuquerque. I thought at first that it was because of Daddy's dying in a strange place, a place I didn't know, and my not having spoken to Daddy before he died, when he had wanted to speak to me so desperately. Of course, it's possible I might have blown the whole thing out of proportion. And yet, there were those other circumstances."

"What circumstances?"

"Well, for example, on the afternoon of the day I had arrived here, I went to the mortuary and asked to see Daddy's body. I was told the mortician wasn't available—that I'd have to get his permission." She stopped briefly in thought. "Let's see, he did give me a specific reason why I couldn't see the body—oh, yes, because they hadn't finished the embalming process. I would have to get the owner's permission. So I told the mortician's assistant that I'd return later, which I did—twice that day—but I never found the mortician there. The next day was the funeral so I never did get a chance to view the body.

"It was at the funeral the next morning, as the coffin was being placed on the base above the grave that for no apparent reason, a thought occurred to me—I suddenly realized that Daddy's body was now being given an ordinary burial."

"What was so unusual about that?"

"In and of itself, there was nothing unusual about it, but Daddy had always wanted to be cremated. He had explained that to me very clearly a few years before, during one of his visits to California. And when Mother was alive, I remember she and Daddy discussing it once or twice. It was evidently something he had believed in."

"Maybe he never told anyone around here about it," Ross said. "Possibly he never got the chance to tell someone. There's nothing strange about that—it's a perfectly reasonable explanation."

"No, Ross, I don't think so. Daddy felt strongly about it. I know he did. He would have left instructions with someone. The heart attack didn't cause his death immediately. He was conscious for a few hours and there was plenty of time to tell someone."

"Maybe he did and that someone goofed up. Or maybe he was cremated and his remains are what were buried. I'll admit I don't know much about cremation but wouldn't they do it that way?"

"I imagine they could. There's nothing that I know of that would prevent them from doing it in that manner. But not usually. Besides, when I visited the mortuary the day before, the person I spoke to there made specific reference to their not having finished with the embalming. So that would rule out cremation. Surely they wouldn't go through the trouble of embalming the body only to have it cremated later. It troubled me then."

"Great scott, Carol, surely that in itself doesn't seem that strange to me. After all, there's—"

"Wait, let me finish—there's more to it than that. For example, there's that place where he used to live and work."

"You mean the place near here where you said he had set up some kind of lab?"

"Yes."

"Does this have anything to do with what you told me earlier about witchcraft?"

"Yes, it does. You see, that afternoon of the day of Daddy's funeral, I visited the place where he used to live. It's a couple of miles from here. The place is owned—or at least, it was then—by an old lady by the name of—I can't think of her complete name but I believe her last name was—yes, I remember; her last name was Hawkins. I remember it because the people around here used to call her Old Lady Hawkins. She had the reputation around here of—of practicing witchcraft."

"And you honestly think your father was tied in with this Mrs. Hawkins in someway connected with witchcraft?" Ross asked unbelievingly.

"Yes." She was eyeing him carefully. "The look on your face tells me you don't believe me." She managed to smile slightly.

"Oh, I believe you may have suspected it. But you must admit, it's rather hard to swallow something as screwy as that about your father. I didn't really take you seriously earlier tonight when you first mentioned it. I always knew your father had his idiosyncracies, but witchcraft! In this day and age, it's difficult to believe a scientist like your father would—well, I mean, it doesn't make sense that a scientific mind would give any credence to matters of the occult and black magic that were prevalent ages ago. Unless, of course, it was some sort of crazy hobby of his; something he studied; something he did just for kicks."

"No, Ross, I'm certain that wasn't the case with him. He took it all rather seriously. You see, it goes much further back than just the two years he used to live on the Hawkins property. It has to do with something that happened to him a long time before that. But I'll tell you about that later. Let me tell you about the time I visited this woman — Old Lady Hawkins.

"I went there because I had been told Daddy had left some of his personal belongings there and I wanted to gather them up and see how much he had there so I could make arrangements for someone to pick them up. He had left them with Miss Hawkins. Anyway, this place she lived in—it was an old house located in an out-of-the-way place—off the beaten path. Hardly anyone ever went there, I was told, because the road leading to her place dead ends a little further down. But the place was enough to give anyone the willies. It gave me the creeps the moment I set foot in it.

"I was there for maybe half an hour or a little more—just long enough to tell Miss Hawkins who I was, what I was there for, and to go through Daddy's things. She hardly spoke to me at first, although I'm sure she had been expecting me. She quietly led me into this room in back of the house and showed me where Daddy's things were. She had already gathered them to one side of the room. Some of his things had been placed in storage boxes, and I told her I'd send someone over for the big boxes later. I asked her also if it was all right with her if I spent some time going through some of the things first, to sort them out. She said nothing, but merely turned around and left me alone in the room.

"I don't know whether it was my imagination or what, but during the entire time I was in that lady's house I strongly sensed that she didn't trust me—that she was suspicious of me. Why, I couldn't say.

"Well, I began looking rather hurriedly through the items that were there, I was looking for something in particular. Daddy's sudden death, his connections with this mysterious old woman, and his work with this experiment of his which has always remained a mystery to me to this day, compelled me to search for this one item that belonged to him. I had known him to keep it with him always. When I couldn't find it, I left the room and went searching for Miss Hawkins, to ask her about it. I went down this long hallway calling out her name several times, and when she didn't respond, I thought she had left the house. I walked into the parlor and called out her name again, but there was still no answer. The room was dark for all the drapes were drawn closed. I turned around to leave and that's when I saw her sitting on a chair in the darkness near the doorway. I had passed right by her. She had been there all that time and quite obviously heard me calling for her, but she hadn't bothered answering.

"She remained sitting there in the dark, even when she knew I had noticed her. I asked her about this metal box I had been looking for—whether all of Daddy's belongings had been placed in the back room. Finally, she answered. Yes, she said, everything Daddy had possessed to her knowledge was there in the room she had showed me. She didn't make any specific reference to the box I had inquired about, but I described it for her and she finally said she knew nothing of a metal box—she had never seen it. I didn't believe her, but of course, there was nothing else I could do so I returned to the back room and took what items I could carry and later sent a moving company for the rest of the things too large for me to carry.

"To this day, I've felt certain that old lady knew something about the box and what had happened to it, because—well, because what was in that box was in a direct way, connected with black magic and the kind of thing one associates with practitioners of witchcraft and that sort of stuff."

"What exactly was in this box you were looking for and how did you know it even existed?" Ross asked curiously.

"It was a small doll—a wax doll." She spoke softly and calmly.

"A doll!" For a moment, he thought he had misunderstood. "This is getting a little confusing for me. Did you say a doll?"

"Yes. A doll made in the image of my father."

"But I don't understand."

"Let me explain. Daddy was a genius in his field. I'm not just saying this because he was my father. It was an accepted fact among his colleagues and the people he worked with. They admired his skill; the way his mind worked. I've been told this by the closest of his associates. But even so—even though he had a brilliant scientific mind, it was nevertheless true that he was an extremely superstitious man. This belief in the supernatural was a special weakness with him. I don't think even he knew exactly what it was that made him that way. But he had been like that as long as I can remember. Somewhere early in his life, before I was even born, he began believing in the supernatural—the occult. Even when my mother was alive, he'd never discuss it with her. She knew, though. We both knew that a terrible fear had grown within him of people who possessed supernatural powers to do harm to others." She paused, as if allowing Ross time to absorb all that she had said.

"This is absolutely amazing. Astonishing. But what does all that you're telling me have to do with this doll you were looking for?"

Slowly, Carol began telling Ross everything she knew of the two years her father had spent in Africa where he had traveled to perform certain experiments involving the genetic structure of several African tribes. She told him of the tragic accidental death of the young African native at the hands of Andrew Borlin and the sworn vengeance of Bangurah, the dead man's father, and of the black magic which he practiced and which her father had grown to fear. She related the subsequent search by her father and his dedicated assistant, Babatundé, for the waxen doll created to bring about the terrible death of her father, and the premeditated murder of Bangurah. Finally, she told Ross of Andrew Borlin's flight from the African continent, the wax doll safe at his side, the dead Bangurah no longer a living threat.

When Carol had finished her story, Ross sat there in disbelief. "But it all sounds so incredible," he finally said. "He *must* have been a true believer in witchcraft, to have killed that native to get his hands on that doll."

"Now you know why I said it wasn't only a hobby with him."

"Yes, I certainly do. How did you ever learn this about your father? Did he tell you?"

"Heavens no," Carol replied. "He would never have discussed it with me. It was something he considered too personal. He never discussed it even with my mother, except at the beginning when he first told her about it shortly after his return from Africa. I wasn't even born yet when Daddy returned to the United States. No one else ever knew about this obsession of his, except, of course, Mother and me. And probably Miss Hawkins—I think that's why he was attracted to that horrid place—why he lived there."

"How did you ever find out about it then, if it was never discussed?"

"I learned about it quite by accident many years later, when I must have been around eight or nine years old.

"One day, I was snooping in my parents' bedroom—you know, like most children that age do. I still remember that day vividly. I had placed a chair in the closet and an old suitcase on top of that so I could reach the high shelf above where the clothes were hanging and there, I found this black metal box. It was a sturdy box with a lock in front and it was locked, but the key was attached right to the lock. I was curious to find out what was inside so I took it down and opened it. In it, neatly in place, I found the doll. My first reaction was that it was a gift my parents had bought for me and were hiding it from me. I could tell it wasn't an ordinary doll and that it was crudely made but I recall the one thing that impressed me the most was that it was a doll of a man and not a woman—something I had never seen before. It fascinated me and I took it out of the box to play with it.

"I was playing with it on the bed when Daddy happened to enter the room and found me there with the doll in my hands. I remember the terrified expression on his face when he first saw me and the anger which came over him immediately after he had taken it away from me. And then he gave me the spanking of my life. It upset me terribly. My mother too became upset when she rushed into the room. She and Daddy exchanged a few angry words and she tried to comfort me but I didn't get over the traumatic experience for several days, during which time I grew afraid of my father.

"But a few years after that incident, when I was older, I still recalled what happened — it was still imprinted in my memory, and finally, one day, when Mother and I were involved in serious conversation, I reminded her of the incident and pleaded with her to explain to me why Daddy had gotten so angry with me that day he found me playing with the doll. Until then, she was the only one aside from my father who knew what had happened in Africa, so she swore me to secrecy even then. You're the first person I've ever told. I guess it doesn't matter now that anyone else should know about it since both my parents are dead. In any event, I thought it'd help you understand why I felt the way I did about Daddy's death if I explained the story about the doll. And now you know why it is I felt he was involved with Old Lady Hawkins in some kind of witchcraft practice or rituals involving this doll. And so I suspect, too, the old lady knew about Daddy's experience in Africa and about the wax doll, but that she didn't care to discuss it with me."

"Do you actually think he might have shared his secret with her?" Ross inquired.

"I can't say for certain. I don't know whether he may have told her about it or whether she learned of it in some other way. All I know is that I never found the doll and that I felt strongly the old lady knew where it was or what may have happened to it. I can't help thinking even now that it might have had something to do with Daddy's death."

"Oh, come now, Carol. You can't honestly believe that. From what you've told me, I'm sure it's true your father was a firm believer in this sort of thing, but his believing in it, no matter how sincere his belief, certainly doesn't have to make believers out of you and me."

He studied Carol. It startled him somewhat that such a primitive superstition should survive in the twentieth century, especially in the mind of a brilliant scientist, even one as eccentric as Carol's father. It was simply incredible to think such things could be taken seriously, or thought to be taken seriously, in the age of advanced technology, where television, jet planes, man-made earth and martian satellites, and moon landings were becoming everyday occurances.

"I'm not saying," Carol countered, "that I necessarily believe in witchcraft, or in the harm that could have been caused by the wax doll Daddy feared so much, but what I actually meant was that he may have believed in it so much that psychologically, it might have had a strong influence on him. To the point, possibly, that his health was affected by it. Many people suffer from psychosomatic illness — they suggest the sickness, even though there may be nothing organically wrong with them. Now there, we're speaking of something believable —simply because it's a scientific thing. And so, in the case of my father, possibly the witchcraft the old lady practiced really didn't work, but it could have affected Daddy in that way."

She paused. They exchanged glances. "Well," she continued, "we'll never know what effect, if any, the old lady's witchcraft may have had on Daddy's death, and it actually makes no difference to me now; it all happened years ago. I'd never discussed it with another living soul except that I wanted you to know exactly what happened now that we're together under these circumstances."

"Well," Ross said, "you've certainly let me in on a lot of information. It's interesting—about your father, I mean." He smiled at her slightly; she smiled back. "What about that metal box you never found at the old lady's house. Did you ever inquire about it further; ask anyone else besides Miss Hawkins?"

"Yes, I did. There was this young man—a caretaker—who lived in a small dwelling on Miss Hawkins' land. He did work for her but I understood he was close to Daddy and helped him as some kind of assistant. He helped in the laboratory. I asked him about the box but he said he didn't know what I was talking about; that he had never seen the box nor the doll. I even asked Daddy's attorney when I was in Albuquerque, but he knew nothing."

"Maybe your father kept it locked up in a safety deposit box at some bank, not necessarily here nor in Albuquerque, but somewhere else. Did you ever check out that possibility?"

"Yes. As far as his attorney knew, Daddy had only one safety deposit box, in a bank in Albuquerque. We looked through his papers to see if there was evidence that he had one in some other bank, but we found no indication of it. We inquired at the other banks. All he had in the safety deposit box that was registered in his name were some bonds and stock certificates and a few deeds to real estate he owned." She shook her head slightly. "Besides, he would never have kept the doll in such a place. He always kept it physically close to him."

She noticed Ross staring off into space, in thought. "Mind if I ask what it is you're thinking about?" she inquired. "Your mind seems to be elsewhere."

Ross turned and looked at her. "Oh, nothing important. It came to my mind that life has many hidden surprises in store for some people—like tonight, for example."

"I don't understand what you mean."

"I was thinking that a few days ago, I would never have guessed that you and I would be sitting here tonight, talking about something that happened so many years ago. But for your phone call yesterday, tonight I would be in San Francisco, doing what, I don't know, but spending a perfectly normal evening. Yet, here I am, sitting in a strange place, listening to you relate an even stranger story about your father and your disappearance from my life twenty years ago."

At that moment, Monica came into his thoughts, and he thought that even though he really didn't know what he might be doing in San Francisco tonight, whatever it might be, most likely the two of them would be together. His thoughts of Monica disappeared from his mind when he became aware Carol was saying something to him. She was asking him whether he had any suggestions what they might do the following day.

"I think, Carol," he replied, "to begin with, we should pay

another visit to the sheriff. What did you say his name was?"

"Dominguez, Bartolo Dominguez. But I'm not so sure he can help us. I wouldn't want to get Carrie in trouble."

"Bar—Bartolo." He had trouble pronouncing the name. "Carol, we might as well face it. Carrie's in enough serious trouble already, and right now, I think the most important thing is to find her before we're too late, and we've got to locate her even if it means getting help from law enforcement agencies. If they should charge her with anything criminally— well, we'll cross that bridge if and when we come to it. I think the sooner we both realize this, the better our chances are in locating her. And after all, that's what we both want right now more than anything else, isn't it?"

"Yes, I guess you're right," Carol said reluctantly.

"But now, I think we both better try getting some sleep." He looked at his watch as he stood up. "I didn't realize it was so late."

"Yes, we have. It's already made me feel much better."

"I can see that."

Carol stood up and they both walked toward the corridor leading into the hotel lobby.

They stopped midway down the hallway at the entrance to Carol's room.

"I meant to ask you earlier," Ross said. "Do you have a photograph of Carrie—a recent one?"

"Yes, I do," Carol said. "It's in my wallet, right here." She raised her purse. "Oh, I forgot, this purse is too small to carry much—only a few cosmetics. I left my wallet on top of the dresser inside. Just a minute and I'll get it for you." She took her key out and began unlocking the door.

"Oh, don't bother tonight. It's late. You can show it to me tomorrow at breakfast."

"All right. What time do you want to get started in the morning?"

"I don't know. I'm sure I'll probably wake up early. Let's say I'll give you a buzz whatever time that is. It that all right?"

"Sure, that'll be fine, then. Goodnight, Ross. And thanks again for coming."

"Sure. Goodnight, Carol, see you in the morning."

She unlocked and opened the door. Ross waited until she had closed it behind her. Then he turned slowly and walked through the corridor into the lobby and upstairs to his room.

Tired. Very tired; his entire body ached with the tiredness of sleep. *Carol is dead.* He wanted desperately to succumb to the blissful, satisfying state of repose.

Finally, sleep came suddenly to him and he was unaware exactly when it had overcome him, only that it had done so after many long hours of tossing and turning—the tumbling, rolling waves of thoughts inside his mind more so than his body.

CHAPTER 12

DAYBREAK came early the following morning but it didn't awaken him. He awakened gradually to the voices of two men conversing on the sidewalk below. He was still drowsy when he opened his eyes; he felt a slight headache. But even in his drowsiness, he recalled vividly the events of the early morning. *Carol was dead.* He suddenly found it all incomprehensible and hostile, his being in this small town.

He took a quick, cold shower, then shaved and put on a newly-pressed suit.

As he walked down the corridor to the stairs, he noticed the old man sitting behind his roll-top desk. The old man looked up as Ross approached him.

"Well, good morning, Mr. Blair," he said. "Did you sleep well?"

"Yes," Ross answered. "Did the Sheriff's office finish with what they had to do in Mrs. Lockwood's room early this morning?"

"Yes. Not long ago, as a matter of fact. Last man out of there left here about an hour ago, I'd say. Fingerprint man, he was. Dusted the whole room for them. He gave me the key to the room before he left. Said not to clean it up nor rent it out to anyone just yet."

"I see."

"Ah—the body was removed from the room shortly after you went upstairs last night. Took it down to the mortuary, they did."

"Yes, I was going to ask you about that. Would you happen to know what mortuary?"

"There's only one in town, Mr. Blair. Tom Richard's place. It's been the only mortuary around this place for years. His father owned it before Tom did. Passed it on to Tom when he died a couple of years ago. You can't miss the place. Just go up the street here on the side of the hotel and turn left at the second stop sign. It's right there half a block down."

"Were Mrs. Lockwood's clothing and personal effects left in the room?"

"Yes, still there. Sheriff left orders to keep the place locked up, though, until he gave the orders to move anything in there." He squinted his eyes as he looked up at Ross. He held his eye glasses in his hand. Now, he put them back on as he stood up and approached the railing.

"I want you to know, Mr. Blair," he said, "how sorry I am about what happened to Mrs. Lockwood. It was a terrible thing to happen. Such a nice lady, she was. Can't imagine who would do a thing like that. Feel awful about it happening here, I do. Now, most of the town folk will be coming by here just snooping around, like vultures, you just wait and see. I wanted you to know how sorry I am about it all."

"Thank you," Ross said. "Tell me, is that lounge-restaurant down the street open this early? For breakfast, I mean."

"Yes, it is. And they serve a mighty good one, too. I've always recommended it to our guests, and they've never complained."

"Thanks. I'll be going out now; be back sometime before noon, I imagine. I've got to go see the sheriff and then I'll have to make some kind of arrangements with the mortuary." He turned and walked out the door.

After having a light breakfast, for he wasn't too hungry, he got into the car and found his way to the county courthouse to meet Sheriff Dominguez. The courthouse was a beige pueblo-styled, stuccoed building. Although it was two stories high, it wasn't a large building, but impressive. The front of the courthouse was beautifully landscaped. Evergreen hedges surrounded the building near its walls and a neatly trimmed lawn spread around the building from the front to the side opposite the parking area. A few large evergreen and mulberry trees lined the edge of the lawn, near the sidewalk and a broad walkway led through a small courtyard and to the entrance. To one side of the entrance to the courtyard, stood a wooden sign post. In red letters painted on a yellow background, it read:

SANDOVAL
COUNTY COURTHOUSE
COUNTY SEAT
ESPERANZA, NEW MEXICO
BUILT 1938

Once inside, he had no difficulty finding the sheriff's office and he was quickly ushered into Sheriff Dominguez' private office by a young, dark-haired girl sitting behind a reception desk at the far end of a hallway.

Dominguez sat behind an old wooden desk. As soon as Ross entered the room, the sheriff looked up from a small pile of papers. He rose to greet Ross.

"Ah, Señor Blair," the sheriff said, "you are just in time to join me in a cup of coffee. I was about to have some." The two men shook hands. The sheriff motioned to an oak chair in front of his desk. "Here, please sit down." He returned to his chair. "Marcela," he said to the young girl who had ushered Ross into the office, "please do me the favor of getting coffee for both Mr. Blair and myself. He turned to Ross. "How do you like your coffee?"

"Black," Ross answered. He smiled at the girl, then sat down.

The sheriff turned to the young girl. "One black, Marcela, for Mr. Blair, and—you know how I like mine."

The girl simply nodded and left the room. She returned shortly with the two cups of coffee on a tray. It was steaming hot. She placed the tray on Dominguez' desk and then disappeared again without a word.

"Enjoy your coffee for a minute," Sheriff Dominguez said as he settled back into his chair, "while I get some of these letters signed and out of the way."

"That's fine, take your time, please," Ross replied.

Sheriff Dominguez began skimming through the papers in front of him. Trying not to be too conspicuous about it, Ross began studying the man seated behind the desk. Ross estimated the man's age to be about forty five, only a few years younger than he. For a moment, he wondered whether persons of Mexican or Spanish descent were like the Negro, who in Ross' opinion, retained a remarkable youthful appearance in their later years.

The sheriff was wearing a long sleeve, khaki shirt similar to the one he had worn the night before, except that his sleeves were now rolled up to a point just below the elbow, displaying muscular arms thickly covered with long, black hair. When he had met the sheriff the night before, in the dim light of the hotel, Ross had noticed a penetrating stare in the man's eyes and Ross couldn't make out what it was about them that gave such an effect. But now, as he studied the man, he noticed he had deep blue eyes which created a vivid contrast with his dark-skinned face.

Sheriff Dominguez looked up abruptly and caught Ross staring at him. Slightly embarrassed, Ross glanced down, brought the cup up to his lips, and sipped the hot coffee.

"That takes care of that," Dominguez said, releasing a long sigh. "Paper work. That's one of the few duties I dislike about this job. But unfortunately, it's one of the necessary ones." He gave a slight laugh and smiled as he picked up the papers to straighten them out. He stood up and stepped around the desk. "Just a moment, please, Mr. Blair, while I give these to my secretary." He disappeared; in a few seconds, he returned and seated himself behind the desk, sipping at his mug of coffee.

"How's your coffee, Mr. Blair?" he asked.

"Fine," Ross answered. "It's good and strong. I like it that way."

"I've been drinking this stuff since I was three or four years old, I guess. My grandmother used to warn me all the time it would prevent me from growing—keep me short and skinny—but bless her heart, I've proven her wrong about that, for I'm anything but short and skinny." He glanced down briefly at his waist, then looked up at Ross, a wide grin on his face. "Ah, well, that's enough of my talk. Let's get down to business, shall we?"

He stood up, walked to one corner of the room and brought back a small, portable cassette recorder. He asked Ross if he minded having their discussion recorded; Ross said no, he didn't mind at all.

Sheriff Dominguez began the discussion with detailed questions concerning any information which Carol may have related to Ross that might have the slightest connection with her murder. He asked Ross about Carol's telephone calls to him in California. Ross related all he could remember about the telephone calls, at times pausing in thought, trying to go into as much detail as he could remember. He held back nothing and told the sheriff what he knew of Carrie's problem with drugs and the recent misunderstanding between Carol and Carrie. Finding Carrie now that Carol was dead was more important to him than at the beginning. His search for Carrie began taking the form of an obsession. And so he revealed everything he knew to Sheriff Dominguez, ignoring for the moment the possibility that criminal charges might be filed against Carrie.

Again, as he had the night before, Dominguez asked Ross if he knew of anyone who might have had reason to kill Carol and whether Carol herself may have mentioned someone to him who may have wanted to harm her. The sheriff's question immediately brought to Ross' mind what Carol had told him of Carrie's growing resentment toward her for having kept his whereabouts from her a secret. He sensed a sudden emptiness —a panic—as he reflected upon the possibility that Dominguez might consider Carrie a suspect.

"No," he finally said. "I know of no one who might have wanted harm to come to her. If there had been, I'm sure she would have mentioned it to me."

The sheriff proceeded with other questions. After almost an hour, he turned off the recorder and leaned back on his chair.

"Well, I believe I've exhausted you, Mr. Blair. Now, let's

turn things around. I thought possibly you might have a question or two to ask me."

"Yes, as a matter of fact, I do have some questions—are you finished? I thought you wanted me to make some kind of written statement?"

"I thought of doing that originally, but I've got it down on tape. That should be all I need for the moment. If the District Attorney should want something in writing later, we can get it done then. You'll comply with his request, won't you?"

"Yes, of course."

"That'll be fine, then. Please go on."

"I'm planning on traveling to Albuquerque this weekend, today, if possible, and I'm going to make some inquiries there about Carol and my daughter. I think maybe I'll try locating some of Carrie's friends to see if they might know where she could be. You see, my ex-wife wasn't certain that our daughter was somewhere around Esperanza. She had reason to believe she might be. So I'd like to satisfy myself that Carrie's not back in Albuquerque.

"In any event, I'll have to travel there to arrange for my ex-wife's funeral and I'll probably be getting in touch with someone who knew her. I don't know if the hotel has her home address, but if it doesn't, I'll have to go through Carol's belongings—her wallet, for example. So I was wondering about her belongings; I understand they're still in the room at the hotel. When would it be all right to have them picked up? I'd like to take all of her things back to Albuquerque with me."

"I don't see why that couldn't be done today, if you wished. We've already gone through all of Mrs. Lockwood's things and I'm sending one of my men over there right after lunch to make an inventory of what we found there. It shouldn't take him long to do that and after he's through, I'll make sure you're permitted in the room. A thought just occurred to me, though —the coroner should be here in my office sometime this morning and I want to ask him if it's all right to open up the room. I'm sure he'll permit it, but in the unlikely event that he should order that it be kept closed, I'm afraid we'll have to abide by his ruling."

"Yes, of course."

"What other questions might you have, Señor Blair?"

"Most likely I'll be making arrangements for the funeral in Albuquerque and I understand the body is presently at the local mortuary. When will the body be released so that arrangements can be made to transfer it to a funeral home there? You told me there would probably be an autopsy, and I've no idea when that will take place."

"Yes, I'm sure the coroner will want one performed, but only he will know when it will be completed. He's a licensed pathologist and he'll be doing the autopsy. He might get started on it sometime this afternoon but most likely won't get finished with it today. But, judging from his work in the past, he'll probably have the results by noon tomorrow. I see no reason why the body couldn't be transported to Albuquerque sometime tomorrow afternoon or if not then, by Sunday morning at the latest."

"That would mean that if I get in touch with a funeral home in Albuquerque today, I might be able to arrange the funeral services for Monday morning."

Ross took a package of Winstons. He offered the package to Sheriff Dominguez, who took one. Each lit his own cigarette.

"Do you think you'll be returning to Esperanza after the funeral?"

"That'll depend on what I should find out about my daughter. I intended checking out of the hotel. It's all right with you if I do that, isn't it?"

"Certainly," the sheriff said. "I didn't mean to give you the impression you weren't free to leave, for most assuredly you are. It's only that I think it would be a good idea that we remain in touch with each other, just in case there are any developments, either in the case of Mrs. Lockwood's death or of your daughter. So, once you find a place to stay there, I'd appreciate your giving me a call."

"I'll do that. Do you want my address in San Francisco?"

The sheriff smiled. "No that won't be necessary, I've got it already." He continued smiling.

"You do? Oh, from the hotel registry."

"Exactly. I asked Mr. Sandoval for it last night after I left your room. Just part of—"

"I know," Ross interjected, smiling, "It's all part of your job, right?"

"Right."

"I'm grasping for straws in going to Albuquerque hoping to find out something concrete about Carrie, I'm sure you can see that, Sheriff Dominguez. I have to find out some things about my daughter for myself; depending solely on what Carol told me just isn't enough now that she's dead. So I've got to start this thing anew. It might be that I'll end up here again."

"You have my complete sympathies, Mr. Blair, about your daughter *and* for what's happened to your ex-wife. We'll help all we can; I want you to depend on that."

"Thanks, I appreciate that."

"We'll keep in touch then, no?"

"Yes, that'll be fine. I'll give you a call shortly after I've registered at a motel there."

"Good."

Ross started getting up but then kept his seat. "Oh, there's one other question that came to mind, Sheriff Dominguez, if you don't mind."

"By all means, Mr. Blair." He relaxed his arms and reclined back on his chair.

"This has absolutely nothing to do with what we've been discussing and you'll probably think I'm silly for asking you about this, but it's to satisfy my curiosity, more than anything else."

"Surely, go right ahead."

"One of the things Carol and I talked about last night was her father. He used to live here many years ago and in fact died here in Esperanza. Anyway, at the time of his death, he lived nearby. He was supposedly a good friend of an old woman who lived someplace around here—an old woman by the name of Hawkins."

"Consuelo Hawkins," the sheriff interposed. "Consuelo *Jurado* Hawkins, to be exact. Old Lady Hawkins, she's known by mostly everyone around here."

"Yes, that's her."

"What about old Consuelo?" the sheriff asked, a broad smile on his face, as if the sound of the name had loosened in his mind fond memories of the lady.

"I was only curious. Is she still around or has she passed away?"

"Ha! old Consuelo is still very much alive, I would say. Just ask anyone around Esperanza, they'll tell you. Still has that same reputation she had many years ago when your ex-wife's father probably knew her."

"You mean the rumor about her practicing witchcraft?"

"Actually, it isn't rumor," the sheriff corrected Ross. It's been a well known fact around here for as long as I can remember that Consuelo Hawkins practices witchcraft." He still had a faint smile on his face as he spoke of the old woman. "Now don't get me wrong, I'm not saying she's been successful at it, but the fact remains nevertheless that she's a practitioner of black magic and all that mumbo jumbo stuff. She's breaking the law doing that—there's both a county ordinance and a state law which prohibit the practice of the occult and other matters related to the supernatural. But what the hell, old Consuelo's never done anyone any harm that I know of and no one yet has ever complained about her. Besides, she stays to herself in the old house of hers and doesn't bother a soul."

He let out a soft laugh. "As a matter of fact," he continued, "it's the other way around. More than once she's called my office complaining about some youngsters from the town snooping around her property—up to some mischief, according to her. It's only a few of the kids who do that—the older ones. I don't think they mean any harm; they're just a bunch of curious kids who wonder about the old lady. Most of the younger ones around here wouldn't dare go near her place. Whether or not the old lady is successful in dealing with the spirits, I don't believe these kids have ever satisfied themselves one way or another. They hear these wild stories about her and most of the young ones become terrified even at the mention of her name. Consuelo, *la bruja*—the witch—the youngsters call her. It's a normal reaction with children."

"Yes," Ross agreed. "Does she actually still live in that same house she used to live in, say—some twenty years ago? According to Carol, the house was rundown even then."

"Yes, she still lives in the same old place. And your ex-wife was correct, it used to look like hell then; badly in need of repair. But I can't honestly say the place has changed a bit since then. It looks the same way to me. Old Consuelo, she's twenty years older and of course, looks it. But that house, twenty years ago it looked like it was ready to fall down and it still does today—but it hasn't. And I don't imagine it will during the old lady's lifetime. And you know, she never has left that place, as far back as I can remember. Hasn't even shown her face in Esperanza for a number of years; not even to see a doctor. It's become a world all her own."

"How is she able to do that; remain so independent there, I mean? Surely, like everyone else, she needs the basic necessities of life—food, medicine, people's company, for example."

"Yes, she needs the things her land can't provide her with, but people's company, she's done without that for all these years. Old Consuelo owns a considerable amount of farm land a short distance behind her house, which she rents out to a fellow by the name of Baltazar Montoya. Montoya's been working and farming the land there ever since I was a youngster. He's pretty much of a hermit himself. Never married. And he's a mighty sharp fellow. Never went to college, but the guy knows his way with words. He can carry on a conversation —something one wouldn't expect of him. Anyway, the old lady lives off the rental that Baltazar Montoya pays her for farming the land. He sells the stuff he grows locally to the produce merchants, but also provides the old lady with a share of the crop. I imagine that's where she gets most of her food.

"Montoya lives in a small adobe dwelling at the far corner of the farm about a mile from where old Consuelo lives. In addition to farming the land, the caretaker does a few chores and errands for the old lady. One of them is coming into town once in a while and doing some shopping for her. He comes into town maybe two or three times a month in an old pick-up truck. In addition to getting items for old Consuelo and for himself, he stocks up on wine—the best he can find. Montoya has gotten to be somewhat of an old wino. And drinks the best. I found that out from Felipe Lujan, the owner of the liquor store where Montoya buys his spirits. He's told me Montoya always gets the most expensive wine the store has in stock—no exception."

"I wonder if that's the same person Carol mentioned used to assist her father in his experiments," Ross said softly, more to himself than to the sheriff.

"Pardon me?"

"Oh, nothing, I was only thinking out loud. That name—the combination's somewhat peculiar, *Jurado—Consuelo Jurado*—it's a Spanish name, isn't it? Is she part Mexican and part Anglo?"

"Yes. And she could pass for either—she's of light complexion and speaks both English and Spanish equally well—not the slightest accent in either language." He smiled once again and shook his head slightly. "In fact, you should hear some of those old Spanish cuss words she uses over the phone when complaining about those kids trespassing around her place. She's still got a mighty sharp tongue and she uses it whenever she feels she has need of it. She's got a sharp mind, too. The years haven't taken that away from her. Consuelo's one elderly person senility hasn't taken hold of and most likely won't before she's in her grave.

"Anyway, you asked about the old lady's name. She's the last surviving member of the Hawkins family, a well-known family name around this part of the state many years ago, around the turn of the century. Her father was a prominent merchant and trader who moved down here from St. Louis in the 1880's, when this was Indian and frontier country. He became successful and made a considerable fortune trading with the Indians and with the settlers in the Southwest.

"He married a Mexican woman by the surname of Jurado—met her in Mexico during one of his many trips down there and brought her here to live with him. He built that house old Consuelo lives in now before she was even born. I understand he supervised the construction himself and used local labor, but he used the architecture of the homes located in the prominent areas of St. Louis and in its early years, that house used to be the swankiest place in the state. Now, you'd never know it, for it's badly deteriorated and in great need of repair. Hawkins and his wife had two children, both girls—Consuelo was the younger of the two. One day, Hawkins, his wife, and their older daughter were up north a ways from here, inspecting a mine he owned. There was a freak explosion or cave-in while the three of them were in a mine shaft and they were all killed.

"The accident happened when Consuelo was in her late teens. Anyway, she was the sole-surviving heir and inherited all of her parents' estate. Big mansion and all, which in those days was still a plush place. I heard she used to throw some big, expensive parties in that house, when she was in her twenties. Didn't think anything of spending her fortune away. I understand too that old Consuelo spent a lot of her time living it up in Europe wasting a substantial portion of her father's money. When she returned, she had very little money left and the mining operations had gone sour due to mismanagement and embezzlement committed by the fellow she had left to run the operation. She sold the mine and mining claims, dirt cheap, according to some accounts. But there was an old rumor passed around that she actually was paid thousands of dollars for the mining claims and that she's hoarding it all in cash somewhere in that old house of hers. I've never believed the rumor, though, but who knows, maybe there is a fortune stashed away there. If there is, it'll all go to the state when old Consuelo dies, for she has no relatives."

Sheriff Dominguez sighed, then puffed on his cigarette. "How she ever got involved in witchcraft and black magic, I've never known, and quite frankly, I've never had the courage to come right out and ask the old lady. I've always been terribly curious about it, though, I must admit." He had been looking down at the floor as he spoke. When he finished, he looked up at Ross. "Why the interest in the old lady?"

"Oh, mainly my curiosity, that's all. Carol had mentioned to me that her father had known her for a number of years before he passed away. She must be an interesting individual."

"She's interesting, all right," the sheriff chuckled. "And, in my opinion, she's always been slightly mentally imbalanced. She acts weird—I think her interest in the occult is indicative of that."

"You may be right; Carol too thought the woman a weird individual when she met her."

Both men stood up. Ross thanked Sheriff Dominguez and

confirmed that he'd be getting in touch with him as soon as he found a place to stay in Albuquerque. The sheriff again conveyed his condolences and wished Ross luck. The two men shook hands and Ross departed.

During the drive back to the Sandoval Hotel, Ross' thoughts were on Old Lady Hawkins. It was an interesting story Bartolo Dominguez had related to him. He thought he wouldn't mind meeting the old lady. But once having arrived at the hotel, he forced the thought of the woman from his mind, for he had other, more important matters which required his attention. He had to make the necessary arrangements with two funeral homes. That, in addition to having to try contacting Carol's friends and acquaintances, and possibly even her husband, was going to preoccupy much of his time. He wanted to get the whole business over with, however cold it might appear, for deep in his mind was that nagging concern for Carrie.

There was one other matter he had to attend to—he must call Ed Parker to let him know he wouldn't be returning to work Monday morning as he had originally anticipated. He would have to take off from work all of the following week; the work at the office would have to wait, no matter how pressing. Once he related to Ed what had happened, he was sure they'd understand at the office.

He wanted to call Monica too. He had planned doing that originally and he knew she'd be expecting to hear from him by now. But he wasn't certain how she'd react to what had happened. She would begin to worry about him. But he had other matters on his mind at the moment and he knew that if he called Monica now, she would have countless questions to ask him. He decided to put off calling his office until Monday morning, when he would have a better idea of what had to be done. By then, he might find out something about Carrie.

As he parked the car along the side of the hotel, his mind was filled with confusing thoughts of what he had to do. How easy it would be to leave this place this very moment, he thought, and fly back to San Francisco, leaving what had happened behind him. But he couldn't walk out of this problem that easily and return to San Francisco, pretending these past two days in his life, and the tragic events they contained, had never existed.

CHAPTER 13

THE funeral was held Monday morning. Ross managed to make all the necessary arrangements during the weekend and had met with the minister of the church Carol had attended regularly. It was from him that Ross learned Carol and her former husband had been divorced many years before, prior to the minister having known Carol. She, Ross learned, had few friends and acquaintances in Albuquerque.

The burial was simple, attended by only Carol's few close friends and fewer of her acquaintances. There was no service or wake held at the mortuary or at the church—only a simple prayer at the cemetery.

After the services, Ross spoke with the minister and a few of Carol's friends who had attended the burial. He explained his presence after Carol's plea for help. None of them was able to provide him with any information regarding Carrie. Ross was surprised they knew nothing of her drug problem nor that she had even left home.

Ross also had made the necessary financial arrangements with the funeral home, but he knew that later, someone would have to inquire into Carol's financial and personal affairs to find out what needed to be done. He and the minister had discussed this matter briefly the day before the funeral and the minister had offered to see to it that the arrangements would be made.

For Ross, the weekend had been two days of misery, for he had thought of the week ahead and whether he would be any closer to finding Carrie at the week's end than he was now.

Early that morning, prior to the funeral, he had called his office and spoken to Ed Parker. Ed had sounded happy to hear from him. Ross related to him the events of the weekend. Before hanging up, he explained he hadn't had time to call Monica and that he wasn't certain whether he should call her just yet in any event. He asked Ed to get in touch with her, convey to her what had happened, and inform her he would be calling her soon. Ed had assured Ross he would convey the message.

Ross was certain Monica would be upset and angry for his not having contacted her by now, but he was as certain she would understand once she discovered what had happened. But he began having second thoughts about not having called her and he experienced a depressing, lonely feeling as he drove away from the cemetery. He couldn't explain why he suddenly felt this way; he was certain only of what and how he felt. At that moment, he desired Monica's presence. He didn't know why, except that he realized he missed her miserably. He was tempted to place another call to San Francisco, this time to Monica; he urged to hear her soft voice. It might give him the lift he now needed desperately. But he had decided against placing the call.

He returned to the car rental desk at the airport to renew the rental contract. Leaving the air terminal, he traveled eastward on Central Avenue toward the University of New Mexico campus. He would start his search for Carrie there. He had thought about going to the local police but had quickly dismissed the idea from his thoughts at least for the time being. It was at the university that he hoped he might be able to get in touch with some of Carrie's friends; he had nowhere else to go.

Traffic on Central was heavy; dozens of stores and businesses lined the broad avenue. Central Avenue was one of the busiest thoroughfares passing right through the heart of the city, and ran for miles, with seemingly endless signs and billboards of thriving businesses—cocktail lounges, pizza parlors, family restaurants, curio shops, and extremely busy motels. The wide avenue finally ends on the outskirts of the city, near the foothills of the majestic Sandia Mountains. On this Monday morning, the mountains were a deep purplish color and slightly hidden by a maze of smog. The pollution and smog of the big cities was now beginning to find its way into this thriving, bustling metropolis of the Southwest.

Soon, to Ross' left, the buildings of the university began to appear. He passed Yale Avenue and approached Cornell Drive. He veered the car onto the turning lane to make a left turn at the next street. He awaited the passage of oncoming traffic on the westbound lanes before entering the campus.

He turned where the street dead-ended, then was forced to make another left, following a road around a small park lined with large evergreens. A few students sat on the thick grass of the park, enjoying the bright, sunny day. Ross slowed down and noticed a large building to his right; a sign post identified it as the student union. He followed the road, attempting to maneuver into the heart of the campus, but was unable to find a way. He returned to Yale Avenue; the avenue continued on toward the campus. It didn't take him long to realize the university was in the process of reconstructing its traffic patterns, leaving the center of the campus free of vehicular traffic.

It took him several minutes to find the location of the building he had been searching—the administration building. He parked his car along a side street and walked the few blocks to the building.

As he walked, he reflected on the architecture of the university structures. The buildings he had seen, particularly the older-looking ones, were of pueblo-style architecture, tan in color, obviously depicting the Indian and Spanish cultures found in the state.

Once inside the building, he spotted immediately a small sign above the first doorway which read: Information Office. There, a young girl sitting behind the reception desk gave him directions to the office of the Dean of Students. Ross thanked the girl and walked down the corridor. The corridor turned, and at the far end of a narrow hallway, he found the dean's office.

The dean was in and within minutes, Ross sat in the man's office. The dean sat quietly as he listened to Ross explain the reason for his visit. Ross wanted to make absolutely certain the man understood the gravity of his problem, so he took a moment to relate Carrie's disappearance followed by Carol's death. He was careful not to mention Professor Conrad's name, for he wasn't certain what would be the dean's reaction. The gentleman sitting in front of him appeared understanding. But would he be willing to cooperate? When Ross had finished, the dean asked him a few questions. Appearing satisfied he knew exactly what Ross wanted, the dean suggested that the registrar's office might be of assistance. He knew no other way to go about it, he said. First of all, from the registrar, he would be able to obtain a list of the courses Carrie had taken during the past school year. Secondly, a list of the students in each of her classes could easily be compiled. Then too, Carrie's personnel file would indicate whether or not she belonged to one of the university's sorority chapters.

Aside from what he had suggested, was there any other way he could be of assistance, the dean asked Ross. Ross told him it was necessary only to provide him with a list of female students who lived in the Albuquerque vicinity, together with addresses and phone numbers. The dean agreed. It was a longshot; but Ross understood that well. The dean stated that if Ross would return in an hour, he would make the information available to him.

Ross thanked the man and said he would return within the hour. The two men shook hands and Ross departed. He walked the distance to his car before realizing he had no place in particular to go. He didn't feel like driving, so to pass the hour away, he decided he'd stroll through the campus and do a bit of sight-seeing. Having walked only a short while, he came upon the university library. It was there that he passed away the major part of the hour, leafing through various books and magazines.

Upon his arrival at the dean's office, he was disappointed

to find Carrie had never belonged to any of the school's sororities. If she had, he was fairly certain he could have found there some of her closest friends.

But the dean was able to provide him with a list of names, addresses and telephone numbers of those female students living in the Albuquerque area who had been enrolled in the same classes Carrie had attended the two prior school semesters. Before Ross departed the office a second time, the dean assured him he was willing to assist him in any other way he could. Ross told him he appreciated what he had already done for him and thanked him again.

With the list of names in his possession, he returned to the car. He remembered the student union building he had passed earlier; there would be public phone booths there. He drove in the direction of the student union.

Inside the building, he found a small lounging area where there were several telephone booths lining the length of the room. A few students sat on couches and chairs. A portable television set was turned on at one corner of the room but no one appeared to be watching the program. At the soda fountain counter, he exchanged a couple of dollar bills for small change with which to make the calls. He chose the telephone booth at the far corner of the room where he felt he would have the most privacy. From his coat pocket, he took the paper containing the list of names. He glanced down the list briefly, then began counting the names.

There were nineteen names of female students who had at least two things in common—each had been enrolled in at least one course with Carrie; secondly, each lived in the Albuquerque vicinity. From this list, Ross hoped he would find at least one student he could talk to about Carrie. He began making the calls, starting at the top of the list. Within five minutes he had called the first five telephone numbers on the list—without success. He received no answer at the first two numbers. At the third and fourth, someone answered but the party he asked for wasn't at home. On the fifth try, the party he wanted answered the phone. He grew nervous with anticipation.

He told the girl he was Carrie's father, that he was in town for a few days and wanted to see his daughter; would she happen to know where he might locate Carrie? To his disappointment, the girl he spoke to explained apologetically that although she knew Carrie, they weren't close friends. She was terribly sorry, she said, but she wasn't able to tell him very much about Carrie; she didn't know her well at all. Did she know anyone else who might have known Carrie, Ross asked. No, the girl said, she didn't. Ross thanked her and hung up.

In this fashion, one by one, he depleted the list of names; either he didn't find the party at home or no one answered or the girl could tell him absolutely nothing or very little about Carrie. In half an hour, he exhausted the entire list and had gotten nowhere. Disappointed, he left the phone booth and walked to the fountain counter where he ordered a Coke. When he had finished the soft drink, he returned to the booth to try again those numbers on the list where he had either received no response or the party wasn't at home. His earlier unsuccessful attempts made him pessimistic that his luck would change, but he realized that at the moment, it was the only method he had to find out anything new about Carrie.

He dialed the second number on the list; this was one of the numbers he had tried several times before but had found no one at home. He glanced at the name to which the number corresponded. The girl's name was Pamela Moxley. He allowed the phone to ring three or four times and was about to hang up when he heard a slight click as someone at the other end picked up the receiver.

"Hello," a voice said softly at the other end. "Moxley residence."

"Yes ma'am," Ross spoke into the telephone. "My name's Ross Blair. I'd like to speak with Pamela Moxley, please. Is she in?"

"Yes, this is Pam." She was panting softly, as if she had hurried to get to the phone.

"Pamela, we've never met before. I'm Carrie Lockwood's father; I'm in town for a few days."

"Yes."

"I've been trying to get in touch with Carrie. I thought possibly you might know where she is or be able to help me locate her. I guess I should explain how I happened to be calling you."

There was a soft laugh at the other end of the line. "Yes, I was about to ask."

"Well, you see," Ross explained, "I was given your name by the Dean of Students. He provided me with a list of names of those students who had taken courses last year with Carrie." He paused briefly, then held his breath as he asked the vital question. "Do you know Carrie, Pamela?"

"As a matter of fact, Mr. Blair," Pamela Moxley answered, "I know her well. She and I *did* have several classes together last semester. But aside from that, we're close friends. Well, I shouldn't say that really—we're not so much now but we used to be."

"Would you happen to know where I might find her?" Ross said excitedly.

"Well, not really, Mr. Blair. I haven't the faintest idea where you might locate her. I haven't seen her all summer; since school let out. You have her home address, don't you? Have you tried there?"

"Yes, I have her address. But that won't do any good. You see, evidently, she went out of town for a few days, or so I've been informed, and I thought possibly one of her friends might know where she's at."

He paused momentarily, wondering whether he should try explaining to this girl, whom he had never met, his real concern for Carrie, and of Carol's death. How much did Pam Moxley know of Carrie's problem with drugs? Maybe she *did* know where Carrie was but had promised not to tell anyone. He had to find out but he couldn't do it over the phone—he wanted to see Carrie's friend in person; to talk to her. Only then would he tell her of Carol's death. If she did in fact know Carrie's whereabouts and was keeping it from him, possibly telling her about the death might persuade her to reveal where Carrie was. It was worth a try.

"Listen, Pamela," he went on, "if you've got a free moment sometime today, I'd like to meet with you and speak to you about Carrie. You see, I haven't seen her in a long time and there's some things I'd like to learn about her. It's important to me. Could we meet someplace where we might talk, even if only for a few minutes? I won't take much of your time."

"Of course, I'd be happy to, Mr. Blair. I have to be at work at one o'clock, though. It'll have to be before then."

"That'll be fine."

"When and where would you like to meet?"

Ross glanced down at his watch. "Well, it's a few minutes before twelve right now. Would it be asking too much to have you meet me in, say—ten or fifteen minutes?"

"Where are you at, Mr. Blair?"

"I'm at the student union on campus."

"That's fine. I live kind of close by and that's on my way to work, anyway. I can make it down there in about five or ten minutes. I was about to leave home anyway. I had just come in to pick up something I'd forgotten. You almost missed me."

"I'm glad I didn't. Where in the building shall we meet?"

"How about my meeting you in a small canteen right next to the cafeteria. Just ask anyone there where it's at."

"Fine, Pamela. I'll meet you there in five or ten minutes." He was about to say goodbye when a thought occurred to him. "Pamela," he asked, "I wonder if you might know of any other friends of Carrie's who might know where she went? Someone who might be able to meet with us. I've tried calling several other students whose names the dean gave me, but haven't had much luck."

"Yes, I do. In fact, Diana Jenkins is working part time there on campus in the journalism department. She's a close mutual friend of ours. If you'd like, I'll give her a call."

"Would you please, Pamela? I'd appreciate it. I'll buy both of you lunch."

Pam Moxley laughed. "That won't be necessary."

"Oh, but I insist."

"All right; I'll call her. And then I can give you a few other names when I get down there."

"That'll be fine, Pamela. Thank you. See you in a few minutes."

"Right. Bye."

"Bye." Ross hung up the phone. He looked at his list and noticed that Diana Jenkins wasn't on it. Standing there for a moment, he felt a certain satisfaction in having made contact with someone who had known Carrie. For the first time since his arrival in New Mexico, he sensed at least some minute quantity of success. Somewhere in his mind, there existed a tiny flicker — a kindled hope — that he might be a step closer to locating Carrie. Surely, through Pamela Moxley and Diana Jenkins, he would learn of others who might know of Carrie's whereabouts. Maybe Diana Jenkins knew. But the thought suddenly occurred to him that Carol had already inquired of some of Carrie's friends, and presumably, she even knew them; through one of them, Carol had suspected Carrie might be somewhere near Esperanza. Had Carol spoken to the same persons whose names Pamela Moxley or the Jenkins girl would provide him with? He hoped not and he dismissed the possibility, for he didn't want to lose the sudden optimism and hope he now felt. For the first time that day, he regained some of his calm.

It was a few minutes after twelve that he was sitting at a corner booth in the canteen Pam Moxley had directed him to. He looked up and noticed two young girls approaching.

"Mr. Blair?" It was the taller of the two girls who spoke. She had long, blond hair.

Ross stood up. "Yes, I'm Ross Blair," he said. "Pamela Moxley?"

"I'm Pam Moxley," the girl who had spoken to him said. "And this is Diana Jenkins—the girl I told you about. She was just leaving her office when I called her; almost missed her. She's on her lunch break now and said she'd be glad to help if she can."

"Hello, Diana."

"Hi." Diana Jenkins smiled at Ross.

Ross returned the smile. "I'm happy that we could all meet together. Won't you please join me? May I buy either of you lunch? I was having coffee, waiting for you before ordering a sandwich myself."

Both of them said they'd have a sandwich and sat down at one side of the booth. Ross sat back down at the other end.

Each of them ordered a sandwich. Ross briefly explained to the two girls how he happened to be in Albuquerque. He spoke candidly; he told them of Carol's death. He related what Carol had told him of Carrie's problem with drugs, studying their reaction—they weren't surprised, for both had known for several months that Carrie smoked pot and used LSD. Both had disapproved, they told Ross, and Pam Moxley confided Carrie's use of drugs was the reason why Diana's and her close friendship with her had become strained. Ross was convinced that neither of them was keeping anything from him.

It was Diana Jenkins who possessed the information Ross had been hoping for. At least it was a beginning. Diana had been with Carrie about three weeks ago, she said; when she had last seen her, Carrie had seemed to have been moody—depressed. Pam and Diana both confirmed what Carol had told Ross of Professor Conrad's influence over Carrie and her professed loved for him. Both girls were certain Carrie's feeling was an infatuation. Pam believed that Carrie saw in the professor a father image and that his influence over her was caused by this fixation more than by the professor's intentions or attempt to control her life.

Ross learned more from Diana Jenkins. The last time she had seen her, she went on, Carrie had confided in her that she would be leaving Albuquerque for a few weeks. She hadn't wanted her mother to know. Diana had asked Carrie whom she was going with, and Carrie had been purposely vague, saying only that she was going with 'friends', but Diana had suspected the professor was going too. The group was first going to Taos, Carrie had told Diana, to one of the hippie communes in the Taos area. They were planning to stay there something less than a week and then Carrie had said she might go on to Mexico for several weeks before registration for the fall semester.

"Mexico!" Ross said abruptly. "What in the world for? Did she say where in Mexico she was going?"

"No, she didn't, and I didn't ask her," Diana Jenkins replied. "But she wouldn't have told me where, anyway, had I asked. The way she spoke, though, I got the impression she was going to a particular place in Mexico, rather than just going there to travel."

"Did she happen to say what she was going to do there?"

"No, she didn't. As I said before, she didn't actually say she was going—she only said she *might* be. Didn't say with whom, except to say 'with friends', or where in Mexico she was going, and she didn't tell me why. I did ask her why she was going and she gave me a very vague, general answer—something like she had never been there before and she was going just to go."

"When were they supposed to leave Albuquerque, did she say?"

"Let me see. I think I saw her exactly three weeks ago this past weekend and I distinctly remember her saying she'd be leaving in about two and a half weeks. So let's see, that would make it—yes—the middle of last week that she would have gone to Taos."

Ross was unable to hide his excitement. "Then she might still be there."

"Yes," Diana Jenkins said, "I remember she said they'd be staying there about a week. But if you're thinking of going there, Mr. Blair, I'm not so sure you'd be able to find her anyway. Why, they could be anywhere within a five mile radius of Taos. Those hippies there are spread throughout a rather large area and it'd be difficult to find anyone there."

"Nevertheless it's the only lead I've got so far. That's a chance I'll have to take." He lit a cigarette. "How far is it to Taos from here?"

"Not too far," Pamela Moxley answered. "It's past Santa Fe a ways, and there's a good highway between here and there. It's about a fifty minute drive to Santa Fe. From there to Taos, I'm not so sure how far it is or how long it takes to get there. Do you know, Diana?"

"No, I'm sorry, I don't," Diana said. "I've been there only once long ago, but I don't remember."

"Carrie's mother," Ross continued, "had been told by someone that Carrie might be up near Esperanza; a place around there which this group frequents once in a while. That's why we were up there when Carrie's mother was killed. Do either of you know anything about that?"

"Well, I do know that Carrie sometimes used to go to a place near there. I don't exactly know where it's at except that it was close to Esperanza. And Professor Conrad too. Since Esperanza is near the highway coming back to Albuquerque from Taos, I imagine they might have stopped off there. But

I can't say I recall Carrie specifically mentioning they were also going to the Esperanza hangout. I'm sorry I can't be of much help, Mr. Blair."

"Oh, but you have. Both of you. In fact, just talking to someone who was close to Carrie; you don't know how good it makes me feel to be able to speak with the two of you.

Their sandwiches arrived and Ross continued with more questions as the hour wore on. He wanted to know about Carrie —her interests—her friends. These were questions that he would eventually have gotten around to asking Carol had he ever had the opportunity. He realized Diana Jenkins and Pam Moxley wouldn't necessarily be objective about what they thought of Carrie as a person, but he was nevertheless curious what their impressions of her were.

It was almost one o'clock when Ross and the two girls finished their lunch. Both Pamela Moxley and Diana Jenkins gave Ross their phone numbers at work in the event Ross later wanted to speak to either of them. Ross gave them the addresses he could be reached at in Esperanza and in San Francisco, in case either of them heard from Carrie in the meantime. He asked them to let Carrie know he was looking for her and to call him at once. She was to leave word where he might reach her if she was unable to locate him.

He accompanied the two girls out of the building. He thanked them again, then walked to where he had parked his car.

CHAPTER 14

AS he walked to the car, he thought of Arthur Conrad. He remembered Carol telling him she had attempted getting in touch with Conrad before traveling to Esperanza. She had been unable to find him at his office. He decided to pay a visit to the professor's office. If, for no other reason, he wanted to confirm that the professor wasn't in Albuquerque, before he journeyed to Taos. He knew little about Arthur Conrad and although he had never met the man, Ross had grown to despise him. The man had poisoned his daughter's mind.

Ross saw his task as the surgeon's—performing surgery on a cancerous tumor of a patient, removing the poisoned, malignant tissue surrounding the body's healthy cells, before the poison spread irreparably to other parts of the body. But was he too late—had the poison already spread? What if now there was absolutely nothing he could do but watch his daughter ruining her life in exchange for a few insignificant moments of false and deceiving pleasure with drugs—a youth robbing herself of life's real and valid pleasures. Life had its curious, ironic manner of being unfair at times. It was being unfair to him now, he thought.

Professor Conrad's office was located on the northern edge

of the campus. The front hallway of the old building was poorly lighted, but Ross saw the sign on the wall indicating the administrative offices. There, he found a middle-aged woman rummaging through some papers stacked on a large table. Ross asked her where he might find Professor Conrad's office. She told him the office was the third one down the hallway in the east wing, adding that the professor wasn't in; he was on vacation outside the city and wasn't expected to return until sometime the latter part of August. Ross inquired further, asking the woman where he might locate Conrad, but he was met with resistance. The old woman told him she hadn't the faintest idea where the professor might be and that even if she did, under no circumstances was she allowed to release that information. She spoke in a rather high-pitched, irritating voice.

Ross then asked the woman where he might be able to find out where the professor was vacationing if the matter were urgent enough, and she told him such information would have to come from the university's academic vice-president; he'd have to inquire there but she added it was against university policy to give out information regarding vacationing faculty members.

The most she would be able to do, the woman continued, was to take his name and an address where he could be reached, and she would make certain the professor would get the message upon his return. Ross told her that he didn't wish to do that, thanked her, and walked out of the building.

He thought of paying another visit to the administration building to inquire about Conrad. But that would take time— time he didn't have, and he couldn't be sure the information would be divulged to him in the first place. Besides, he would have to make certain strong allegations against the professor; allegations he wasn't prepared to prove and which he couldn't actually substantiate at the moment.

Instead, another idea came to mind, one that had occurred to him earlier—he would visit the district attorney's office. It wasn't for the purpose of asking for help in finding Carrie that he thought of going there but to inform that office of Conrad's illicit activities. He weighed the pros and cons. It didn't take him long to make up his mind—he would go there.

He was back on Central Avenue headed toward downtown and he pulled the car over into a gasoline station where he asked directions to the county courthouse. He found it was located in the downtown area.

He was curious to find out how much, if anything, the district attorney's office might know already of Arthur Conrad's activities. If they knew nothing of the man, he'd provide them with what he had discovered. Granted, he knew very little; but wasn't that enough to justify some kind of an investigation which might lead to evidence against the man. But would they listen to him? He wouldn't know the answer to that until he tried. What would he tell them, though? That the professor smoked pot and probably encouraged young kids to use it too? That he experimented with LSD and possibly other illicit drugs; and that he was corrupting the youth of society—specifically his daughter Carrie? Or that the professor had taken his daughter against her will? He knew that wasn't true, for Carrie hadn't been forced to go anywhere; she had gone of her own volition. And what about the rest of the information he thought he possessed about the professor? He had no proof. Only suspicions; less than that, actually—only Carol's suspicions. And it had been second-hand information, even in her hands.

He had no difficulty locating the Bernalillo County Courthouse; the sandstone building stood out conspicuously a few blocks off Central Avenue. He was still slightly unsure of himself as he drove the car into the courthouse parking lot. Nevertheless, he parked the car, and went into the building.

Once in the district attorney's office, Ross asked for the district attorney. He was informed by a young receptionist in the front office that the district attorney was out of town. Cordially, she told him that if he would sit down, she would have Mr. Meyers, one of the assistant district attorneys, speak with him. Ross said that would be fine and he sat down.

The *few minutes* the girl had asked him to wait turned out to be exactly half an hour. Ross was growing slightly impatient when he heard the rumble of voices coming from a narrow corridor. Soon a man entered the room. He glanced over to where Ross was seated and then began walking towards him. The man appeared to be in his middle thirties and possessed curly, black hair. Ross stood up to greet the man.

"Mr. Blair?" the man asked.

"Yes," Ross said.

The young man extended his hand. "I'm Tom Meyers."

"Ross Blair, Mr. Meyers."

They shook hands.

"I understand you wish to discuss something with me. Won't you please step into my office?" He indicated toward the hallway.

"Yes, thank you, Mr. Meyers."

The assistant district attorney offered Ross some coffee but Ross thanked him and said no.

"What is it you wish to see me about, Mr. Blair?" Tom Meyers asked as he sat back in his chair.

Ross felt slightly nervous. He took out his cigarettes. "Mind if I smoke?"

"Not at all. Go right ahead." He pushed an ashtray setting on top of his desk toward Ross. Ross offered the man a cigarette which he declined.

Ross didn't quite know where to begin, but he decided he would start with Carol's phone call and tell the man everything that had happened since his arrival in Esperanza. He quickly summarized all that had happened. Finally, he told the assistant DA of his attempt to get in touch with the professor.

Tom Meyers sat back in his chair listening patiently and with obvious interest. Only when Ross had finished did the prosecutor say anything. Ross noticed he possessed a deep, resounding voice, with a certain inflection of formality.

"First of all, Mr. Blair," he was saying, "let me convey my condolences for your ex-wife's death. Unfortunately, the county where it happened is out of this office's jurisdiction, so we can't be of much help to you in that respect." He paused to light a cigarette.

"About this matter that you've told me about the professor, I think you'll be happy to know we've already compiled quite an extensive file on him. In fact, we have a couple of undercover agents working on the case. They've been working it for several months now. So far, all our investigators have been able to turn up are complaints — suspicions, hearsay —

very much the same thing you've told me about. But nothing concrete to justify the filing of formal criminal charges against the man, I'm sorry to say."

"That's what I was afraid of," Ross said disappointingly. "But at least I know my ex-wife's suspicions about him were well-founded. I'm glad, too, to hear you have men working on the case. They report to you regularly, do they?"

"Well, I'm not actually involved with this particular case. It's assigned to one of the other assistants in the office; he's not in at the moment. But each of the attorneys in the office is generally familiar with the cases the others may be handling and it's only that knowledge that I'm relating to you now. But I'm afraid I couldn't discuss the contents of the file with you; I'm sure you'll understand why they're kept confidential."

"I understand." He stared briefly at Tom Meyers. "Actually," he continued, "I didn't come here to discuss my daughter's problem, but now that I'm here, I might as well ask you about it. Is there anything you would be able to suggest? Would your office be in a position to help me?"

"We're only too happy to help any person we can, whenever the occasion arises, Mr. Blair, but from what you've told me about your daughter's case, I'm sorry to say I don't think we could help in any way at this particular time."

He paused. "You see," he explained further, "what you've told me so far about your daughter doesn't, in my opinion, justify this office taking steps to enter the case. Your concern for her is certainly understandable, and believe me, I sympathize with your position, and I certainly don't mean to be minimizing the problem.

"But you see, all you've told me is that you suspect your daughter's involved with drugs. Aside from that, there's no concrete evidence that she's breaking the law, even at this moment. And even though she's admitted to others in the past that she has smoked marijuana and has experimented with LSD, this is not the kind of thing that will justify this office's investigation of the case. The law is clear that we can't go around prosecuting people based solely on their admissions that they did something wrong sometime in the past; the law requires corroborating evidence.

"Unfortunately, we don't have the resources to go searching for your daughter merely because of the rather remote possibility that if and when we find her, we'll just happen to catch her in the act of doing something illegal." He stared again at Ross. "Am I making any sense to you, or am I making you feel I'm avoiding handling a case?" He displayed a smile.

"No, not at all. I'm listening and understand exactly what you're getting at. Please go on."

"This office picks up hundreds of rumors or suspicions that a particular person may be using narcotics or marijuana, or breaking the law in some other way, but that just isn't enough, and unfortunately we have neither the time nor the money to track down each rumor that we may hear. So we stick to clear-cut cases that we have, and believe me, Mr. Blair, we have plenty of those to keep us busy. It's difficult to keep up with the back-log of cases we do have." He paused to stub out his cigarette.

"Besides, I'm sure you wouldn't want this office filing criminal charges against your daughter even if we did happen to find her for you."

"The thought of your doing exactly that has entered my mind," Ross said emphatically. "That might not be a bad idea under the circumstances. It might be just the thing that would make Carrie take a long, hard look at what she's been doing— maybe that would make her see things in a different light."

"Maybe. But not necessarily." He lit another cigarette. "We might be able to be of some help if you told me that you had reason to believe she had been taken someplace by Conrad against her will. Then we'd have something to go on. But from what you've told me, it seems your daughter is with him voluntarily. That is, if in fact she's with him, which we don't really know. If she were younger and a juvenile under the law, which she isn't, then possibly the professor might be guilty of contributing to her delinquency, which in this state is a crime, but such isn't the case. I truly sympathize, Mr. Blair, that your daughter is in fact involved with this man, in view of the suspicions we have about his activities in connection with drug abuse.

"Also, from what you've related to me, there's no basis for

believing foul play is involved. If that were the case, or if her disappearance couldn't be explained otherwise, then without question we'd immediately investigate the case and try locating her. But at the moment, we've absolutely nothing to go by, Mr. Blair. However, please rest assured that should you come up with something else that throws new light into the case, let us know and we'll see what we can do to help."

The two men spoke a few minutes more. Finally, Ross stood up and thanked the assistant district attorney. The attorney had been correct—Ross was strictly on his own.

He spent the remainder of Monday and the daylight hours of Tuesday in Taos, searching for some lead to Carrie and Arthur Conrad. He checked everywhere and every place he could think of—motels, hotels, kitchenettes, restaurants, bars, lounges, even some that were rat holes—any place he thought they might be. He asked for them by name; he also used the photograph of Carrie he had taken from Carol's wallet. Although he had formed an image of the professor in his mind, nevertheless he had no description of him; nor of Carrie, for that matter, except what he could tell from her photograph. The fruitless search made him wonder what had made him believe he could have ever found them there to begin with. It had been a trip made in total desperation. He was groping—he knew it—for some miracle that he would somehow casually cross Carrie's path.

In the small town of Taos, he inquired of the locations of the various hippie communes. He visited all of them and was appalled at what he saw—the type of life in existence there. Even the city slums and ghettos and barrios he had seen elsewhere were nothing compared to the stench in the air, and the filth and the miserable living conditions which he found existed in the colonies.

It depressed him as he witnessed hundreds of young people wasting their lives away in an existence of their own choosing, apparently confused by what they saw in life elsewhere. Even some convicts in the country's penitentiaries led more productive and fruitful lives, emotionally and physically. It was difficut to believe anyone could ever endure, day by day, what he saw. He wondered how long this kind of existence was endured by those who chose to live it, before they moved on to some other type of life elsewhere. Were they hypocrites? They seemed happy enough when he spoke with some of them; others roamed about endlessly or sat in one place for hours doing absolutely nothing but staring off into empty space. How many of them, deep down inside, were truly unhappy, lonely people, looking with contempt at the world outside? Ross sensed a deep pity for the miserable creatures.

Where was the blame? Whose fault was it that they were even there to begin with? Was there anyone in particular to blame at all, or was it just plain life or society that must take the blame for allowing it to happen in the first place? There were no simple answers to the questions that occurred to him as he drove along the highway away from it all. Nor had anyone found any answers, he thought. Was it now too late for even that?

It was dark when Ross reached the turn-off to Esperanza— the place this nightmare had begun. When he had left Taos, he thought of returning to Albuquerque. From there, he was planning to telephone Sheriff Dominguez to inquire if there had been any developments. He changed his mind, for it was already late and he was tired. He'd spend the night in Esperanza and visit with Dominguez in the morning.

Besides, he had given Ed Parker the phone number of the Sandoval Hotel, and there might be a message waiting for him. But there was one other, more important reason for stopping in Esperanza—the possibility that Carrie or Arthur Conrad, or both, had stopped there since Ross had left the previous Saturday.

CHAPTER 15

FOR some unknown reason, he was relieved to be back in Esperanza. He wondered if it was because of the day the prior week when he had driven from the airport to the little town for the first time. Then, though he was nervous in anticipation of meeting Carol, nevertheless the confusion he now exprienced hadn't set in. Carol's death had precipitated it. So much had happened since he had first set foot in Esperanza.

He considered for a moment that somehow he felt an unexplainable attachment to the small town, in spite of the fact that it was where Carol had been murdered. As he turned off the main street of the town, toward the hotel, he told himself he wouldn't mind returning here someday, when his life permitted such leisure. At this moment, he wished not to have a care in the world; he hoped that in one swift second, he could release from his mind all that had forced itself there during the past few days. If only that could be.

Immediately upon entering the hotel, his eyes came upon the old man seated behind the desk, squinting his eyes through his bifocals as he sorted letters and other papers scattered on the desk top. He wore a wrinkled white shirt with sleeves rolled up to the elbows.

The sight of the old man sitting there amused Ross; it seemed symbolic of the solitude and privacy which the quiet town had displayed to him when he had first arrived the prior week. The old man apparently hadn't noticed Ross enter the lobby, his mind obviously elsewhere in thought.

"Hello, there," Ross said softly so as not to startle the gentleman.

The old man jerked his head up. There was an expression of surprise on his face as he studied Ross for some sign of recognition.

"Why, hello," he finally said. "Hello, Mr. . . . Mr. Blair; that's it. For a minute there, your name slipped my mind. Sorry about that. Old age, it is."

"Oh, you appear to have a number of years ahead of you."

The old man stood up. "Quite nice of you to say that, young man. Mighty nice. But sometimes I'm not sure about that myself."

The old man paused and stood to the side of the desk now, leaning across the railing in an effort to get closer to Ross. "Tell me, Mr. Blair," he said, almost in a whisper, "was the funeral service for Mrs. Lockwood held yesterday as you had planned?"

"Yes," Ross said softly. "The minister of the church she belonged to conducted a brief, but nice burial service."

The old man nodded approvingly. "Like I said before, Mr. Blair, I wish I could have been there, but I hope you understand, that was close to impossible."

"I understand."

"I knew you would. Haven't been out of this village in years; in fact, it's been so long ago now that I can't honestly remember the last time I left town."

He shook his head and smiled, then dipped his hand into his shirt pocket and brought out a cigarette that was wrinkled and badly bent out of shape. He took the cigarette in the fingers of both hands and attempted getting some of the wrinkles out. "I'd offer you one," he said, "but it just so happens it's the last one I've got." A puckish expression set on his face. "It's my ol' woman," he explained, in a whisper. "Can't let her see me smoking; she won't permit it. Gotta keep these things loose in my pockets, otherwise she'll notice the bulge of the package and take them away. Many a time I've lost them to the clothes washer 'cause I forget to take them out of my pocket. Doctor's given me strict orders—they're bad for my heart and arteries, he says." He took a long wooden match from the top of his desk and lit the cigarette.

"Yes, I know what you mean," Ross said, smiling, unable to hide his amusement. He took out one of his own cigarettes and lit it.

The old man sat back down on his chair, the cigarette hanging from his mouth and a thick cloud of white smoke rising from where he sat.

"Nice to have you back, Mr. Blair. You checking into the hotel or did you just come by to see if you had any messages?"

"No, I'll be staying the night, so I'd like to check in. Possibly for two nights if I should decide to stay through tomorrow." He slipped his hand inside his coat and pulled out a pen from his shirt pocket.

The old man waved the pen away. "No need in your filling out a new card, Mr. Blair. I've still got the old one back there and I'll just pull it back out and use it again. That is, if you don't mind staying in the same room. It's vacant."

"That'll do just fine. May I have the key to it then? I'd like to freshen up a bit and take my things in there before I go out to grab a bite to eat."

"Surely can." The old man pushed himself up from the desk and walked back to get the key.

"By the way, *are* there any messages for me?"

"Nope, no messages at all." He returned with the key. "Here you are, Mr. Blair."

Ross took the key. "Thanks," he said and started walking down the lobby toward the stairway.

"For goodness sakes, I almost forgot to tell you. No messages for you, but you've got a visitor."

Ross stopped abruptly and turned around. "Pardon me?"

"I said you got no messages but there's someone here that's been looking for you."

Ross walked back to where the old man was standing. "Whom would that be—Sheriff Dominguez?"

"Nope. Person who's been looking for you is checked into the hotel as a guest. Staying in the room two doors past yours. Person's there right now, matter of fact." He gestured upstairs.

"Well, who is it? Surely the person gave you a name."

"Yep, sure did. But I was asked not to give it out should you happen to come by; said to tell you just go on up."

Ross was confused by the old man's behavior but he said nothing else; he turned around and moved quickly through the lobby and up the stairs. He hurried through the narrow corridor past the room he would be staying at and stopped two doors down the hallway. He looked down into the lobby over the railing toward where the old man stood. He was watching Ross and nodded his head.

Ross knocked softly.

He heard the sound of footsteps coming toward the door; then the door opened. There, staring at him was the one person he would never have guessed he would see in Esperanza.

"Monica!" Ross exclaimed. He stood there bewildered for a moment. He was staring into a pair of lovely, sparkling eyes, and then he saw the bright smile which had formed on Monica's face. "What in the world are you doing here?" Ross asked. "Why, you're the last person I was expecting to open that door."

Monica Ashley formed a slight frown on her forehead. "Don't I deserve a better greeting than that?" she asked.

"Of course you do, you crazy nut," Ross said happily. He smiled at her, moved away from the door and closed it, then placed his arms around her. He drew her closer to him and caressed her, almost making her feet leave the floor as he pulled her up tightly. She returned his embrace.

"Oh, Ross, Ross."

He kissed her softly on the mouth. "I can't believe this is happening and that you're actually here. Are you sure you're not just a dream?"

She laughed and squeezed him again. "I promise I'm not."

He released her slightly, then held her by her shoulders, smiling down on her. "My, you have a sneaky way of dropping in on a person; just when he least expects it." He shook his head. "But I'm terribly happy to see you, darling. I've missed you miserably."

"And I've missed you, Ross. And besides that, I've been terribly worried about you; *and,* may I add, angry too."

"I'm sorry for what's been happening, Monica. I was sure you'd be angry at me for having left San Francisco without explanation. Then, of course, for not having called you."

"Yes, you're absolutely right. I *had* expected to hear something from you by now, darling. At least, to let me know a little of what's been going on. But I'm not angry anymore; if I had been, I wouldn't have come. I wasn't that angry with you anyway. Most of all, I was worried about you." She looked up at him with sad, but beautiful eyes. "Ross, I'm so sorry about what happened to Carol."

"I take it Ed Parker told you all about it?" He sat down on the edge of the bed; Monica sat next to him.

"Yes, he did. I called your office yesterday morning thinking surely I'd find you there. You can't imagine my surprise when Mrs. Jones told me you had called in that morning to say you wouldn't be in all week. Immediately, I guessed something terrible had happened. Ed wasn't in the office when I first called and Mrs. Jones was unable to tell me anything about what you had discussed with him. In fact, I didn't reach him until after lunch—that's when I found out about Carol.

"Ross, I'm sure it came as a terrible shock to you. I got so nervous and upset over it that I had to leave the office early."

"Poor Carol. It's been an experience I'll never want to go through again. It happened that same night I got here."

"I know. And what about Carrie? Ed told me you had found out very little about her. Have you learned anything else since?"

"Nothing much; hardly anything at all, really. I've been coming up against one wall after another." He shook his head in disappointment as he gazed down at the floor. He turned to Monica. "Let's wait on that though; I'll tell you all about what's happened later. Have you had anything to eat yet?"

"No. In fact, I was getting ready to go out for a bite to eat when you knocked."

"Neither have I. I know a good place we can go. But first, I have a few questions I'd like to ask."

"But I should be the one asking the questions," Monica said laughingly.

"Well, I've got a few of my own." He couldn't hide the smile on his face.

"For instance?"

"Like for instance, the one I asked when I first laid eyes on you a moment ago. What in the world are you doing here? What made you decide to come?"

"I knew that would be one of the first things you'd ask me if I was lucky enough to find you, so I've had plenty of time to think of an answer." She pulled out a cigarette from her purse; Ross lit it for her.

"I'm waiting for the explanation," he said.

She laughed. "Honestly, Ross, I think I know you much better than you give me credit for. To begin with, I thought of how you must have felt after Carol's death; Ed Parker told me you had told him you knew nothing, or at most very little, about where Carrie might be, and as I said a moment ago, I was upset and terribly worried about you. Surely you must understand my concern after I spoke with Ed. Besides, he said you sounded 'down in the dumps'. It was yesterday afternoon at home that it occurred to me that too much had happened to you during such a short span of time—it was enough to get anyone feeling low, even you. And then, or course, you were all alone here, not knowing a soul. That's when I decided you needed someone down here to give you some encouragement and moral support."

"Someone like you, I take it," Ross said.

She grinned. "Yes, why not? I thought I fit the description more than anyone else."

"You crazy, loveable creature," Ross interrupted. He began laughing and Monica laughed with him. "Leave it to you to think of something like that to say," he went on. "And then just packing up your bags overnight and flying down here without even knowing whether you'd find me or not. How did you know about this place?"

"From Ed Parker. You left the name and address of the hotel with him when you spoke to him yesterday, remember? I called him last night."

"What did he say when you told him you were coming?"

"He didn't think I was serious at first. Then when he found out I was, he said he thought I was nuts."

"And that didn't dissuade you in the slightest?"

"Not at all."

He took her in his arms and squeezed her lovingly. He pulled away and looked down at her. "You flew down, didn't you?"

"Why, of course, silly. You don't think I drove all night in that old, sorry-looking jalopy of mine, did you?"

A boyish grin lit up his face. "I sometimes honestly don't know what to make of having a lovely woman like you loving me—and, I might add, putting up with me like you do." He kissed her on the forehead. "Tell me, how did you manage to get away from your work. I'm curious to know what you thought up to tell them."

"I didn't actually have to think up anything. I just told Dick Blanchard the honest-to-goodness truth. It was going to be an especially light week, anyway, I could tell by my schedule. So I called up Dick last night and told him a little of what had happened. I managed to convince him I was almost caught up with my work, and besides, I would get very little done at the office all week because of worrying over you. I also reminded him I was owed a week's vacation from last year."

"And he gave you off the rest of the week—just like that?"

"Just like that," Monica replied, snapping her fingers. She smiled, then burst out laughing. "Well, it wasn't exactly as easy as I'm trying to make it appear. I'm half-kidding, of course. One reason, I think, why I was able to persuade him, was that I promised him I'd be working extra hard when I returned, and you know Dick, he'll probably be on my back all of next week making sure I keep my word."

They both laughed; then there was silence and they stared into each other's eyes. He brought her closer to him. They kissed and their tongues touched. Her lips were moist and tender, and she moved her tongue slightly around his.

They parted and he gazed into her sparkling eyes again. "Oh, my darling," he said softly to her, I'm so happy to see you. Your coming down here means more to me than just moral support. But then too, I hate to get you involved in this, especially now that Carol's dead; there's no telling where I'm going from here. I'm certainly no closer to finding Carrie and —well, what I mean is, under all these circumstances, I've got mixed emotions whether you should have come down here. There's no telling what's—"

"Hush!" Monica said softly, and placed her fingers to his lips. "If you're happy that I'm here, then don't start giving me all kinds of reasons why I shouldn't be here. Let's just be happy that we're together, all right?"

"O. K."

She closed her eyes and kissed him again. She stood up.

"Come on," she said, extending her hand down to him. "Let's go get a bite to eat at this place you say you know of and then you can tell me all about what's happened. I want you to tell me everything that's happened to you from the moment you stepped off that plane to the moment you walked in that door a moment ago."

He took her hand and stood up. "To tell you all that, darling," he said, "will take considerable time."

"That's fine. Time, as the saying goes, is one thing we have plenty of. We've got all night if it takes that long, darling, and I promise I'll be a good listener."

Ross went back to his car to get his luggage and clothes. The suit he was wearing was soiled after his roaming the country side in Taos that day, so he took a cold shower and got into a clean set of clothes. Within half an hour, he and Monica were in the same lounge he and Carol had dined at only a few nights before.

"Oh, this is nice," Monica commented as they entered the restaurant. "Nice atmosphere."

"Yes."

Absent-mindedly, Ross was about to select the same table he and Carol had sat at the week before, but he quickly caught himself and moved to another table.

"Let's sit over here," he said to Monica as he pulled out a chair for her.

"Thank you."

They ordered a cocktail. After a second round of drinks,

they ordered from the dinner menu.

Having placed their order, Ross immediately explained to Monica all that had happened since his arrival in Esperanza. He spared no detail; he spoke at length about the discussion he and Carol had concerning her father, his death, and the reasons for her coming to New Mexico in the first place. He told her what he had learned about Carrie, from Carol herself and from Pamela Moxley and Diana Jenkins in Albuquerque. He related his visits to the dean's office and to the District Attorney's office before leaving Albuquerque the day before. Finally, he spoke of his trip to Taos and of what he had seen there.

Monica sat there quietly, apparently spellbound with the tale related by him. She said nothing until he had finished all that he had to say.

"It's simply unbelievable that all of what you've told me has actually happened. I still find it hard to believe that anyone would want to hurt Carol, much less kill her."

"It certainly is. I too have posed the question in my mind countless times. It doesn't fit in, why anyone would want her dead."

"Maybe it had to do with something she knew. Something someone was afraid she'd reveal to you."

"But that's what's got me confused. What would that be? It doesn't make sense. And why would that someone wait until I got here to do it."

"Maybe they didn't know you were coming."

"That could be."

Monica took out a cigarette from her purse and offered one to Ross. He took one and lit both cigarettes. "Poor Carol," Monica went on, "does anyone have any idea who might have done it?"

"Not the slightest," Ross answered. As he spoke, he thought of his earlier suspicions that Carrie's group might have had something to do with Carol's death. He cringed everytime the thought occurred to him. "That's one of the reasons," he continued, "why I decided to stop by here tonight instead of driving through to Albuquerque."

"Well, I'm certainly glad you decided to do that; otherwise, we would have missed each other."

He smiled. "I'm glad too. I want to go see the sheriff in the morning to find out whether he knows anything new on the case. I also want to ask about Carrie, and particularly about Conrad. There's a good chance that tip Carol had gotten from Carrie's friends might be true; I'm speaking of the possibility Carrie might be in the area with the professor. They may have stopped off here on their way back from Taos. Even if the sheriff has heard nothing, I still want to ask him about Conrad. I'd like to find out how much he might know of the professor's visits here."

"You think he may have already found out something about Carol's death?"

"I don't know. Probably not, the way things seem to be going."

"Oh, darling, I know things don't seem to be going well for you, but please try not to be so pessimistic."

"You're right, I guess. I shouldn't let my hopes down."

She said nothing else for the moment.

Ross brought the cigarette to his lips and inhaled deeply, letting out a long stream of smoke. "What do you say we have another drink? Shall we?"

"Let's do."

"Fine, what'll it be—an after-dinner drink or another martini?" He beckoned the waitress.

"Yes, another martini, please."

Ross ordered two martinis. Monica was ready to change the topic of conversation.

"You know," she said, "that hotel we're staying at certainly is interesting."

"In what way? You mean the pictures and relics and all that other stuff they have in the lobby?"

"Yes, all that. The building too. There's quite a history behind it, you know."

"The building?"

"Yes."

"It doesn't surprise me," Ross said. "It's an ancient building too, from the looks of it."

"That's what gives it character, darling."

"Yes, I suppose you're right." He began to laugh.

"What's so funny? Are you laughing at me, Ross Blair,—"

"No, I'm not laughing at you. I was thinking — poor Monica, waiting for me in that hotel all afternoon; you must have gotten bored. What did you do — spend all afternoon finding out about the hotel's history?"

She grinned. "Not the entire afternoon. I spent the early part of it in my room, reading, but I grew restless; not actually bored. Then I went down into the lobby. There was hardly anyone there except that little old man. He's so cute."

"Yea, he's quite a nice fellow."

"Terribly nice, I think. Charming man."

"That little old man's got a lot of character; that's one thing you find little of today in most people."

"That's exactly what I was thinking. Anyway, I walked up to him and before I knew it, he started up a conversation and then even went so far as to offer me a chair. I sat down and that's when he really started talking—the man loves to talk. And I just happened to ask him about the hotel and he started going; that's all he needed and there was no stopping him. He told me all about how the building's almost a hundred and twenty years old and that his great-grandfather had built it with little labor and a lot of sweat. He told me about all of the famous and interesting people who've been guests there. It used to be one of the main stops of the Wells Fargo Company, he said. Part of it was even converted into a jail at one time, when the old county jail burned down." She put out her cigarette.

"I imagine the town has a colorful history," Ross said. "And you know, I was thinking about it as I was driving into town earlier this evening—I like this little town. I know it's the place where all my troubles began, but nevertheless, I enjoy the pleasantness."

"You know, darling, the place struck me the same way too," Monica said. "It's the kind of place you always hear about but one you've never been to. Seeing an automobile here, for example, is like a —Oh, what's the word I'm searching for? You know, when something is placed in a time it actually doesn't belong to."

"An anachronism."

"Yes, that's it —an anachronism. Anyway, cars do seem out of place—out of their period. Everything else looks so much older. It's almost as if I expected to see horse carriages and stagecoaches coming down the street."

"It's not that old-looking, you silly nut."

"To me it is." She paused. *"Esperanza.* I even found out what that means in Spanish."

"You did? What?"

"It means 'Hope'," she said proudly. "But it's also a woman's name."

"Did the old man at the hotel tell you that too?"

"Yes. He talked his head off. Doesn't he like to talk a lot with you?"

"No." He looked at her and grinned. "But then," he added, "I don't have a pair of lovely legs like you do. I bet that's why he brought the chair over for you—so he could stare at your beautiful legs."

"Oh, Ross, he's ancient — probably doesn't bother with things like that anymore."

"Don't be so naive. Would you want to bet on it?"

"Oh, you stinker. Anyway, after that interesting discussion with the little old man, I decided to take a walk. I hadn't intended to walk for too long a time, but you know that I was out there for about two hours and walked practically clear across town."

"Really! All that distance."

Monica could tell that the drinks were affecting Ross, for he was beginning to kid with her; martinis always affected him in that way.

"My goodness, darling," Ross continued in the same jesting tone of voice, "it's not as if you crossed the city of San Francisco from one end to the other."

"Of course not." She too laughed, to show him she was taking his teasing in stride. "Honestly, though, it's quite a long distance to walk. I got pooped out, as a matter of fact, you big smart aleck! I bet you haven't walked that much since you've arrived." She smiled faintly.

"No, to be truthful, I haven't." They both laughed. "I'm just teasing, hon. I know it must be a long walk. I had to pay the sheriff a visit last week at the county courthouse but that's not very far from here. I could tell the town went on a lot further, though."

"I'm glad I took the walk." She paused in thought for a moment. "You know," she went on, "there's one thing in particular that attracts me to this little town. I felt the attraction this afternoon as I was walking down the street but I couldn't quite place my finger on the reason I felt that way; now it's come to me—it's the pace. It's slow. The people here simply take their time in doing things. They're not in any big hurry, like us. None of the rat-race you find in the big cities like San Francisco." She waited for Ross to say something but he didn't. "You and I should move down here, where a person seems to be able to relax all he wants."

He laughed. "Yes, the advertising business should be extremely good here. Booming—in fact, we ought to make a quick million, you and I. Turner's Dry Goods down the street there ought to be good for a least a quarter of a million dollars worth of advertising in a year's time." He looked at Monica with a big grin stretching across his face and then he burst out laughing.

Monica couldn't help laughing. "Oh, Ross, but you think you're such a smart guy, sometimes, coming out with those sarcastic remarks. You know quite well what I mean—what I'm getting at. That's exactly my point—the advertising business couldn't exist down here, not only because there's no need for it, not the way you and I know it, anyway, but because it just simply doesn't fit in with the slow pace I'm referring to. They aren't compatible. There's absolutely nothing about this little town that causes a person to rush here and there practically all of his waking hours like I find myself doing most of the time. Don't you agree—surely you must?"

"Yes, putting all kidding aside for the moment, darling, I must say I agree with you. It's an extremely peaceful place where life's lived slowly, I won't deny that at all."

"Or maybe," Monica added, "we'd be singing a different tune if we actually lived here. Who knows, we might get bored, since you and I are so used to the hustle and bustle of big city life. We'd probably find it difficult to change our life patterns."

"I'm not so sure that would necessarily be the case with you and me. I think it's all a matter of a person's attitude, and his ability, as well, to adjust to his surroundings; even new surroundings, no matter how abrupt the change. You take the people around this place, for example—they seem perfectly happy and content with themselves and in that way, if one considers a person's emotional contentment as a barometer of success in life, which I happen to believe, then these people here have been successful. They will have led full, satisfying lives. It's true that individually they won't make any imprint on man's history, but collectively, who knows. I think it depends on what standards one uses to measure success; and the standards I happen to be talking about have absolutely nothing to do with materiality."

"You're so right, darling." She placed her arm on the table, then reached across and affectionately placed her small hand on his. "You certainly do have the ability of putting across your thoughts so clearly." She carressed the back of his hand.

He eyed her thoughtfully and then his stare dropped down to a point beneath her neck and shoulders, around her breasts, where her white blouse was clinging provocatively to her firm, but soft skin. He smiled awkwardly at her when he became aware that she caught him staring at her body. What made him feel awkward was not simply the fact that he was staring at her physical form but the manner in which he was doing so. His eyes betrayed his carnal thoughts, and he realized she knew he wanted her; she had seen him with that same burning look in his eyes many times before.

He took her small hand and wrapped his around it. "My precious, beautiful darling," he whispered. "I love you."

"And I love you, Ross."

"Let's go back to the hotel, all right?"

"All right, let's," Monica replied softly.

Upon arriving at the hotel, they went to their separate rooms; Ross wanted to take his suit off and put on a pair of slacks and a sport shirt. When he had changed, he slipped back into Monica's room. He wasn't surprised to find Monica too had changed into something more comfortable.

She had slipped into a white chiffon, knee-length night gown which made her look both beautiful and appealing. It was a high-waisted gown so that it pushed up on her firm breasts, revealing the soft upper roundness of them and making them appear larger. Ross was filled with ecstasy as he watched her walking about the room, turning all the lights out except for the small lamp on top of the dresser. They were in semi-darkness.

Trembling with desire for her, slowly he walked up to where she stood waiting for him. Gently, he took her soft face in both hands and kissed her smooth, wet lips. She kissed him back, offering him the tip of her tongue. He could sense her growing desire for him.

Suddenly, she threw her arms around him and held on to him tightly, kissing him passionately. His desire for her increased; he couldn't recall any other time when he had desired her more than he did this moment. But he restrained himself; he wanted their desire for each other to grow and grow until he could feel the two of them bursting with a craving for each other.

They parted momentarily. He walked over to the small lamp on the dresser and turned it off so that they were completely in darkness. He opened the venetian blinds. Returning to where he was standing, he took her by the shoulders and lowered her with him to the bed. He could stand the craving within him no longer. She waited for him temptingly. Slowly, he began to undress her as they kissed; she began unbuttoning his shirt.

He struggled with her sleeping bra; he couldn't unhook it. She waited. Finally, she pushed him back playfully when it was apparent to her he was unable to loosen the bra strap.

"Oh, Ross," she said in a jesting, yet sarcastic tone of voice. "How absolutely unromantic you can be all of a sudden." He couldn't help laughing at her remark.

She sat up on the bed, quickly unhooked her bra, and let it fall to the floor. She sat there for a moment in silence, looking down at him. From where he was lying on the bed, he could see the silhouette of her lovely body. In the darkness of the room, with only the moonlight entering through the window, reflecting off her face and smooth shoulders, she looked to him more beautiful than ever. The soft moonlight on her face added to her beauty, giving the skin of her naked body a certain magical quality which now stirred his growing desire for her even more. But he waited and watched her sitting there for a moment longer; then he took her gently by the shoulders and pulled her down to him.

In the blissful world of love-making, the two of them lost sight of all else—of what had brought them to this little town of *Hope* and of the sudden, unexpected turn of events of the past week. It wasn't that they suddenly didn't care, but only that they were now in a different world of ecstasy where, for that moment at least, nothing else mattered.

CHAPTER 16

THEY slept late the next morning. It was nine o'clock when Ross left his room to knock on Monica's door. Monica was still in bed, but had awakened moments before she heard the rapping on the door. She got up only to let him in the room, then she quickly returned to the bed and motioned for him to sit beside her on the edge of the bed. He complied.

They spoke for only a moment; Ross wanted to call Sheriff Dominguez to ask if he could see him that morning. He asked Monica to take a shower and get dressed so they could have breakfast before going to the sheriff's office. He returned to his room after having made certain Monica was out of bed. He had taken a quick shower before going into her room; he shaved and finished getting dressed before calling Dominguez. They spoke for several minutes on the phone. The sheriff would be happy to visit with him that morning at whatever time was convenient to Ross. Dominguez also spoke briefly about an incident which had occurred during the weekend that might be worth following up.

"I'm curious to know what that look on your face is all about, darling," Monica said to Ross as they drank their coffee at the restaurant. "You've hardly said a word since we left the hotel. I take it you've spoken with the sheriff?"

"Yes," Ross said. "While you were getting ready." He glanced down at her dress. She was wearing a navy blue dress he had never seen before; it was sleeveless with a low neckline, revealing her soft, white shoulders. "But first let me say you look exquisitely lovely this morning, darling."

"Thank you." She smiled brightly at him. "What did the sheriff have to say?"

"He told me that Carrie may have been here a few days ago. That is, *if*—she's with Arthur Conrad."

"I'm afraid I don't understand."

"There's no certainty in what I'm saying," Ross said and shrugged. "A lot of it is nothing more than speculation on our part, I suppose. Sheriff Dominguez told me a few minutes ago he had learned over the weekend that a professor from the university was here sometime last week. There were other people with him, young people, probably students, he said, but he didn't know exactly whom they might be."

"And you think Carrie might have been with them, is that it?"

"Yes. I'd be surprised if she wasn't with Conrad."

"How did Sheriff Dominguez find all this out? Did he actually see or talk to this professor?"

"No—no, he didn't. Actually, he doesn't know for certain that this university professor he heard was in the area is the same one we're looking for."

He sipped some of his coffee. It was still hot. "You see, Dominguez only learned quite by accident, that some professor from the university—identity unknown—was in the area. Evidently, this man paid a visit to Old Lady Hawkins. You remember, the woman I told you about last night."

"You mean the elderly woman who practices witchcraft?" She took a drink of her coffee.

"Yes."

"That's odd. What connection could there be between the two of them?"

"Who knows? Sounds peculiar, doesn't it? But of course, we might not be talking about Arthur Conrad. There's a remote possibility, yes, but it could be entirely someone else and not

Professor Conrad. Besides, I'm not at all convinced Dominguez' source of information is reliable. Neither does Dominguez."

"What do you mean?"

"You remember this fellow Montoya I referred to last night? Baltazar Montoya, I think his name is."

"You mean the caretaker—the one who farms the Hawkins land?"

"Yes, that's him. Anyway, I think I may have told you last night about this fellow coming into town from time to time to do some shopping for the old lady and for himself."

"Uh huh."

"Well, it seems he was in Esperanza yesterday doing exactly that, and Dominguez happened to run into him. Dominguez had been making inquiries about Carrie and the student group, and he happened to pose the question to Montoya, thinking the caretaker might have seen the group out in his part of the country. Evidently, from what the sheriff has been able to piece together so far, this hangout the group is supposed to have here is somewhere in the vicinity of the Hawkins place."

"Oh, really?"

"In the conversation, Baltazar Montoya happened to mention this man who had been at the Hawkins place last week. He told Dominguez he didn't get a good look at the stranger but that there were other persons with him in a car—possibly students."

"But how would he know this stranger was a university professor?"

"The old woman told him so. Evidently, Montoya was at the old lady's working in her yard when the group drove up —Montoya spoke to the old lady about it afterward. But Montoya told the sheriff something else, which I think adds to the possibility that it was Professor Conrad he saw out there."

"What's that?"

"He told the sheriff that although he couldn't be absolutely sure about it, he thought he had seen the same man there a few times before."

"But why would that make you suspect it was Arthur Conrad who was there?"

"Because it would be too much of a coincidence. Can't you

see? If the man Montoya saw there has been in the vicinity various times in the past, he could well have been Conrad, since Conrad too has been here before. It ties in."

"You're right, now that you mention it, it does seem too much of a coincidence. But what if in fact it was Arthur Conrad Montoya saw there. I'm curious as to what possible connection there could be between him and Miss Hawkins. You don't think she could be involved with him?"

"You mean in connection with drugs?"

"Yes."

"The same thing occurred to me and I posed the question to Sheriff Dominguez. He said he didn't think so—it didn't sound like the old lady, he said. Whatever connection there may be between the two of them, he didn't think it was that. He reminded me that we couldn't be certain the man Montoya saw was Arthur Conrad. Secondly, he said, and of course he's right, we really don't know much about the professor's activities around here. The sheriff is extremely interested in the case now, though, and he assured me he's going to look into it further. One important possibility did occur to him, though, and that was that if it was Conrad who was at the Hawkins place, it's conceivable that the group may be conducting its illicit activities somewhere on the old lady's property without her knowledge."

"But where; surely she would know if they were?"

"According to Dominguez, the old lady's farm has several small unoccupied dwellings at the far end which were used a long time ago to house transient farm workers and their families." He paused and finished what was left of his coffee. "What Dominguez said seems possible. I'd sure like to find out about it soon."

"Is Sheriff Dominguez going to question Miss Hawkins about all this?" Monica asked.

"No, he's not. Not right now, anyway. He doesn't think it would be wise for *him* to do that. He feels the old lady would be suspicious of him if he were to go there asking questions of that sort, simply because he's the sheriff. He thinks she would clam up if he were to go. He's suggested something else—that I go visit her and let her know I'm looking for my daughter and then mention that I've got reason to believe she might be with a professor from the university. Then I can explain that I had heard a certain university professor had paid her a visit a few days ago and that I was curious if it were the same man I was looking for."

"Do you honestly think she'll talk to you?"

"Dominguez seems to think she'll cooperate."

"What makes him think that?"

"He didn't say over the telephone, except that maybe he feels the old lady will tend to sympathize with me when I tell her I'm looking for Carrie, rather than if he were to appear at her place asking questions."

Their breakfast came. Neither of them said much as they ate. When Ross had finished, he moved his plate to one side and lit a cigarette. "Incidentally, I told Dominguez about you; that you would be coming with me to see him this morning."

"Oh." She drank some of her coffee and pushed the cup aside.

"Yes, he's quite anxious to meet you. He even insisted that I bring you along when I asked if he'd prefer I went alone."

"Gee, that was awfully nice of him. I think I'll like Sheriff Dominguez." She laughed softly.

"You'll like him, I think."

Sheriff Dominguez was sitting behind his desk in his private office when Ross and Monica were ushered into the room by Marcela, the young girl Ross had seen there the week before. Dominguez was enjoying a hot cup of coffee and perusing papers on his desk.

"Well, well, Señor Blair," Dominguez said, standing up to greet his newly-arrived visitors. "It's a pleasure to see you once again." He walked around the large desk to shake hands with Ross. Immediately, he turned his attention to Monica, who stood at Ross' side.

"And this lovely lady," the sheriff continued, a gleam in his eyes, "she must be the visitor from San Francisco who arrived so unexpectedly and of whom you spoke about over the telephone." He offered both hands to Monica in greeting. She extended her hand to him and he wrapped his hands around it.

Monica smiled at Dominguez.

"Ah, but Mr. Blair," the sheriff said, turning to Ross, "why did you keep something as lovely as this back in San Francisco? I surely would not have done such a thing had I been in your shoes."

The three laughed.

"She may not believe this," Ross explained, smiling at Monica, "but before she showed up, I was beginning to feel sorry I had left her there."

"Oh, but what a pleasant surprise it must have been for you when she suddenly appeared so unexpectedly." He turned again to Monica. "It's a pleasure meeting you, Señorita—"

"Ashley," M o n i c a volunteered. "Monica Ashley. It's a pleasure meeting you too, Sheriff Dominguez."

"Ah, but the pleasure is all mine, Miss Ashley," the sheriff replied. "It's such a lovely name, you have—*Monica Ashley.*" He pronounced the name slowly and with a Spanish enunciation. He looked up at the ceiling momentarily, as if contemplating the name. "Yes, I like the sound when one says your lovely name—Monica. Such a name is befitting such an attractive young woman as you."

Ross watched Monica with interest and could see that she was beginning to blush.

"Why thank you, Sheriff Dominguez," she replied, still smiling. "It's nice of you to say that."

"Oh, but there's nothing to thank me for, Señorita Ashley, for I'm simply making a factual observation." He turned to Ross. "Am I not correct, Mr. Blair? I'm certain you'll not disagree."

Ross and Monica laughed.

"No," Ross said, "I don't disagree."

'Please sit down and join me in a cup of coffee," Sheriff Dominguez said. Still holding on to Monica's hand, he led her to one of two chairs setting in front of the desk. Ross sat down in the other one.

The sheriff returned to his chair and buzzed his secretary on the telephone intercom. He asked her to bring in two more cups of coffee and another one for himself. "Just a moment, Marcela," he said into the telephone. He turned to Monica.

"How do you like your coffee, Señorita Ashley?"

"Black, no sugar," Monica answered.

"Marcela, two coffees black and one with cream and sugar. Yes. Thank you."

Moments later, Marcela brought the three cups of coffee and left them setting on a tray on top of Dominguez' desk. Dominguez handed two cups to his guests and he took the third cup for himself.

The sheriff then proceeded to ask Monica whether her stay in Esperanza had been comfortable so far. Monica assured him that it had been. The three conversed in small talk for a few minutes before Dominguez began explaining how the investigation into Carol's death was progressing. He was blunt about the fact that not much had been learned since Ross had left for Albuquerque. The only progress, if in fact it could be considered that, had been one of the elimination of possible clues. The fingerprints, for example; several had been lifted from the furniture and several items of personal property found in the room where Carol was shot. All prints had been checked. A few had belonged to Carol, which had been anticipated. Some of the others belonged to the cleaning woman employed by the hotel. The rest of the fingerprints had belonged to the prior occupant of the room, a salesman from Colorado Springs. His name and address had been obtained from the registration card at the hotel. From there, it had been simply a matter of contacting the law authorities in Colorado Springs to ask for their cooperation in locating the man. When a set of these prints had arrived, they were compared against those found in the room—they belonged to the same person.

Dominguez next discussed the weapon. A preliminary check with ballistic experts indicated that the bullet which had been removed from Carol's body had come from a .32 caliber pistol. The hotel and the immediate vicinity had been searched thoroughly, in hope the killer had hidden or thrown the gun away while leaving the scene. It was an unlikely occurrance, but a slight possibility existed that the killer had panicked and so it was checked out. It was even less likely that the gun would be found elsewhere, unless, of course, the killer was found, and so far, there were no suspects. Dominguez assured Ross that everything would be done on the case to insure all possibilities were exhausted, and that he would continue his own personal efforts to find the murderer. Ross told the sheriff he was satisfied the case was in good hands.

Monica sat quietly as the two men spoke; they returned to their earlier telephone conversation during which Dominguez had told Ross about the visitor to the Hawkins residence. The sheriff reiterated that he thought it was better if Ross, not someone from the sheriff's office, visited Consuelo Hawkins in an attempt to elicit from her information about the visitor. Too, he might be able to discover if the old lady knew anything about her visitor's activities in the Esperanza area.

"Monica and I were discussing it on the way up here," Ross said to Bartolo Dominguez. "We're planning to go over to the Hawkins place shortly after we leave your office. I imagine now will be as good a time as any, what do you think?"

"Yes, of course," the sheriff said. "That's very good; there's no reason to delay your visit. The sooner, the better. I'm extremely curious now to find out whether old Consuelo will be able to tell you anything useful. I'm anxious to find out if you'll learn anything that might help you get closer to discovering your daughter's whereabouts, but from the standpoint of my duties as sheriff, I'm also interested in learning more about the professor's activities in the county. If he's in any way broken the law in the past, it's my job to see to it that he doesn't do so again."

Ross next discussed with Sheriff Dominguez his recent trip to Taos. He also told him of his attempts to locate the professor at the university. Finally, he related his visit with the assistant district attorney in Albuquerque.

"Well, Sheriff Dominguez," Ross said when he had summarized his activities of the past two days, "I'm sure you have other business to attend to and we've kept you from it long enough. I must apologize if we've caused you any inconvenience this morning." He stood up and shook hands vigorously with Dominguez.

"It was no inconvenience, Mr. Blair," the sheriff answered. "I'm only too happy to be at your service." He turned to Monica and gave her another of his bright smiles. "And of course, it was indeed *my* pleasure to visit with you this morning, Mr. Blair, for I got the opportunity to meet your lovely *señorita*."

Monica smiled at the sheriff.

"Well, I think we'd better pay Miss Hawkins a visit now," Ross said. "We might be able to learn a great deal from her."

They exchanged goodbyes.

Ross promised Dominguez he'd let him know what, if anything, he learned from Consuelo Hawkins. Dominguez accompanied them out of his office and into the hallway. There, he wished them luck and bid them farewell again.

CHAPTER 17

THE old house in which Consuelo Jurado Hawkins lived was in a secluded area along a hidden countryside road. Twice, Ross had missed the turn-off from the main road, but finally, after stopping on two occasions to ask directions to the old lady's place, he found the narrow path. The difficulty they had experienced in finding the way was proof to Ross that the place was truly in far-off spot where a scientist would indeed treasure the privacy necessary to perform secret experiments, as Andrew Borlin had purportedly done so many years before. Should the old lady be willing to talk to them, Ross said to Monica as they traveled up the dusty, winding road, he would also ask her about Andrew Borlin. Carol's tale about her eccentric father had left a strong impression on him, and he was curious to find out exactly how much accuracy there was to Carol's belief concerning her father's involvement in witchcraft. He still believed Carol may have unintentionally blown out the proportion her father's interest in the occult.

They came to a turn in the road where the brush and grass were thick to each side and the tall trees were so close together that they hid the view beyond. Ross slowed down when Monica pointed out an old mailbox to the side of the road. He had to leave the roadway to get nearer. The mailbox was heavily corroded, but even through all the rust, he was able to decipher the name which had been crudely painted on the side of the box. The name was unmistakable—it read: *C. J. Hawkins.*

"This is the place!" Ross said excitedly to Monica. "Keep your fingers crossed."

"Wow, it certainly looks creepy enough," Monica said. "Ties right in with what people say about her."

Ross laughed at her. "I assume you're referring to her being a witch."

"Uh huh."

"Oh, Monica, don't be silly."

Several large weeping willow trees partially hid the house. A wide ditch ran alongside the road. In the middle of the ditch, only partly filled with water, there were thick clumps of water reeds which obscured the view of the house from the roadway. Large cypresses on the near side of the ditch, along with the willows, hid the remainder of the Hawkins farm.

The car wheels made a thumping noise as Ross drove the car over an old wooden bridge crossing the irrigation canal.

"My God!" Monica exclaimed as the large house came into view. "Look at that place; it gives me the willies." She turned to Ross. "Ross, I really don't think we should have come here. You may think I'm being terribly childish but I don't mind telling you I've just now, very quickly, grown afraid of this place—and this Hawkins woman."

"Oh, Monica, be sensible," Ross said. "Surely you're not going to let the appearance of the place affect you that way. It doesn't make the old lady evil. She's just an eccentric old woman who happens to like seclusion." He stopped the car and studied the house before them. "And," he continued, "from the looks of the place, one of her eccentricities is to permit the house to fall apart, like Dominguez said. What could possibly happen? The worst is that she'll slam the door in our faces, and if that's the case, then we'll take the hint and leave—no fuss—no bother."

He placed his hand on Monica's lap, attempting to reassure her. "We've come this far, honey, let's not turn back now. After all, don't forget the reason why we came here; she just might have the information we want."

She looked at him and attempted a smile. Then she sighed. "Oh, all right. But let's not stay too long, all right, darling?"

"We won't."

He brought the car to a stop in front of the residence, along a gravel driveway full of weeds from lack of use. He exited the car and walked around to open the door for Monica. They both stood there awed for a moment, as if their eyes had come upon the sight of the two-story mansion for the first time.

It was a wooden frame house, in desperate need of repair. Some of the wood siding along the walls was warped and splintered with age. The wood had been painted white once, one could tell by close inspection, but now, the paint had yellowed and peeled badly and in some places, had come off completely, leaving the bare wood to show. An ancient wooden porch ran the entire length of the front of the house, with a wooden railing at its edge. Some of the ornamental pieces attached to the railing had decorative carvings. They appeared to be hand-carved but it was difficult to tell, for they were splintered and cracked.

The house itself was built high off the ground, on a brick foundation, and to get onto the porch, one had to climb a stairway of fifteen or so steps. It was a large house, Ross thought as he stood there beside Monica; he remarked he couldn't imagine a little old lady like Consuelo Hawkins living alone in such an enormous place.

There wasn't a cloud in the sky so that the sun lit up the surrounding countryside vividly, but the area immediately surrounding the Hawkins home was so abundantly filled with shrubbery and tall trees thick with leaves that the house and adjoining yard were shaded from the hot sun. A gust of wind which had swept noisily through the leaves of the trees now came down upon the two of them standing there and they felt the soft touch of the breeze, cooled by the shade of the gigantic trees.

"Come on," Ross said softly to Monica and he reached out, taking her by the hand. "Let's get this over with."

They walked up the steps and onto the creaky porch. Monica hesitated for a moment and Ross had to move her out of the way to reach for the doorbell. Even through the heavy, thick door, they could hear the sound of chimes inside. They waited for what seemed a long minute and Ross was beginning to think no one was in, but he remembered Dominguez had said the old lady never left the house. Again, Ross pressed the button. This time, before the chimes had stopped, they heard the sound of someone releasing the door chain and latch on the other side. Both of them waited for the door to open but there was a stillness again, as if whoever had unlatched the door hesitated.

Finally, the door opened slowly and stood ajar. Still, no one appeared; Ross and Monica stood there puzzled. Suddenly, a face appeared out of the darkness. It was the face of a large woman. Ross had expected to meet a small and elderly, frail-looking woman, but the face with deeply-set eyes that he saw belonged to a rather tall, medium sized lady. She held the door open only five or six inches, so that although Ross couldn't see the face plainly, he was able to see that even though it posses-sed a few wrinkles, it didn't give the appearance of belonging to a very old woman. On the contrary, the face was dark and healthy-looking, nothing at all like Ross had expected, causing him momentarily to suspect it wasn't Consuelo Hawkins who was peering at them through the crack in the doorway. Her long hair, which she wore braided, was completely white.

The woman stood there, without uttering a word, as if studying her unwelcomed visitors.

"Yes, what do you want?" the old woman finally spoke, her loud voice crackling.

"Miss Hawkins?" Ross said hesitantly.

"Yes. Yes, I'm Miss Hawkins. What is it you want with me?" She appeared not to move her lips at all as she spoke.

"Miss Hawkins," Ross said again, "my name's Ross Blair and this young lady is Miss Ashley—Monica Ashley. We're not from this area but for the past few days, we've been here trying to locate my daughter. We have reason to believe that—"

"Your daughter, you say," the old lady interrupted coldly. "I know absolutely nothing of anyone's daughter. There's no-body who lives here but me. I'm extremely sorry, but you've certainly come to the wrong place looking for your daughter,

Mr. Barnes."

"It's *Blair*," Ross corrected her.

Consuelo Hawkins glanced at Monica curiously, then returned her glance to Ross. "Well, you won't find your daughter here, Mr. Blair," she snapped. "Now, if you'll excuse me, I've—" She was about to close the door.

"Please, Miss Hawkins," Ross said desperately. "Please wait. If you'll allow me a moment to explain." He swallowed, then cleared his throat. The old woman looked at him curiously and waited. He'd better say what he had to say while he had the chance, he thought. "We were told that sometime last week you had a visitor here — a professor from the university in Albuquerque, I believe. It's this man we're trying to locate if he's the same professor we're looking for. You see, Mrs. Hawkins, we have good reason to believe my daughter's either with him or that he may know where she can be located."

The old woman looked at Ross suspiciously. "I know nothing of any professor visiting me last week either," she explained. "No one's visited me here in months, young man." She watched both Monica and Ross rather impassively now. "And I don't know what you're talking about or where you got your information but there's been nobody here to see me recently. No one that I'd care to tell you about, anyway. Now if you'll please—"

"We have a reliable source, Mrs. Hawkins, that—"

"It's *Miss*, young man, not *Missus*!"

"I'm sorry, *Miss* Hawkins. I apologize. As I was saying, we have a reliable source who we understand saw this man we're looking for here on your property. Now it could be that you know nothing about this man and that our source of information is incorrect, and if so, I would appreciate your telling us."

"Reliable source, you say?" Consuelo Hawkins snapped back, ignoring Ross' inquiries. "Just who in blazes is this reliable source you refer to, anyway?"

"I believe you have a man by the name of Baltazar Montoya working here on your land."

"Yes, that's right, he farms my land. What about him?"

"It seems he was in town early this week and he's the one who told—"

"Baltazar! So that's your reliable source. Now, that's a laugh; him—reliable! That no-good drunkard. A wino—that's all he is; he's not reliable at all. Why he's probably suffering from delirium tremens right this moment, as much as he drinks."

"He told Sheriff Dominguez back in Esperanza not only that he saw this man here on your property but that he saw you speaking to him."

"That man should mind his own business, I tell you. There's no telling what Montoya may see around this place. He's lucky he manages to remain sober enough during the growing season to work the land."

For an old lady, she was extremely sharp with her words, Ross thought.

"But we have reason to believe that this man—this professor we're looking for — was someplace around the Esperanza area, Miss Hawkins, and it appears to be too much of a coincidence that Mr. Montoya would make up a story about seeing someone from the university here last week."

"What university are you referring to anyway, young man?"

"The University of New Mexico." He thought he noticed a change in her tone of voice, as if she were suddenly becoming more receptive and less hostile to her uninvited visitors.

"It's my understanding," he continued, "that Montoya said he's seen this same man here before—several times before."

Consuelo Hawkins opened the door wider, so that both Ross and Monica could see her more clearly and they noticed a heavy frown form on her forehead. "You say Montoya's been talking to the county sheriff about this?"

"Well, yes," Ross began to explain. He was relieved that the old lady now appeared to be showing some interest in what he had to say. "You see, Sheriff Dominguez is helping me locate my daughter and he's been making inquiries in the area. One of the persons he's talked to is Baltazar Montoya."

"He must be referring to Arthur Conrad; he's a professor at the university and he—"

"Yes, that's him, that's the one!" Ross said excitedly. He's the one we're looking for. He *has* been here to visit you, then?"

"I wouldn't consider him a visitor. He's more of a trespasser, now; came here uninvited last week. Wanted me to let him use these two dwellings I own back further on the farm. I actually spoke to the man only a few minutes. He's been here before, of course, as Montoya said. I used to let him use these two small houses I have in back. He used to come out here a few days at a time and would usually bring a group of his friends along with him."

"Did he stay in one of those houses last week, do you know?"

"Certainly not! I didn't permit it; ran him off. Told him I didn't ever want to see him near this place again."

"Why did you do that, Miss Hawkins?"

"Never mind about that, young man." She raised her voice slightly.

"I don't want you to think I'm unnecessarily prying into your personal affairs but it's important for me to find out about this man. And I'd like for you to give me a chance to tell you why—please."

"Very well, young man. I'm listening, but be quick about it!"

Ross began his tale, telling Consuelo Hawkins of Carrie's relationship with Arthur Conrad and the reasons why he suspected she was with him. He told her about the drug problem. As Ross spoke, Monica thought she noticed the coldness in the old lady disappear and in its place, there was beginning to appear a touch of understanding.

"You certainly have a legitimate gripe against the professor, then," the old woman said when Ross had finished.

"I think I do too. That's why I want to find them as soon as possible."

"Now that I've heard what you had to say, Mr. Blair—it's a sad thing about your daughter—I'd like to help you, but I'm afraid I can't. You see, I've no idea where Professor Conrad went to after he left here—no idea at all. At the time, I couldn't have cared less. But I'll tell you that it's possible your daughter was with him for there were several young people with him; someone was always with him."

"Did you get a good look at any of them?"

"I'm afraid not. You see, they were in a car and only the

professor got out. They were only here a few minutes."

"And you say he didn't give you the slightest idea where they might have been going?"

"Not the slightest. I told him that under no circumstances did I want him hanging around my land. I wouldn't permit it —ever again!"

"I'd certainly appreciate your explaining that to us, Miss Hawkins. Did the two of you have some disagreement in the past—during his last visit here?"

"Disagreement!" She chuckled loudly. "That's a nice way of putting it, young man. But yes, I guess you might call it that. It had to do with what you spoke of earlier."

"His use of drugs?"

"Yes—disgusting. I didn't appreciate his making use of my land for such rot!"

Ross then went on to tell Consuelo Hawkins what he knew of the suspected hangout near the area which the professor used for pot parties and LSD trips. He asked the old lady whether Conrad had been using her property for that purpose. Was the hangout he had heard of on her property?

"Young man, for a person who came here specifically for the purpose of asking questions, you surely do seem to have a lot of the answers yourself!" She studied him again, but her suspicious nature seemed to have disappeared.

"Yes—yes," she went on. "I discovered he was using one of my houses out back for all those terrible things. I confronted him with the matter and told him I wouldn't permit such things taking place on my property. And so I ran him and his group off; I even threatened to turn them in when I had my doubts they would leave. I didn't, though. Now, I kind of wish I had after what you've told me about your daughter."

"Was it this past week that all of this happened?"

"No, no, this happened several months ago, when I first found out about their activities. Then, he has the gall to show up again last week—after he had been told he wasn't wanted here."

"I see."

"I used to like the man when we first met. That was several years ago. But not after I found out he was up to no good."

She paused, as if reflecting on a thought. "If that answers all of your questions, Mr. Blair, now if you'll excuse me—"

"Wait, Miss Hawkins, please," Ross said. "There's one other matter I wanted to ask you about. It's not related to Arthur Conrad but concerns something that happened a long time ago."

"Yes—yes, what is it?" the old woman asked impatiently.

"It has to do with someone I believe you knew quite well a while back—almost twenty years ago."

"Yes, go on. Whom might that be you're speaking of." Again, she wrinkled her brow.

"A man by the name of Andrew Borlin." He waited to see what reaction the name would bring to the old lady's face. "Do you remember him?"

"I certainly do," she replied after some hesitation. "I knew Andrew Borlin—what about him? How very odd that you should happen to mention his name."

"Why is that, Miss Hawkins?"

"Oh, never mind, I was only thinking out loud."

"Miss Hawkins, would you mind if we came in for a moment?" He sounded excited once again. "That is, if you don't mind answering a few questions about Andrew Borlin."

"Please tell me, young man, why would you be interested in learning of him. This business about coming here to see me about the professor and your daughter—that wouldn't have been just an excuse to—"

"Not at all, Miss Hawkins. My questions were asked in good faith. But you see, it happens that Andrew Borlin was my ex-wife's father. In fact, you met her once; you may not remember her, though. She came here to your house to pick up her father's belongings shortly after he died." He kept watching the old lady and saw a sudden spark of recollection come to her eyes.

"Yes, I remember meeting her. An attractive girl, she was too." She turned to glance at Monica, who had been standing there quietly. "Borlin's daughter was your ex-wife, you say?"

"Yes," Ross replied. "We were divorced many years ago. In fact, she actually wasn't my wife when she visited you." He paused, expecting the old woman to say something else but she only stood there. "Miss Hawkins, *may* we come in for a moment?" he asked politely. "So that we may discuss Andrew Borlin, I mean."

"Well," Consuelo Hawkins said, sighing, "you've already taken up this much of my time, I guess a few more minutes won't matter now." She formed a frown but almost instantly it was gone and Ross thought that for the first time, he had noticed the woman smiling.

She opened the door wide. "Come on in then and have a seat in the parlor." She shut the door as soon as they had entered. She turned and led them through a dark corridor toward the back of the house. She walked slowly with a hunched back. She wasn't a heavy woman but was big-boned and the black and white flowered print dress she wore made her appear larger. Draped over her shoulders and held by both hands was a hand-wovened, black shawl which reached down to her waist.

She turned at the first doorway on the right; Ross and Monica followed closely behind. This particular doorway led into a large, extremely old-fashioned parlor; the room too was dark—much darker than the hallway, even though it had a large front window—the dark, thick curtains were drawn closed, preventing the daylight from entering the room. A large chandelier hung from the high ceiling, but the lights weren't turned on. Consuelo Hawkins walked up to a small, ornamental table lamp and flipped the light switch; it was the only light in the room she bothered turning on. In that same, high-pitched, crackling voice, she asked them to sit down on a long sofa near the center of the room.

Immediately, Monica felt a thick layer of dust covering the sofa. She noticed too that the coffee table in front of her and the end table at the far end of the sofa were covered with dust. Poor woman, Monica thought, it was too large a house for a person her age to handle. She suddenly became aware she was now feeling sorry for the woman she had feared earlier. Ross had been right — Miss Hawkins was only an eccentric, but harmless elderly woman; she now felt slightly ridiculous for having permitted the gloomy surroundings and Ross' story of witchcraft to affect her. She was conscious that the old lady was watching her as she glanced about the large room.

"Now, Mr. Blair," Consuelo Hawkins said, clearing her throat. "What exactly do you wish to know about Andrew Borlin?" She was sitting in a large arm chair which enveloped her totally.

"Well," Ross began, "could you tell me something about these experiments he's supposed to have conducted? I understand he had a special laboratory."

"Yes, he used part of my property to conduct experiments. He built a small structure at his own expense; it didn't belong to me. He paid me rent, though, for the use of my land. I actually knew very little about what these experiments of his consisted of, however, for he never spoke to me about them and I never bothered asking him. It was all too scientific—something I find difficult to understand. But that fellow you mentioned a moment ago—Baltazar Montoya."

"Yes, what about him?"

"He worked for Andrew Borlin, helping him with his experiments."

"My ex-wife told me that."

"He helped Borlin out in the lab, cleaning up and getting supplies for him. So I don't think he actually knew what the experiments were all about either. But then again, he may have known much more than I give him credit for. Borlin confided in him, actually, I remember that distinctly—why he relied on that old buzzard, I don't honestly know. But I remember he liked Montoya and they got along well. All of this, of course, was before Montoya became an old drunkard like he is now. He would have been no use to Borlin then."

"Tell me, Miss Hawkins, whatever became of his experiments?"

"Nothing became of them—nothing at all. Borlin never did complete them as far as I know. He died while he was still at work. His heart attack was a sudden thing. After his death, Montoya set fire to the building where Borlin had his laboratory and all of his equipment, notes, records—he burned it to the ground, contents and all. Thousands of dollars worth of property turned to ashes."

"But why would Montoya do that?"

"I wondered the same thing myself; thought he had been

driven mad when he did it. But he told me later Borlin left specific instructions with him to do it. He said Borlin wanted all of his notes and important records and the laboratory destroyed—wanted nothing left of his experiments. Montoya always did what Borlin told him to do. He was an extremely faithful and devoted employee and Borlin trusted him to the limit."

"But why would Borlin want all his notes and work destroyed, after he had spent so much time working on the experiments? I understand he had friends who were also scientists. One would think he'd have left his work to someone to carry it on further."

"I don't know the answers to those questions, Mr. Blair. Why he would want his notes and the laboratory destroyed— your guess is as good as mine."

Ross watched her carefully and was surprised to find her grinning. She laughed softly at him.

"You're wondering why I appear amused by all this."

"Yes, I am."

The grin vanished as she continued. "I was laughing because of Borlin's secrecy—he was extremely secretive with his experiments. But then there were other matters and interests of his which he too wanted to keep secret. He was that kind of man. There was one interest in particular he and I had in common which wasn't scientific by any stretch of the imagination—not in the sense that we use the word today, anyway."

"I'm afraid I don't understand, Miss Hawkins."

"Come now, Mr. Blair," the old woman said, almost chuckling, "surely you didn't come all the way up here to see me and to ask questions without first having inquired about me and discovering that I'm known as the old witch by everyone in Esperanza. For instance, you've indicated you spoke with Sheriff Dominguez and I assume you spoke to him too about the fact that Montoya saw the professor on my land."

"Yes."

"Well then, he must have explained to you that I'm a true believer in the occult and the ancient art of witchcraft."

Ross and Monica exchanged glances. Suddenly, Monica became uncomfortable and felt a rebirth of the fear and nervousness she had sensed earlier.

Ross smiled at Consuelo Hawkins. "Yes, we did happen to learn of the rumor in town that you practice witchcraft." He was extremely careful not to confirm the old lady's suspicions that it was Sheriff Dominguez who had provided him with the information.

"It's no rumor, Mr. Blair, for it's true enough. Please don't feel you'll offend me. By definition, I imagine you could call me a witch or sorceress, whichever term you'd prefer to use. But it's the truth—I do practice the black arts."

A strange smile appeared on her face and she turned to Monica. "You seem nervous," she said. Monica didn't answer but managed a slight smile.

"What is your name again, young lady?" the old lady asked her.

"M—M—Monica," Monica replied faintly. She cleared her throat. "Monica Ashley."

"Yes—Ashley. You're a lovely woman, Miss Ashley. And I like you; I like the two of you, as a matter of fact. So there's no need to be nervous or even afraid of what I'm saying to you. You needn't worry—I'm not going to harm you." She was smiling again.

"It's true that the inhabitants of the town think of a witch as one who does other people harm by casting evil spells against them, but I want you to know I've never harmed anyone with my magic." She looked at Monica with reassuring eyes; then she turned to Ross. Her eyes glistened even in the darkened room. "It's strange—coincidental, one might say," she went on, "that you should happen to come see me this very day to inquire of Andrew Borlin, my companion of the past."

"Why is that, Miss Hawkins?" Ross asked. He was witnessing an abrupt change come over this woman sitting before him. First, she had met them coldly at the door, but now she seemed eager to talk to them.

"Because of my activities of the last two weeks. I'll explain that to you in a moment. First of all, let me go back to what I said a moment ago about my having a common interest with Andrew Borlin. You see, he too was a student of black magic and things pertaining to the occult."

So Carol had been right, Ross thought.

"Through the years," the old woman continued, "since Andrew Borlin's death, I've attempted rituals for the purpose of conjuring up his spirit." She stared deeply into Ross' eyes. "Do you happen to know what that means, Mr. Blair?"

"I've only a vague idea."

"Let me explain then. It means to bring back the spirit of a person from the dead." She paused and watched for their reaction. "I don't believe you're taking me seriously."

"Do you mean returning a person physically from the dead?"

"No, not physically. Not the ritual I conduct, anyway. Let me explain further. In witchcraft, there is a certain practice referred to as 'necromancy' which legend has it means the reanimation of a recently defunct corpse—the actual physical body of the dead. I do not mean it in that way. When I speak of bringing Andrew Borlin back from the dead, I am speaking of his spirit only. Some call this 'necromancy'. That is why, because the term is often referred to as the conjuring up of a corpse physically, I prefer to use the term 'sciomancy' to signify that only the spirit is brought back to life.

"I've spent the necessary thirteen days in preparation of the final ritual and today is the fourteenth and final day of preparation. That is why I said that it was coincidental the two of you should come this very day inquiring of Andrew Borlin. Tonight, as the new moon ascends, I'm prepared to perform the ritual."

She sat forward in her chair. "Since you've shown an interest in Andrew Borlin and in his experiments, Mr. Blair, maybe you and Miss Ashley would care to join me tonight. It may well be that we could ask Borlin questions concerning these experiments so that you may learn what they were all about."

Ross was beginning to like this eccentric but interesting old woman.

"Of course, I may fail again tonight, for I'm sorry to say that my attempts in the past have failed to conjure up Borlin's spirit. But please don't misunderstand, for I've succeeded in these rituals many times before with the spirits of other persons; but Andrew Borlin has presented a peculiar problem to me, for reasons I don't care to discuss at the moment.

"My meditation will begin sometime between seven thirty and eight tonight, when the new moon begins to ascend."

"Are we to understand you wouldn't mind our presence here tonight during this ritual you've planned?"

"Certainly I wouldn't mind. It would be extremely important, however, should you wish to witness the event, that you arrive here before I begin the ritual, for once I've begun, I cannot under any circumstances be interrupted. Would you and Miss Ashley care to come witness this extraordinary event, Mr. Blair? I assure you, you'll find it most interesting." She smiled and her eyes looked at him intently.

Ross glanced at Monica for a brief moment. She was watching Consuelo Hawkins. He then faced the old woman himself. "We'd be only too happy to come. I'd be extremely interested in witnessing the ritual."

Monica immediately turned a surprised face toward Ross. She didn't say anything to him but she didn't have to for he read in her eyes that distinct look of disapproval he had seen in them before.

"Good, that settles that. I'll be expecting you then. And now, I'm sorry to say that I must cut short your visit." She stood up slowly. "There is still much I must do in preparation for tonight's meditation so you must excuse me. Before you leave, however, I wish to apologize if I acted suspiciously or rudely when you first arrived. But I'm always suspicious of strangers. It was when you told me about your daughter, young man, that I became less suspicious of you. I must admit your mentioning your interest in Andrew Borlin, an old friend, helped rid me of suspicion."

She accompanied them to the front door. Ross opened it.

"Then I can expect the two of you tonight?" she said.

"Yes," Ross answered. "We'll be here." He took Monica by the arm.

"Goodbye now."

"Good day, Miss Hawkins," Ross said. "And thank you for your time."

Consuelo Hawkins merely nodded and smiled at them as she closed the door.

Once inside the car, Ross immediately noticed the look of disapproval in Monica's face. He was about to say something to her but she cut him off.

"*You* might be thinking of coming back tonight, Mr. Blair," she said in an angry tone of voice, "but *I'm* certainly not."

Ross started the engine. "Oh, Monica, honestly," he said, attempting to sound apologetic, "I didn't think you'd mind returning here tonight. Besides, I couldn't very well have asked you in the old lady's presence whether you'd like to come. If you'd prefer not to come, darling, I could always give her some excuse why you couldn't make it." He drew a deep breath. "But aren't you even the slightest bit curious to find out about Miss Hawkins and her witchcraft. Just think—a legitimate and authentic witch ritual. How many persons are able to say they've ever attended on in their entire lives?"

"And I'd be willing to bet that not very many would care to, either," Monica retorted. "Yours truly, for one." She took out a cigarette from her purse and lit it.

"Monica, darling, I actually thought you'd find all of this interesting and exciting, even if we don't expect her to succeed with this crazy idea of hers that she can speak to the spirits of dead people. Don't spoil the fun of it."

"Oh, Ross, honestly, I sometimes find it so difficult to understand you. For the life of me, I can't possibly see what interest you'd have in whatever ritual this Hawkins woman would want to conduct. So what if it concerns Andrew Borlin. What information can you possibly expect to get anyway, from this ridiculous thing tonight? I'm sorry, but I for one can't see any possible value in it."

Ross turned the car onto the paved road, heading back into Esperanza.

"Darling," Ross explained, "I was only trying to be nice to the woman. You must remember, whether we take any of this seriously or not, *she* does, and couldn't you tell by that look on her face that she was just dying for us to accept her invitation?"

"No, I can't say that I did."

"I did and I was afraid that if we didn't accept her invitation, she would have been offended. And that, I wouldn't want to do for I feel strongly we can get more information from her about Carol's father."

"But Ross—why should you so suddenly be concerned about Carol's father; about something that happened to him long ago? That's what I don't quite understand. What does finding out more about Andrew Borlin have to do with finding Carrie? After all, that's why we went to see the old lady in the first place. Or have you forgotten that?"

"Oh, Monica, really—of course I haven't forgotten. But I felt that since we weren't actually planning on leaving until tomorrow morning, it wouldn't hurt to visit with the old lady again tonight to see what else we may find out. Do you remember my telling you how suspicious Carol was of the old lady; she suspected the old lady was involved in her father's death?"

"Yes, I recall." She inhaled smoke from her cigarette and let it out quickly, waiting for Ross to continue.

"I think the old lady will be able to answer some questions about his death which might clear up some of the questions Carol posed. I think there's some perfectly valid explanations."

"But what should any of it matter now that Carol's dead?"

"Only that it would certainly satisfy *my* curiosity. Although before she died, Carol explained to me why she had left San Francisco so suddenly, there are many questions left unanswered. I'd feel more satisfied if I were able to learn more about the circumstances surrounding his death.

"I honestly think Consuelo Hawkins will be able to provide us with at least some of the answers. You'll recall I said Carol had told me the old lady hadn't been too receptive when she went there to pick up her father's belongings. Well, that was a long time ago and maybe the old lady did have something to hide from Carol."

"And what makes you think she'll reveal something to you when she didn't to Carol?"

"That was twenty years ago and any reasons which the old lady may have had for not cooperating with Carol may not be significant today. So maybe she would be willing to openly discuss Andrew Borlin. His sudden phone call to Carol, for example. Or, the secrecy of these experiments. His sudden death. Carol not being able to find that wax doll he always kept with him. All of these questions to this day remain unanswered."

He paused. "And," he said as an afterthought, "if she's unable to provide us with some of the answers, maybe this fellow Baltazar Montoya will be able to; I wouldn't mind paying him a visit too, if we have time. But first, I'd like to find out what else the old lady has to say."

Monica didn't say anything else for a long while. Then she broke the silence. "Well, you'll have to do it on your own, then, because I'm not going back to that place with you tonight."

They were silent the rest of the way into town.

At the hotel later that afternoon, Monica attempted persuading Ross not to return to the Hawkins place; but she got nowhere with him as he was determined he would go with or without her. When she realized she wasn't able to change his mind, she resigned herself to this fact and she finally decided to accompany him.

"That's my girl," Ross said happily and he put his arms around her, squeezing her lovingly.

"Oh, Ross," she said, returning his embrace. "You're so set in your stubborn ways sometimes."

CHAPTER 18

THAT evening, they arrived at Consuelo Hawkins' at twenty minutes past seven. Although the sun had set fifteen or twenty minutes earlier, the sky on the western horizon still possessed a bright red color. The evening was without shadows and it was becoming difficult to see clearly without light. It was that time of day when darkness moves swiftly and so the sky had darkened considerably during the period it had taken them to get from the hotel to the old lady's house.

The old lady's face lit up with a bright smile as she opened the door for them. She invited them in.

"You barely made it—aren't any too early, anyway," she said as she ushered them through the darkened corridor leading toward the rear of the house. She proceeded walking, obviously in a hurry.

"I was beginning to think you had changed your mind about coming." She glanced back briefly as she spoke but then quickly turned around as she continued to move hurriedly down the hallway.

Ross and Monica followed closely behind.

"It would take something else very important, Miss Hawkins," Ross said, "to make me turn down your gracious invitation to witness the ritual." He threw a quick glance at Monica. She looked up at him and attempted a smile but he could tell she was somewhat sullen because of his determination to come. He smiled back at her and then took her by the hand as they walked behind Consuelo Hawkins.

"We must hurry," the old woman continued, sounding slightly out of breath. "I was in preparatory meditation only a few minutes ago when you rang. That's why it took me so long to answer the door. For as you may have already surmised, much more time goes into the preparation for this sort of divination than for the actual ritual itself. Here we are!"

They had turned into a second, much narrower and darker corridor. The old woman opened the only door leading from the hallway.

Having followed Miss Hawkins into the room, Ross and Monica stood by the doorway, their eyes momentarily transfixed by what they observed. The walls and the ceiling were painted a dark, penetrating red. The only light in the room came from two candles burning slowly on a table set in the middle of the room. The low candlelight caused dark shadows on the red walls, making them blend into the room, so that one momentarily lost his depth perception. The hardwood floor, unlike the walls and ceiling, was painted black. It hadn't appeared a large room when they had first entered, but as their eyes slowly adjusted to the dim light of the candles burning away on the low table, they could see that they were indeed in an enormous room.

Consuelo Hawkins bolted the door behind them. The room had three large windows, two on the west wall and another on the north. Beautifully made draperies, also red in color, hung ornately at each window; black shades completely covered the windows, so that the room was secluded. Consuelo Hawkins walked briskly to each window, and released the binding which had kept the curtains to the sides of each window. Now the draperies covered the windows and shades completely. It was fairly obvious the old woman wanted as much privacy as she could possibly attain.

She approached Ross and Monica. "Now," she said to them in a low whisper. "I've placed these chairs here for the two of you. Please listen carefully—you must remain seated here at all times no matter what may happen. Under no circumstances should you attempt to move. And please remain completely silent throughout the ritual; that's important also. I must have complete silence lest all may be for naught." She again indicated the chairs and remained there until both of them sat down. "You won't disappoint me, I'm sure."

"We'll certainly try not to," Ross said. He turned and nodded at Monica.

"All right now," she went on, standing in front of them. "Let me briefly explain at least a part of what you are about to witness. For many years now, I've performed the ritual you are about to partake. I speak of summoning not only the spirits of the dead, but in communicating with non-human entities. Possibly the most famous conjuration of non-human entities is one in which the sorceress summons Vassago, one of the seventy-two demonic intelligences that exist in the spirit world—a world of demons. Much has been written of Vassago, and some who have studied witchcraft in the past several hundred years have known him well, but today—and I speak of this century—I dare say that no other living witch knows his spirit as well as I do." She appeared more excited with each word she spoke, totally involved in what she was telling them. The tone of her voice changed abruptly, and they were no longer listening to the woman who possessed that high-pitched, crackling voice with which they had been greeted earlier that day. Her eyes became alive, containing a vivid reflection of the candlelight.

"Vassago!" she said in a sharp whisper; she then repeated the name jubilantly. "Vassago! The mighty prince of the nature of Agares, who declares things past, present and to come, and discovers that which has been lost or hidden.

"So great is the power of almighty Vassago that he is not bound by any sidereal or solar rules of time, and therefore may be summoned at any hour of the day or night. And I myself call him only in matters of extreme perplexity, when all lesser methods of divination have failed me. He is one of the seventy-two demons; he is a being formed out of primordial fire eons and eons before man evolved into his present shape, and he is of an intelligence far superior to that of most men alive today.

"Ah, it appears I've been much carried away in speaking of the prince Vassago, for you didn't come here to witness his summoning. No, for tonight, the two of you will witness not the summoning of Vassago, but the summoning of the spirit of Andrew Borlin. This is sometimes a much more delicate and dangerous operation, strange as it may seem to you, than the summoning of demons."

Her eyes gleamed with excitement. "Now, I must ready myself, for I can sense the time is near. Now then, if I may have from you complete quiet."

Having said that, she turned her back to them and walked to the small table in the middle of the room.

Since walking into the room, Monica hadn't had the opportunity to examine its contents, including various items which she had seen on the table; now, as she sat there silently next to Ross, she began looking about the room.

The table in front of them was arranged as some kind of altar; it was covered with a black silk cloth which almost touched the floor on the sides. Near the front of the table was a rod made of wood, approximately eighteen inches long; it was connected with a fine piece of twine to two other wooden rods extending from each end of the first rod to the back of the table, where the two pieces met, forming an equilateral triangle. The triangle pointed east. To the right side of the table was a stick or wand of lacquered wood of about twelve inches in length. On this stick, as if with a wood-burning iron, had been inscribed certain lines and symbols which Monica could barely make out. Inside the triangle was a small rectangular platform which looked like a jewelry box; on top of this platform was a heavy stone of glass or crystal which was slightly hazy but transparent.

On each side of the table and slightly behind the triangle formed by the three sticks, were the two candlesticks which contained the burning candles. The candlesticks were also wooden and engraved with the same letters and symbols carved onto the wooden wand.

A crude, white ring or circle had been painted on the black floor, completely encircling the altar, leaving a space of about three feet extending from the line to the edge of the table. A few inches outside the west arc of the circle was another equilateral triangle which had also been painted onto the floor. It was much larger than the one formed by the wooden rods on the table. Inside it was a human skull, or the replica of one. Monica wasn't certain Ross had seen it, so she nudged him and pointed to the skull. He turned to her and merely nodded, acknowledging he had already seen it.

Consuelo Hawkins remained hunched over the small table, but Ross and Monica couldn't see what she was doing. Monica felt somewhat ridiculous sitting there, waiting for the old woman to begin the ritual. She was growing uncomfortable in the stuffy room and already, she was becoming bored. Out of the corner of her eye, she studied Ross to see whether she could tell how he was reacting to all this. As she had anticipated, he sat there almost motionless, watching the old lady, and apparently taking his presence in this room seriously, awaiting the happening of some momentous occasion—an event surely he had no reason to believe would arrive.

On the table were various objects, including what to Monica appeared to be two incense burners and another container. Consuelo Hawkins took one of the containers and began placing a white powder into one of the burners, causing it to smoke. Immediately, a strong odor began filling the room. It was a strange, almost repugnant odor, which Monica was certain would remain with them, for there appeared to be no ventilation into the room.

The old woman took an object from one of the pockets of the black robe she wore, and placed it inside the triangle formed on the table. Ross could make out it was a photograph of someone, but the old woman was blocking his view and he couldn't identify the face. Finally, she turned around and approached Ross and Monica. In her hands, she carried two chains, with a heavy brass object in the shape of a pentacle attached to each. Hurriedly, she placed one of the chains around Monica's neck, then placed the other around Ross' neck.

"Wear these during the ritual," she whispered, "for otherwise harm may come to you. Do not be afraid—this will protect you from the possibility of evil spirits entering your body and possessing your soul."

Ross only nodded. Looking up at Consuelo Hawkins, he noticed that she too was wearing around her neck a brass pentacle similar to the one she had given each of them. Before she turned away, he noticed the old woman's eyes. Earlier that day, when he had first laid eyes on the woman, Ross had dismissed them as insignificant, but now he realized he had been wrong, for her eyes were now very much alive, seemingly burning in anticipation of the sight of something awesome that was to come.

As the woman walked back to the table, Ross turned quickly to look at the photograph. It was badly worn around the edges and yellowed and cracked, but he could now vaguely make it out—it was a picture of Andrew Borlin. Although he had only met the man a few times, and then, only for short periods, he still remembered the face.

Consuelo Hawkins approached the west side of the altar and again bent slightly over it, facing east. She took a small metal container and moved it over the photograph; a few drops of water trickled from the container onto the photograph. She then lifted the incense burner, which was now smoking heavily, and moved it too above the photograph, allowing the smoke to surround it momentarily before it lifted.

She put the burner aside and then took the wand with the carved inscriptions. Holding the wand in her right hand above the photograph, she traced an imaginary cross in the air and then surrounded the cross with an imaginary circle. Her eyes penetrated into the invisible objects she was forming with the wand. And now, another sudden change seemed to come over the old woman, as she began to speak in a low voice. She was half-speaking, half-singing, the strange words that came from her mouth.

> Colpriziana Offina Alta Nestera Fuaro Menut
> I name thee Andrew Borlin;
> Thou art Andrew Borlin.

When she had completed these words, still carrying the wand in her right hand, she cautiously picked up the photograph in her left hand, and then proceeded to walk backwards in a clockwise direction to the rim of the circle at the other end of the table. There, facing away from the table, toward the east, she held the wand over the photograph and began the incantation once more:

> Spirit of Andrew Borlin, deceased,
> thou mayest now approach the gates of the east
> to answer truly my liege demands.
> Berald, Beroald, Balbin!
> Gab, Gabor, Agaba!
> Arise, arise I charge and command thee.

Having finished the recital, she moved backward once more, again clockwise around the rim of the circle; this time she stopped at the south end of the table. Here, she repeated the exact words she had said moments before, except that now, she referred in the incantation to the gates of the south. When she had finished, once more, she continued moving completely around the table, ninety degrees at a time, and each time facing outwardly, until finally she had completed the four quarters of the circle.

Then, staring beyond the space in front of her, as if she were looking beyond the red wall into some faraway place, she began once again uttering strange ritual words, this time in a sharp and high-pitched, almost wailing voice.

"I conjure and command thee, O Spirit Andrew Borlin, by Him who spake and it was done by the Most Holy and Glorious Names Adonai, El, Elohim, Elohe, Zebaoth, Elion, Escherce, Jah, Tetragrammaton, Sadai. Appear forthwith and show thyself to me, here outside this circle in fair and human shape, without horror or deformity and without delay!

"Come at once from whatever part of the world and answer my questions. Come at once, visibly and pleasantly, and do whatever I desire, for thou art conjured by the Name of the Everlasting Living and True God, Heliorem. I also conjure thee by the real name of thy God, to whom thou owest obedience, and by the name of the Prince who rules over thee."

Finally, she stood there in silence. She remained in that same position, without apparent movement—not even as much as taking one short breath. She appeared to be waiting—waiting for something to happen.

Ross and Monica had been sitting there obediently, listening to the bizarre chants and utterings coming from the old woman —seemingly mesmerized by what they witnessed. After two or three long minutes of silence, the woman began to move once again; she took incense from another container and placed it in a thurible to burn. As it began to smoke heavily, a smile of apparent satisfaction crossed her face. She had set the photograph back on the table and she now placed the wand over the photograph. Again came the weird jargon from within her. As she finished each line of the chant, she would strike the photograph gently with the end of the wand. Her voice became even lower now and it seemed no longer a human voice at all, but of some strange and unknown animal crying in the night.

> By the Mysteries of the deep,
> by the flames of Banal,
> by the power of the east,
> and by the silence of the night,
> by the holy rites of Hecate,
> I conjure and exorcise thee, spirit Andrew Borlin,
> to present thyself here,
> and answer truly our demands.
> So mote it be!

She replenished the thurible with more incense and powder. Then suddenly, with two quick breaths, she put out the two candles, plunging the room into total darkness.

In the darkness, a sudden fear overcame Monica. She quickly turned to Ross, but it was pitch dark and she couldn't see even a shadow or his silhouette. Immediately, she sensed a panic come over her when she feared he was suddenly gone. Quickly, she reached toward the place where he had been sitting and her hand came upon his shoulder. She felt relieved and immediately held on to his arm. Ross realized she was afraid and he placed his hand over hers reassuringly, but said nothing.

A minute or so passed since the old lady had put out the candles. Then they heard the old woman's voice again; this time it came from somewhere near the place where they had noticed the large triangle with the human skull inside it.

Although Ross and Monica could not see her, Consuelo Hawkins was kneeling down facing the large triangle painted on the floor. She crossed her arms to her breast, saying, "Allay Fortission, Fortissio, Allynsen Roa!"

She repeated these same words twice, then remained kneeling in complete silence, again apparently in some kind of meditation.

Monica's eyes hadn't yet adjusted to the dark and she thought they never would; she felt tempted to light a match or to turn on the light switch. Even with Ross at her side, his hand holding on to her, she was overcome by a strong sensation of fear. She wanted the ritual, which had as yet failed to produce anything but the fear within her, to come to an end.

After a considerable length of time had passed, there came first a spark of light and then a burning flame as the old woman, having risen from the floor, struck a match to relight the candles. She had returned to the table. Once having lit the candles, she closed her eyes, and nodded, as if acknowledging the sudden appearance of something or someone else in the room, but neither Ross nor Monica was able to see anything.

In that deep, resounding voice that was not hers, Consuelo Hawkins slowly pronounced Andrew Borlin's name three times. "Andew Borlin. Andrew Borlin. Andrew Borlin." She extended both arms out to each side to form a cross. She then opened her eyes wide and stood there with an expressionless stare on her face, waiting for something to happen; they waited and waited, but nothing occurred. Soon, the old lady's face registered disappointment and Ross knew immediately that the ritual had failed to produce the spirit of Andrew Borlin.

She let her arms drop slowly to her sides and walked backwards to the east end of the table, facing west across and beyond the altar. She took white powder once more and again placed it above the burning coals in the thurible; as she did so, she uttered:

Go, go, departed shade Andrew Borlin
by Omgroma Epin Sayoc
Satony, Degony, Eparigon
Galiganon, Zogogen, Ferstigon.

We license thee depart into the proper place
and be there peace between us evermore.
So mote it be!

When she had finished, she faced Ross and Monica. She stood there, as if in a daze, and said absolutely nothing to them; she appeared extremely tired and emotionally exhausted from what had transpired during the last hour. Still without saying a word, she walked over to the wall near the doorway and switched on the ceiling light. Monica appeared relieved that it was all over; she attempted not to show it, for she suddenly felt sorry for Consuelo Hawkins. The old woman returned to the table and extinguished the flames before walking to where Ross and Monica remained seated.

"Did either of you," she asked in a weak voice, "feel the presence of anyone or anything foreign in this room near the end of the ritual?"

"I didn't," Ross said. He looked over at Monica.

The old lady turned her attention to Monica and simply waited for her reply.

"Neither did I," Monica said softly. "Were we supposed to?"

"Not necessarily," Consuelo Hawkins answered. "But it was entirely possible that one of you might have, young lady, aside from myself. It would depend, of course, on whether your power of concentration was centered around what I was attempting to do." She sighed and paused to catch her breath. "Andrew Borlin's spirit did not appear before us tonight," she went on. "I'm sure you have assumed that much, by now, for you neither heard nor saw anything that would have led you to believe otherwise. And how true that is. I've failed once again.

"But, someone or something was here tonight. That is why I asked if you had felt its presence. I did! Yes, tonight was much different than the other failures. On this occasion, I felt a strong, magnetic pull emanating from the east—from some unknown spirit which I'm certain entered this room. It wasn't Andrew Borlin, of that much I'm sure. But someone or something else came here, attempting to communicate with us. Are both of you positive you felt nothing at all—no foreign or strange thoughts in your minds—no one attempting to speak to you or think for you?"

Ross and Monica both shook their heads.

"Whatever was here conveyed something to me about Andrew Borlin. Something having to do with his not being available to appear and that he never would be, because—because he did not belong to the world of the dead. Only faintly was I able to receive this strange and perplexing message. But now I'm sure of it; I was right!"

Ross and Monica glanced at one another, puzzled.

"I don't understand what you're getting at, Miss Hawkins," Ross said.

"I'm sorry—I must be talking in riddles. Let me explain. It's as I suspected long ago. And if we assume as true what I've always suspected to be the case, it would surely explain his spirit not appearing tonight and why I've failed in the past. After all, it shouldn't have been a difficult matter arousing his spirit, for we knew each other well. You see, in rituals such as the one I conducted tonight, it is easier to communicate with those we were close to or knew well here in the world of the living." She paused, watching Ross and Monica with extremely tired eyes.

"What is it you've suspected before?" Ross asked. "What do you mean when you say Andrew Borlin does not belong to the world of the dead?"

She turned and lifted her gaze up toward the ceiling. She still appeared tired but by now, she had regained some of her strength and she managed a smile as she stared upward.

"I mean," she replied slowly, "that I strongly suspect Andrew Borlin is not dead but is very much alive! Here, on this earth, like you and me."

CHAPTER 19

ROSS and Monica exchanged glances, thinking they had either misunderstood what the old woman had said or that she was joking. Ross smiled at Consuelo Hawkins. "You're speaking figuratively, of course," he said.

"I most certainly am not, young man," she answered, a stern expression on her face. "I meant exactly what I said, quite literally." The ceiling light appeared to be bothering her for she squinted her eyes. "That's the only possible explanation that can follow from what's happened tonight. I tell you positively there was some spirit here in the room with us a moment ago and it communicated with me. And of course this would explain why I've failed in the past. I would have succeeded, I tell you. If he were dead, that is."

She paused in thought. "But he's not dead; I'm certain of that. The spirit was correct."

"Are you saying you spoke to a spirit a minute ago and that it told you Andrew Borlin wasn't dead?" Ross asked.

"No, I can't truthfully say *I* communicated with it. But *it* communicated a message to me; it wasn't a message from Borlin. Communicating with the spirits isn't a simple matter, for they often speak in vague and ambiguous terms, so that this spirit didn't actually tell me that Andrew Borlin wasn't dead as you. put it. But what it did say was that he would never appear for he didn't belong to the world of the dead. Can't you see, he couldn't be summoned tonight, nor at any other time, for that matter, simply because he isn't dead—he's alive!"

"But how can you say that? Andrew Borlin died some twenty years ago."

"These matters aren't that simple to explain, Mr. Blair. Witchcraft and black magic are arts that require a tremendous amount of skill and feeling before one is truly able to understand them at all—and terribly complicated arts, at that. Only a handful of us are knowledgeable enough to handle it well. What I'm getting at is that spirits don't always communicate with us, the living, by the use of words, as you and I communicate in our world. Spirits sometimes implant thoughts in us and feelings too that wouldn't otherwise be there. Premonitions, some believers theorize, for example, are actually messages sent by a spirit, warning a living person of some danger or some tragedy that is to come to him or to a close friend or relative. That manner of communication is unknown to us, but the means of communication is there nevertheless. The fact that we the living have been unable to develop the ability to use it doesn't negate its existence; it lies in the mind dormant. Spirits are superior to us in that way for they know how to use the power."

She moved her eyes from Ross to Monica, then back again. "So then, what I'm saying is that it was a thought implanted in my mind by this spirit that has informed me Andrew Borlin is definitely not among the dead."

"But why would this spirit you speak of suddenly appear at all," Monica asked, "when you didn't even intend to summon it?"

"Because," Consuelo Hawkins replied, "this spirit was only trying to be helpful. It's not unusual in these matters—it happens often enough that a spirit that is not being called comes forth for some reason or another. This particular spirit must have heard my calling out to Andrew Borlin and it only wanted to communicate to me that I wouldn't succeed."

"And you assume from all this that Andrew Borlin is alive

and that he didn't die years ago as we've been led to believe?"
It was Ross who spoke.

"That's correct, Mr. Blair."

"But it can't be, Miss Hawkins," he stated incredulously.
"It just can't be. My ex-wife attended her father's funeral. She
witnessed the burial. He had called her to come to him because
he was in poor health and didn't expect to live. And when she
arrived here, she found she was too late—he had died. She
later obtained copies of the death certificate, certified by a doctor."

Consuelo Hawkins laughed. "I see by what you're saying
that I must explain some other matters to you—other things
I've always suspected about Borlin—before I'm able to convince you that what I speak of is in fact the truth."

She turned away from them. "Come, it's rather stuffy in this
room. Why don't we go into the parlor where I can serve the
two of you some hot tea while we talk. You'll be much more
comfortable there, I'm sure."

They left the room; Monica was relieved for she felt the
beginning of a headache, caused, she was certain, by the lack
of ventilation in the room. They returned to the front of the
house by way of the long hallway. The old woman accompanied them into the parlor. There, she asked them to sit down
and then excused herself. She went through the corridor and
disappeared into some other part of the house.

Ross and Monica sat down on the dusty sofa. Monica appeared eager to speak to Ross but she waited until she was
certain the old lady wasn't within hearing distance.

"The thought hadn't entered my—" she began loudly, before Ross stopped her.

"Shhh, not so loud!" he said to her. "I don't want her to
hear what we might say."

"The thought hadn't entered my mind earlier," Monica continued, this time in a low whisper, "but now, after what happened back there, I'm wondering whether the old woman's
suffering from some mental imbalance. I disagree with Sheriff
Dominguez; I think she's becoming senile."

"Not necessarily," Ross whispered back.

"Do you realize what she's asking us to believe?" Monica

said, speaking louder.

"Shhh. Keep your voice down; she might hear us."

"I don't care if she hears us." She was back to a whisper. "I think it's about time we let her know we're not believers of any of this mumbo-jumbo stuff she's talking about."

He grinned. "I was certainly beginning to think back there a moment ago that *you* were beginning to believe in it. You were a little scared back in that room, weren't you?"

"Of course I was; I won't deny it. But that doesn't mean I was beginning to believe in what she was trying to do."

"Honestly, Monica, I don't think she's trying to make believers out of us. She's merely explaining to us what *she* believes, and I think she couldn't care less whether or not you or I believe any part of it. After all, why should she care if we do or don't?"

"I think I detect in your tone of voice that you're falling for all of this—including her rather absurd assertion that Carol's father is alive."

"No, of course I'm not falling for it. But let's hear her out. Don't you think it's rather interesting?"

"I can't say I consider it necessarily interesting; I'd say her assertions are more the product of an unusually strong—and slightly warped—imagination."

"Well, I consider it interesting—unusual, yes—but interesting, nevertheless." He watched Monica carefully and smiled. *"And* scary," he continued. "You must admit, the ritual back there affected you."

She didn't return his smile. "Of course it affected me. It would have anyone. But I still get the impression she's trying to pull the wool over our eyes—*and,* that you're falling for it. Besides—"

"Be quiet!" Ross interrupted. "She's coming. I understand how you feel, darling, but please try not to say anything that might offend her. I want to hear all she's got to say about Carol's father, and I'm afraid she won't if she realizes how you feel about this. In fact, it might be wise if you said nothing at all. Let me ask all the questions, and you just listen, all right?"

"All right, if you insist."

He placed his hand on hers. "That's my girl."

Monica couldn't help smiling at him. She could tell he was absolutely fascinated by the old lady and was enjoying every minute of the evening.

Consuelo Hawkins walked into the room. In her hands, she carried a tray with three settings and the tea in a small container. She set the tray on the coffee table.

"Please help yourselves to the tea," she said as she walked back to a chair and sat down. "Excuse my not serving you some, but I'm suddenly exhausted. You don't mind, do you?"

"Of course not," Monica said. "I'll be glad to pour." She leaned forward to reach the tray and begin pouring.

"You'd like some, wouldn't you, Miss Hawkins?" Monica asked.

"Yes, please, but only half a cup. I take mine without sugar, please." She smiled at Monica as she took the cup that was offered to her. "Thank you, Miss Ashley. There's cream there too if you prefer your tea with it." She leaned back on the chair cautiously, being careful not to spill the tea. She sipped slowly.

"I'm most anxious for you to go on with what you were telling us, Miss Hawkins," Ross said.

"Yes, I was sure that you would be, Mr. Blair. I knew I'd arouse your interest." She paused in deep thought. "Let's see, where did I leave off?"

"You were about to tell us about some earlier suspicions you had concerning Andrew Borlin's death."

"Oh, yes, so I was." Cautiously, she took another sip of her tea and leaned back once again, apparently relaxed. Well," she continued, "I suppose you're wanting me to get on with it." A faint smile came to her face as she contemplated Ross' interest. "You see, tonight isn't the only time I've suspected Andrew Borlin was still alive. I've suspected that much from the beginning, soon after his death was supposed to have occurred."

"You sound positive and determined that he was never dead," Ross said.

"Yes—I am. Now more so than ever before. I believe that before I left to fetch the tea, you stated that your ex-wife had been to her father's funeral and that she saw copies of the death certificate."

"Yes."

"But even so, and even if she saw Borlin's body, it doesn't necessarily mean it was her father who was buried. It was merely his body—not Andrew Borlin."

Ross shot a puzzled look at the old woman. "As a matter of fact," he volunteered, "she told me she never got the opportunity to view the body. She tried to, but was never able to."

"But what's the difference, anyway?" Monica asked, thinking the conversation was becoming ridiculous. "What I mean, Miss Hawkins," she went on, "you said Carol might have seen her father's body buried but not Andrew Borlin. That doesn't make any sense to me." She looked at Ross. "I'm sorry, but I just don't understand what you mean. What's the difference?"

The old woman laughed. It was prolonged laughter. "Ordinarily," she explained, "to people who think of death in only one way, as I'm sure both of you do, there's no difference whatsoever. I'm speaking of death in the conventional sense. You think of it in that way only because you think of a person's soul belonging to one and only one body and that is all, without realizing that the soul and the body are two separate entities. The soul always exists and is able to live on even when the physical body dies in the conventional sense.

"Usually, then, a person thinks only in terms of one person possessing one body and never another." She paused as she sipped the tea. She directed here eyes at Monica. "Have you ever heard of the term *transmigration,* Miss Ashley?"

"Why, yes," Monica replied softly. She looked up at Consuelo Hawkins. She noticed the woman was waiting for some definition. "As I understand the word, it means moving from one country to another—doesn't it?"

"I think, Monica," Ross broke in, "that Miss Hawkins is using the word in a different context. Am I correct, Miss Hawkins?"

"Yes, precisely, Mr. Blair," Consuelo Hawkins replied. "The term, Miss Ashley, may of course be used to mean what you've just indicated. That's the word's broader meaning. But in black magic, the term is a highly technical one and is only used when one speaks of the passage of the soul at death into another person's body. It means literally to be reborn at death in someone else's body." There was an extremely somber expression on her face.

Ross was intrigued; he wanted the woman to continue. "And that is what you believe happened to Andrew Borlin?" he asked.

"Not just happened, Mr. Blair," Consuelo Hawkins corrected him. *"Transmigration* of the soul doesn't ever just *happen* to anyone. It is planned!"

"Planned?"

"Yes—planned; you heard me correctly. In this case, by Andrew Borlin himself. I'm convinced of it now, after what happened tonight."

"And you were going to tell us something of Andrew Borlin that made you suspect this even before tonight."

"And so I shall, Mr. Blair. It has to do with those experiments. He led everyone to believe that the experiments were purely scientific, since he was a scientist. But he also was a student of the occult, remember. I'm now convinced that he was actually making the necessary and complex preparations to enter someone else's body. Remember what I told you earlier, that he studied witchcraft. And I recall that once, long before his death, he made inquiries of me concerning *transmigration.* I myself know very little of this old art, except the basics—but I referred Borlin to several old references which gave detailed accounts of it. I'm now satisfied that he discovered the secret of this rare art. I dare say few persons are alive that know it well." She was watching Ross carefully. "You, Mr. Blair— you've given me the impression you knew something of transmigration before tonight. As I've explained it, that is."

"I've heard of its practice in ancient times. But I must be honest with you, Miss Hawkins, I've always considered it nothing more than a superstition carried on through the centuries. It's like reincarnation. What you're saying is so unbelievable, though. I certainly hope you don't mind my saying so; I appreciate what you believe in, Miss Hawkins." He glanced briefly at Monica. "We both do."

"You needn't worry about hurting my feelings, young man —I don't mean to force my beliefs on anyone, but I'm certain that if you knew enough about what I'm talking about, you'd certainly begin to believe it. It's always difficult for those who know little of the black arts to believe in the existence of supernatural powers—especially something as powerful as transmigration. Only because such people fail to understand the nature of such power, do they not believe in its existence. It is only those who are able to use the power who truly believe in it."

"What body do you suspect the soul of Andrew Borlin to have possessed?"

"That, Mr. Blair, I cannot tell you, for I don't honestly know." Her eyes weren't on Ross or Monica but were looking past them, staring into empty space beyond the wall. "But," she continued, "Baltazar Montoya helped Borlin in these experiments of his, and I suspect he helped him prepare for the actual soul transfer, so I wouldn't be at all surprised if Montoya knows. Since Borlin had the utmost confidence in him, if there was such a soul passage, then Montoya had to be in on it. Borlin needed someone's help—of that, I'm absolutely certain, for he couldn't have carried it out by himself. And Montoya, I think, is the person who supplied that help."

"What kind of help?"

"I'm sure the thought has already occurred to both you and Miss Ashley that transmigration requires the sacrifice of someone else's body; that is, the body which has been selected to be possessed by the soul. And it may readily be assumed that force will have to be used, for it would be rare indeed for one to give up his body willingly. So a body had to be taken."

"You mean murder!" Monica exclaimed.

Consuelo Hawkins gave out a soft chuckle. "Murder, you say, Miss Ashley? Well, not exactly in the way legal scholars define the word, for in performing the ritual, it is absolutely necessary that one not injure or damage the body that is to be possessed. The body chosen, of course, must be intact and otherwise perfectly healthy. But once the transfer has been completed, the person who originally occupied the body sacrificed ceases to exist, in a manner of speaking. Putting it rather simply, one might explain it by saying that another's body is stolen in the process. The body, after all, even though it is physically alive, is only something that contains something else within it that is also alive—the soul. In the sense then, that the soul of some person is substituted for that of another, it may be called murder, Miss Ashley. The body is kept alive and well, but the soul originally in it is robbed of it, and cannot exist in this world without it."

"Do you honestly believe that Baltazar Montoya helped Borlin perform this soul transfer," Ross said, "and that he's kept this secret since?"

"I wouldn't be surprised if he knows everything there is to know about it, for as I've told you, Andrew Borlin required help—it would have been impossible for him to have done it alone—and of course, the fact that he confided so much in Montoya. And then too, I wouldn't be at all surprised if Borlin paid Montoya a substantial sum of money to maintain his silence. If I confronted Montoya, I would think he'd speak of what he knows. But there is something else that happened once concerning Montoya that I haven't told you about. Once, not too long ago, when he was drunk, he happened to come in here to discuss matters involving the farm. Somehow, Andrew Borlin was mentioned in our conversation—yes, I remember now, Montoya was inquiring about an earlier ritual I had attempted to conjure up Borlin's spirit. Anyway, as I said, on this particular occasion, Montoya was terribly drunk indeed, and he began praising Borlin and in the process, he mentioned something to the effect that Borlin's black magic was better than mine, for *he* had found a way to live on forever, and I would some day be dead like everyone else. I remember asking him to explain himself but he said no more about it. I placed little significance then in what he said for I thought him too drunk to be making any sense. But now, in a different light, I know what he meant." She sighed deeply. "I must speak to Montoya. And I'll get him to tell me the truth." She smiled. "To think the old drunkard has managed to keep all this from me for so many years."

Ross' interest in the discussion became more intense and he kept asking question after question of Consuelo Hawkins, not only about transmigration but of Baltazar Montoya. Ross was curious about him now. What kind of person was he? Where exactly did he live on her farm? He too, Ross told the old woman, was interested in what Montoya had to say of Andrew Borlin's experiments. There was only one other matter, Ross said to the old lady, that he wished to inquire about.

"And what is that?" Consuelo Hawkins asked.

"My ex-wife, Carol, mentioned to me a certain doll made of wax. Did Andrew Borlin ever discuss with you this doll that he was obsessed with? Supposedly, it was made in his likeness."

"Ah, the waxen image he would have protected with his life if he had to, and which he never let out of his sight."

"You *did* know of it, then. Did you and he ever discuss it?"

"We certainly did—numerous times. That doll definitely became an obsession with him, as you indicated. It turned out to have a tremendous effect on his life. The image was actually one of the reasons why he and I became good friends, and why he chose this place to conduct his experiments. He had studied witchcraft before I met him, of course, and he had learned of me through someone where he used to work and that is how he happened to come here—to see me about the doll. He was interested in reversing the curse cast upon it.

"That doll was always in his thoughts and dreams." She stopped and glanced at Ross. "I assume you know of the doll's history?"

"Yes, Carol told me about it and how he had come to fear it."

"He grew terribly afraid of the spell. He feared its destruction or damage and this is why he guarded it with his life."

"What ever happened to it? My ex-wife told me that when she came here to see you about gathering her father's belongings, she looked for the box in which he had always kept the doll and she didn't find it."

"What didn't she find, the doll or the box?"

"Neither. She asked you about the box but you told her you knew nothing about it. It was a small black box she was looking for."

"Yes, I do remember her inquiries—a small black box. But I didn't relate what she was looking for with the image. Did she think she'd find the doll in that?"

"That's what she told me. She said she remembered her father keeping it in that box."

"That's strange. I don't recall such a box at all. When I first learned of the doll, he kept it in a medium-size, fire-proof container. It was a gray metal container, not black, and not small, as you've mentioned."

"He must have changed containers sometime after Carol last saw the doll."

"I suppose so. Didn't your ex-wife ever find the doll?"

"No—she didn't. The fact that it wasn't found appears to bear out your theory of transmigration."

The old lady's face displayed an impish smile. "Yes, it does, doesn't it? Only one person would have taken it—Andrew Borlin in another person's body." She spoke with a tone of confidence.

"You said a moment ago," Ross remarked, "that Borlin had initially contacted you with the purpose in mind of countering the spell placed on the doll by the witchdoctor."

"Yes."

"Did you ever make any attempt to overcome the spell?"

"On numerous occasions. I conducted rituals to counter any spell which might have existed. At the conclusion of each event, I assured him that whatever spell might have existed had been nullified and overcome by my magic. But I was never able to convince him that I spoke the truth—his fear of the waxen image was too great to overcome. That is, if in fact there ever was a curse on it. Borlin never actually knew for certain that there was, you know."

"Oh. No, I didn't know that."

"Yes. You see, when Borlin got his hands on the doll, it had been completed, yes, but he actually had no way of knowing whether the witchdoctor's ritual casting the spell had ever been performed. That was impossible to learn, for the witchdoctor was killed in the struggle for the doll. You knew of that, I assume?"

"Yes, I knew."

They spoke a while longer and finally, when Ross noticed Consuelo Hawkins appeared extremely tired, he knew it was time to go.

"Miss Hawkins," he said, "we certainly appreciate your generous hospitality and your invitation. It's been an interesting evening, I assure you, but now I think we've been imposing on you for too long and it's time we were on our way."

He and Monica stood up.

"It's been my pleasure having you as my guests tonight, Mr. Blair. I'm tired, of course, but I've enjoyed the conversation." She ran her fingers through her coarse hair. "Although, I know I'm a long way from convincing either of you that what I said tonight is the truth."

Ross and Monica exchanged glances again and smiled at the old woman. They were standing at the front door. Consuelo Hawkins opened it for them. "I certainly hope you find your daughter, Mr. Blair."

"Thank you. I appreciate your concern. Thank you again for a most enjoyable conversation."

"As I said, the pleasure was mine."

Before they said goodbye, Ross asked the old woman that should she learn of Arthur Conrad's whereabouts, he would appreciate her contacting Sheriff Dominguez. She assured him that she would, but reminded him it was unlikely the professor would reappear.

Consuelo Hawkins stood by the open doorway as Ross and Monica walked down the wooden stairway of the porch.

CHAPTER 20

ON the return to Esperanza, Ross spoke of the old woman's strange tale. Monica seemed unimpressed and reiterated her opinion that Consuelo Hawkins suffered from senility. She was convinced her opinion was borne out by the old woman's fantastic tales of 'conjuring up spirits' and transmigration of souls.

Upon reaching the outskirts of the town, Ross became silent, but Monica still spoke of her impressions of the old lady. Ross was in deep thought as he listened to only bits and pieces of what Monica was saying. He reflected on what had happened back there at the Hawkins home. Something was beginning to bother him.

He pulled into a service station. We're almost out of gas," he said, breaking the silence. "It's a good thing I noticed— needle's on empty."

A young attendant appeared; Ross asked him to fill up the tank and to check under the hood.

"There's a Coke machine," Ross said to Monica, nodding toward the filling station building. "Wouldn't you like a Coke?"

"I'm a little thirsty, but not for a whole one," Monica said. "Would you split one with me?"

"Sure." He opened the door. "I'll be right back. Anything else? I see a snack vending machine in there."

"No, thanks. Just a Coke."

He left the car and walked to the soft drink machine. He returned to Monica's side of the car. Standing by the open window, he took a drink and then handed the bottle to her. He stood there momentarily, then entered the car.

"You know," he said, taking the Coca-Cola bottle from Monica, "I've been thinking about what happened back there tonight. I can't get it out of my mind." He took another drink.

"So I've noticed," Monica replied. She grinned. "What else is new?"

"Seriously, Monica, I bet you're going to think I'm out of my mind for saying what I'm about to say, but please bear me out."

"I'm listening, darling."

He cleared his throat. "I think we should pay a visit to that cemetery where Andrew Borlin was buried. It's around here somewhere."

"What on earth for?"

"Here's where the crazy part comes in—I'd like to dig up his grave to see what we'll find—or don't find, whichever."

Monica turned to him in disbelief. "You've got to be kidding, Ross!"

"No, I'm not—I'm serious. I knew you'd think I'd flipped my lid."

"You're absolutely right about that. What you're saying is wild—crazy. I'm amazed at you. You're not going to tell me you're honestly beginning to believe what the old woman told us back there, are you? Darling, we're living in the twentieth century, remember? Not back there during the Salem witch hunts when apparently everybody believed in witches. What she told us about Carol's father being alive because of this transfiguration that's supposed to have taken place long ago, or whatever, it's too fantastic a thing to swallow."

"The word is *transmigration,* darling."

"Well, whatever it's called, for the life of me I can't believe you're talking this way. It's as if that ritual she performed back there has affected you somehow."

He laughed softly. "It's true that our discussion with the old lady has affected me, but only in that it started me thinking about a couple of things that have never been completely clear to me to begin with."

"But what if—"

"Please, darling, listen to me for a minute, O.K.?"

"Oh, all right."

"I'm not saying that what the old lady told us is true—it's extremely unbelievable, I agree."

"And impossible, I should add."

"But I'm firmly convinced she believes it herself not as a product of the delusions of an old woman suffering from senility but as a product of her belief in witchcraft."

"What's the difference?"

"The difference is that a belief in witchcraft, no matter how absurd one might consider it, isn't necessarily the product of senility. And what I'm getting at is that if one believes in witchcraft to the extent that one practices it, then one can easily believe in this thing called transmigration."

"It's still pretty way out, no matter how one looks at it—you'll have to agree, Ross."

"Granted. But Consuelo Hawkins still possesses a sharp mind, I think. Surely you could see that much in her, if you were to forget for the moment that she practices witchcraft, something that's looked down upon by the average person."

"I don't think one should totally ignore that fact."

"Anyway," he continued, ignoring her remark, "what she said about Andrew Borlin having possessed someone else's body started me thinking about something that's bothered me."

"What's that?"

"I'm sure you recall what I told you about Carol being somewhat mystified by what she considered to be unusual circumstances in connection with her father's death—and, the funeral. I think it's significant that she never did see the body, in light of what the old woman has told us."

"In what way?"

"Carol made several attempts to get the mortician's permission to view the body, remember. Each time, the mortician, very conveniently, wasn't there. Carol implied that she was intentionally being kept from seeing the body. And the question is—why?"

"It could be purely coincidental."

"It could be, I won't deny that. But then there's something else that bothered Carol—the fact that her father had always desired to be cremated. If so, why wasn't this wish carried out? People who believe in cremation usually take whatever steps are necessary to assure that it's done. So, if Andrew Borlin felt that strongly about it, surely he would have made certain before his death that someone he trusted would have taken care of it—someone like Baltazar Montoya, for example—the man who befriended him."

"Maybe he did entrust Montoya with the request, and Montoya simply failed to carry it out in the confusion after the death. Or possibly Andrew Borlin didn't get the chance to tell anyone. There are several possibilities."

"That's right. But the ones you've mentioned don't ring true, the way I look at it. You're forgetting, for example, the confidence Borlin placed in Montoya. I think we can be fairly certain of that and too, that Montoya must have earned this confidence. It follows that he would have made sure Borlin's last request was carried out. A friend just doesn't forget a dying request.

"As for the second possibility you've mentioned, that Borlin didn't pass on his last wish to anyone, that too is remote, since you'll recall that Carol's father was already ill when he telephoned her. He had already suffered the first heart attack, and therefore would have had plenty of time to tell Montoya.

"So darling, I won't be satisfied until I take a look at Borlin's grave. Tonight."

"Tonight?"

"Yes, tonight. You coming with me?"

"Ross, honestly! You're not really thinking of going to dig up a grave at the cemetery *tonight?*"

"Sure, why not?"

"Well, if for no other reason, because you might get caught doing it."

"Exactly—that's why we've got to do it while it's dark. It's against the law, you know, digging up graves without court order."

"That's what I'm getting at. You've got to see Sheriff Dominguez about this, if you really want to go through with it."

"We don't have time for that. Besides, I doubt seriously that Dominguez would have the authority to O.K. it himself—we'd need a judge's O.K., most likely, and I don't think we could get that, even if we had the time to do it."

"But how will you manage to do it—you'll need some equipment—something to dig with?"

"There's an old mercantile store on the other side of town that I noticed last night. It might still be open. If it's not, the place looked to me like someone lived there—maybe the owner." He glanced at his watch. "It's not that late; the owner probably won't mind opening up just long enough to sell us a shovel. I'll make it worth his while by offering him something extra. A shovel's all we'll need. That—and a little muscle." He smiled at her. "What do you say, you'll come with me, won't you?"

"And what happens if I say I won't?"

"Then I'll have to take you back to the hotel and leave you there while I go do it myself, I guess."

"I figured that much," Monica said, and she sighed deeply, knowing she wouldn't be able to dissuade him from what he had already set his mind on doing. "Oh, Ross, you know I'd rather go with you than sit back at the hotel wondering what may happen."

"It's settled then, we'll go."

Before leaving the station, Ross confirmed with the attendant that there was only one cemetery in the area, and asked directions.

It took them a couple of minutes to get through town and Ross turned onto the highway. To the right of the road, past the outskirts of the town, stood the old, wood-framed building housing Hillman's Mercantile and Hardware Supplies.

"It's closed, Ross."

"There's a light up above. Someone's still up."

"But I'm sure they won't appreciate you—"

"I'll go knock on the door," Ross said and he opened the door to get out of the car.

Monica protested again but to no avail. "Ross, we can probably find another store that's open."

"Are you kidding? We might find another store open, but not a hardware store, the only place where we'll ever find a shovel."

"Ross, you're being terribly inconsiderate."

"I'll make it worth Mr. Hillman's while for whatever inconvenience I cause him."

And he did make it worth Mr. Hillman's trouble, even though he had gotten the man out of bed. After paying him for two shovels, two pairs of working gloves, and a flashlight complete with batteries, Ross gave the old man an extra ten dollar bill. The man eagerly accepted Ross' kind offer, convinced he had earned it, although he had originally displayed displeasure for having been requested to re-open the store.

Monica continued her protests, pleading with Ross to abandon what she considered an incredible and ridiculous plan. "But Ross, you won't be able to do it alone. It's too much work for one person."

"You know, I thought of that while I was in there. I bet I can find someone to help me. That's why I bought two shovels."

"I can't believe any of this!"

Ross said nothing more. Instead, he drove back into town and after circling around fruitlessly for almost half an hour, he located his accomplice. He was a middle-aged man who had just left a bar and was getting into his car when Ross approached him. Monica waited in the car and although she couldn't hear what Ross was saying, she saw him display a $100 bill. She noticed the man nod his acceptance. Smooth talker, she thought of Ross.

"Is the man even sober?" Monica asked sarcastically when Ross entered the car.

Ross couldn't help laughing. "Yes," he answered. "He's agreed to follow us in his car."

"How in the world did you talk him into pulling off something like this?"

"I managed to hide the truth a bit. Told him I was an insurance investigator on a case, inquiring about a person's death. He fell for it. Before that, I simply assured myself he needed the money badly enough to risk it."

"But how can you trust a total stranger? He might turn you in."

"When he's been an accomplice? I doubt it. But even so, honey, let's face it, we're taking a risk as it is. Someone's bound to find out the grave's been tampered with, sooner or later. Besides, I plan to tell Sheriff Dominguez after it's all over with."

They had no trouble finding the cemetery. It was only a mile from the edge of town, off a dirt road which continued into rolling terrain and several small villages. They easily spotted the cemetery grounds from the highway. Ross drove the car through the entrance and continued down a narrow roadway to a point near the far end of the cemetery, underneath the sprawling branches of several large elms. The man in the second car pulled up alongside, exited the car, and waited silently for Ross' instructions.

"It's a good idea to make sure the cars won't be spotted from the road," Ross explained to Monica when she asked why he had parked where he had. He got out of the car, but noticed Monica made no effort to move. "Aren't you coming?"

She looked at him with pleading eyes. "I wish you'd change your mind about this, Ross. Won't you please reconsider and leave it to Sheriff Dominguez?"

"Now, Monica, we've gone through that already. It's out of the question."

He didn't wait for a response but walked to the back to remove the shovels and flashlight from the trunk. He returned to the front of the car shortly. Monica still hadn't gotten out.

"We've come this far, darling. Besides, I've already invested in this equipment." He rested the shovels against the car and began unscrewing the flashlight to insert the batteries. "So why don't you get out?" He opened the car door. The man who had accompanied them still said nothing, but he appeared surprised at Monica's reluctance.

Monica finally stepped out of the car. She stood to one side, while Ross readied the flashlight. She looked around. She could see, even in the dark, that the cemetery was located on several small hills. They had parked only a few feet away from the first grave markers. A chill came over her as she thought of Borlin's grave.

She turned and looked away from the cemetery toward the clump of trees further down the hill. A slight breeze picked up and created the rustling of leaves on the gigantic trees.

It was cool and the ground underneath her feet felt moist and soft. When the cool breeze had passed, it became still except for the sharp chirping of crickets coming from somewhere beyond the trees.

Monica turned to Ross. "You don't honestly think we're going to find his grave easily, do you?" she whispered.

He smiled at her but she couldn't see him. "You needn't whisper, darling. You won't wake anyone up out here."

"Oh, Ross, this is no time for your silly jokes."

He laughed. "I thought I was being rather witty, myself." His laugh tapered off. "It shouldn't take us long to find it. This flashlight will be useful." He looked around briefly. "But I had no idea the cemetery would be this large. I'm sorry I didn't get another flashlight. That way I could have started at one end, and you at the other."

"*No sirree,* not on your life, I wouldn't. I'm staying next to you, just in case."

"Just in case what?"

"Just in case anything should happen."

"Come now, nothing's going to happen."

"I wouldn't be too sure about that."

He didn't answer her. He screwed the flashlight cap back on and turned the switch. It gave a strong beam of light across a portion of the cemetery.

"Come on, let's get started. We'll start at this end up the hill here and work our way down toward the highway, then we'll come back on the next row of markers." He turned to his helper and motioned for him to follow them. Ross was grateful for the man's silence. Maybe it would remain with him once their task was completed, he thought.

Slowly, they began their search. Monica found it difficult walking on the soft ground, for her heels kept sinking into the moist soil. They went through the first row of the marked graves without success, then through the second and the third

—no marker. The depth of the cemetery had been deceiving in the night and it took them half an hour to cover the first five rows. Finally, on the sixth, they found the large granite monument they had been searching for.

"There it is," Ross said excitedly. He ran the beam of light through the letters and numbers chisled into the stone. They could see the name clearly:

ANDREW BORLIN
Born—April 12, 1891
Died—November 5, 1957

A cold chill ran down Monica's spine as she stared at the name on the marker.

"We may as well get started," Ross said and he handed the flashlight to Monica. He gave one of the shovels and a pair of gloves to the man. "Better leave the flashlight off so as not to draw any attention, Monica, should someone happen to come down the highway. We can see all right without it, and we can use it from time to time to see how we're progressing."

"It'll probably take you half the night to do this," Monica said impatiently. "Did you even stop to realize that?"

"I don't think it will," he replied confidently. It'll tire us, that's for sure. But I think the two of us can be through in two hours or so."

"Two hours! That's long enough."

He said nothing more as he and the man began to dig. The soil was moist and soft and Ross was relieved. Monica stood nearby watching the two men heave the dirt to one side. But she soon tired of this and began walking within the immediate vicinity. She became nervous and occasionally, she gazed up toward the highway, expecting the headlights of a car to appear at any moment.

Both men worked steadily for half an hour without resting. Ross stopped and took off his gloves to light a cigarette. He offered the man a cigarette.

"I don't smoke," he said softly.

They were the only words the man had spoken since they had arrived at the cemetery. He's probably thinking the less said, the less trouble, Ross thought and smiled in the darkness.

Ross took only a few puffs and then stomped out the cigarette before they resumed their work. After forty five minutes or so, Ross asked Monica to shine the light where they had been digging. She did so and was surprised at the amount of dirt that had been removed.

On and on the endless digging continued, until finally, their heads were flush with the ground. They would disappear into the hole momentarily, each time they bent down to shovel. The rhythmic sound of the shovels each time they forced them into the ground, followed by the thud of the dirt as it hit the pile which now surrounded the hole, became a part of the night sounds, along with the crickets chirping beyond the grouping of trees, and the far-off sound of a dog howling somewhere.

Finally, there came from the hole a loud, echoing thud as Ross' shovel struck an object.

"We've hit it," Ross' tired voice came from below. "I've hit the coffin."

Monica quickly walked over to the high pile of dirt.

"Give me some light down here, Monica!"

She focused the flashlight down to the bottom of the deep hole.

"My God, Ross, how creepy," she shuddered. "I'm scared to death."

"Not half as creepy as what we may find inside," Ross said as he began scraping and moving the rest of the dirt off the top of the coffin.

"Oh, Ross!"

Finally they had dug enough dirt to the sides of the coffin so that they could place their hands and feet to either side.

"O.K.," Ross said, "that's done. Here, Monica, would you please take the shovel?" He lifted it up to her; she took it and placed it next to the pile of dirt which had been accumulated. "We've made barely enough room to each side to stand in so that we can open it. You'll have to shine the light down here so we can see what we're doing."

"I can't, Ross!" Monica said sharply. "I don't want to look in it and I don't have the slightest intention of doing so."

"Now, settle down, Monica. You won't have to. You can aim the light down here so it hits the coffin and you turn away if you wish. But make sure you keep the beam of light steady. We'll have our hands full." He waited for her to move closer. "Get up here, near the edge—be careful, though. There. O.K., now turn the light on and shine it right down here while we try pulling up."

Monica stood near the edge cautiously; she braced herself before closing her eyes. She could hear the two men grunting and moving about as they tried forcing the coffin lid open, but she didn't dare open her eyes. Several minutes passed and the men were still tackling the lid.

"It's frozen shut after all these years," Ross finally said. "Probably corroded." He was out of breath, panting heavily.

"Or maybe it's locked," Monica volunteered. She had opened her eyes. "Some have locks on them."

"That may be, but I don't think so; it's probably just stuck with rust. I'll need something to pry it open and I can't use the shovel—it won't fit in here sideways." He thought for a moment. "Monica, would you please go to the car. You'll find the car keys there in my coat pocket. Take the flashlight along with you—you'll need it. Inside the trunk, you'll find a crowbar. Please bring it to me; that'll do it."

"All right." Monica left and walked cautiously back to the car, opened the trunk, and searched for the lever to the tire jack. She found it underneath the spare tire. Within a minute, she had returned to the open grave. She lowered the crowbar to Ross.

Almost immediately, she heard the scraping sound of the crowbar against the coffin. Suddenly, there was a sharp, snapping sound.

"Ah, I've gotten it!" Ross said.

"Ross, couldn't you get back up here and open it with something from up here. You could use a rope."

"Don't be silly, Monica," he said defiantly. "Whatever's down here has been here for twenty years. Being here or up there certainly isn't going to make any difference. Now, would you please shine the light down here so I can see?"

Monica did as he requested, turning her eyes away from the beam of light. She heard the creaking sound of the lid as Ross opened it slowly. Then, there was silence. She waited for Ross to say something but he didn't. She was still afraid to look down.

"Well, I'll be damned!" Ross said finally. "Just as I thought. Take a look, Monica. Can you see?"

She was still grasping the flashlight, her head turned away. "I'm scared to, Ross."

"There's nothing to be afraid of, silly. There's nothing down here but a pile of rocks!"

Slowly, Monica turned and looked downward; she opened her eyes. The lid had been pulled open to one side and the beam of light disclosed the contents of the coffin. The light was shining on a pile of rocks of various sizes. It took several seconds for her mind to register what exactly it was she was gazing at. But she was unable to comprehend the meaning of it.

"I don't understand," she said softly. "What does it mean?"

"I don't know exactly what it means," Ross said, "except that we can be fairly certain now that Andrew Borlin was never buried here. Whether he's still alive as the old lady claims he is, I don't know, but one thing we can be sure of—he was never buried at the funeral Carol attended."

"What's going on here?" the man finally spoke again, obviously perplexed by their discovery.

"I can't really say," Ross replied. "But even if I knew, you're better off not knowing."

The man simply nodded.

Ross examined the contents carefully to make sure he hadn't missed anything. Only then did he close the lid and proceed to climb out with some difficulty. He rested half an hour on the pile of dirt they had removed, talking to Monica about the meaning of their discovery. The man sat across from them on the other side of the grave.

It took them very little time to shovel the dirt back into the hole, but even then, it had grown late.

"Is this what you expected to find?" the man asked.

"I wasn't sure," Ross replied abruptly. He took out the $100 bill from his pocket and handed it to his nameless accomplice. "Thanks for your help."

"Don't mention it, fellow." He said nothing more and began walking in the direction of the cars. Within half a minute, he was on the road leading away from the cemetery.

Ross drove slowly back into town.

"What now?" Monica asked.

"I think that in the morning," Ross replied, "before we leave town, we better have a talk with Baltazar Montoya. He has a bit of explaining to do about what we found back there."

CHAPTER 21

BALTAZAR Montoya lived in a dilapidated, two-room wooden dwelling at the east end of the Hawkins farm. Ross and Monica had no difficulty finding the narrow road leading to Montoya's hideaway. Ross' eagerness to speak with the caretaker was only surpassed by the anxiety he felt to get on with the search for Carrie and his planned visit to the university campus once again. There, he planned seeing the academic vice-president. He hoped that once he explained the urgency of his problem, and Conrad's illicit activities, the vice-president would reveal the professor's location and this, hopefully, would lead them to Carrie.

Once they had cleared the heavy brush and trees along the path, their eyes came upon the modest house near the crest of a small hill overlooking the farm. The narrow road terminated at a point approximately one hundred yards of the house. Ross brought the car to a halt there. They saw a man in a straw hat and Levi overalls at the far side of a pasture. He was squating down, working on a piece of farm machinery. The man stood up, watching his unexpected visitors.

"That's got to be him," Ross said softly to Monica as he opened the door. "Do you want to come with me?"

"No, I'll stay here."

He was about to get out of the car when she placed her hand on his shoulder. "Darling?"

He turned to her.

"Please be careful and promise me that if he doesn't want to cooperate, you won't make a fuss."

"Don't worry, darling. I can handle it. I'll be careful not to lose my temper if he's uncooperative."

She nodded.

Ross took long strides walking up the hill toward the man in the straw hat. He hadn't moved; he was still standing there, eyeing Ross curiously as he climbed the hill.

"Mr. Montoya?" Ross asked when he was within a few feet of the man in overalls. "Baltazar Montoya?"

"Yes—yes, I'm he," the man said, nodding his head.

"How are you?" Ross extended his hand and the two men shook hands.

"I'm fine, thank you," Montoya replied, a look of puzzlement on his suntanned face. "What can I do for you?"

"My name's Ross Blair, Mr. Montoya," Ross said. "I hope I'm not coming to see you at an inconvenient time."

"I'm busy, yes, but I can spare the time; got all day to do what I'm doing." He motioned to the piece of machinery.

"I'd like to ask you a few questions, if you don't mind."

"A few questions concerning what?" Montoya asked. He placed his cupped hand just above his eyes to block the sunlight from obscuring his vision.

"About a man you knew a long time ago; a man you used to work for."

"And who might that be?"

"His name was Andrew Borlin. I understand you knew him well when he lived here." He studied Montoya, surprised the man had reacted rather casually at the mention of Borlin's name.

Montoya nodded and wrinkled his brow. "Yes, I knew Andrew Borlin—long ago." He stopped, waiting for Ross to continue, but Ross said nothing. "What is it you wanted to know about the man?"

"It'll take some time for me to explain, Mr. Montoya.

Could we possibly go inside your place to chat for a minute? I'd like to spend a little time telling you something about me and why I'm interested in learning about Andrew Borlin. I feel I owe you at least that much before hitting you with questions."

Montoya stood there silently.

"It's important to me, Mr. Montoya," Ross added.

"Yes, we'll go in if you wish," Montoya finally began. "You've aroused my curiosity by bringing up the name of someone I knew a considerable number of years ago. I don't know what information you want, Mr.—I'm sorry, I didn't catch your name."

"Blair—Ross Blair."

"Let's step inside, then, Mr. Blair."

Ross wasn't certain whether he noticed a tone of apprehension in Montoya's voice. "Thanks," he said.

Inside, Montoya offered Ross a cup of coffee, which Ross accepted. It was an extremely small kitchen they were in, with a narrow doorway leading into another, slightly larger room. There wasn't a door, only a faded curtain hanging from the ceiling, separating the two rooms.

Ross studied Baltazar Montoya as the man poured coffee into two mugs which he had set on the table. He appeared a much older man than Ross had expected to meet. Ross guessed his age at about the mid-fifties. He was of dark complexion and his face displayed a considerable number of deep wrinkles throughout, especially below and to the sides of his dark brown eyes. Ross could tell the man spent considerable time in the sun, for the wrinkles on his face were accentuated by a lighter color than the rest of his skin. He had a slightly squatted nose which was large and round at the tip. Ross noticed Montoya's hands as he gave Ross a mug of hot coffee—they were extremely large hands, heavily calloused.

Montoya offered Ross a chair at a small wooden table in the middle of the room. He joined Ross at the table.

"Now, Mr. Blair, at least here we are out of the sun. I get too much of that anyway and I'm always glad when there's some excuse that brings me indoors. Now, what exactly is it you want to know about Andrew Borlin?" He leaned back on his chair, eyeing Ross quizically.

Ross began his explanation of how he came to be in Esperanza, his conversation with Carol Lockwood prior to her death, and his visit to Consuelo Hawkins' house the night before. He didn't mention the old woman's suspicion that Borlin was still alive. Too, he was careful not to imply Montoya was connected in anyway with Borlin's alleged death. He mentioned nothing of the discovery at the cemetery the prior night. That was his ace in the hole—to be used later only if he found Montoya uncooperative.

"So that woman who was found shot last week at the hotel was Andrew Borlin's daughter," Montoya said when Ross had finished. "That's strange."

"What's strange about it?"

"Oh, I was only thinking out loud. What I meant was that I would have never guessed she was Borlin's daughter. It's a coincidence, that's all, that she was killed here. She wasn't from here, from what I heard."

"That's right—she lived in Albuquerque."

"Was she his only daughter?"

"Yes. Why?"

"Because I know now who she was." He noticed a look of surprise on Ross' face. "Oh, don't misunderstand, I didn't know her personally, but if she was Borlin's only daughter, then she's the one who came here when he died. But I never met her."

"Yes, she came here. Her father had asked her to."

"I remember vaguely that he had." He drank some coffee. "Strange, I would never have made the connection." He paused and looked earnestly at Ross. "Have they any idea who might have killed her?"

"None at all. They've found absolutely nothing to go on. It's all too puzzling, I'm afraid. And terribly frustrating—this business about my daughter."

Montoya said nothing. Ross offered him a cigarette.

"No, thanks, I don't smoke," Montoya said.

Ross lit one for himself. "No one seems to know much about the experiments Borlin had been conducting for a number of months prior to his death. I understand you helped him with them. I was hoping you'd be able to tell me something about them."

"Why would you want to know about them after all these years?"

"Let's say I'm the curious type, that's all. You see, I'm trying to clear up a few loose ends that bothered my ex-wife. And now they bother me."

Baltazar Montoya looked at Ross suspiciously. "Yes, I helped him with his experiments. But not in the technical, scientific sense, if that's what you mean. I only ran errands for him, cleaned up the lab, rinsed out and cleaned off the equipment—just small, minor stuff."

"Did you have even the slightest idea what his experiments were about? Surely he must have spoken to you at one time or another about his purpose—what he was trying to do?"

Montoya merely shook his head.

"I was told he confided in you," Ross continued. Immediately, he noted the look of surprise in Montoya's face.

"That's true, so he did."

Aside from what Consuelo Hawkins had told him about Montoya's relationship with Borlin, Ross knew very little about that relationship except that Borlin confided in Montoya. But he wouldn't reveal to Montoya how little he knew, for he hoped Montoya himself would provide him with the information he didn't possess. He was hoping he could force Montoya to fill in the gaps. If his plan didn't work, then he had no other choice but to confront his host with what he had discovered in Borlin's grave.

"It's difficult to believe that if Borlin had that much confidence in you, he wouldn't have let you in on the secret of what he was working on."

"As I said, I won't deny that he confided in me. After all, he and I got along fine. He always seemed pleased with my work. But I never meddled in his affairs nor did I ever inquire of him the purpose of his experiments. My only concern was to help him in whatever way I could, but I had no interest in what he was attempting to do. Besides, he never bothered to volunteer any information about his work. He was always secretive about everything he did, and that included his experiments. We never discussed them."

"Not even casually?"

"Not even in that way."

Ross decided to change his approach, at least for the moment. Old Lady Hawkins was wrong, he thought, when she said Montoya was just an old drunken fool. The man was certainly articulate and more importantly, chose his words carefully. Ross remembered that Sheriff Dominguez had told him that much. "Tell me, did he ever tell you about the wax doll he kept with him or did he happen to keep *that* a secret from you?"

Montoya said nothing.

"I'm told," Ross went on, "that he feared harm would come to him if the doll were damaged or destroyed. Did you know about that?"

Montoya sat there very still, staring at Ross, frozen momentarily to the chair. Ross' reference to the waxen image had apparently stunned him.

"Yes," he finally said. "I knew about the doll. He told me all about it. Very few persons knew." He had been avoiding Ross' glance and now had his eyes fixed on the table. He raised his head and looked at Ross for only a brief moment, then looked away again. "How did you learn of it?"

"Carol Lockwood told me about it the night she was killed."

"Oh," Montoya said simply. There was a momentary pause, then he continued. "I didn't realize she knew."

"She learned of the doll quite by accident one time when she was very young. I don't think Andrew Borlin ever found out that Carol knew."

"I see," Montoya remarked, attempting to sound casual but Ross could tell he was nervous.

Ross prodded with question after question, becoming more determined that Montoya was keeping something from him, Ross persisted that Borlin must have revealed something to Montoya about his experiments. Montoya grew equally insistent that Borlin never had. With each question, he displayed increased distrust for his audacious visitor. But Ross sensed it wasn't the displeasure of a man being falsely accused, but of one afraid the truth would eventually have to be told. Finally, Ross thought, it was time to let go with everything he had, for Montoya was weakening.

"Consuelo Hawkins," Ross said, "thinks Borlin is alive; that he was never buried at the funeral my ex-wife attended."

Montoya laughed nervously. "Ha, that fool!" he exclaimed. "That crazy old woman doesn't know half the time what she's talking about. She gets so involved with her black magic that she's gotten to believe everything can be explained by the supernatural." He laughed again. "The old woman always suspected Borlin was up to something akin to her magic when he was working on his experiments. Well, the old witch couldn't have been any further from the truth!"

"Let's talk about the supernatural for a minute," Ross said emphatically. "You won't deny Borlin professed himself a believer in witchcraft."

"I won't deny that."

"And there's that wax doll, for example. He believed in such evil."

"What you're saying is true, but the experiments he conducted, I assure you, were along different lines. They were strictly scientific in the true sense of the word; not experiments dealing with the occult and all that hogwash, like the old lady would have you believe." He paused and picked up the pot of coffee. "More coffee?"

"No thanks, I've had enough." He watched carefully as Montoya poured himself more coffee. "Andrew Borlin obviously didn't consider the occult 'hogwash'."

"He was entitled to his beliefs—I'm entitled to mine. The man was a scientist above all, however. Those experiments he was working on when he died proved--" He stopped abruptly.

"Yes, please go on. What did they prove?"

"All I was going to say is that the fact he was working on true scientific experiments proves he was a scientist above everything else."

"Yes, that may be true, but it obviously didn't prevent him from believing in the supernatural."

Montoya shrugged.

"You know," Ross continued, "I don't have any facts at the moment to prove Andrew Borlin is alive as the old lady claims, but I *have* found convincing evidence that proves to me he wasn't buried in the cemetery at the funeral my ex-wife attended."

The time had come to put Montoya to the test. Ross soon hoped to find out exactly what it was the man was keeping from him. His host sat there quietly now, growing pale.

"What evidence are you referring to?" Montoya retorted, attempting a laugh. His face appeared to grow paler. "If you mean that ritual at the old lady's house last night, I'd hardly call *that* evidence."

"No, something much more convincing than that." Ross was beginning to get impatient with the man. "You see, Montoya, I myself did something out of the ordinary last night. I went to that cemetery where Borlin's burial supposedly took place. And, I found the pile of rocks in the coffin. For some reason, someone wanted to create the impression that Borlin had died and had been buried at that cemetery. I think you were involved. The rocks in the coffin—that's proof that Andrew Borlin was never buried there, wouldn't you say?"

Baltazar Montoya's mouth suddenly sagged awkwardly. "I don't believe a word of what you're saying."

"I think you do, Montoya; otherwise, you wouldn't be sitting there looking at me like that. You know I'm speaking the truth because you've always known the coffin contained a pile of rocks. I'm convinced *you* had something to do with the deception that took place twenty years ago."

Ross continued his attack, throwing bits and pieces of information at Montoya; without interruption he confronted the man with question after question. He threatened to turn him in to the authorities. Ross knew that soon, Montoya would break.

"Now, Montoya," Ross snapped angrily, "are you going to tell me what you know, or am I going to have to give the sheriff what information I've already uncovered and let him take it from there? I think he'd be delighted to know what's back there at the cemetery. And you'd be right in the middle of it all!"

Montoya considered what Ross had said, then spoke. He drew out his words slowly. "All right, Mr. Blair, you needn't go through the trouble of getting the sheriff in on this. I'll tell you what I know. I'm not so sure you're going to believe what

I have to say but so help me God, what I'm about to tell you is the truth." He stopped and looked into Ross' eyes.

"O.K., I'm listening."

"You're right—Andrew Borlin was never buried back there in the cemetery. It was all part of the plan."

"What plan?" Ross asked. "Wait a minute! Is Borlin still alive as the old lady claimed? He never did die back then, did he?"

"No, he didn't. He was very much alive then. But who knows whether he is now? I myself haven't seen him since a couple of days after that fake funeral took place. He disappeared from here and I never laid eyes on him again. He might be dead now for all I know."

"But why would he go through such an elaborate plan to deceive others, including his own daughter?"

"For you to be able to understand that, I'll have to explain to you about the experiments."

"So you *did* know the nature of his experiments?"

"Yes."

"Did he conclude them after all?"

"Yes, we concluded them. He succeeded, for the final test of the experiment worked—at least partially."

"Partially?"

"Yes. You see, Mr. Blair, the—"

"Would you please wait a minute—I'd like to ask Monica to join us. She's the lady out in the car."

"I wouldn't mind at all."

"I'll be right back."

"I'll make some fresh coffee."

CHAPTER 22

ROSS left Montoya in the kitchen and went to the car to get Monica. He was back shortly and introduced her to Montoya.

"Please go on," Ross said anxiously.

Montoya finished putting some new coffee into the coffee pot, then brought another chair from the next room and joined Ross and Monica at the table.

"To continue with what I was about to tell you a moment ago about the experiments," Montoya began, "Andrew Borlin, a few months before I first met him, by sheer accident, made what he considered to be some startling discoveries concerning an experiment he was conducting at the laboratory up in Los Alamos. I don't know much about chemistry and physics and those other matters Borlin was a genius at, but this discovery of his, he told me later, had something to do with an element he had found. It was an element which most scientists, for many years, had considered extinct. I can't remember its name, it's been so long ago.

"Anyway, as I said, quite by accident, Borlin discovered that by injecting a chemical made up of this rare element into some laboratory mice, it slowed the growth of body cells. By injecting the serum he produced into these mice, he was able to get them to live for a period of time much longer than their average life span. This is because they grew at a slower rate than mice which had not been injected with the serum. Needless to say, Borlin was overwhelmed by his discovery, and like so many of the things about him, he kept it a secret—even from his fellow colleagues at Los Alamos. His assigned work at the lab, however, didn't permit him the time to carry on with this discovery of his, so he quit the lab and came down here, where I met him.

"He liked this place because it was secluded and he could work in privacy and secrecy which he cherished so much. He had known Consuelo Hawkins for a long while before quitting work at the laboratory and he worked out some rental arrangements with her. He worked hard for months and months, without relenting, although there were times, he would tell me, when he didn't think he'd be successful in perfecting the serum. He was a determined man, and there were times when he thought he was close to a discovery, but then something would go wrong. This built up his frustrations and so he would stop for a few days to rest and to catch up on his sleep. Then, determined as ever, he would go back to his test tubes and continue on with his work. Finally, after many months of trial and error, he accomplished what he had been attempting to do. He succeeded, partially, as I said a moment ago. But by then, he had tortured his body and mind; he had drained every ounce of energy from his body, going for days without sleep or anything to eat. He had become obsessed with the experiments, as he had with that wax doll.

"But he had overworked himself into both physical and mental exhaustion. That's probably why he suffered that first heart attack. That's when he called his daughter in California. He *was* actually dying when he called her. He wasn't deceiving her."

"But what about his discovery?" Ross asked. "You said he succeeded. What exactly did he succeed in doing?"

"This is the part both of you will find difficult to accept, Mr. Blair, but so help me, it's the truth I speak to you. I told you a moment ago that while at Los Alamos, the chemical he injected into the laboratory animals only slowed their growth. Borlin theorized that once perfected, the serum might go further. And his theory was correct, for he was able to discover a serum so powerful that when injected into the body of living animals, it immediately reversed, not only slowed down, the growth process of the cells in the animal and within a matter of seconds, the injection returned that animal to a form it had been sometime in its past. When Borlin injected mature, adult mice with the serum, for example, in seconds it returned the mice to the body they had possessed only a few days after birth. It gave them back their youth."

"Unbelievable," Ross said, a look of bewilderment in his eyes. "Absolutely amazing!"

"I agree—it's so very unbelievable. I myself would never believe such a thing had I not seen it with my own eyes. Nevertheless, that's exactly what Borlin succeeded in doing."

"Are you saying that Borlin tried this serum on himself?"

Montoya nodded. "He hadn't intended to, yet. But then the heart attack came and of course, he couldn't continue perfecting his discovery. He needed more time, he kept telling me, and he knew he wouldn't last much longer—he saw death staring him in the face. That's when he decided to use himself as the first human guinea pig. He injected himself with the chemical, not actually knowing what to expect, for he realized as a scientist that a human being might react to it much differently than did the mice. But he didn't have time to perform preliminary tests and so he decided to try it without them. As he himself told me, he had very little to lose, for he was dying anyway."

"And what happened? Did it work?"

"What happened, Mr. Blair, explains your finding those rocks in his coffin back there in the cemetery. Yes, it did work. I still find it difficult to believe, for I was present when he injected himself with the serum. I was there when the injection began taking effect on his body. Before my eyes, Andrew Borlin began changing in appearance. First his hair began turning slowly from white to black, then his face changed drastically and the wrinkled skin that had been there began to disappear, and finally, his ailing body changed its shape. In minutes, there was suddenly another person there in the room with me. He stood up and ran up to me, shouting excitedly. The tired and ailing, white-haired old man that moments before had been withering away, dying of a heart attack, had turned into a young, vigorous-looking and handsome man somewhere in his middle twenties. Physically, the man had changed completely. I stood there stunned, unable to utter a word."

"But if that's so, if he changed and became younger, no longer an old man suffering from a heart attack, why is it you say the experiment only worked partially?"

"Because," Montoya began slowly, "aside from changing him physically into a much younger person, the serum had changed him in another, more vital manner—a way that he had never anticipated. He still retained his memory. He knew who he was and what had taken place, and also of his past. But yet he said he felt strange, as if he were an entirely different person. He was shocked when he looked in the mirror and found that his face wasn't the face he had possessed when he was a young han in his middle twenties. Instead, he saw a complete stranger staring at him in the mirror. It was not himself he saw, but a different person—a new being.

"You see, he had theorized that the serum only changed the cell structure from old to younger ones; he went one step further, however, for he also theorized that the younger cells were the same cells, the identical cells that had been there before. In other words, the reverse of the growth cycle. He had no way of knowing there might be side effects. And of course, immediately he found out there were. The serum had somehow changed the cell structure of his brain in such a way that not only did he possess a younger body different from that he had possessed as a young man, but he also had an entirely different personality. It was as if a new man had been created.

"He not only spoke differently but thought and acted differently. He just wasn't the same man. For example, originally, immediately before he had taken the serum, he had told me he intended to continue working toward perfection of his experiments, if the serum worked, but he no longer seemed interested in that once the process had been completed. He held a different outlook on life—new ideas, interests, emotions. As I said, he was a different person. He was no longer the scientist. He retained the technical knowledge he had acquired and learned but not the interest in science. He knew, for example, that his daughter was coming to see him. But he was no longer interested in seeing her. To him, it was as if he had no daughter. No affection, no feeling towards her. It dawned on him, of course, that she would be unable to comprehend all this and that she would certainly be affected by it, and he rebelled at the idea of having to carry on ties to the past. That's when he realized he must try to forget his past and the people in it, including his daughter, and to start a completely new life, just as if he had been reborn. It was then that he swore me to secrecy.

"Everything was planned then—he was to disappear—begin a new life somewhere far away from here. No one, least of all his daughter, he said, was to ever know what had actually happened to him. He wanted those who had known him to believe he had died of a second heart attack. It was Borlin who thought up the idea of the fake funeral. To do that, he needed the cooperation of the local mortician—which, he was able to obtain. For a considerable sum of money, he took the mortician into his confidence and persuaded him to stage the funeral. The mortician is dead now, but he too was sworn to secrecy. Only three people ever knew the truth—what really happened to Andrew Borlin. Borlin himself, the mortician, and of course, me. Until today, no one else has ever known. Not to my knowledge, anyway."

"But what about the death certificate? Carol saw certified copies of it."

Montoya smiled. "That was no problem—those too were faked. It was the mortician who made the arrangements to obtain those, somehow. But no doctor ever verified the death. Everyone just accepted that Borlin had died—they had no reason to doubt it, I guess. The truth of the matter is that it became an easy deception to accomplish once we were able to obtain the mortician's cooperation. Without him, of course, it would have been next to impossible."

"Incredible," Ross said. "Simply incredible."

Monica too sat there stunned by Montoya's fantastic tale.

"And you say you never saw him again after he disappeared?" Ross asked.

"Not once. He disappeared completely. Never even heard from him again. It was as if he had vanished from the face of the earth—there was no longer an Andrew Borlin. Besides, I probably wouldn't recognize him today even if I were to see him. It's been twenty years. And I'm sure he's changed much —aged. And then, too, he might be dead—who knows?"

"This is too unbelievable," Ross said again.

They sat there talking a while longer. Ross asked more questions. But Montoya had very little else to tell them. Finally, Ross stood up to leave. He thanked Montoya and apologized if he had appeared forceful. Montoya assured him he understood and that there was no need of an apology.

"And," Montoya continued as he accompanied Ross and Monica outside his home, "I hope *you* understand, Mr. Blair, why at the beginning, I withheld any information from you. After all, I was sworn to secrecy and I respected Andrew Borlin's request that I never divulge to anyone what actually happened. That's why I haven't told a living soul all these years. But now, what difference will it make to anyone—Borlin's daughter is dead. Besides, you knew too much already. Prior to your mentioning the rocks you had found in the coffin, I didn't see any reason for telling you the truth."

He eyed Ross thoughtfully. "Will you promise me one thing, Mr. Blair?"

"Sure, what is it?"

"All this happened so long ago and I would rather not have to answer any more questions about what I've told you. So would it be asking too much that we keep this discussion to ourselves and that you say nothing to Sheriff Dominguez about it."

Ross thought for a moment. "I don't see why I'd have to tell Dominguez. You're right, it happened years ago and there's no reason why he has to be told."

"Thank you, Mr. Blair. I appreciate that."

"Well, goodbye, Mr. Montoya. Thanks again."

The two men shook hands. Monica said goodbye and Montoya nodded a farewell.

Montoya stood there watching them from the top of the hill as they walked down to the car. He was still standing there when they drove out of sight.

Before leaving Esperanza that morning for Albuquerque, Ross telephoned Sheriff Dominguez. He decided calling him rather than paying him a personal visit, for he was anxious to leave for Albuquerque. He reported to Dominguez their two visits with Old Lady Hawkins of the day before. Dominguez seemed amused when Ross related to him the ritual the old lady had conducted. He was tempted to tell the sheriff about their visit to the cemetery and of the startling revelations of Baltazar Montoya, but he had made a promise and intended keeping it.

Arriving in Albuquerque, they drove to the University of New Mexico campus, going directly to the administration building where they asked for the academic vice-president. It was already half past one when they were ushered by the receptionist into the vice-president's office. The man they met there was friendly and likeable. Ross was impressed by the man's manner. He wanted to make absolutely certain the vice-president realized the importance of his dilemma in his search for Carrie, so he detailed every small fact he had learned of the professor and of Carrie. The man sitting behind the large desk listened intently as Ross spoke. It was imperative, he told the vice-president, that he find Carrie as soon as possible.

When Ross had finished, the vice-president had a few questions to ask concerning Ross' belief that he would find Carrie with Conrad. When he appeared satisfied, he placed a telephone call. He spoke softly but confidently to the person at the other end. Just prior to hanging up, he jotted something down on a note pad. He tore off the white sheet of paper he had written on, folded it, and handed it to Ross.

"There's the place where you're most likely to find Professor Conrad," the man said. He extended his hand to Ross. "I certainly hope you find your daughter, Mr. Blair."

Ross stood up and shook the man's hand.

"Thank you," Ross said. "You've been most helpful."

Once outside in the hallway, Ross stopped to look at the note the vice-president had handed to him.

"Look, Monica!" he said loudly.
Ross gave the note to her. It read:

Arthur Conrad
Hacienda Villa del Sol
El Camino Seco
Ruta 3, 1321
San Cristobal, Mexico

"Oh, no," Monica said disappointingly. "He's out of the country."

"That's no problem at all. In fact, I know where that place is; I've been near there before. But you're missing what I'm getting at. Now I'm certain we'll find Carrie with the professor."

"Oh, why of course. How stupid of me. Carrie's friend— she told you Carrie had said something to her about going to Mexico."

"Exactly. And I'm willing to bet she was referring to going down there with Conrad. That's got to be it. It'd be too much of a coincidence for the two of them to go down there their separate ways."

Quickly, he folded the paper and placed it in his coat pocket. "Come on, let's find a telephone and check on a flight to Puerto Rafael."

"Where's that?"

"A Mexican resort town only a few miles south of the place Conrad's staying." He took her by the arm. "Let's not waste any time."

CHAPTER 23

THEY caught a flight out of Albuquerque to Tucson early that evening, but failed to make connections for the last flight of the day from there to Puerto Rafael. They spent the night at a motel near the airport, and early the next morning, they boarded the first flight to the Mexican resort town.

Shortly before ten o'clock, they arrived in the village off the coast of the Gulf of California. At the Puerto Rafael airport, they rented a car and drove the short distance to the small village of San Cristobal.

Having arrived there in the blistering heat of mid-morning, they immediately looked for a place to stay. In the business district of the village, across the street from the town plaza, they found a small, but clean hotel. It was a quiant plaza, where several of the older people sat in park benches underneath the shade of the trees, passing the morning away. The hotel was connected to a restaurant and bar next door which had a sidewalk cafe.

Ross knew very little Spanish—Monica, none at all—but the man behind the hotel counter spoke some English. They registered as husband and wife.

It was a miserably hot morning in San Cristobal but the

sidewalk cafe had large, colorful patio umbrellas protecting each table from the hot rays of the sun. They had missed break-fast in Tucson and so they decided to have a brunch at the cafe.

San Cristobal reminded them of Esperanza, except that it was much smaller and lacked paved streets. The commercial buildings around the town square were made of adobe clay, only some of which were plastered over with stucco. The struc-tures did indeed appear quite old, some as old as the village itself. They noticed too, as they sat there waiting for their meal to arrive, that the town experienced a minimal amount of vehicular traffic.

Having finished, they remained at the table, each enjoying a cigarette. A cool breeze swept across the cafe and they sat there enjoying the relief it provided from the heat of the day.

"Well, there's no reason to postpone our trying to find that place Arthur Conrad is staying at," Ross said, rising from his chair. "Shall we go and see?"

"Let's do," Monica replied.

He helped her up.

At the hotel desk, Ross displayed to the clerk the slip of paper containing Conrad's address. The man told Ross he knew where the road was located, and he pointed in the general di-rection, but he wasn't familiar with the address itself. It was a rural address, he said, but all he could inform them was that the place was somewhere out of the village. He suggested they make further inquiries at the post office, located on the oppo-site side of the plaza.

At the post office, they were unable to find anyone that spoke English, but finally, with what little Spanish Ross knew, and by showing the postal clerk Conrad's address, he was able to get a vague idea where the place was.

They traveled down a narrow village street, passing through a residential area congested with dwellings clustered one on top of the other. The path was unleveled, full of puddles of stagnant and dirty laundry water.

The car they had rented at the Puerto Rafael airport had no air conditioner, and so they moved along the narrow street with the car windows rolled down. The heat was miserable. Children playing and hollering in the street, stopped to gaze curiously at Ross and Monica as they crept along on the mud-puddled street.

"This doesn't seem like a street leading out of town," Monica said, sounding slightly annoyed. "Are you sure we're on the right one?"

"I think it's the street the fellow at the post office told us to take," Ross replied. "But I too am beginning to wonder."

Finally, the houses became scattered and the road grew wider to a point where it turned into an unpaved country road. Further down, they came upon an intersection, and Ross noticed a sign along the side of the road.

"Look," he pointed out, "that's the street." He read from the sign. "Camino Seco."

Immediately, he took out the slip of paper and looked at the address. "Yes, that's it. The number we're looking for is 1321."

"A lot of good that'll do us," Monica remarked. "We don't have a reference point to go by."

"We'll have to do our best. Keep your eyes open for that number."

This deserted, dusty road led through barren countryside of rolling sand hills filled with dry desert brush. The tires of the car rolling along the dirt roadway easily loosened the dust from the path, so that the car left a trail of billowing dust behind it. Some of it found its way into the car, much to their dismay. There was nothing in sight but the rolling desert hills and Ross, for the first time, worried that the address he had obtained didn't exist at all. What if Conrad had made up the address? No doubt about it—they were in desolate desert country and there didn't appear to be a residence for miles around.

Monica had rolled the car window partially up, attempting in vain to keep out at least a part of the choking dust which, together with the heat, made their journey extremely unpleasant.

They continued moving up and down the rolling desert hills a few miles until finally, the road leveled off. A few minutes later, about two miles ahead of them, Ross noticed what appeared to be the outline of a structure off in the distance. But he wasn't certain, for it was difficult to see clearly because the rising heat created flickering waves along the horizon, obscuring the view. As they neared the structure, their eyes focused on the trees and vegetation around it, setting it off from the barren surroundings.

"That might be the place we're looking for," he said. "What do you think?"

"It might be," Monica answered. "I certainly hope so. There doesn't seem to be another place for miles."

"We'll soon find out."

The house they had observed in the distance appeared to be about half a mile from the road. Ross kept watching for a turn off. They came to a clearing which opened up into an intersecting road. A small wooden sign stood a few feet away. It read:

> J. W. Rountree
> Ruta 3, Numero 1321
> El Camino Seco

"That's the address!" Monica said happily.

"It's the address, all right," Ross agreed. "But who the hell is J. W. Rountree? Let's hope that whomever he is, he knows a fellow by the name of Arthur Conrad or we've come down here for nothing."

Monica could tell he was dismayed by the thought of a fruitless journey. She turned and began studying the house from a distance. "Wow, it's a big place. And it *does* look like one of those Spanish haciendas or villas one always hears so much about. But I'd never have guessed you'd find one around here." She gazed at the surrounding countryside disapprovingly.

"Neither would I. It's enormous. Have you noticed that other building to the rear? It looks like separate sleeping quarters for servants."

There were trees throughout, completely surrounding the grounds, with a thick, smooth carpet of lawn surrounding the main house.

"Look at the landscaping in this place, will you," Ross said as they passed the first row of tall Arizona cypresses. They moved along a graveled entrance road, the car tires crunching noisily over the gravel.

Ross brought the car to a halt on the circular driveway, within a few feet of the front entrance to the mansion.

CHAPTER 24

THEY sat there in the car for a moment. It was indeed an enormous house, with thick, stucco-adobe walls. It reminded Monica of the large homes of Mediterranean and Spanish architecture she had seen from time to time in lower California. She was unequivocally impressed. It was a two-story structure with narrow arched windows on the second level. Decorative wrought-iron bars covered each window. Elaborate rows of intricate shrubbery and flowers had been meticulously planted around the front of the house. There was a portion of the second story which overlapped the first story walls for approximately half the distance of the width of the house, the overlap supported by several massive wooden girders held up by five colossal wooden columns along the front edge of the house. This structural overlap created a large porch or veranda underneath the supporting girders, heavily shaded from the sun by the large trees in front. The porch floor was some two feet above the ground and made up of large squares of highly-polished red tile. Large round beams protruded out some two or three feet from the wall above the porch and continued on higher for the remaining front of the house.

"I certainly hope this is the right place," Monica said as

they stepped out of the car. "Professor Conrad must know some very wealthy people, from the looks of this mansion."

Ross nodded as he walked around the car. He took her arm and they walked up the steps to the entrance.

"Oh, Ross, just look at those magnificent doors, will you!" Monica whispered, referring to the double walnut doors decorated with beautifully hand carved designs, and reaching up to the height of the porch ceiling.

Ross placed his hand to the heavy metal knocker, lifted it and let it swing back against the door. It gave a resounding, echoing sound. "Here goes. Hold your breath."

In a few moments, they heard the clicking sound of leather heels on the floor inside, then the rattling noise as someone disengaged the door latch. One of the doors slowly swung open.

An extremely huge man appeared. He was a tall man, and he looked down at them. He was dressed in a white, long-sleeved jacket, with white buttons running all the way up the front to a Nehru-type collar. The man had short, kinky hair and unusually big, thick lips. Everything about this man at the door looking down at them was big, Ross thought. He had seen the man's counterpart playing left tackle for the San Francisco Forty-Niners.

"Yes, may I help you, please," the large man said in a resounding, vibrating voice. His large, dark eyes looked first at Ross, then at Monica.

Ross cleared his throat. "We're looking for Professor Conrad," he explained. "Arthur Conrad. We were told we'd find him here. Is he in?"

The big man didn't answer for a moment, his eyes watching Ross cautiously. "Yes, the professor is in. He is resting in his room at the moment and cannot be disturbed." He paused, glancing quickly at Monica, then returned his gaze to Ross. "He was not expecting any visitors. You may come back later in the afternoon, if you wish, but I cannot say for certain whether he will be in then. He left instructions not to be disturbed during the morning and noon hours."

"Please, it's important that we see him. It's extremely urgent —and, we've come such a long way to see him."

"Are you friends of the professor's?"

"No—we're not friends at all. But it's terribly important that we speak with him. We're trying to locate someone and we have reason to believe Professor Conrad knows where we might find this person. In fact, we've reason to believe this person is staying in this house."

"This person you're looking for—what's his name?" He spoke in yet a deeper voice and with a slight accent.

Ross glanced at Monica, then back at the man. "It's not a man we're trying to find. It's a woman; a girl, rather. Carrie Lockwood. She's around nineteen or twenty years of age."

The man said nothing.

"Is she staying here?" Ross finally asked.

After another moment of silence, the man spoke. "Wait here, please. I will go see if the professor will speak with you. What is your name again, please?"

"Blair. Ross Blair."

The man said nothing more nor did he invite them in. Instead, he closed the door and left them standing there. They heard the clicking sound of the door latch locking the door.

Ross turned to Monica. "He's certainly a trusting fellow, isn't he?" he said facetiously.

"Yes, isn't he though," Monica said. "Terribly suspicious. What's he afraid of—that we'll go barging in uninvited?"

"We might find ourselves having to do just that. I'm beginning to get a little nervous. To think Carrie might be in there after going through the past week batting zero."

"I understand how you feel, darling." She tried smiling at him. "You think Conrad will talk to us?"

"It's hard to say after that cool reception we got from that giant."

"Isn't he enormous?"

"Agreed." He turned to survey the place. "I must say, though, I didn't expect anything as plush as this." He gestured to the surroundings. "A colossal castle in the middle of nowhere; servants answering the door. I really thought we'd find our professor in some little adobe hut, puffing away on a marijuana joint along with a bunch of hippies." He frowned. "*And* Carrie," he added disgustingly.

"Why would he come all the way down here, do you suppose?"

"I don't know." He shrugged. "Probably just for a change of scenery—to get away from his academic surroundings, which I imagine can become tiring after a long school year."

"He certainly chose an unlikely spot."

"Not really, if what he wanted was seclusion. Stop to think about it; this place certainly has that."

"Yes, I guess so. But there's plenty of other places back in—" She stopped when she heard the sound of the latch moving.

The door opened slightly and the big man appeared again. "The professor cannot see you," he said, holding the door slightly ajar. All they saw of the man was his head and the top of his white jacket, for he refused to open the door further. "He is not seeing anyone."

"But we must see him!" Ross said, raising his voice. Suddenly he grew angry—desperate. "Did you let him know I said it was urgent. Did you tell him whom we were looking for?"

"Yes, I certainly did, and he instructed me to inform you that he does not know a person by the name of Carrie Lockwood. He also asked me to tell you he does not wish to see anyone at this time. Now, if you'll excuse—"

"But that can't be," Ross interrupted, his voice forceful. "The professor damn well knows Carrie. I strongly suggest you go back there and tell him that if he doesn't see us, I can assure him I'll be returning shortly—this time, with the police."

The big man hesitated a moment, then shrugged. "Be that as it may," he said, "but I have my orders and—"

"Let the gentleman come in, Paulo!" a loud, vibrant voice came from somewhere inside.

The big man turned around, then slowly opened the door completely. Through the open doorway, Ross and Monica could see clearly into a large, high-ceiling entryway which led into a much larger room. At the far end of this room, was a wide, carpeted stairway; midway up the stairway, Ross saw a man standing there, in a smoking jacket, his hand resting on the railing. The man glared at Ross deprecatingly.

"What is it I can do for you, Mr. Blair?" the man said loudly. He began walking slowly down the stairs. "I assure you, I see no need whatsoever in your threatening to call the police. There's no justification for something as drastic as that." He reached the floor and approached the open door.

Monica grew frightened by this sudden confrontation.

"Please come on in, Mr. Blair," the man continued. "Both you and your lady friend." He glanced at Monica.

"Thank you," Ross replied softly. He gently took hold of Monica's arm and led her into the large entryway. "This is Monica Ashley," he said to the man. "I'm Ross Blair." He wasn't sure whether to shake hands with this man but finally it was the man who limply extended a hand to him.

"And I'm Arthur Conrad," the man said, shaking Ross' hand, "as you may have already deduced." He turned to Paulo, the servant. "It's quite all right, Paulo. You may go now and carry on with what you were doing."

The big man hesitated momentarily and glanced at Ross. "Yes sir, Professor," he said softly and then disappeared down the large room.

Conrad turned his attention to Ross and Monica. "Would you please step into the study." He led them into a large, carpeted room containing a wide variety of oil paintings and elegant pieces of fine furniture. On the far wall were built-in book shelves from floor to ceiling, filled with what appeared to be thousands of assorted books. Two large windows facing the front of the house were covered with elaborate draperies which darkened the room considerably.

Conrad walked up to a lamp next to a long sofa and switched on the light. "Please," he said to Ross and Monica, gesturing to the sofa, "please sit down—both of you." He himself sat down in a large arm chair. Ross and Monica sat down.

"Now," Conrad began, "I understand you came here looking for Carrie Lockwood."

"That's correct, Professor."

"Tell me, Mr. Blair, why your interest in Carrie?"

Something about the manner in which he asked the question led Ross to believe the man already knew the answer.

"She's my daughter," Ross answered. He looked inquisitively at Conrad. "Your servant told us a moment ago that you didn't know Carrie."

"I must apologize for Paulo's tendency for abruptness. He's indeed a faithful and hard-working servant to this household. He's worked for J. W. Rountree for many, many years. Mr. Rountree, if you're wondering, is a very dear and close friend of mine. You won't find him here for he leaves this place during the summer months; he's kind enough to allow me the use of the house for three or four weeks during the time he's away. He's also gracious to leave the servants behind.

"Paulo must have misunderstood me for I didn't tell him I didn't know Carrie; I do very well indeed. He did communicate to you correctly, however, that I instructed him I did not wish to be disturbed, and to inform you also I could not see you. But, for reasons I shall not discuss at the moment, I changed my mind after he had left my room. I hope you don't interpret my initial and rather hasty reaction, I might add, as being one of rudeness, Mr. Blair." He spoke in an extremely formal manner. It made Monica somewhat uncomfortable.

"No, I won't—I certainly respect your right to privacy. But then again, I do consider it rather important that I speak with you."

"Yes, about Carrie Lockwood, I presume?"

"Yes. She's here with you, isn't she?" What he said sounded more like a statement of undisputed fact rather than a question.

"Yes, she did come down here with me to stay a few weeks. She's not in the house at the moment, however." He gave Ross a sober stare. "In fact, to be more precise, she's not actually in the area at all, for she left yesterday with Paulo's wife—she too is employed here as housekeeper. Paulo's wife went down south to a small village where she has relatives. Carrie decided to drive her there, and they won't return until sometime tomorrow night, I'm afraid." The man spoke in a pompous manner.

"Well, I'd like to see her when she returns," Ross said somewhat emphatically. "Would you mind very much if we returned tomorrow to see my daughter, Professor Conrad?"

"As a matter of fact—" He hesitated. "I'll be quite frank with you, Mr. Blair—I don't believe now's the time for you to see Carrie. Believe me, I say this realizing fully well your deep interest in seeing her. You see, Carrie is—"

"Not the right time, did you say?" Ross retorted, trying to hide his displeasure. "I'd like for you to know, Professor Conrad, that I haven't seen my daughter in almost twenty years." He was suddenly angry at the audacious manner of this man sitting before him, especially in view of what he had learned of the man's detrimental influence over Carrie. He had grown to hate the man sitting there confidently. "And I might as well speak quite frankly myself, sir, and come right down to why I'm here.

"I happen to be extremely concerned about Carrie's present health and well-being, which I believe is being endangered by her past association with you and your kind, and more specifically, by her being here with you now."

Ross glared at Arthur Conrad. The professor was a much older man than he had expected to find. He approximated his age to be around forty-five, but he supposed the man's extremely long hair, which had prematurely begun to turn gray, was deceiving. Ross expected the man at any moment now to demand he and Monica leave the house immediately. Instead, Conrad leaned back in his chair, apparently studying Ross. He sat there cool and somewhat reflective, as if Ross had said nothing offensive. He had striking blue eyes which, even in the dim light, he squinted as he gazed at Ross.

He had a long, narrow nose and a wide mouth with a thick lower lip. He was clean shaven but one could still discern the dark shadow of the heavy beard which he possessed. Even so, there appeared to be a certain look of femininity about him that bothered Ross. He didn't know what it was that gave Conrad that appearance, unless it was the silk smoking jacket that he wore. One other physical trait stood out strongly—the man possessed distinguished hands.

Ross thought he detected a flicker of amusement in the man's eyes.

"If you'll let me finish what I have to say, Mr. Blair, I'll try to explain," Arthur Conrad continued, ignoring Ross' reference to his private life. "As I was about to say before you interrupted, Carrie is presently going through a serious and highly emotional problem that she herself must contend with—alone —and I think it's purely a matter of time now before she resolves this problem of hers. I'm quite aware of the fact that you've never seen her since she was only a few months old. More importantly, of course, is the fact that she has never known her father."

"How would you know that? It's something I doubt you'd care to know."

"I've learned that and much more, from Carrie herself. She and I have struck a close relationship—one of complete confidence."

"Is *that* what you call it?" Ross snapped.

"I beg your pardon, Mr. Blair?"

"Look, Professor Conrad, I came down here hoping that I would get some cooperation from you and that there'd be no need for name-calling and some rather nasty remarks, but frankly, I think I better put things plainly to you. Your not wanting me to see Carrie shows me very clearly where you stand.

"You see, I know about Carrie's problem with drugs. I learned of it from her mother. That's how I happened to wind up in New Mexico. And I also learned of your reputation around the university with drugs and pot. I've learned also that you had a great deal of influence in getting Carrie started on drugs. So based on what I know about you and your habits, Professor, am I supposed to sit here calmly and leave here without seeing Carrie? Whatever emotional problem she may be going through is most likely a direct result of her association with you and your kind!" He appeared slightly nervous but his hands were steady.

"Obviously, *you're* not going to remain calm, Mr. Blair. First, then, let me say that *I* certainly will try to, at least for the moment. Secondly, what I do with my own personal life is strictly—and I wish to emphasize the word—*my* concern and not yours or anyone else's and—"

"It certainly is someone else's concern," Ross interjected. "Society's *and* mine, when your life is conducted in a way that is not only violating laws but is directly responsible for corrupting innocent people's lives, like Carrie's, for example. You're certainly no paragon of virtue in my book, Professor." He became white with anger.

"That's a matter of opinion, which you're entitled to have, Mr. Blair, and moreover, a matter which involves some value judgment. I happen to strongly disagree with your opinion. Besides, Carrie is an individual with a mind of her own and with her own will and wants. Whatever she has done in the past and is doing now is certainly something she did of her own volition—nobody has forced her to do anything, I assure you. She came down here voluntarily, for example. I didn't force her; she certainly wasn't abducted. I've never forced her to do anything in her life. She knows exactly what she's doing and she has all along. So your threatening to call the police a moment ago means nothing at all to me."

"But you've influenced her when it comes to smoking pot and using drugs," Ross blurted out angrily. He felt more than faintly resentful now. Monica felt a pang of hurt in her heart because she knew only too well how and what he felt.

"There again, Mr. Blair," the professor said coolly. He measured his words. "I can't help it if I influence other people to my way of thinking, my way of life, by my actions. I am what I am, and if I happen to have the ability to influence others to my philosophy of life, then so it must be. But never have I attempted to control anyone's life, nor to force my beliefs on others, and that includes Carrie. I can't help it if I've influenced her to do what you obviously think is bad, even though I don't agree that it is necessarily.

"Carrie herself must make up her own mind whether she wishes to accept what she has been doing as something which she feels strongly about, or whether she should abandon it completely and seek pleasure out of life in some other way. That is her decision—her choice, not mine, and quite frankly, not even yours, even though you are her father. That is why I sincerely believe you shouldn't see her at this particular time. It's imperative that she be given sufficient time to iron out the problem once and for all, in her own mind—without the help of your influence, or even mine, at this juncture. She'll be back in the States within a few weeks and you may see her then—it's not that I wish to take that right away from you."

Monica noticed Ross watching the professor with increasing irritation.

"You needn't be pretentious about it. That's all easy for you to say, for you've been influencing her up till now, when I've never had the opportunity to make whatever impression I can make on the girl's mind. I think I'm entitled to that opportunity now, before it's too late." He gazed at Conrad for a moment.

"Surely," he went on to say, "you don't doubt my good intentions in trying to help Carrie when I've come all the way down here?"

"I've never inferred during our discussion that I ever doubted your sincerity. I know you mean well. I believe we both have Carrie's well-being as our prime concern. But whether you like it or not, Mr. Blair, you must accept the fact that for now, anyway, I know Carrie very well, and that you don't know her at all. Based on these two facts alone then, even as difficult as it may be for you to accept, you're going to have to rely on my judgment of what may be best for Carrie at the moment." He sighed meaningfully.

"And, it happens to be my strong opinion," he went on, "that until that time comes when Carrie has resolved her emotional problem by herself, without any influence coming from anyone, you should not see or speak to her. I believe that seeing you now, after all these years, considering the state of mind she's in, would only confuse her miserably.

"And I promise you, Mr. Blair, that I'm leaving her alone to arrive at her own decision and that I haven't spoken to her about it since we've been down here. She had become rather depressed during the last month or so and she and I discussed the matter thoroughly before coming down here. In fact, that was the reason I decided to bring her with me, for I felt it was a place where she could have the time and peace to examine her conscience and resolve the problem once and for all. Just like some religions have retreat houses where persons go in solitude to examine their conscience as it relates to God, so must Carrie remain alone, without interference from the outside, whether it be you or me."

"Suppose we let her decide whether she wants to see me or not," Ross demanded.

"That would be impossible, Mr. Blair. It would not be in

her best interests to see you at this time. I've made up my mind."

"*You've* made up your mind!" Ross mouthed off angrily, but disconcertingly. "What in God's name gives *you* the right to decide?"

"I won't go into that discussion with you, Mr. Blair, for it is fairly obvious you and I disagree about that also. Suffice it to say that I feel I have sufficient basis to make that decision. I appreciate the fact that as Carrie's father, you have reason to be suspicious of me because of the things that I do that you believe are immoral and wrong, aside from being illegal, but nevertheless, the fact remains that you must now put your trust in me, a total stranger, in seeking what is best for Carrie.

"Believe me, Mr. Blair, you would only place an additional strain on Carrie's mind should you speak to her now. I dare say that because she would realize that too, she might refuse to see you, and since you have known absolutely nothing about her problem, you might interpret that in a way that will hurt you. And I should tell you too that I've become aware Carrie has missed terribly not having a father and one matter that's always caused confusion in her life is that she wanted desperately to learn of you—to know you.

"I suspect that it might have been this very strain that caused her to turn to drugs. If this in fact was the case, then she turned falsely to that kind of life and she should therefore re-evaluate her decision. Again, let me say that we must let her do it alone."

He glanced at Monica and then turned to Ross again. "And now, Mr. Blair—Miss Ashley—if you'll excuse me, I have some things to do." He gave Monica a thin smile and stood up.

Monica lifted herself from the sofa. Ross hesitated but then, knowing there was little he could do now, he too finally stood up.

"You haven't convinced me, Professor Conrad," Ross said, attempting to sound forceful. He looked tortured. Monica had seen that same look in his eyes before.

"I didn't really think that I would, Mr. Blair," the professor answered, "but nevertheless I thought it would be worth a try. I wish you'd reconsider and leave here—I mean San Cristobal—now, this moment."

"I wish *you'd* reconsider. Unfortunately, I happen to be in this house and there's nothing I can do about that, so Miss Ashley and I'll leave for the moment." He felt a certain indignation having to leave.

"Have it your way," Conrad said and he began walking them out of the study.

At the door, he bid Ross and Monica good day and remained standing at the doorway watching them as they entered the car. Then, he slowly closed the door.

On the return to San Cristobal, Monica tried calming Ross, who was still angry.

Her thoughts were on the confrontation; on what Conrad had said back there at the *Villa del Sol*. One thing stood out clearly in her mind—she had never expected Arthur Conrad to have reacted in the manner that he had. Why did she think that now? Because, she kept telling herself, she had expected to find a man *indifferent* to Carrie's problem. Yet, the man they had met, irrespective of his pompous and confident nature, didn't seem to fit the picture of the ugly professor she had formed in her mind previously.

Somehow, Arthur Conrad had not acted the part of the professor who corrupted the minds of innocent youth with drugs and false hopes, and who had been responsible for poisoning Carrie's mind.

CHAPTER 25

IT was almost one o'clock when they arrived back at the hotel. Feeling an uncleanliness from the dust they encountered on the trip, Monica decided to take a quick shower. Afterward, she slipped into a clean set of underwear and a lounging gown. Ross was sitting down on the bed where she had left him. He was smoking his second cigarette, staring out the window past the plaza below and toward the large, mushrooming clouds gathering on the horizon.

"Looks like we might get some rain," he said almost automatically, forcing himself to make conversation.

She could tell he was distraught, wondering what to do next. He appeared lost.

She walked to the edge of the bed and sat next to him.

"Darling," she said softly, "we'll think of someway to get to see Carrie." She wanted to console him desperately but wasn't exactly sure what to say. "Don't think about what happened back there. It'll only make you feel worse. As difficult as I know it must be to do, try blocking it out of your mind for the moment."

"If I only could, Monica," he answered despairingly. "But I can't. What Conrad said back there keeps running through my mind. I can't shut off his words. The audacity of it all. So help me God, Monica, I'll find a way to see Carrie if it's the last thing I do."

"I know you will, darling." She raised her hand and stroked his hair gently. "But first, why don't you try not thinking about it, even if for only a few minutes." She stood up. "Why don't you take a shower now; it'll make you feel better?"

He simply nodded, took one last puff of his cigarette and stood up. He walked into the bathroom and closed the door.

They ate a light lunch later that afternoon in the restaurant downstairs. When they had finished, they walked across the street to the plaza and there sat on one of the park benches underneath the shade of a tree, watching some youngsters playing on the skimpy grass a few yards away.

Only once did Ross break the silence. "You know, Monica," he said, "I've been sitting here trying to give some meaning to what Conrad told us, but I can't. And I can't believe Carrie wouldn't want to see me, as he suggested."

She hated to see him this way—it made her extremely sad.

"I'm sure Carrie would see you if she knew you were here, darling," she said. "And I agree with you, there would be absolutely nothing wrong in your seeing her."

But even as she spoke these words, she realized only too well the possibility existed, however remote, that Conrad was right—that Carrie might not want to see Ross at this particular time due to—what is it the professor had called it—her highly emotional problem. Whatever that meant. She considered unfair the manner in which circumstances had placed them in this strange land, forced to play the game by Conrad's rules. Ross deserved much more than that. She knew Ross had considered that aspect but had apparently brushed it aside, for he wasn't one to feel self-pity. As they sat there on the park bench, she didn't know whether it was contempt or despair she saw in his eyes.

They finally left the plaza and began walking through the dirt streets of San Cristobal, apparently not too concerned with the heat of the afternoon. They strolled the streets for at least an hour, going nowhere in particular, passing the time away. Upon their return to the hotel, they had a cocktail in the restaurant. By then, Ross appeared more at ease and, Monica thought, was regaining the calm which had left him momentarily after the confrontation with Conrad. But he now appeared tired. When they had finished their second drink, Monica suggested they go back to the room and lie down to rest.

They spent the remaining part of the afternoon in bed. Monica closed her eyes and dozed off into a light sleep. On one occasion during her sleep, she awoke half-way, opened her eyes and saw that Ross was fast asleep. They were exhausted and slept for two hours. Upon awakening, they discovered a light rain had fallen while they slept.

The sun had just lowered itself below the horizon, throwing long, striking rays of bright, orange sunlight onto the high clouds moving away to the northwest off in the distance, and the first glimpse of night began to show itself, slowly creeping its way from the east. They had awakened with an appetite and they went downstairs to the restaurant.

It was much cooler now after the rain. They found a refreshing breeze blowing across the cafe's terrace, and so they chose to have dinner there.

Ross sat there through his second martini before dinner, staring absently across the plaza. Suddenly, his eyes twitched as they caught a glimpse of something or someone across the street. Monica immediately noticed his sudden attention. She tried following his gaze to see what it was he was watching. She saw several villagers on the square and across the street, passing the evening away in conversation. She then noticed the young girl who had exited one of the buildings. The girl, who appeared to be American, walked hurriedly to a small foreign car parked alongside the building. She got into the driver's seat.

"That's her!" Ross said loudly.

"That's who?" Monica asked, puzzled. "You mean that girl who just got into the sports car?"

"Yes," he said excitedly. "That's Carrie!"

"Are you certain, Ross?"

"Yes, I'm positive. She looks a little different from that photograph Carol showed me of her. But it's her, all right." He stood up. "Come on, let's follow her."

Monica stood up awkwardly. "But—"

"Come on, let's not waste time or we'll loose her." He kept looking across the street; the car was now slowly moving onto the street, away from them.

"Waiter!" Ross called out to the man who was serving a table nearby. "We have to go." He forced a twenty dollar bill into the waiter's hand. "That should cover what we've ordered; keep the change."

He quickly took Monica's hand and started toward his car.

Soon, they were in the car headed in the direction the girl had taken.

"Ross, how in the world can you be positive that girl was Carrie? After all, from a photograph, it's hard to get a good likeness sometimes."

"I'm sure she was, Monica."

"But what would she be doing here? Professor Conrad said she was out of town and wasn't expected back until tomorrow night."

"I don't care what he told us. That was Carrie and that's all there is to it, so we're following her. I hope we haven't lost her."

He turned off onto the road the girl had taken. "How stupid of me. I should have realized that if he didn't want me to see Carrie at all, he would even lie to keep us away from her. He probably made up that story about her being out of town so I wouldn't keep insisting on seeing her. She was there in the house while we sat there talking with him. That Goddamned, lying bastard!"

Although it was considerably darker now, they could see the small car up ahead of them, a trail of dust behind it.

"Be careful, darling," Monica cautioned.

Ross was driving as fast as he could without risking an accident but the little car was gaining on them.

Through the rolling hills, they would momentarily lose sight of the car as it disappeared behind each hill. Ross knew where it was headed. The car turned off and disappeared into the road connecting to the *Villa del Sol*. The hacienda stood silhouetted against the dim, reddish sunlight still creeping past the horizon.

The small car had disappeared somewhere behind the big

house. The girl was nowhere in sight.

Ross brought the car to a screeching halt in front of the main residence and hurried out of the car. He was already rapping the knocker noisily against the door when Monica reached the entrance. In a matter of seconds, Paulo, the huge servant, appeared. He said nothing.

"Tell the professor I want to see him!" Ross snapped at the servant. "Now—this instant!"

"I'm sorry, sir," Paulo began to say humbly, "but Pro—"

"I won't accept any excuses this time, you big goon! You may be big, and I've nothing against you personally, except that at the moment, you're standing between me and the professor so if you don't mind—" He pushed with all his strength against the servant's chest and gained entrance.

He had taken Paulo by surprise. The servant appeared confused and glanced at Monica, who was still standing outside the open doorway. Then he slowly turned around to face Ross, who by now was standing in the middle of the large foyer.

"Sir, I am going to ask you now, in a nice way, to leave immediately. Otherwise, I will—"

"I'm not leaving this place until you summon Professor Conrad," Ross shouted angrily. His voice echoed into the larger room.

Paulo shouted back something undecipherable and rushed towards him, when a voice called out from the rear of the house.

"Paulo! Leave this to me!" It was Arthur Conrad.

The big servant turned around. Arthur Conrad stood at the bottom of the stairway.

"Professor, sir, this gentleman has forced himself in, insisting—"

"It's all right now, Paulo. I'll handle it."

Paulo bowed slightly at his approaching master and then disappeared.

"Now, Mr. Blair," Arthur Conrad said angrily, walking up to Ross, "just exactly what do you mean by barging your way into this house when I've asked you once to leave, and have made it quite clear that you're not welcome here."

By this time, Monica had entered and she now closed the

front door behind her. She stood there terrified, staring at the two men hurtling angry words at each other.

"You're a rotten liar, Professor Conrad," Ross shouted. "A Goddamned liar!"

"And what exactly makes me a liar, may I ask?" the professor asked loudly.

"Because, professor, you conveniently told us this morning Carrie wasn't here, that she was out of town and wasn't expected back until tomorrow night." He was glaring at Conrad with angry eyes.

"And?" Conrad said in a cool manner.

"And, we've just followed her here from town. So *that*, Professor Conrad, makes you a liar!"

"But you're wrong, Mr. Blair, for Carrie couldn't have gone downtown. You must have mistaken someone else for her. I told you this morning, and I'm telling you now, Carrie's away."

"I've made no mistake about it. I recognize her from the photograph her mother showed me before she died."

Arthur Conrad appeared to freeze momentarily. "A photograph—before she died, did you say? Is Carrie's mother dead?" He took Ross forcibly by the arm.

Ross was puzzled. What had suddenly come over this man? "Yes, she died in Esperanza."

"But how? Tell me how she died, Mr. Blair."

"She was shot. A .38 caliber pistol."

"Where in Esperanza?"

"She was killed while staying at the hotel in town. She had been searching for Carrie there."

"Oh, my God!" Conrad said. He choked. "When did this happen? What day exactly?"

"It happened early Friday morning of last week—around two or three in the morning." He stared at the professor, unable to comprehend why the man was suddenly asking these questions. Ross glanced briefly at Monica, then turned to Conrad. "But why are you asking all this? Do you know something about Carol's death?"

Conrad didn't answer him. "Paulo!" he shouted instead into the other room. "Paulo, come here, immediately!"

Almost instantly, the servant appeared. "Yes, professor?"

Conrad turned around to face Paulo. "Has Margaret gone to San Cristobal during the past hour or so?" he asked the servant. "And if so, has she just returned from there?"

"Yes, professor, I saw her return through the rear entrance just before Mr. Blair knocked on the door."

"Where is she at the moment?"

"I believe she went directly to her room, Sir."

"Go there quickly and bring her here to me at once."

The servant stood there, evidently confused. He made no attempt to move.

"Go, now! Bring her into the study."

The servant turned and hurried down a narrow corridor running to the rear of the house, and vanished behind the stairway.

"I think we had better go into the study, Mr. Blair—Miss Ashley," Conrad said to Ross and Monica and he hurriedly led the way into the room.

The man seemed extremely nervous, and not the same calm man they had met that morning. He asked them to sit down, and they complied. He went to the desk and leaned against it.

Ross and Monica sat there puzzled by the sudden turn of events. Monica was too nervous to speak out or ask any questions.

"Professor—" Ross began to say, "what—"

"Please, Mr. Blair, I ask you to have patience."

"But—"

"Please—I will explain all of this in a moment, as soon as —here they are now!" He was looking toward the entrance to the study.

Ross and Monica turned and saw a young girl entering the room. Paulo followed behind, entering noiselessly into the room. It was the same girl Ross and Monica had seen enter the sports car in San Cristobal. It was definitely the girl in the photograph. Ross was tempted to speak out to her immediately, but he held back—Conrad had insisted this girl was *not* Carrie. But who was she, then?

"Is this the girl you thought was Carrie—the one you say you followed here from the village?" Arthur Conrad asked Ross.

"Why, yes," Ross said, by now deeply confused. He and Monica exchanged glances.

"And you said a moment ago Carrie's mother displayed to you a photograph of this girl. Exactly when did she show you this photograph?"

"It was after I had come into her room—a minute or so after she had been shot. She was lying on the floor and she could hardly talk. But she was able to bring to my attention the wallet which she held in her hand. It was open to this photograph. She wanted me to see the picture."

"But why would she want you to see this particular picture?"

"Because," Ross replied, "earlier that evening, before she had gone into her room, she was going to show me a photograph of Carrie so I would know what she looked like."

"And so of course you assumed the picture she was referring to was a photograph of Carrie?"

"That's right. It was the photograph she had intended showing to me earlier."

"I believe you were mistaken, Mr. Blair, for you see, that picture she was referring you to wasn't of Carrie but of the person who only moments before had been in that same room with her. It was the only way she could tell you who had shot her—the photograph she was pointing out to you was of her murderer!"

Conrad turned and faced the girl who had entered the room with Paulo. "Isn't that so, Margaret?" he said to her. "You killed her, didn't you? That night in Esperanza when you left the group, still feeling the effects of 'acid'—the *trip* you had been experiencing earlier that evening. That's why when you returned later that night, you refused to tell me where you had been, and became almost hysterical when I asked you about the gun you had fired. But you knew she was there in Esperanza staying at the hotel—and you went there. What made you think you could get away with it?" He continued glaring at the young girl with angry, piercing eyes. The girl stared back meekly, seemingly ready to explode with cries.

"Well, Margaret, answer me, damn it! You killed her, didn't you?"

"Yes—yes!" the girl finally shouted back. It was a half-cry, half-shriek. "I killed her! I killed her! And I would gladly do it again, even without the effects of 'acid'. That's what you want to hear, isn't it?"

She watched Conrad for a moment, as if expecting him to hurtle words at her. Instead, he stared back at her.

Suddenly, she burst into tears. "She deserved it," she cried. "I swear she deserved it! For what she did to me. I'm glad I did it! I'm actually glad she's dead, and nothing you say is going to make me feel any different."

She was shouting and crying uncontrollably—it was difficult to make out her words. She ran toward Conrad, still crying, and began hitting his chest with her clenched hands. He tried holding her back. She swore at him violently.

"For God's sake, Margaret," Conrad shouted at the young girl, "act and talk sensibly. You bitch! You've killed my daughter. Murdered her!" He quickly turned to Paulo. "Paulo, come here and help me with her!"

"What are you saying?" Ross cried out.

Conrad turned to Ross. "My God, man, don't you realize who I am? I'm Andrew Borlin!"

The servant moved swiftly toward the desk where the struggle continued. But not swift enough. The girl cried louder now and appeared more hysterical. She went wild. Suddenly, she picked up a long letter opener from the desk, drew it back, and with all her strength, brought it forward.

Arthur Conrad wasn't quick enough, and the opener caught him below the rib cage. He let out a terrifying gasp, his eyes opened wide, the letter opener plunged deeply into his chest. His face grimaced with pain.

It had happened quickly. Ross had gotten to his feet only seconds before the girl had thrust the weapon into Conrad. He managed to grab her. Paulo helped him subdue the girl.

Monica sat there terrified, unable to move, for her entire body seemed momentarily paralyzed by the incredible event that was taking place.

Paulo having taken hold of Margaret, Ross rushed to where Conrad had fallen to the floor. The injured man had withdrawn the letter opener from within his body. Ross knelt beside him and his first thought was that the man was dead, but then his eyes opened. He stared up at Ross, his face twisting in agony.

"I will go lock her up in her room and call a doctor," Paulo said, to no one in particular. The young girl had succumbed to Paulo's strong grip, her hysterical crying having subsided, but she was sobbing and gasping for air as he dragged her from the room.

Ross turned to Monica. "Come give me a hand," he said to her. "Help me get him onto the sofa. Take his legs."

Monica took hold of Conrad's legs as Ross began picking him up carefully around his back. They lifted him off the floor. "Easy now," Ross said. "Easy, don't move him too fast!" They carried him to the sofa.

Conrad's eyes were closed again, but within moments, they were open. By now, his face had grown extremely pale.

"I—I—wish to talk to you," he said to Ross. "I have something to tell you." He paused momentarily, as his face became distorted with pain again. "Please come down here close to me, so that I can make myself heard."

Ross quickly turned to Monica. "Go find where Paulo went; he might need some help. Make sure he calls a doctor quickly."

Ross knelt down near the edge of the sofa, next to Conrad's face. Very slowly, the dying man began speaking to him.

Monica left them there, in search of Paulo, and so she did not hear what it was Arthur Conrad said to Ross.

CHAPTER 26

THEY had been sitting in a booth of the bar-lounge.

"But it all sounds incredible," Monica was saying to Ross. They had been sitting there maybe half an hour, after their return from the *Villa del Sol*. It was late and they hadn't bothered eating dinner. They had spent most of the night at the villa. There had been the usual questioning by several civilian representatives of the local police authority. The interrogation had taken considerable time because of the language barrier, and Paulo had been called upon to act as interpreter.

The girl, Margaret, had been taken into custody by the police—held on an open charge of homicide. One of the investigators wanted also to take Ross and Monica into custody as material witnesses, but through Paulo, Ross convinced the man that he and Monica would cooperate and make themselves available the following evening. The detective reluctantly agreed. He assured Ross it was a fairly routine matter. But Paulo confirmed Ross' fear that it was anything but routine and had even encouraged Ross and Monica to slip away the next day as quickly and quietly as possible. Ross intended doing just that.

"Ross," Monica said. "Ross?"

"Oh, I'm sorry, darling," he finally answered. "What is it you said?"

"I was saying how completely incredible all of this was."

Ross' thoughts had been on the events of the evening, and —on what Conrad had said to him.

"This entire affair, from the beginning, back in Esperanza, has been incredible," Ross acknowledged. He took a drink of his scotch. "It's all so difficult to comprehend."

"So tell me exactly what Arthur Conrad said to you before he died," Monica said. "My mind's still not clear about some things."

"Don't feel alone, darling; mine isn't either."

"Start at the beginning again, now that it's calmed down a bit in here."

Ross had begun a few minutes earlier relating to her his conversation with Conrad, but a group of eight or ten persons sitting at a table in the middle of the lounge had been loud and boisterous, and Monica had found it difficult to hear what Ross was telling her. The group had left. Now, there was only the rumble of a few voices in the lounge.

"You were telling me about this girl, Margaret," Monica reminded him.

"Oh, yes," Ross said. "Naturally, you were as curious as I was to learn how Margaret Lockwood fit into the picture—why I had mistaken her for Carrie. That's one of the first things Conrad managed to clear up for me just before he died. How stupid of me not realizing why Carol had drawn my attention to that photograph minutes before she died. To think she was pointing the finger at her killer."

"But you had no way of knowing that, darling—naturally, you mistook—"

"That's right," Ross interrupted her, "Carol had said nothing to me about Margaret." He paused. "If only she had. Anyway, Margaret, it seems, was Carol's daughter—born to her illegitimately. You'll recall Carol told me she had remarried, and of course, she went by the surname of Lockwood. But the truth is, I learned from Conrad, that this Lockwood fellow never married Carol. In fact, he deserted her even before Margaret was born.

"Margaret was an illegitimate child but Carol gave her Lockwood's name. As a matter of fact, she did the same with Carrie soon afterward. Margaret and Carrie are about the same age—Carol had this affair with Lockwood only weeks after arriving in Albuquerque." He paused in thought. "Poor Carol —she was probably embarrassed to tell me all this. I think she would have later, though, had she lived."

"But why would Margaret want to kill Carol?" Monica asked.

"Because," Ross explained, "quite by accident, only a few months ago, Margaret learned she was a bastard child. Carol wasn't the one who told her; she had kept it a secret. She actually had made both Carrie and Margaret believe that Lockwood had abandoned them shortly after Margaret was born and that she later had divorced him on grounds of desertion. Carrie, of course, had been too young to remember anything about the man.

"So, when Margaret learned the truth, she confronted Carol with it and they had a bad argument over it. Margaret left home as a result of the disagreement. Carrie and Margaret had never been very close half-sisters so Carrie didn't leave with Margaret—not then, anyway. But the two of them did have one thing in common—both of them knew Arthur Conrad from school, and too, they were both smoking pot and using drugs. Carrie sympathized with Margaret's position and this caused her to feel resentment towards Carol and also, it regenerated the anger she had always felt towards her mother for refusing to reveal my whereabouts or even divulge my name. All of this built up to a point where finally, the two of them had it out and that's when Carrie left home. Soon thereafter Carol began her search. The rest, you know."

"And that's when Carol called you?"

"That's right."

"Carol was truthful with you except for keeping from you the fact that Margaret even existed."

"Yes, it's too bad she kept it from me—but, can you blame her? Undoubtedly, it would have caused her some embarrassment."

"But what you've related about their disagreement doesn't

appear to justify Margaret taking Carol's life."

"Who knows? Chances are, even Margaret herself doesn't know the real reason why she did it. I'm sure that's the justification she gives herself. She probably had grown to hate Carol, I guess, for having kept her illegitimacy from her and it began to build up in her eventually. *And*, don't forget, Margaret was taking drugs—that must have affected her thinking considerably, enough to do what she did."

"But how did she know Carol was staying at the hotel? And why did she go there that night?"

"Conrad said they were in Esperanza that night Carol was killed; actually, a few miles from there—near the old lady's place, as a matter of fact. Margaret was still on an LSD 'trip' when she disappeared from the camp. It was late when she had left them. Somehow, both Margaret and Carrie knew Carol had been looking for them in Esperanza. It was then that Margaret must have gone to the hotel to speak with Carol; they argued, and she shot her." He stopped, recalling the voices he thought he had heard that night in his sleep.

"But what about the pistol? Where did she get that?"

"It belonged to Conrad. He had been concerned because she had taken it that night. Later, when she returned, he took it away from her and noticed it had been fired. He confronted her with it but she only laughed and said something about shooting at a coyote. The group left Esperanza early the following morning so they never heard about the shooting." He stopped for a moment, in thought, then shook his head disapprovingly.

"What?"

"Oh, nothing. I was only thinking about that photograph; my assuming it was a picture of Carrie. If Carol had only told me about Margaret's existence, we probably wouldn't be here now and more importantly, Conrad wouldn't be dead."

"That *if*, darling, is a big word."

"Yes, isn't it."

The two of them were silent for a moment. Monica finally spoke.

"And who would have thought," she said, taking a sip of her drink, "that the mystery of Andrew Borlin's disappearance would be solved upon finding the evasive Arthur Conrad. That's the part most difficult to believe."

"That Conrad and Andrew Borlin were one and the same man?"

"Yes."

"It's incredible, isn't it, even after what Montoya told us about the experiment. So the old lady turned out to be right after all."

"You mean about Andrew Borlin being alive?"

"Uh huh."

"Yes, she was, but she was wrong about the way he had managed to do it."

He laughed. "Her talk of transmigration of the soul—it *was* pretty hard to swallow. But so is what actually happened."

"But why did he keep the discovery a secret and make Carol believe he had died?"

"For the same reasons Baltazar Montoya gave us. Conrad had very little to add to that. The part about Borlin becoming an entirely different personality was true. Conrad corroborated Montoya's account. That funeral twenty years ago in Esperanza ended the life of Andrew Borlin and began anew the life of Arthur Conrad."

"But did he become Arthur Conrad right away?"

"No, not right away, actually. He left New Mexico soon after the funeral and was gone several years before returning to live in Albuquerque—as Arthur Conrad. By then, he had formed a basis in his mind for his new personality."

"But why did he began teaching—philosophy, no less, something entirely different from what he had become accustomed to doing all his life? And what about his teaching credentials?"

"Keep in mind what Montoya told us earlier about the serum changing not only Andrew Borlin's features, but also changing his personality altogether. Conrad explained it to me by saying the serum somehow made some physical change in the genetic structure—the chromosomes which control personality make-up. As to his credentials, I thought of that too and asked Conrad. He said that was easy—simply a matter of forged documents. New birth certificate, school transcripts and false papers certifying he held a Ph.D.

"It's in essence a rebirth, isn't it, but different from reincarnation in that one has retained the memory and knowledge of a prior existence. How strange it must be to be reborn as a mature adult. It's difficult to conceive what it would feel like."

"Only one man has experienced how it must feel," Monica said. "Arthur Conrad—and he's now dead. What happened to his notes—the formula for the serum? Did he ever reveal the secret to anyone else?"

"No—only he knew it. All his notes were destroyed when Montoya struck a match to the lab. The secret was locked up inside Conrad's mind, and now it too is gone." He finished his drink. "Unless," he said as an afterthought, "someone else stumbles onto it someday as Borlin did—the legendary fountain of youth." He smiled at the thought.

"It was much more than that—I think it was something ugly. The thought of it gives me the jitters. It's too unnatural. Besides, who would want to live on forever? I would think life would eventually become dull. It's like that story I heard when I was a child, about the young boy who wished that every day would be Christmas and his wish was granted. So every morning of each day, when he awakened, he would find the Christmas tree still there, full of unopened presents and toys underneath, until all of the excitement was gone and he began to tire of it and wished life would become normal once more."

"Well, one thing's for certain—people would never approve of it in the manner Borlin did it."

"What do you mean?"

"Conrad told me that in addition to use of the extract from the plutonium he discovered, he needed a certain chemical which existed only in the petuitary gland of another human being. And to do that, it became necessary for Borlin to kill someone."

"Did Conrad tell you that?"

"Yes. I don't understand why he found it necessary to. That mortician Montoya told us about cooperated with Borlin in yet another way. It seems he would allow Borlin to perform some kind of operation on the bodies he received for burial, sometime before the actual embalming took place. Borlin would extract the gland fluid from the body of a person who had died recently. But no matter how quickly he managed to do it, it proved not soon enough, for usually the person had been dead several hours before Borlin was given access to the body. So he found it necessary to extract this fluid from the body of a person who had been dead only a matter of seconds, before death affected the petuitary gland through the process of rigor mortis. There was only one way he could do that—it was necessary to sacrifice someone else's life."

"And so they killed someone?"

"Yes, they were careful to select a person who stood little chance of being missed by anyone in Esperanza. So they picked a stranger that was passing through—a hitch-hiker, hitch-hiking his way across the country."

"How awful."

"Montoya was careful to keep that part from us, wasn't he?"

"I can't say I blame him. He helped Borlin with it, I take it?"

"Yes. I imagine we should tell Sheriff Dominguez about all this."

"You'd almost have to."

"I doubt he'd believe one word of it. And even if he does, I don't think he can make any type of case against Montoya after all these years."

"Did Professor Conrad say anything to you about why he turned to using LSD and other illicit drugs?"

"No. But he didn't have to; it's fairly obvious. He was the type of individual who believed that use of marijuana and hard drugs, such as LSD, was the choice of the individual and not an activity to be censured or controlled by the government. I think it was that simple with a man like Conrad. It's typical thinking with these fellows toward drug abuse. He couldn't have cared less, for example, what you or I may have thought about it. It was his own conscience and belief that were important, not the conscience or belief of others or of society in general, which were irrelevant—to him, anyway."

"You're probably right," Monica said. She took out a cigarette from her purse. Ross lit it for her. He lit one for himself.

"Would you like another drink?" he asked.

"No, I don't think so." She drew from her cigarette and exhaled, letting the smoke out slowly. "Did Carrie know about this—that Arthur Conrad was actually her grandfather, I mean?"

"Was he really, though?" Ross inquired.

"Well, of course he was—by blood, anyway."

"I guess in the traditional sense, one would have to consider him Carrie's relative, even though he did become a different person." He took another puff of his cigarette. "She didn't know," he said.

"And was there ever any romantic tie between the professor and Carrie? I mean physically."

"Not according to what Conrad told me. It was simply an infatuation on Carrie's part. Evidently, Conrad wasn't exactly the ugly, disgusting person we had pictured him to be."

"But he knew who Carrie was all along—his granddaughter."

"Yes, he did."

"One would have thought he'd feel some guilt about getting Carrie—and Margaret too—started on drug abuse; or at least, encouraging the use of drugs."

"Well, stop to think about it for a minute, though. Remember that he himself believed there was absolutely nothing wrong with it. Now, if he felt that way, then it would follow that he would think there was nothing wrong with either Carrie or Margaret using them, even though they happened to be his granddaughters." He watched Monica's eyes sparkling. "We might not have agreed with what he was doing, but of one thing I'm quite certain—he wasn't a man who believed in double standards—Conrad was no hypocrite, whatever else he may have been in our eyes or anyone else's."

He pondered for a moment. "Nor was he the liar I accused him of being earlier this evening, for he had told us the truth about Carrie—she *is* out of town where he said she was."

"Did you say earlier Paulo left to go get her?"

"No, he's leaving early in the morning. The village she's at isn't far from here. It's a small town the other side of Puerto Rafael. They'll probably return here by midmorning. I asked Paulo if it'd be all right if we waited for them at the villa."

"You must be terribly anxious to see her after all that's happened."

"Yes—very." He gave her a smile of satisfaction.

"Have you decided whether or not you'll tell her about Arthur Conrad?"

"You mean about whom he really was?"

She nodded.

"No," he said. "I see no reason for ever telling her. Do you?"

"Not at the moment. She'll probably be taking her mother's death hard." She watched him carefully. She could tell by the look in his eyes that he had misgivings about whether Carrie would accept him, now that he had found her. She sensed his mind was filled with mixed emotions about their meeting the next day.

"Darling," she said softly to him, "everything will turn out just fine between you and Carrie. You wait and see—I know it will."

"Let's hope so." He smiled at her.

There was momentary silence.

"Oh, I'd almost forgotten to ask you," Monica said. "Did Arthur Conrad say anything to you about the wax doll?"

Ross looked up abruptly. "The waxen image! I'd forgotten all about it. It's out in the car."

"What are you talking about?"

"The doll! Conrad told me where I'd find it. I asked him about that—as if to show me proof positive that he was Andrew Borlin, he told me where I'd find it. In the confusion earlier when the police were asking all those questions, I gave it to Paulo and asked him to put it in the back of the car." He stood up. "Come on! Let's go take a look at it."

Ross paid the waiter and led Monica out to the car. There it was, in the back seat—a small, but heavy, metal box. He carried it back to the room as if he were holding something sensitive and fragile.

He placed it carefully on the bed. "The latch is locked. I tried opening it before giving it to Paulo but I couldn't find the key. It should be fairly easy to open, though." He glanced around the room and spotted a can opener on top of the dresser.

He took the opener and began inserting it into the locking apparatus, attempting to pry it loose. After a minute or so of heavy prying, the lock gave and the cover was loose. Slowly, he opened the box.

Inside, carefully wedged into a thick layer of soft cloth, was the waxen image of Andrew Borlin. It looked ancient but well preserved. It was a crudely made doll, but even then, Ross saw some resemblance between it and the Andrew Borlin he vaguely remembered.

There was a small object glistening on the upper portion of the doll, a few inches below the neck. Ross drew it closer to him and he noticed the large sewing needle stuck through the middle of the image.